D1150581

WHAT I

"We circled to the East ... ... The cloud-steeds won't fly over it. The Great Maze to the South is full of very old Magic too, but somehow that doesn't bother the cloudsteeds.

"I could see three Magicians on top of the tallest pillar—two old men and a woman, wearing robes. I don't know exactly what they were doing, but, all of a sudden, thunderheads raced up. It had been as clear as water, and then there was a full-blown storm right overhead. The eerie thing was that once the clouds were there, they stopped moving.

"There was thunder and wind; peals of thunder from stock-still clouds. Then one of the Magicians raised his Staff. The moment he did it, bolts of lightning started coming down. The lightning was attacking the boxes. That's the only place it was landing. I swear that the old man was doing it. I swear he was aiming at them." He looked at Darius, his eyes pleading for belief and Darius nodded encouragement.

"The Magician in the middle kept that Staff pointing up, but the other one collapsed. He just seemed to crumple up, and after that it started to rain. I've never known rain like that, never. It was as if the clouds were angry, growling and flashing and hurling rain down. The rain was coming down so hard, bouncing up so high, that it seemed to be raining upward."

Also by John Lee from Orbit:

THE UNICORN QUEST

Futura

An Orbit Book

Copyright © 1988 by John Lee

First published by Tor Books in the USA in 1988

First published in Great Britain in 1989
by Futura Publications, a Division of
Macdonald & Co (Publishers) Ltd
London & Sydney

*All characters in this publication are fictitious
and any resemblance to real persons, living or dead,
is purely coincidental.*

All rights reserved.
No part of this publication may be reproduced,
stored in a retrieval system, or transmitted, in any
form or by any means without the prior
permission in writing of the publisher, nor be
otherwise circulated in any form of binding or
cover other than that in which it is published and
without a similar condition including this
condition being imposed on the subsequent
purchaser.

ISBN 0 7088 8304 4

Reproduced, printed and bound in Great Britain by
Hazell Watson & Viney Limited
Member of BPCC Limited
Aylesbury, Bucks, England

Futura Publications
A Division of
Macdonald & Co (Publishers) Ltd
66–73 Shoe Lane
London EC4P 4AB
A member of Maxwell Pergamon Publishing Corporation plc

the
Unicorn
Dilemma

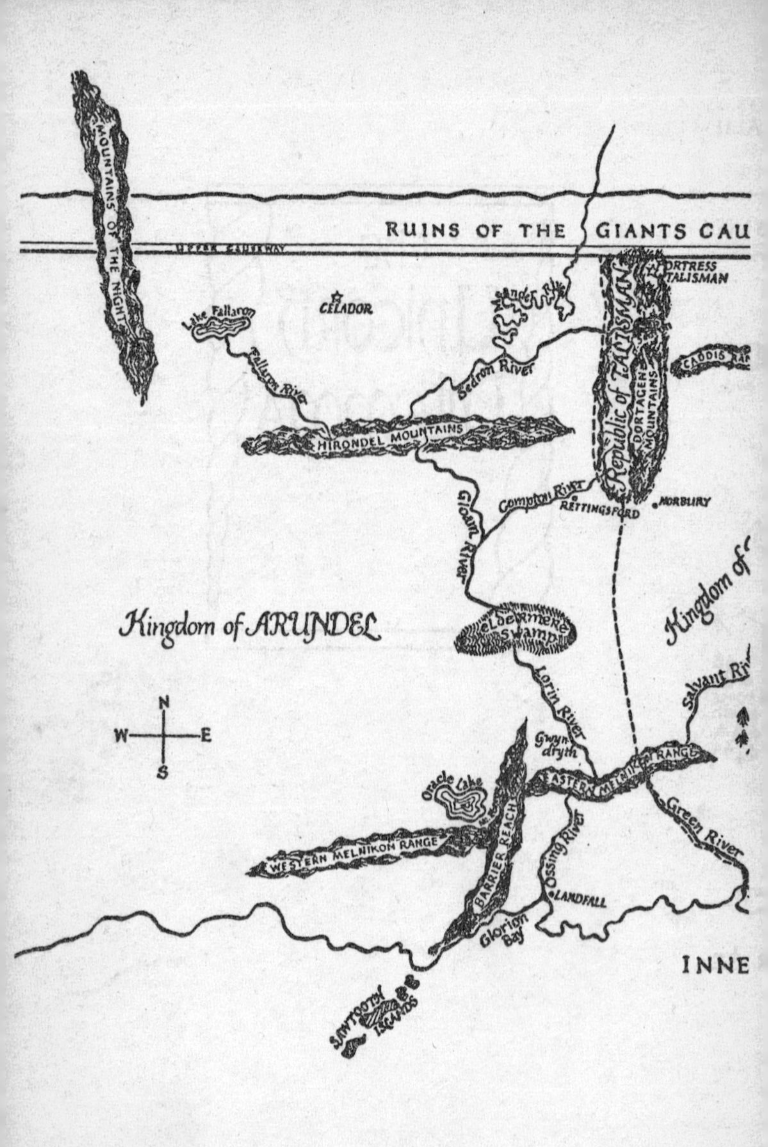

MOUNTAINS OF THE NIGHT
RUINS OF THE GIANTS CAU
ORTRESS TALISMAN
CELADOR
Lake Fallaron
Fallaron River
Sedron River
HIRONDEL MOUNTAINS
Republic of TALISMAN
DORTAGEN MOUNTAINS
CADDIS
Compton River
RETTINGSFORD
NORBURY
Gloam River
Kingdom of ARUNDEL
Eldermere Swamp
Kingdom of
Lorin River
Gwyndryth
EASTERN MELNIKON RANGE
Oracle Lake
BARRIER REACH
WESTERN MELNIKON RANGE
Ossing River
Green River
LANDFALL
Glorion Bay
INNE
SAWTOOTH ISLANDS
N
W
E
S

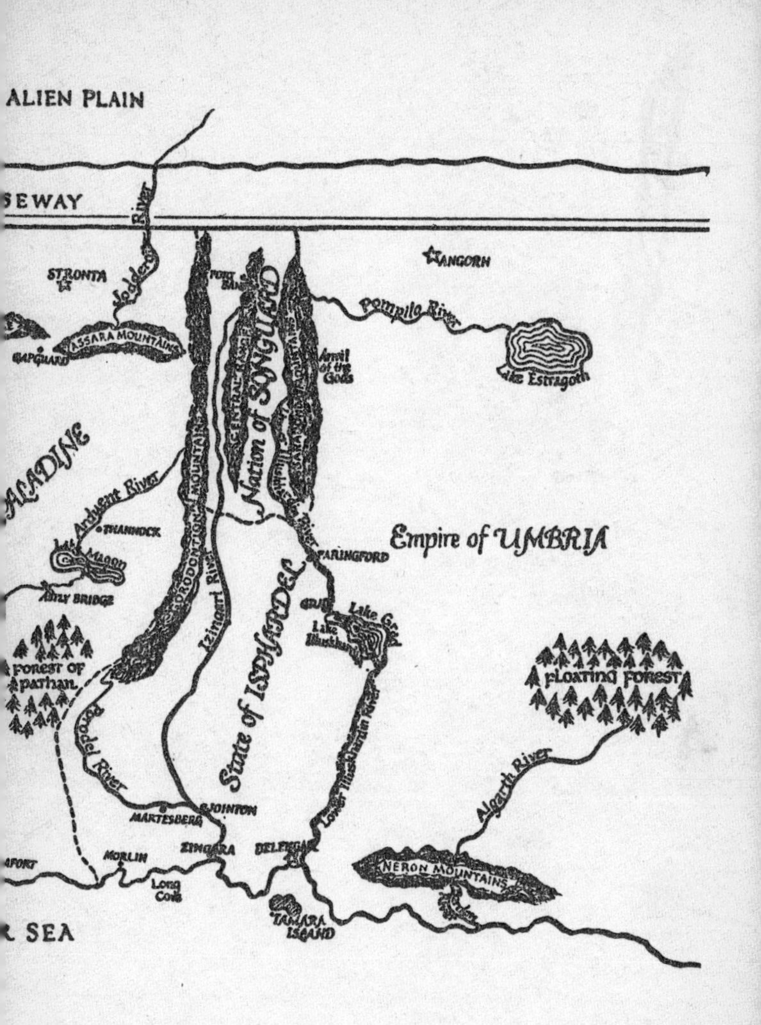

ALIEN PLAIN
SEWAY
STRONTA
ANGORN
Pompilo River
ASSARA MOUNTAINS
Anvil of the Gods
Nation of SONGUARD
CENTRAL RANGE
Ardvent River
THANNOCK
Empire of UMBRIA
FARINGFORD
State of ISPHARDEL
Izingari River
FOREST OF pathan
FLOATING FOREST
Algarth River
JOINTON
MARTESBERG
ZINGARA
MORLIN
Long Cove
NERON MOUNTAINS
TAMARA ISLAND
SEA

chapter 1

Darius of Gwyndryth was in a bad mood. He scowled at himself in the clouded piece of tin that served as a looking glass. The room behind him wavered around his reflection. Coming to Court was always an ordeal, but they usually housed him comfortably. This time, with every royal, Magician, and notable in the world in attendance, all he rated was this misbegotten cubbyhole. The bed was too small and there was scarcely room for his servant's pallet.

The milky image that glared back at him was too pale to do him justice and, like the bed, incapable of holding all of him. He was broad and fleshy, without being fat. The hair, though bleached by the sun and the years, was still red, and the color was repeated in a face that told of a life lived out of doors. He tugged at the lace collar that was supposed to be the fashion.

Damned foolishness, he thought. He had no business in palaces. His place was at Gwyndryth or in the field with his regiment. He had had such high hopes of this trip too, but it had been a disaster. What a time to try to introduce his daughter at Court. She was stuck in a room at the other end of the castle that was even smaller than this one. She hadn't even been able to unpack her gowns.

The scowl deepened. He'd guessed wrong about everything. He had welcomed the summons to the Conclave. It would be a purely ceremonial occasion, and all the eligible young men would be there. He had held Marianna back too long as it was. Other girls her age had babies already. It was time to look to the future of the Holding. That's what he had thought, but the Conclave had turned out to be all Magic and terrible Magic at that; a nightmare wrapped in a chimera.

The call to attend the Council of War had come as a relief. At least that was an area that he understood, and it was an honor to be singled out to discuss strategy with the King of Paladine and the Thane of Talisman, let alone the Emperor of Umbria. That was heady stuff.

He moved his concentration to the jacket. Why did they make it so difficult to get all the little hooks set? The tip of his tongue emerged as he struggled with the fasteners. Why had he opened his mouth at the Council of War? He had made a spectacle of himself, and in front of those people. They had been polite, he had to give them that. Well, what else do you expect from Princes? he asked himself sardonically. Made you so comfortable that you got up without permission and tramped up and down the room lecturing them.

He closed the waistband of the jacket and looked up again. "Thought you'd got away with it too, didn't you?" he asked himself. "Got right off the table into the stewpot, that's what you did."

He had offended somebody, Varodias of Umbria most likely. Why else would the Princess Regnant demand his attendance? And for the privilege of a royal reprimand he had to get himself up like some fancy boy and use the plummy tones and artificial phrases of the formal mode. He turned sideways and plucked at the silk slashed into the arms. This was the first time he had allowed Marianna to pick his clothes and it would be the last.

Where was that fool man of his when he needed him?

He was in enough trouble as it was without being late for the audience. He hooked the short cape to the shoulder pads, his thick fingers fumbling at the eyelets, and then clapped the hat on his head. He hated hats; they made him look ridiculous. The plume on the hat nodded agreement.

Darius had guessed wrong again. The anteroom was crowded with courtiers, but the Presence Chamber held only the Princess and three ladies-in-waiting who were grouped behind the throne doing needlework. Arabella of Arundel managed to look both regal and comfortable. Royalty was a public state and he had expected to be dressed down in front of an audience. This might not be as bad as he had feared. A slim hand beckoned and he marched down the carpet. He halted the prescribed ten paces from the throne, swept off the offending hat, and went into his court bow.

''We welcome the most noble Holdmaster of Gwyndryth,'' the Princess Regnant said in the clear, quiet voice that he remembered from the Council of War. ''You may approach us.''

He came out of the bow and moved closer. He didn't know if he was supposed to look straight at her, probably not, but he found himself staring into her eyes. They were large and squill blue. The gaze was calm and direct. A most impressive young woman, he thought. This close, he could see the shadows beneath the eyes. The Conclave had left its mark on her after all. With the long, fair hair, it was difficult to think of her as a Magician. He found that somehow comforting. She was beautiful, he decided, but she wasn't pretty.

''We are delighted to have this opportunity to meet with you privily,'' she said. ''We have had good reports of you, my Lord.'' She smiled the smile that had been a feature of her portraits since she was a child.

Here comes the "we are all the more surprised therefore" speech, he thought and inclined his head.

"Reports that were amply borne out at yesterday's Council meeting." He looked up to see if a mocking expression accompanied the words. She seemed sincere and a cautious optimism took root.

"Our Cousin Varodias," she continued, "was much taken with you."

"The Emperor of Umbria, Ma'am?" The moment the startled question was out, he knew he shouldn't have spoken. Would he never learn? He tried to look contrite, but the smile was back and there was nothing condescending about it.

"The very same, my Lord. He has, in fact, made a most unusual suggestion. He feels that the gravity of the situation revealed in the Archmage's vision calls for greater cooperation among the members of the Alliance and, to that end, he has offered to have an official observer from the Magical Kingdoms at Angorn." Darius's eyebrows rose and he watched the Princess carefully.

"You look surprised, my Lord," she remarked, giving him tacit permission to speak.

"I am, Ma'am. The Empire has always kept very much to itself. The only travelers they welcome are Isphardi."

"Quite so, and we applaud our Cousin for this change of heart. Now, my Lord, can you guess why we have sent for you?" Arabella sat back and watched the emotions play over his face; puzzlement, enlightenment, and disbelief. Varodias has picked well, she thought, this one cannot dissemble. I shall have to send someone good with him to keep him out of trouble.

"If my Liegelady is suggesting that I . . ." he began. "I mean, if your Majesty is looking to me for counsel on the appointment, I must confess that I am totally unqualified in such matters.'' His Marches burr was beginning to creep into his delivery and he stopped abruptly.

''You are too modest, my Lord. The Emperor himself brought your name forward. We are afraid it is a position that you cannot refuse. Our Imperial Cousin is seldom so forthcoming, and what the Alliance needs most at this juncture is harmony and unanimity of purpose. The Emperor has made a significant gesture. Besides''—there was no smile now—''you are our sworn man.'' She paused. ''You have done us homage for your Holding. You are bound.'' There was iron in the voice.

Darius was stung by the implication. He was proud of his house's loyalty to the Crown. His ancestor had helped put hers on the throne and his own father had served briefly under Archmage Ragnor on her Council of Regency.

''As my Liegelady commands,'' he said formally. He bowed low.

''Congratulations, my Lord Observor.'' She was gracious once more. ''Since you are to be our envoy, we shall bestow upon you the Order of the Ruby Crown.''

''Your Majesty is most generous.'' Darius's reply was automatic. His mind was filled with questions.

''Have no fear, my Lord,'' Arabella said, misreading his face. ''If this mission is a success, and we are sure that it will be, you will be rewarded with something more substantial.''

''May I be permitted an inquiry, Ma'am?''

''You may ask, but we may not vouchsafe an answer.''

''How long will this assignment last?''

''Who can say? It is at the Emperor's pleasure.'' She gave him a mischievous little look. ''They do say that quicksand is more constant than the Emperor's favor.'' She laughed, bright and high, and Darius was quick to join her.

''No matter how long or short your visit turns out to

be, it would benefit our realm to know more about the Umbrians.'' The momentary levity was gone. ''All we have now is merchants' gossip. How do they really live? How secure is Varodias? What are the alliances? What are these new weapons that they are developing? We of the West are protected by our Magical arts, but that does not mean that it is wise to be ignorant.''

''I shall do my best, Ma'am. One further question if I may. . . ?'' She nodded. ''When must I leave?''

''The Emperor returns to Angorn in two days. Why do you ask?''

''Well, Ma'am, I must make arrangements for Gwyndryth and I also have a daughter . . .''

''Ah yes, the Lady Marianna, is it not?''

''It is, Ma'am.''

''And she is with you at Celador.'' It was a statement. ''Excellent. As to your Holding, do you trust your Senechal?''

''Absolutely. He served my father before me.''

''You are fortunate. Write to him, my Lord: send him your instructions. You may use our Royal Messengers to have them delivered. Did you bring bunglebirds from the Hold?''

''Yes, Ma'am.''

''Be sure you take them to Umbria with you. We shall loan you a pair that home on the Imperial capital and you may send them to him as well. That way you will be able to keep in touch with your lands while you are away.'' She surprised Darius by standing up.

''You are most thoughtful, Ma'am,'' he said and bowed. The audience was obviously over.

''There is another matter,'' she said. She looked over her shoulder at the ladies-in-waiting and then stepped down toward him. ''My flowers are without thorns, but they have sharp ears. Do you escort us to the window seat so that we may take advantage of the Winter sunshine.''

He turned and offered his left forearm. She rested her hand lightly on it and they walked slowly to the window. What in Strand is going on? Darius wondered. You didn't have to be a regular at Celador to know that this was highly unusual. The Princess Regnant seated herself and patted the cushion next to her. He sat gingerly on the edge of the broad sill. He was nervous again.

''We wish to talk to you about your daughter, my Lord.''

''About Marianna? Has she done something to offend, Ma'am?''

''No, my Lord, you need not trouble yourself on that account.'' She smiled at him and saw that the smile had its habitual effect. ''We have an embassy of sorts in mind for her as well. It seems that the throne finds itself much in need of the services of the Gwyndryth family.''

''The House of Gwyndryth is ever at the disposal of the Crown.''

''Spoken like a true vassal. We are most fortunate among Princes. Now, tell us, has your daughter ever shown any manifestation of the Talent?'' The question was sharp and direct.

''No, Ma'am. There has never been a Magician in our family.'' He remembered that she was a Thaumaturge and added, ''More's the pity.''

''Excellent. Is she still a virgin?''

Darius's eyes went wide. ''Majesty?''

I must remember, she thought, that I am talking to a Marches Lord. ''There is no reason to look so shocked, Holdmaster.''

''But she is unmarried, Ma'am.''

Remarkable, she said to herself, he really does believe that the two are inseparable. ''Ah, indeed.'' She managed to make it sound as if his statement were explanation enough. "We have good reason for our question, you may be sure." Gently, the man is nervous and this is too important. "We have a mission for her that may well prove to be even more important than your own." She drew back and looked him over measuringly. "It concerns Magic and must remain secret. That is essential." She paused. He waited.

"There was a meeting of the High Council of Magic. During that meeting, the Princess Naxania fell into a trance and proclaimed a verse about the discovery of a unicorn. You were at the Conclave, were you not? Well then, you can readily understand why the High Council thinks that it might be an answer to the future that the Archmage foresaw."

"And my daughter was mentioned in the verse." It was an acceptance.

"Not exactly, my Lord. How much do you know about unicorns?"

"I had never realized that they were more than fancies. If the ballads speak true, then they are beautiful, gentle, and constant."

"Every country has its legends," the Princess agreed. "In the Empire, we are told, they are reputed to be fierce fighters. One trait seems to be universally agreed upon. They can be tamed by virgin girls."

"And that is why you questioned me about my daughter." He was at ease now. He knew where things were leading.

"Just so."

"But why Marianna, if I may be allowed to ask?"

Good, she thought, he is coming around. He has accepted the idea of the unicorn. "There are many reasons," she said judiciously, "not the least of which is that she is here. She has never been to Court before. Can that be entirely coincidental? Then consider the aptness of her virtues and accomplishments.

"It is the judgment of the High Council that the creature will be found in some remote area. It is a shy beast by all accounts. We must tell you frankly, my Lord, that the search will probably be full of rigors. We need an exceptional young woman. Your daughter, by merest chance, is an excellent horsewoman and has an adventurous spirit. She is in excellent health and old enough to be responsible. She has never lain with a man. There are few women in Celador who can fulfill those requirements." She permitted herself a tight smile.

"My flowers would wilt a hundred leagues from Court and the rest are too old, too fat, or married. The High Council thinks that the Lady Marianna is the one for the task. What think you? Are we wrong?"

"No, of course not, your Majesty," Darius replied, wondering where the Council had got its information. "She will be most honored to be considered worthy, though I am sure that there must be others in the land who are her equals."

"We do not have the luxury of time, my Lord, you saw that in the vision. Besides, you will be far from Arundel on state business, and the Lady Marianna is at, ah, a vulnerable age to be left idly at home. The Emperor, alas, has limited your party to a squire and a cloudsteed escort of four, so you cannot take her with you."

Darius sat there trying to marshal his thoughts, and Arabella watched him closely. "Where will they be looking, Ma'am? How big is the search party?"

"Given the nature of the unicorn and the need for secrecy, we felt that two would be best. They will be provided with a guide in Songuard. The Council felt that the mountain fastnesses would be the most likely place."

"So small?"

"Would you rather a troop of soldiers?"

"In truth, Ma'am, I do not know what I want."

"But you know where your duty lies, Holdmaster."

This was the sovereign speaking. "I am ever your Majesty's servant to command."

"It is settled then."

He bowed his head in knightly submission and she felt relieved. For a moment she had been afraid that he would balk. His head came back up and he looked directly at her. Don't count your peas before they are shelled, she thought. "You may speak, my Lord."

"Thank you, Ma'am. I wondered if I might know the name of the other girl?"

"There is no other girl. Her companion will be a young Magician. He is a student at the Collegium, a protégé of the Mage of Paladine. It is essential that Magic be represented."

"That's all very well, Ma'am, but I cannot say that I am taken with the idea of my only child roaming the wilds of Songuard with two men." And one of them a Magician, he added to himself.

"You need have no fear on that account," she replied, guessing that it was the men that bothered him and not the wilderness. "Jarrod Courtak, an Apprentice, comes from an excellent family. He's a ward of Robarth Strongsword of Paladine. Besides, he too is a virgin and must remain one. He is sworn to it."

"Shall I be allowed to meet him?"

"It is best if you do not." She looked at him sympathetically and reached over and patted his sleeve. "This is a time of great peril, my Lord, and much will be demanded of us. It is not just we who have need of you, all of Strand has need of the service of the House of Gwyndryth, and we are proud that you are Arundelians. We know that both you and your daughter will bring fresh glory to an old and much respected name."

He rose impulsively and went down on one knee before her. There, she thought, that should do it. She got to her feet and looked down at him. Affection welled. They were good people, her Arundelians, and she was fortunate to have vassals such as this.

"Rise, Lord Darius. We are much pleased with you. Our Cousin Varodias has chosen well. Be assured that there will be a place at Court for you upon your return." She dangled the prospect of advancement before him and waited until he was standing. Then she moved with him toward the door.

"Say nothing, as yet, to anyone about these matters. Do you bring the Lady Marianna here to us upon the morrow. We shall give it out that she is to be presented. Since her father is to leave so soon on royal business, it will cause no comment." She stopped in the open doorway and smiled conspiratorially at him. She was in plain view of the courtiers assembled in the antechamber, and Darius was aware that it was a signal mark of favor that she had come so far from the throne with him. Such things were never done casually, and he was grateful.

"Until tomorrow then, my Lord Observor." This time the use of the title startled him.

"As my Liegelady commands," he replied.

"There must be more to it than that. She must have told you more. You wouldn't have agreed to it unless she had." Marianna of Gwyndryth was sitting on her father's bed. Her hair, a darker red than his had ever been, hung round her shoulders. The green eyes were fastened on him and the mouth was determined. Darius knew the look. She was going to be stubborn.

"I've told you everything I know, and that's more than

I should have done. The Princess will doubtless tell you more. As far as anybody else knows, you are simply going to be presented, so wear the special gown you brought and remember to behave properly. It would be best if you pretended to know nothing about this unicorn thing.'' He was gruff.

''Very well, Papa, if you won't tell me, you won't.'' She leaned back on her elbows. ''There seems to be an awful lot you won't tell me these days.''

''I beg your pardon, young lady?'' He used his sternest voice, but she paid it no heed.

''You refuse to discuss what happened at the Conclave with me.''

''I do not discuss it because I choose not to discuss it,'' he said stiffly. ''There are things I would as lief not remember,'' he added by way of explanation.

''Then leave out the nasty bits,'' she said practically. ''It's obvious that this unicorn hunt you're going to send me off on has something to do with what went on at that Conclave. Don't you think I should know before I go chasing off after a mythical beast?''

''The High Council seems to think it's real, but you do have a point You're bound to hear rumors sooner or later anyway, and I suppose it would be better if you heard the truth from me.'' He paused and seemed to drift away in thought.

''What was it like when you went in?'' she asked to get him going.

''What? Oh, it was passing strange. The whole place was filled with benches and they were packed. People stood along the walls. It seemed as if every great man in the world was there. There was no way to get the doors closed and the banners were fluttering in the draft. The Mages and our Princess were up on a dais at the far end. They were sitting in chairs of state and they didn't move.

Their eyes were open, but they didn't blink. It was as if they were dead.

"Then, from one minute to the next, everyone was quiet. It was as if somebody had called for silence. At that selfsame moment, the Magicians came to life. That's the only way I can describe it." He paused, remembering.

"What happened next?" she prompted.

"The Archmage got up. He looked old and ill, not his usual self at all. He stood there, leaning on his Staff. He was wearing a gown with complicated patterns and there were lights running over it. He told us that he had seen the future and that it was terrible. Then he showed us."

"How? How did the Magic work?"

"I don't really know. He called on the Mage of Paladine and unhooked a big gold chain. They stood back to back and he put the chain over both their heads." He smiled grayly. "It was a poor pairing. Ragnor is tall and thin, and Master Greylock is not much above normal height. They started to chant, but I cannot tell you what words they used or if they used words." His voice trailed off as if the spellcasting had claimed him once more.

"Go on."

"A cloud grew round them," he said reluctantly. "It stretched clear up to the tracery, and the windows threw patches of color on it. The Magicians were swallowed up in it. There were pictures. Places, people, animals swirled around. They came and went and came back again." His hands moved in illustration.

"One scene began to dominate, to become more solid. It drove out the weaker images until it filled the end of the Hall. I can't remember if it was here or Stronta, but it was a battle. The Outlanders were fighting without hoses and were using terrible new weapons. They were burning us down and butchering us." He broke off and shook his head.

"There were many scenes like that," he went on softly. "No one was spared. The Umbrians had strange weapons of their own, but we watched them being consumed. I saw many men die; some of them I know."

"Did you see yourself?" she asked with the cruel directness of the young.

"No, I did not." The reply was quiet and even. "I take no comfort in that."

"Why not? It might mean that you will be spared."

"It might mean that I was already dead." His voice was flat and final, and she knew that she would get no more out of him.

"And the High Council thinks that the unicorn may be able to change all that?" she said, shifting tack.

"I am not, as you well know, a praying man, but if I were, I should pray that they were right. Otherwise there is no hope." He attempted a smile. "That is why I must go to Umbria and you must go to seek a unicorn."

"Do you believe in unicorns, Father?"

"I never have, but I never believed that the Outlanders could attack us without hoses. Now I shall have to believe in both." He looked down at her, sprawled on the bed, and this time the smile was real. "If anyone could tame a unicorn, it would be you."

"Oh, Father!" She was all mock annoyance.

"You'd badger it into submission," he added, and she stuck her tongue out at him.

The "presentation" was undoubtedly the high point of their visit to Celador, but the ball that same evening was a disaster. It started out well enough. Marianna was in high spirits and looked very becoming on his arm. He wore his new decoration and people deferred to them. The Great Hall had been made to look festive. The banners were gone and the pillars had been covered in fluted white fabric. There were curtains on the lower windows and green soskia boughs were hung everywhere. There was gay music and beautiful women paraded in ornate gowns. The only shadows here were induced by candlelight.

He led Marianna out to dance a corrante and was aware of the eyes that followed them. She was beautiful and graceful, there could be no doubt about it. He saw it confirmed in the faces of other men and knew that he must get her safely married soon. The Princess had been right. The dance ended, and as they made their way off the floor, young men he did not know came and introduced themselves. That was when everything started to go wrong.

Marianna was soon dancing again, and he found that he was not comfortable seeing his daughter smiling up into the face of her partner. He was not comfortable either with trying to make smart conversation with young men who spoke to him, but watched Marianna. When she disappeared from the floor and did not rejoin the group, he became both uncomfortable and anxious.

He excused himself and went looking for her under the guise of getting something to drink. The mountains of Songuard would be a much safer place than Celador. There were more snares here for an unwary girl than in any wilderness. Besides, the boy would be bound by oath and Magicians did not forswear themselves. He looked around at the leaping couples on the dance space, but Marianna was not among them. He pushed his way onward toward the buttery.

In the event, it was she who found him. She was unaccompanied and she was upset. She demanded that they leave and refused to give a reason. Darius knew that some man had tried to take advantage of her inexperience and felt his anger rising. He put a protective arm around her and steered her through the throng and out into the cold night air.

"Do you want to talk about it?" he asked gently as they made their way back toward her end of the castle.

"I'm not going on the hunt for the stupid unicorn and I don't want to talk about it."

Darius pulled up in dismay. "Who is the blaggard? I'll kill the son of a bitch."

"Calm down, Papa. His name's Jarrod Courtak and he's quite impossible, but I don't think that he deserves to die."

"Jarrod Courtak? But that's the– "

"That's the boy I'm supposed to go to Songuard with," she finished. "He's a child. He's a long, awkward, gangly clump. He won't last a day on the trail." Her anger and disappointment blazed out.

Darius relaxed, tucked her arm into his, and resumed the walk. "I'm sure he's quite capable, or the High Council wouldn't have picked him. You mustn't judge him by the first impression. Not all men are at their best on formal occasions, especially if they're young. I'm sure you'll find that he's a nice lad once you get to know him." He tried to be soothing.

"I have no intention of getting to know him," she said firmly. "I am a loyal subject, but I'll be damned if I'll play nursemaid in the middle of Songuard."

"You are not to talk like that," he reprimanded, dropping her arm. "Who are you to question the High Council of Magic? The Archmage has seen the future. I told you that. If they have chosen this boy and picked you, it is because you complement one another. Now I want no more talk of backing out of your obligations. We have both given our word to our Sovereign and a Gwyndryth does not renege. Do you hear me?"

She was surprised by his anger, but unwilling to back down. She said nothing.

"Look," he said in a gentler tone, "you know how important this is. The Princess Regnant has told me that your mission is more important than mine. We both have a chance to serve the throne and that is good, but you have the chance to serve all of Strand. You cannot refuse it.''

He looked down at her and she saw the intensity in his eyes. He seldom laid down the law to her, but when he did, experience had taught her that he was unbudgeable.

''Oh, very well,'' she said ungraciously. ''Perhaps you're right. He may be better on a horse than he is in a ballroom.''

They reached the bottom of her staircase, and he kissed her on the forehead. ''You will be a credit to us all, I know it. Try to keep an open mind about the boy. The two of you will have to depend on each other for a lot of things. It will be easier if you like each other.'' He gave her a lopsided little grin, but it elicited no response.

''Good night, Father.'' She dropped a curtsy, turned, and made her way up the stairs.

Darius watched until she disappeared around the first turn. He shook his head. The quest would probably do her a lot of good. She needed a safe outlet for all those pent-up energies. He turned and resumed his walk. What would Angorn be like for him? he wondered. She only had a young Magician, a seemingly harmless young Magician, to deal with. He would have an Emperor.

chapter 2

Angorn looked powerful and secure from the air. Massive walls enclosed the castle. Houses had sprung up outside and crooked little streets wound through them. At some later date a curtain wall had been erected to protect the transmural community. Though the whole was larger than Celador, there were far fewer turrets. There were towers at the corners of the original fortress and one on either side of the oversized gateway, but that was the extent of it. Good, solid, no-nonsense place, Darius thought. There was no magic in this land to confuse the mind.

He pulled back gently on the reins and the cloudsteed's wingbeats slowed. They were circling and he should be thinking about the strength of the wind and the direction of the final approach, but he decided to leave such details to the professionals. His mount would follow them down no matter what he did. Besides, this was the last time he would be alone in anything other than a curtained bed and he relished the freedom and the privacy of the skies. He inhaled deeply through his leather helmet and fancied he could smell the smoke from the myriad chimneys. Angorn looked manageable from up here, but he knew he would not be able to encompass it once he was on the ground.

How had he allowed the Princess Regnant to talk him into this? Not just this. His only child was off on a hunt for a nonexistent animal. With two men. With nothing to protect her except a vow of chastity. He had been rendered as pliant as a country bumpkin in Belengar. He had been dazzled by the aura of power. He had been an easy pullet to pluck. Had she used sorcery? Quite possibly.

No point blaming himself now. He was serving the Crown, as he was sworn to do. He had acted honorably and that's what mattered. "See and report as much as you can," she had said. "Try to get the ear of our Cousin," she had said. The first part would be easy if it didn't depend on the second. And then there was this motherless speech in Umbrian that he had been practicing every night since they had left.

They glided down around the edge of the updraft generated by the buildings below. He was going to miss the cloudsteed and its strong wings. Hunting produced a coursing excitement, but flying had induced a sense of serenity that, until now, he had only found at Gwyndryth. That was gone. The tiny dolls gathered at the landing platform would be smiling, life-sized problems in a minute. He started to recite the opening sentences of his reply to the inevitable speech of welcome and then abandoned the effort. Better to concentrate on bringing off a dignified landing.

The deputation that awaited the Lord Observor was mercifully small, and a quick scan of the upturned faces confirmed the fact that the Emperor was not among them. He released the straps that held the rope ladder and climbed down. A short, richly dressed man with thinning gray hair detached himself from the group and Darius came down the steps to meet him. The Umbrian showed his palms and Darius returned the salutation.

"Varodias, by the behest of the Mother, Emperor of Umbria and Elector of Anduin, has bidden me welcome the illustrious Lord Observor from Arundel to this his realm." The words were fulsome, but the man spoke in accentless Common and in the ordinary mode. Darius found himself instinctively liking the fellow. He decided to abandon his prepared speech. Better to save it for the Emperor.

"On behalf of my Royal Lady, Arabella, Princess Regnant of Arundel, I thank you," he said simply.

The older man drew closer and looked up at him. "I am Phalastra, Elector of Estragoth, Councilor to his Imperial Majesty, and I join him in welcoming you. You have had a long and doubtless tiring journey, so I have taken it upon myself to keep the ceremony to a minimum. I hope you don't mind. No disrespect was intended."

"Polite, but not effusive," the experts back home had told him. "Remember, the Umbrians are more reserved than we are and look on public displays of emotion as unmanly and a sign of weakness." "I think it very considerate of you, my Lord Phalastra," Darius said, and could not help but smile.

"I hoped you would feel that way. Professional diplomats"—Phalastra accented "professional"—"are so protocol conscious. My personal theory is that they do so to compensate for . . . Well, no matter. I'm afraid there are some obligatory introductions, but we'll have you settled in your apartment in no time. It would be different, of course, if his Imperial Majesty were here, but, unfortunately, he is engaged in a series of experiments that are at a critical point. Now"—he indicated the waiting men—"let us get the formalities out of the way. All you need to do is show your palms and bow."

They went down the short line, and Darius smiled and bowed and said "My Lord" to each man. All had military titles. He remembered none of the names.

"I am sure that there will be many new things for you to see," Phalastra said after the last bow had been made, and steered Darius deftly toward the entranceway to the right-hand keep. ''Angorn is very different from Celador.''

''That was apparent even before we landed.''

''The keeps are about six hundred years old, built during the joint reign of the Angorn brothers. The building that joins them was added later. The Emperor is housed in that one.'' He pointed to the tower on the left. ''Everyone else is squeezed into the rest, but I am sure that you will find your quarters comfortable.''

''I'm certain I shall.''

''Since you are come to learn of our ways, we have left the apartment as it is, but if machines bother you, we can have them taken out.''

''Oh, that won't be necessary. I haven't a smidgen of the Talent, and as far as I know, magicians are the only ones who are affected. What kind of machines?''

''Oh, simple things,'' Phalastra assured him. ''All our clocks are mechanical and, if I may say so, infinitely more reliable and accurate than water or tallow, or the sun for that matter. Gas lighting has been installed throughout the palace, and you may find our water closets a little strange.'' Darius nodded as if he understood and followed his guide into the palace.

Despite the warning, the apartment was spacious. There was a small anteroom, a large bedchamber, a small cabinet with desk and writing materials. Lighted globes were attached to the walls and a fire burned in each room.

''I trust it is to your liking, my Lord Observor.''

''Yes, indeed. And it is very kind of you to take the trouble to accompany me all the way here.''

''A pleasure, my Lord. Your man should be up shortly with your belongings, and your escort will be taken good care of. We shall meet again at dinner. I shall be on your right tonight and his Imperial Majesty, should circumstances permit, on your left. Orders and decorations are always worn at Hall, whether or not the Emperor is present."

"I look forward to it," Darius lied, and accompanied the Umbrian to the outer door.

The Hall, when he finally located it, was imposing enough to warrant a dress code. It ran from the front to the back of the "new" building and was larger than its counterpart at Celdor, though the ceiling was not nearly as high. In Celador the windows were down either side, but here tapestries covered those walls and the windows were at either end. At the head of the central table, beneath the North window, there was a large chair with the Imperial arms emblazoned above it. A smaller version occupied the place to its left. The table itself held a rich display of plate that gleamed in the candlelight. The scent of crushed herbs rose from beneath Darius's feet as he surveyed the room.

"Excuse me, your Excellence, but would you be the foreign Lord?" Darius looked down and saw a young page.

"I am the Lord Observor from Arundel, if that's what you mean," he said stiffly.

"Your pardon, noble Sir. This is my first Hall and I wasn't sure. I didn't recognize the sash, so I thought you might be the distinguished visitor." The last two words came out in quotation marks and Darius smiled in spite of himself.

"You supposed to take me to my seat?"

"Yes, Excellence. The Steward said he'd have my hide if I made a mess of it."

"Let's go carefully then and keep your hide intact. Where am I sitting?"

"Right next to the Emperor." The boy was clearly impressed.

"Lead on then."

He followed the page to the top of the room and greeted the Elector of Estragoth as he took his place before his chair. He began to speak, but was silenced by a gong. He turned toward the Elector and raised his eyebrows in inquiry. For answer the old man lifted a finger to his lips. They stood and waited for what seemed a very long time and then a second gong sounded. Darius glanced round and saw that the company was preparing to sit. He followed suit. A fanfare rang and the first course was paraded in.

"It seems that their Imperial Majesties will not be joining us tonight," Phalastra said as he shuffled his chair closer to the table. "Some urgent matter of state no doubt. I'm afraid you'll have to make do with my poor conversational skills. Not that the Emperor says very much at dinner, strange though it may sound. I'm not sure, even after all these years, that he's entirely comfortable when on public view. Does it make you uncomfortable that everyone has taken a peek at you and that, foreigners being a rare and exotic commodity in Umbria, they will continue to watch? Oh, dear. I see that it does, but you mustn't let it bother you. Courtiers have a notoriously short attention span."

"I'll do my best," Darius replied. "I maintain state at home, of course, but that's different somehow. I've not much practice in palaces. I confess I'm more at home in a mess tent."

"I know what you mean. It's one of the curses of rank and the prices of success."

"I fear so," Darius said with a little sigh. "By the way, what were the gongs for?"

"They mark off a period of seven minutes during which the Emperor will make his entrance if he so chooses. Once the second gong has sounded we know that he won't be coming. I'm sorry that you won't get to meet him tonight, but you'll see him tomorrow. Your audience is set for the eleventh hour, by the way."

"So soon? I'd hoped to have a little more time to practice that motherless speech I have to deliver. I haven't spoken Umbrian since Dameschool, and I never was much good at the formal mode."

"I'm sure you will be word perfect, but you might remember one thing. Maternism is the state religion here, and what you consider simple profanity is blasphemy in our country."

"I do beg your pardon. I just wasn't thinking. I do hope I didn't offend. I had no intention of doing so." Darius was embarrassed and contrite.

"No offense taken," the Elector replied easily. "Just remember that his Imperial Majesty does not permit swearing in his presence, even when there's a battle going on. It's one of his quirks."

"I shall keep a curb on my tongue, and I thank you for the warning."

"Ah. Here comes the fish," Phalastra remarked, moving smoothly to safer ground. "From the look of it it's kingklip. They're raised in the Imperial ponds. Isphardel's the only other place you can get them. Try one. I think you'll like it."

He kept the flow of chatter neutral right through to the savory and then walked Darius back to his apartment before bidding him good night.

Morning found the Lord Observor pacing and reading aloud, watched impassively by his new squire, Otorin. He was wearing his newly designed uniform, and the empty scabbard jounced at his hip. Carrying weapons inside the palace was an offense punishable by death, but the lack of one gave the outfit an unfinished look. A tapping at the door halted his performance, and he waited while Otorin admitted the Summoner. He collected the gift that he was to present to the Emperor and suffered the squire's last-minute ministrations.

"Good luck, my lord," the man said quietly as he stood back. Darius gave him a wan smile, squared his shoulders, and followed the functionary out.

The upper levels of the Imperial keep were far brighter than the other portions of the palace, or at least than any he had seen so far. There were broad windows up here with the clearest of glass. The individual panes must have been at least two feet square, another sign of the superiority of Umbrian manufacturing. The Presence Chamber was on the topmost floor, and the Summoner was puffing slightly by the time they reached it. He stopped at the threshold and checked his armclock. He turned to see if Darius was ready and then marched into the room.

Nothing had prepared Darius for the Imperial Presence Chamber. It was large, that he had expected. It was partially filled with courtiers and dominated by the throne, as he had imagined it would be. He had not expected them to be standing in a forest clearing. Frescoes covered the walls. A boar hunt was in progress all around him. The beams that supported the ceiling were painted to resemble the branches of trees. Leaves, twigs, and snaking vines reached up over the curving edges. Roots and grass and fallen leaves were realistically re-created on the floor.

"His Excellency the Lord Darius of Gwyndryth, Lord Observor of Arundel and Knight of the Royal Order of the Ruby Crown, craves audience!" The Summoner's voice stilled the discreet murmurings that their entrance had caused. He swung aside and bowed deeply.

Darius advanced through the clusters of nobles and entered the semicircle of space before the throne. With the Princess's gift clamped firmly under his left arm, he did his Court bow. Gloved fingers motioned him upright. The

Emperor studied him with hard, bright eyes. So did the falcon on his left wrist.

"Be welcome, my Lord Observor, to this our Court and to our Imperium." The voice was clear and precise, and Darius found his Umbrian easy to follow. Varodias paused and turned to soothe the bird. Darius waited, but the Emperor seemed to have lost interest in him.

The Arundelian glanced nervously to left and right for some kind of cue. Two men in their twenties stood to the right of the throne, staring impassively into space. Darius assumed they were two of the Emperor's sons. Phalastra of Estragoth was on the other side and smiled encouragingly when he caught his eye.

"We long to hear of our fair colleague and fellow ruler, the Princess Arabella." The high voice jerked Darius's attention back. The Emperor's mouth was smiling, but the eyes remained raptorlike. "You have our leave to speak to us." Darius cleared his throat and bowed again.

"Arabella of Arundel, by the grace of her people, Monarch, Bearer of the Royal Touch, Wisest of Wisewomen, to Varodias, Emperor of Umbria, Lord of the Mountains and Overlord of the Waters, greeting." His accent sounded ludicrous in his ears, but he pressed on. "Greeting most amiable and affectionate. Thus my most revered Sovereign bids me speak. By my unworthy hand hath she sent a gift that she trusts will find favor in your sight and that she doth beg your Imperial Majesty to accept." He paused for breath.

"I, her humble messenger, hight Darius, Holdmaster of Gwyndryth. I am her vassal and liegeman. I add my thanks to the words of my Royal Mistress for the privilege bestowed on me by your Imperial Majesty's invitation, and do wish to render your Imperial Majesty all service due this cherished gesture." He bowed once more and, head still down, held out the ornate box.

The Emperor snapped his fingers, though the gloves precluded sound, and one of the sons came down and took the case. Varodias transferred the bird to a perch beside the throne and unhasped the proffered gift. He lifted out a glittering coat of mail.

"Our Cousin is most thoughtful. Beauty of workmanship and utility combined; most admirably conceived. You may assure the Princess Regnant that we shall not hesitate to wear it upon occasions ceremonial. We thank her for her munificence." He was clearly pleased, and Darius felt emboldened.

"An it please your Imperial Majesty . . ." The Emperor looked up from his examination of his present.

"You may address us." And you better get this right, Darius thought.

"An it please your Imperial Majesty, the mail is made of a special metal wrought with Magic's aid, melzanite by name. It is as strong as it is light. Should you desire to wear it into battle, it would serve you well."

"Say you so, good my Observor? Say you so?" Varodias's quickened interest was signaled by the narrowing of his eyes. He paused to ruminate and then permitted himself a quick little smile of satisfaction.

"It may be that this gift is more timely than your Mistress could know. We are even now experimenting with a new way to bring destruction to our foe. It would be an excellent test for our projectiles. Yes, a goodly experiment indeed." He looked over his shoulder at Lord Phalastra. "Think you not so, Estragoth?" he inquired.

"Your subjects would doubtless applaud your bravery, Sire, but, with all due regard for the skill of the smiths of Arundel, I feel I must caution your Imperial Majesty that the Princess Arabella's splendid gift was not designed with such weapons in mind."

Varodias's smile was kit cruel. "Oh, have no fear, my

old gray fox, we have no intention of being in the mail. There must be some criminal, some traitor, awaiting death who is of our proportions. If he survives, he lives." He returned his attention to Darius and handed the suit back to his son.

"You may convey our gratitude, my Lord. We trust that you will find your visit among us both enjoyable and instructive. We have arranged for you to tour most of our installations. If there is anything in particular that you wish to see, you have but to ask." The Emperor nodded graciously and Darius knew that the audience was over.

He bowed and backed from the presence as he had been instructed to do. He felt the tactful guidance of the Summoner and was grateful for it. Relief was the feeling uppermost in his mind. It was over and he had not disgraced himself. When he was safely in the corridor again, he called back the Emperor's words from his memory and, for the first time, felt shock at Varodias's suggestion for the armor.

The Emperor was as good as his word, at least where the Lord Observor was concerned. An equerry appeared at ten o'clock the next morning to take Darius and Otorin on a tour of a nearby encampment. It was the start of a daily routine that took them through the Imperial Forests South of Angorn to one camp or another. Paved roads radiated from the capital. Ideal, Darius thought, for troop movement and essential for the steam chariots that chugged past and spooked the horses. The posts were all impeccably maintained and none seemed to carry the telltale signs of hasty sprucing. Recalling the sprawling canvas and unruly atmosphere of the Farod's encampments at home, he felt envious.

There was one exception to the orderly nature of Umbrian military affairs and that was the Rotifer Corps. They had taken over a farm. The house and the outbuildings remained, but all resemblance to things arable stopped there. The buildings were dwarfed by hills of coal and hills of slag. Dust coated the grass so that it looked gray. Out in the fields gray shapes squatted, their drooping metal topknots giving them the look of a flock of ailing birds. Men hurried or sauntered, but no one marched. Darius made a mental note to visit them again.

Each evening Otorin dressed him in finery and listened to him grumble about it. Each evening Darius stood in front of his chair and hoped that the second gong would ring. Each evening Phalastra made the same smooth apology for the Emperor's continued absence. He dispensed with it on the eighth night.

"His Imperial Majesty attended a fascinating experiment this afternoon," he announced as soon as he was seated. "I am happy to say that the Princess Regnant's remarkable gift came through with flying colors. The Emperor was quite delighted."

"The prisoner lived, then?" Darius inquired politely.

"Oh no, but that was never in the cards. The extraordinary thing was that the mail was unharmed. No other material has been able to withstand the cannon, and yet his Imperial Majesty assures me that the suit weighs little. The Magicians of Arundel are to be commended on their alchemy."

"I am glad that his Imperial Majesty was pleased by the gift," Darius said, and hoped that the Elector would miss the irony that he failed to keep out of his voice.

"If an old man may be permitted to offer advice . . ."

"I should be grateful for it, my Lord." Darius was on his guard.

"You have an unusual opportunity here, Lord Darius. I have served the Emperor for a good number of years, and I served his father before him. Never, in all that time, has a foreigner been invited to Court except for State Occasions. The Isphardis come and go, of course, but they are mere merchants.'' He paused and looked directly at his guest.

''If you are truly to observe us, my Lord, you must leave your prejudices at home. You must see us as we are, not as you have been told we are, not as you feel that we ought to be, but as plainly as you are able. Our two countries lie at opposite sides of our world and our traditions are so very different.'' He accompanied the final words with a smile that had no rebuke in it.

He's a good man, Darius thought, and smiled back. ''You are absolutely right, my Lord, and I am deeply sensible of the honor that his Imperial Majesty has accorded me. The truth is, there are so many new things for me to take in that I have difficulty keeping my bearings some days. I was not trained in courtly ways and I fear that I misspeak all too often.''

''I must confess that I find you a refreshing change, though I know full well that you can be dangerous.'' There was a twinkle in Phalastra's eye when he said it.

''I, my Lord?'' Darius expostulated, taking the bait. ''Dangerous? How can that be?''

''Now that I am too old for combat, there are only two kinds of men I fear; those who are more guileful than I and those, like you, my Lord, who have no guile at all.'' He laughed at the expression on Darius's face and turned to do his conversational duty to the diner on his other side.

chapter 3

Darius came awake with a start. A tornado? This far North? He clawed the bedcurtains aside. It was still dark, the mechanical clock unreadable. He lumbered around chairs and threw back the shutters. He leaned forward into the arrow slit, shivering in the cold draft, and peered down into the courtyard. As he did so the noise died and the air ceased to thrum. All he could see was dust swirling in the pewter light. He sat down on the cold ledge and twisted sideways to get a better view. He heard voices and boots on the flagstones, but saw no one. A little later, hooves clattered and somewhere in the distance a bell was rung. Then all was quiet once more.

Darius heaved himself out of the embrasure and padded into the anteroom to rouse Otorin and send him down to the kitchens. The pot of chai was a pretext for gossip, but Darius was glad of it when the squire returned. He sipped the hot liquid while Otorin made up the fire. He poured the man a bowl and pulled up a chair.

"Get yourself something to sit on and tell me what's going on."

"The night shift's all abuzz," Otorin said, dusting off his britches. He went and got a stool and set it across the hearth from Darius. "The scullery maids are standing around watching three men from a rotifer eat. It seems that they have an urgent message for the Emperor, but it is too early to disturb him. So says a Gentleman of the Bedchamber with a fondness for sweet rolls straight from the oven.''

''Did he know what the message was?''

''No, but the undercook says that there's a lot of movement in the Outland atmosphere. All the juice she's passed on to me so far has been accurate. Then there's a footman on breakfast who seems to have taken an interest in me. He said that messengers rode out at least a half of an hour ago.''

''You seem to have established quite a network of friends.''

''I should hope so, my Lord. After all, that's why they sent me.''

''I wondered how I had become so fortunate. I put it down to your fluent Umbrian,'' Darius said dryly. ''Well, it would all seem to add up to an attack in the making. D'you agree?''

''That was my conclusion, Sir.'' He swiveled on the stool as Darius got up and started to pace.

''If the bastards use the newfangled horseless chariots we saw in the vision, Varodias will have something worthwhile to try his cannons on.''

''I wouldn't like to be up in a rotifer. I remember what happened to them.''

''Might not be the same battle. The Archmage's projections weren't necessarily in order, I'm told.'' He stopped and poured himself some more chai.

''Whatever kind of battle it is, we have to be there to see it. D'you think you'll be able to finagle it, Sir?''

''Don't see why not. I was invited here to observe, and I have the feeling that his Imperial Majesty wishes to impress me with the superiority of his forces and methods.''

''I shall have to accompany you. A squire's place is beside his lord and your rank demands nothing less.''

Darius gave him a jaundiced look. "If it means you won't ask so many damned-fool questions, I'll be happy to have someone to polish my armor. In the meantime, get back to the kitchens and get me some breakfast along with any new information you happen to come across."

"Yes, Sir. And, if I may be so bold, I should like to suggest that when the hour comes when a gentleman may, with propriety, be seen abroad, your Lordship take a stroll in the long gallery and mingle a little with the locals?"

Darius took his advice, but the experience proved frustrating. There were too many people standing and talking in front of the pictures for exercise to be a realistic excuse for being there. He drifted from one group to another, conversations dying at his approach and springing up, redoubled, in his wake, until the barricade of polite bows and smiles defeated him. He retreated to his quarters to wait for the equerry. No equerry came.

He fared no better at dinnertime. When he broached the subject of the rotifer, Phalastra was theatrically disingenuous. A training exercise, no doubt. The Corps was rather unorthodox in its methods. It was, after all, breaking new ground in the art of warfare. And it was proof that the armed forces were in a constant state of readiness. Did the Lord Observor feel that the Magical Kingdoms were handicapped by the lack of standing armies?

He doesn't intend me to believe a word of this, Darius thought. He's telling me that he isn't allowed to tell me. Damned convoluted place.

He was kept in limbo for four days. There were no tours and no summons from the Emperor. Lord Phalastra did not attend Hall and his place was taken by the Oligarch Smouha, head of an Isphardi trading mission. He was full of news from other parts of the world, but knew nothing, or pretended to know nothing, about recent developments in his host's country. For all that, Darius was aware that troops were moving toward the Upper Causeway. They could be seen from the battlements. Otorin's talent for friendship proved indispensable and details filtered in. On the fifth night Phalastra appeared beside him again at dinner.

"I fear," the Elector said after they were seated, "that our gloomier prognosticators have been vindicated for once." He smiled encouragingly at Darius.

"And how is that, my Lord?"

"It seems that there is a pattern of disturbance within the Outland air. The head of the Rotifers—a good man—says there is no way that it can be a natural phenomenon." He turned his head and looked up sharply.

"They're going to attack." The Arundelian was blunt.

"It would seem so." Phalastra did not sound unduly concerned. "At the very least, we have to treat it as a fullscale threat. Especially in the light of the, ah, advanced warning that we received at Celador." He sipped fastidiously from his wine goblet and Darius sat back to let the footman clear.

He was going to have to approach carefully. The past few days had proved how little weight he carried here. The Elector was the closest thing he had to an ally at Court and he was going to have to play him as gently as a tickled trout.

"I've a boon to ask," he said cautiously. Phalastra looked up blandly from his fish. "I'm a man accustomed to action and I must confess that sitting around in palaces—even as beautiful a one as Angorn—irks me." He glanced at the Elector and saw that the man was smiling broadly.

"I must arrange some hunting for you," Phalastra exclaimed.

Darius shook his head in mock disbelief. "You already know what I'm going to ask for, don't you?"

"His Imperial Majesty has authorized me to invite you

to accompany me to the front. You may bring your body-servant, but I'm afraid that the cloudsteedsmen will have to stay at Angorn."

"You are most gracious, my Lord Elector. All this fine food is beginning to make my new clothes tight. I could do with a couple of days in the saddle."

"You are most welcome. We leave at Daymoonrise the day after tomorrow." He smiled again and added, "Body armor and a sharp sword are a good idea, but you need not wear them until we get to the front."

"Is the Imperial army short of men, my Lord?" Darius asked teasingly.

"A formidable swordsman is always welcome, but I do not think that his Imperial Majesty intends to make you earn your keep."

"I am here to do as the Emperor commands," Darius said seriously.

"Well said, Sirrah. But you will not see as an Umbrian sees, and that could be most valuable."

They both made ironic half bows to each other and finished the meal in high good humor.

The sun was up, but it was chilly as they rode out, single-shadowed, under the barbican. Daymoonrise was still the better part of an hour away. Darius wore standard mail under his surcoat. Otorin, banished to the rear of the troop, had his master's armor tied lumpily around his horse. Between them rode twenty knights and about twice that number of retainers. Phalastra was well cloaked against the cold, but sat his horse yarely and set a goodly pace.

They rode in silence, cowls up against the wind, and Darius felt the old surge of excitement that riding toward battle always brought. This was not his battle, he reminded himself. He was here merely to watch. If asked for his opinion, he must be circumspect and, above all, diplomatic. The Umbrians were said to be a touchy race. If he got himself sent home for opening his mouth too wide, the promise of a place at court that Arabella had dangled before him would be quick forgot.

They slept beside the road under canvas that night, though sleep was made difficult by the creak of supply wagons taking provisions to the front. They were early away once more and made good progress until they came up to a company of infantry. The Elector reined in his horse and stood on the stirrups. Seeing no easy way round, he summoned his standard bearer. The personal flag of the House of Estragoth was shaken out, the trumpeter blew, and the troops in front of them gave way.

They rode unchallenged to the Upper Causeway and were finally halted at the foot of the ramp beside the Angorn Gate. Phalastra reached into his cloak and pulled out the wax seal of the Emperor's laissez passer. He said nothing. He simply held it out and rode on past the sentinel. The standard bearer spurred to precede him and the rest of the party fell in behind.

The horses picked their way up the steep zigzag to the roadway at the top. They dismounted at a stretch of empty hitching rail on the South side and Darius waited while Phalastra conferred with one of his men about the disposition of his retinue. That done, the Elector beckoned him over.

"Come, my friend," he said as Darius came up, "let us go over to the Imperial Enclosure and watch the troops being deployed. Your man will be looked after."

"How long d'you reckon we'll be here?" Darius asked, adjusting his stride to the shorter man's pace. He was still not sure that he would be permitted to stay for the engagement itself.

"That rather depends on them, doesn't it?" Phalastra replied, pointing to the smudge of foreign atmosphere on the horizon. "There are tents for us below, and I'll wager you were more comfortable on a pallet last night than you've been for a while."

"I'd be a fool to take the bet."

"For myself, I made sure we brought a well-strung bed with us. I've done my share of fighting and living rough and I'm happy to be too old for it at last. Now all I do is advise and provide troops. Oh, and find the wherewithal to keep my men in the field. That is a year-round proposition."

"You're better off than we are in some ways when it comes to that. With a standing army, you know exactly what your workforce is going to be. With us, the Farod can be called away at any time and you're left with the old, the very young, and the women to tend the fields. I've been arguing for a regular army for years, but the agricultural tradition has too firm a hold. There are precious few knights within my own fief who are prepared to be away from their holdings for a full year."

Darius was looking around as he spoke, trying to take in as many details as he could. The basic structure of the Causeway was the same here as in Arundel. The roadway seemed to have a pinkish tinge, but the line of crenels fading away into the distance was the same. Four chariots could race down it abreast and have the same room as at Celador. There were chariots here too, but a name and wheels were all they had in common.

"Not much farther now," Phalastra said and indicated a roped-off area ahead where silk tents strained at the blocks that anchored their skirts. "On second thought, a stop at this particular marquee would be a good idea. Come, join me in some mulled ale. These old bones could do with something warming after that ride. You're too young to feel those kinds of aches yet, but you will. Besides"—the corners of his mouth curled up—"you will have the pleasure of meeting his Imperial Majesty in a little while."

"I shall?" Darius ducked under the blue and white awning. "In that case I shall be more than happy to join you. You might have given me a little more warning, you know. I'm scarcely dressed for an Imperial audience." They seated themselves at a table hard by a brazier and conversation stopped while they gave their order.

"You need have no fear on that account. The Emperor keeps no state up here. Nor would a warning have helped you prepare something to say, for I have no idea if the Emperor will address you, let alone on what topic. Just remember not to swear." They sat in silence and drank the hot, spicy brew.

"That's better," Phalastra said as he put his empty flagon down. He wiped his mouth with the back of his hand. "Ready, my Lord?"

"As ready as I'm going to be. No, no. I insist on paying, but I'd be grateful if you would take whatever is necessary." He held out his purse. "I haven't mastered your coins yet."

They continued on to the canopied gold square that was the Emperor's tent. Drawn up beside it was the most elaborate steam chariot Darius had yet seen. A liveried footman, wearing light gray gloves, was stoking it from a leather bin. No time to admire it now, the Elector was already entering the tent. Darius straightened his shoulders and his cloak and followed him in.

The inside of the tent seemed to glow as the sun came through the silk and burnished the carpets that covered the floor. The far end of the tent was open and flush against the battlements. The throne blocked out the center. It was set on a platform of steps and faced out over the plain. The Emperor was invisible, but a kester hawk shifted feet along a perch just to the side of the throne. Phalastra walked toward it without hesitation. Darius tagged unenthusiastically along. The Elector turned, faced the throne, and went down slowly on one knee. Darius caught the slight wince the effort provoked and wondered how old Phalastra really was.

"Bid you good morrow, my good gray fox. We trust your journey hither was a pleasant one?" The high voice sounded pleased with itself.

"May the best of the day be before my Liegelord. A very pleasant trip an I thank you, made the more pleasant by the knowledge that each passing league brought me closer to this spot." The Elector's face was serenely innocent as he made the remark and Darius could not see enough of the Emperor's to gauge his reaction to such patent flattery.

"If your Imperial Majesty permits . . . ?" Phalastra looked up for permission to proceed before continuing. "I should like to bring to your Imperial attention the presence of the Observor from Arundel, the most noble Lord Darius of Gwyndryth." The Emperor leaned forward and looked around. Darius stepped forward and bowed.

"Be welcome in our presence, my Lord Observor. We may yet have something for you to see."

"Ah, Majesty, I have already seen wonders of mechanics and invention," Darius heard himself say. He took a deep breath and plunged in again. "I look forward to seeing how modern warfare should be conducted." He stopped himself and took a couple of surreptitious deep breaths. His hands were clammy.

"In that case, my Lord, we shall not keep you from your instruction." The Emperor turned his attention to the kneeling figure before him. "Estragoth, do you take our guest to some point of vantage from whence he can view our forces. See that he does not lack, my Lord. On this we charge you.'' He waved a gauntleted hand at each in turn and the hawk uttered a sharp cry.

''As your Imperial Majesty commands,'' Phalastra said and levered himself to his feet. Both men bowed and backed away, careful to keep their faces to the monarch for as long as possible. The Emperor was busy soothing his pet.

Phalastra looked at his armclock as soon as they were out of the tent.

''You handled yourself very well,'' he said. ''I knew that you would. Let's go down the Causeway a bit. I'd like to be fairly close to the gate. My boys should be passing through soon and I like to watch them all go past. After that, we can visit that other tent again for victuals. What say you?''

''I say lead on.'' If the impromptu audience had been a test, Darius thought, I must have passed.

They positioned themselves West of the gate and Darius stared out. The ruins of the Giants' Causeway had been cleared away on either side of the gateway. Cavalry were pouring through and wheeling left. He leaned out and looked down. There was a row of five black tubes below, mounted between large wheels. They did not look particularly menacing, but he knew them for the Emperor's newest weapons. He tried to imprint the picture on his memory. Otorin was bound to want all the details.

''There are so many strange uniforms,'' Darius said, pushing himself up. ''I shall rely on you to point your men out to me.''

''You should have no trouble. They will be wearing the colors of my house.'' The Elector gestured elegantly to the blue and burgundy of his cloak and clothing.

''Very handsome too, if I may say so.''

''They represent spilled blood under a clear sky. Our motto is 'Be vigilant.' '' He turned and looked toward the gate, glanced back and added, "I do my best to follow the precept." Darius had no idea what to say and settled for looking out at the troops again.

The Imperial black and silver were everywhere. Men marched in step and executed maneuvers neatly. His eye was caught by a troop in green with white sashes. Their leader rode a white charger and his armor flashed in the sun. He was accompanied by a herald and three trumpeters. Phalastra followed his gaze.

"Ah, yes. That's the Elector of Ondor. He prefers the dangers of the battlefield to the rigors of science or the welfare of his vassals. He cuts a splendid figure, one must admit that." It was clear that the admission was grudging. "The combinations of his ancestry have been good to him. He is much sought after by the ladies and has the bad taste to show off his mind." There were deep currents here, and Darius resolved to put Otorin to work in the kitchens when they returned to see what he could find out.

"Surely," he interjected, "those are your men coming through the gateway now. Are those not your colors?" Phalastra turned to look. "I must say," Darius continued, "they look very smart and well trained, too. They've a fine swing to the arm and their weapons look all of an angle." Phalastra did not answer. He was busy with something at his belt. He drew out a spyglass and put it to his eye. "Do you know where their station will be?" the Holdmaster asked.

"It is our honor to hold the center," Phalastra replied, his attention on his men. "My older son commands them. He's a scrappy fighter and the men adore him." He lowered the glass and looked around at Darius. "Makes me jealous every now and then," he confessed, "but he'll get to make his share of unpopular decisions in due time." He shook his head and smiled to himself. "You know, Gwyndryth, it's like a big tapestry: one of the ones that take generations to complete? The same patterns keep cropping up. The colors change as the years pass, but certain designs recur.'' There was pride and warmth in the voice now.

''Let us stand here and converse as we have been doing,'' he went on. ''Your height will mark you out, and they will think that I am discussing weighty matters with the man from the land of legends. It will impress them.'' He gave Darius a conspiratorial smile, one overlord to another. The Holdmaster threw back his head and laughed.

''Tell me, is there anybody you don't use?''

''Only those I have no use for,'' Phalastra replied good-naturedly.

''Your boys are marching straight ahead,'' Darius said, changing the subject back. ''Does that mean that the cavalry will try to outflank the enemy in a containment effort, or does it betoken battle in an extended line?''

''Not exactly. We expect to outnumber them, as always. The idea is for the center, my men in fact, to take the brunt of the sortie and give ground while slowing the attack. At a signal from the Emperor, the ranks will break and appear to flee, thereby drawing the enemy away from their support base. If they are hose-attached, it will enable the cavalry to attack the flanks and get at the hoses. If they are not, my boys will peel off to either side and herd them toward our new weapons.''

''The ones drawn up below us?''

''Those are the Emperor's new cannon.'' Phalastra agreed. ''There are more on the other side of the gate.''

''What if they use their new weapons?''

''With all due respect to your Archmage, we shall wait until we see them with our own eyes. Anyway,'' he added offhandedly, ''the plan will work equally well against their conventional weapons or anything new they may have come up with.''

"I certainly hope you're right and I hope you have enough of the cannons."

"It is true," Phalastra admitted, "that they have not been used in combat yet, but they performed very creditably during the testing." He broke off. "You must excuse me for a while: the regiment is approaching."

Darius glanced down and saw a figure riding toward the Causeway. The horseman pulled up and swept out his sword. The Elector drew his own blade and held it out into the sunlight. "That is my older boy," he said.

The tableau held until Phalastra brought his sword down. The heir to Estragoth sheathed his weapon, wheeled about and galloped back to the head of his command. Phalastra rescabbarded his own blade.

"One of the penalties of office, I fear," he said with a sigh. "It's getting harder to hold that sword out." Despite the words, he was plainly pleased by the courtesy his son had shown him. He looked up at Darius.

"You know what the two biggest problems with hereditary titles are?" he asked. "You can't turn them down and you can't retire. There are no former Electors. If you're born to a title, you have to die to it, too.

"Well now," he said with a touch of self-mockery, "that is quite enough of that. Have you seen enough? My contingent will be the last to deploy for a while." He looked at his armclock and Darius automatically checked the sun. "A spot of luncheon perhaps?"

"That would be most welcome. The morning's ride has put an edge on my appetite."

"Good. Let's eat at my headquarters rather than in the mess tent. The food will be good, I can promise you that. I took the precaution of sending my own cook ahead with a wagonload of provisions." He smiled. "I have been at this game for a very long time."

* * *

The Elector had been modest about the quality of his food. The lunch had been simple, but delicious, and dinner had been better than any meal Darius had had at Angorn. The wines had been from the family demesne and had been poured with a liberal hand. As a result, Darius had slept early and heavily. He was up at dawn nevertheless, his mouth dry and his eyes gritty. Otorin was snoring on his pallet and Darius decided that a ride to the top of the Causeway would clear his head.

The stars were just beginning to dim when he tethered his horse. Campfires glittered in the blackness of the plain. They were at once brave and futile. Even here in Umbria there was no feeling that mankind was destined to live beyond the wall. The Causeway had become a boundary rather than a starting place. He stamped his feet to get the circulation going.

A damp wind pressed his cloak against his back. A Southerly, aimed straight at the Outlanders, was a harbinger of battle. At least it would have been in Arundel. Here it was no more than happenstance. He looked East. There was a green tinge to the horizon. It would turn pink soon and the day would be upon them. There would be fighting: he was sure of it. It was in the air as surely as the acrid fumes of stale lees from the striped tent. Out on the plain the fires began to die.

"Give you goodday, my Lord Observor. Oh, forgive me. I did not mean to startle you."

"May the best of the day be before you, my Lord of Estragoth. I was musing on the weather. You are early abroad." He spoke lightly, but he wondered if the Umbrian was spying on him. Nothing was certain in this country.

"When you know that the clock weights are on their final descent sleep seems such a waste of time. Could it be that you, my Lord, have succumbed to the softness of the bed at Angorn and found that straw makes for an indifferent stuffing?''

''My bed, I assure you, was most comfortable. Besides, your excellent wines ensured that I slept well, straw or no straw.'' Darius was feeling meanspirited for his suspicions.

Phalastra raised the lantern he was carrying and peered up. ''Methinks I see a man in need of a victory to celebrate.'' The eyes gleamed in the yellow light. ''Let us not wait upon events.'' He lowered the lantern and linked an arm through Darius's. ''Sack, I think, would help.''

''A little early for that, I fear.''

''Nonsense. Just think of it as a stirrup cup.'' Lamps bloomed inside the mess tent. ''And our timing is immaculate.''

''I have a feeling that there will be hunting today, though I cannot tell you why I think so,'' Darius said as he held the tent flap aside. The vinegar stench assailed the nostrils.

''We are both old hands. We have seen too many battles, you and I. To survive so long, a man develops respect for such feelings. I, too, feel that there will be an engagement, but I do not think that it will amount to much. There will be feints and sorties all along the line to test our strength. My boys must convince them that the main bulk of the army is concentrated behind them. The decoys must act like hunters. It is a time for hot blooded young men to distinguish themselves in the manner best suited to the impetuousness of youth.''

''I can readily understand that kind of warfare,'' Darius said as the sack arrived. He winced as the first mouthful went down, but the warmth that grew in his belly felt good. ''I'm used to being down there in the thick of things,'' he continued. ''What I am going to find difficult to adjust to is warfare from up here. I'm not used to seeing things from above and far away. When I was watching the troops deploy yesterday, I couldn't help thinking how much more like a game it seems from up here. Not knowing the soldiers helps, of course. To me, those aren't people out there. They're squadrons and units."

Phalastra took a pull at his sack. "I know how you feel, my friend. I had to make that transition too, and it was not an easy one. You draw up the order of battle, you make contingency plans in case the enemy changes its tactics, you make sure that your commanders understand them all, and then you have to stand back and leave them in the hands of others. There may be more chances for bodily harm on the field, but command above the field is not without its perils. A mistake down there can mean the loss of a head up here . . ." He let the sentence trail off. "But you, my Lord," he resumed on a more cheerful note, "have come here to observe and there is no better place from which to do that."

The sack was having the desired effect and Darius felt better. "You're right," he said, "of course you are. I must learn detachment. I have always been . . ."

He was cut off by a blare of trumpets. He closed his eyes. They were very close.

"It appears that the enemy has also risen early today," Phalastra remarked calmly. "It is a theory of mine that the Outlanders are troubled by bright light. I have known them break off an engagement on a clear day when the sun and Daymoon were overhead. They live in a perpetual murk, so it would be strange if it were otherwise."

"A good point, my Lord. And speaking of light, how did the trumpeters know what was happening at the front?"

"There are riders with flags who signal us."

"Very ingenious. Should we go out and see for ourselves?"

"We have time for another sack. This stage takes hours." The trumpets contradicted him. "The Regiment must have done an outstanding job, or else the skirmishing began before it was light," Phalastra temporized. "The trumpets say that the center is falling back. Perhaps it is not too soon to go and find a vantage point."

The Upper Causeway was in an orderly turmoil when they emerged. Messengers trotted to and from the ramp. Men were moving purposefully. Everyone seemed to be en route to a designated place. No one was staring out over the battlements. They made their way against the tide until Phalastra found a spot that suited him. He got out his spyglass. Below, carts full of iron balls were being dragged into place.

"Too fast," Phalastra muttered. "They're giving ground too fast." Darius squinted. The growing light was rose and gold, but it did little to illuminate the goings-on a league away.

"What's happening?" he asked. For answer, Phalastra thrust the glass at him. Darius put it to his eye and fiddled with it until the circle came clear. There was movement in the center and it was far from orderly. A knot of horsemen fought with something still shrouded. There was a flash of light, and Darius snatched the glass from his eye and bit back a curse. Phalastra retrieved the instrument. Darius swabbed his eyes with the edge of his cloak and heard the Umbrian gasp.

"What is it, my Lord?"

"The Archmage was right. Here, see for yourself."

Darius focused once more and began to swear in earnest. There was a tugging at his sleeve and he looked down.

"My Lord, you must forgive me, but I am bound to leave you. The Emperor may have need of me."

"Of course. I can fend for myself and I promise not to get in the way."

"Do you keep the glass. It will help you keep track of things."

"Thank you. I shall take good care of it."

Darius took the proffered instrument and the two men bowed to each other. The Elector walked briskly away and Darius swung his attention back to the battlefield. He blinked his right eye to hasten its clearing and cautiously refocused the glass. A riderless horse bolted across the circle. He lifted the front end a trifle and men came into view. They were dropping back all right and they were drawing the enemy in the direction of the waiting guns, but burning hair and uniforms were no part of any Umbrian plan.

Beyond them, more riderless horses were galloping around in front of an oncoming cloud of dust. It began to fray as if the wind were shredding it and an ugly, questing snout appeared atop a moving metal box. He had seen the thing before; in the conjured nightmare at Celador. A knight rode up, crouched over his lance, and spurred at it. The impact threw the rider back over the rump of his charger and the vehicle lumbered on unharmed. Useless, Darius thought.

The long nose moved from left to right and spat flame. Darius was ready this time and had the eyepiece away in time. When he looked back there were fires on the plain once more, but he was loath to speculate about the fuel. There were more of the boxes now and if there had been a plan for dealing with them, none was apparent. He scanned the wings, but all he could see was dust.

A rout was in progress and the action had moved close enough for the shouts and screams to be heard. Trumpets brayed to his right, but he had no idea what they meant. He could see five of the enemy wagons now, crushing their way over charred bodies. Men scrabbled at their sides and were ignored or brushed away by flame. The spyglass brought them shockingly close. It was as if they were at the gate already. He lowered the glass and blinked.

There was intense activity around the guns below. The trumpets blew in unison, but had no effect that he could see on what went on. They blared again and this time the guns roared in answer. Roar was not the right word, but he did not know how to describe the sound. The effect was obvious enough. The salvo cut furrows through the milling horses and the running men. Darius swore and watched the panic escalate. Riders and foot soldiers scrambled to get out of the line of fire.

The crawlers belched, and while they did not have the range of the cannon, they did their part to clear the way for the coming confrontation. The guns spoke again, and the leading vehicle slewed abruptly and came to rest at a drunken cant. A second ball punched a hole in the exposed side, releasing a cloud of brown. A ragged cheer went up. It was drowned out by screams as the other crawlers swept the area with flame. The guns were firing at will and adding their quota to the dead and maimed.

There was nowhere left for the men to flee. The haven of the gate was denied them. Some tried anyway, but most threw themselves down to await whatever fate their prayers could not ward off. Above them, heat crackled and metal flew. The guns had the longer reach, and the attackers were battered as the ground beneath their treads grew too slippery to maneuver on. They bogged down in a churn of mud and flesh. There was no cheering when the last of them was broached.

The guns fell silent at last and Darius could hear the snapping of the flags and the moans of the dying. It was a frozen moment and he felt as if he were looking at a painting by an artist with a diseased imagination. Then hooves clattering on the roadway broke the spell.

He scanned the horizon anxiously, but the enemy did not appear to be following up on its advantage. Perhaps the cavalry had intercepted them while he was concentrating on the battle for the gate. And what an extraordinary battle it had been. Otorin should have been with him. There had been too much going on for one man to take in; so much that was new.

He glanced down the Causeway and saw the Elector of Estragoth approaching. The head was up, the back was straight, but the gait was unsteady and the eyes unseeing. The face was drained of blood and emotion and he gave no sign of noticing Darius. The Arundelian reached out a hand and halted him.

"Ah, my Lord, my Lord." The voice was low and napped in sympathy. "They did wondrous well, those men of yours. Without their valor, that advance could never have been stopped. But for their courage, the Angorn Gate would now lie in ruins." The Elector looked up at him and examined his face as if he were a stranger.

"But the cost, Gwyndryth, the cost." He sounded as old and attenuated as an unshrived ghost. Darius put an arm around his shoulders in mute consolation and found them as rigid as the man's composure.

"My son commanded them." The eyes were open wide, the gaze elsewhere.

"I know, my Lord. I saw him." The old man said nothing. "I have had to talk to the parents of boys who have been lost many times, too many times, and I still can't do it well. What can a man say? Mayhap he is not dead? We do not know for sure? There are many men in the Wisewomen's tents who cannot remember their names?"

"The House of Estragoth, my Lord Observor," Phalastra cut in, pride reviving in his voice, "has always led its retainers from the van."

"It would be better for you if you could weep for him," Darius replied. Phalastra shook free of the encircling arm and looked up sharply.

"To do so would be to admit that he was dead and that I will not do until I must." He held Darius's eyes with an intense, but unfocused, stare. He put a hand out and patted his sleeve, then he inclined his head curtly, turned on his heel, and made his way to the hitching rail.

Darius watched him go with admiration and pity. It is not meet for a man to bury his child, he thought. One knows the risks of war, but there is no defense against the loss of a son. Marianna came into his thoughts and he felt her absence. She was the only child he had and he didn't even know where she was.

chapter 4

The aftermath of the battle was as chaotic as the battle itself and seemed almost as bloody. He found Otorin easily enough, but their tent and their spare linen had been commandeered for the Wisewomen. The Elector's retinue had the unenviable job of reclaiming bodies in burgundy uniforms. The unimportant and the unrecognizable were buried in a common pit. There were few left to mark their passing and Phalastra was nowhere to be seen. The Arundelians did what they could to help and then returned to Angorn. It took them far longer than had the Northward trip. The roads were clogged and there was no standard bearer to clear a path.

The palace was a cheerless place. Attendance at Hall was sparse and the conversations he overheard were perfunctory. He would have preferred to sup in his rooms with Otorin but, fearing that the Emperor might put in a sudden appearance and take his absence amiss, he went anyway. He spent his mornings discussing the fighting and helping Otorin write a report for the Princess Regnant. In the afternoons he walked in the town or on the leads. When it rained, as it frequently did, he tramped up and down the galleries.

The monotony was broken by a service of thanksgiving, held in the Chapel of the Mother. It was a large building, set behind the Emperor's tower, and made remarkable by the number and beauty of its colored windows. Darius found the ceremony impressive and incomprehensible. The ritual movements and costumes meant nothing to him and, since the service was conducted in Umbrian, he was only able to catch one word in four. It did provide his first glimpse of the Empress Zhane, a large blonde with a passive face, and of the Mother Supreme. The latter, in padded robe and wimple, sat on a throne on a level with Varodias and above the Empress. The Church was said to wield great power because of the land and wealth it controlled, and he wondered if the symbolism of the seating reflected political reality or a compromise in an ongoing struggle. The Darius who had come to Angorn would never have thought along those lines. He congratulated himself sardonically and resolved to take lessons in Umbrian.

After that the days hung heavy again. Once a sennight he joined the cloudsteedsmen in a boar hunt and caught up on barracks gossip. Otorin reported that the Emperor had secluded himself in his workshops, that the master baker's son had succumbed to his wounds, and that the commanders were blaming each other for the "victory." It was with a feeling of relief and trepidation that Darius received the news that he was to present himself to the Emperor.

He was dressed to Otorin's satisfaction and ready for the Summoner well before the appointed hour, but when the knock came, his guide was a Gentleman of the Bedchamber. He was not taken to the Presence Chamber, but was ushered into a smaller, paneled room with weapons, arranged in patterns, on the ceiling. Even here there was a throne and a perch for a hunting bird, but the throne was close to the fire and the perch was empty.

Varodias was dictating to a scribe who sat on a footstool by his feet. The throne was old and dark with the kind of luster that only generations of conscientious polishing can produce. Varodias was dressed for it. He wore light gray with dark brown piping. The cut was simple, no puffed sleeves or pantaloons, and, as a result, the Emperor stood out clearly, as if posed for a portrait. Behind him, two gentlemen-in-waiting played cup and ball by the window.

Darius advanced across the opulent carpeting and bowed low. He held the position until a gray gloved hand wagged him upright. The Emperor continued with his dictation as his hand waved Darius into the empty chair across the hearth. He dismissed the scribe and the man picked up his stool and disappeared behind the throne. The Emperor stared at his visitor for a long time before he broke the silence.

''We are pleased to see you once again, my Lord Observor. We trust that you remain well?'' The question was affably asked and the already nervous Darius felt a thrill of alarm.

''Most well. I thank you, your Imperial Majesty,'' he replied with a little bow from the waist. The Emperor was being cordial, which was dangerous, and he was being allowed to sit during an audience, which was unprecedented. He didn't like it at all.

''We are pleased.'' Varodias paused, heightening the tension. ''You are aware, no doubt, that we have been inordinately busy. We shall not hide from you the fact that our recent, most glorious victory cost us dearly. The Mother, may Her name be revered, teaches us that with great joy comes pain. This battle was perfect proof of Her abiding wisdom. Had we not developed our new armament in time, She would have had to vouchsafe us one of Her miracles. You witnessed the fight, my Lord, would you not agree with us?''

''Indeed I would, your Imperial Majesty.''

''What were your impressions? What conclusions did the Observor from Arundel draw?'' The questions were sharp and staccato; more like the Varodias that Darius had expected.

''It was like nothing I have ever encountered, Sire. Of course I did see those contraptions in the cloud at Celador, but that was not the same at all. There was no way that the Imperial Forces could have prepared for them.''

''Think you not, Sirrah? Think you not? Do you consider it then mere chance that we rushed our cannon to completion in time?''

''No, Sire, not at all,'' Darius said hastily. ''I was going to add that I thought the placement of the long guns was a stroke of genius.'' He was rewarded with an ambiguous smile.

''What would you have done in our place, my Lord?'' The question was innocently put, but Darius was aware of the trap.

''Not near so well as your Imperial Majesty. Had I been in command, we would be manning yon battlements now.''

''You are more the courtier than we were led to expect, my Lord Observor.'' The compliment was clearly ironic, but Darius sensed that the Emperor was pleased. The gray thumbs were stroking the ends of the armrests as if they were lapkits. ''And what have you learned from watching the battle?''

''That the enemy may be using the weapons of tomorrow, but he is wasting them on the tactics of yesteryear.''

''Say you so?''

''I do, Sire. They denied themselves half their firepower by attacking in the old formation. Out in the traditional triangle and slap down the middle. They might as well have had hoses to protect.''

''Interesting.'' Each syllable was said separately and Darius suddenly felt cold. ''What, then, are we to expect? Will they learn?''

"Has he learned? That is the question, your Imperial Majesty. That he will learn is certain. We, for our part, must adapt even more swiftly."

"We too are learning, my Lord Observor. It is what we have been slaving at since our victory. For the first time, we have samples of their writing." The Emperor leaned forward. There was a spot of color in each cheek. "The vehicles themselves are most ingenious. We have not fathomed them yet, but they are, after all, the first such artifacts to have fallen into our hands. They are a most remarkable race, those accursed Others." His eyes glittered in the firelight and the left hand wove an independant conversation around his words. "They have become mechanized overnight and in such a sophisticated fashion." There was admiration in the voice. "They are a worthy opponent for us." He stopped and gave Darius a measuring look. He sat back.

"Scribe!" There was a brief shuffling and then the little man appeared.

"At your service, Exalted."

"We have digressed. Where were we?"

The scribe turned back a page and scanned it. " 'Will they learn?' "

"No. Before that."

" 'What, then, are we to expect?' "

"Just so. Our thanks, scribe." The man ducked his head and scuttled back behind the throne. Darius had not realized that the conversation was being recorded, and the knowledge did not make him feel any more confident. He held his hands out to the fire.

"Well?" Varodias said.

"I think we can expect them to attack in an extended line or from several points across a broad front. I do not know how far those things can go, but if the unthinkable happened and they got behind the Causeway, there is no telling how much damage they could do.''

''We have been trying to ascertain the range of their battle craft, but it is well nigh impossible until we understand more about the engine. They are puny compared to the ones that run our steam chariots, but we must confess that they worked well enough in the field. It is a complex and fascinating problem. There is much work to be done.'' The Emperor broke off and watched the fire for a while. Darius waited uneasily. The Emperor looked up again.

''What thought you of our cavalry, my Lord Observor?''

''I thought they acquitted themselves with great bravery, Sire.''

''Oh, aye. When it was too late.'' Varodias was openly contemptuous. ''What you mean, Sirrah, is that, while they may be admirable warriors, they lack leadership and discipline.''

''I should never have said anything like that, your Imperial Majesty,'' Darius objected.

''Of course you would not, my Lord, but you would have been right had you done so.''

What's going on? What does he want from me? Darius wondered.

''I fear that this sudden change in warfare caught them at a disadvantage, Sire,'' he said carefully. Varodias stared at him. ''I do have a suggestion with regard to the cannons,'' Darius continued, goaded by the eyes. ''If your Imperial Majesty permits,'' he added hastily.

''Cannon, my Lord, cannon. There is no *s*. You may proceed.''

''Thank you, Sire. What I have to say is especially important if the enemy attacks in an extended line, but I think it is a good general principle. I think you should put the, ah, cannon and their boilers on proper mountings and harness them behind teams of horses. If you had stations for coal and projectiles along the walls, you would give the guns mobility.''

The shadows cast by the firelight deepened the creases in the Emperor's face. He looks tired, Darius thought. Why doesn't he say something? The fire licked itself and popped. In the ensuing stillness the scratch of quill on parchment formed a ground and the clack of wood on wood, as the gentlemen-in-waiting whiled away the time with their game, was the counterpoint. The Emperor might have been asleep, but for the drumming of his fingers.

''Very good, my Lord Observor, very good. We shall heed you.'' The words, when they came, were said so quietly that Darius leaned forward. The Emperor sat straighter. ''You have confirmed us in a decision to ask a favor of you.'' The head was up and the eyes suddenly direct.

''We took many casualties.'' The voice was back to normal. ''We have asked our vassals for extra contingents. They will grumble and they will drag their feet, but they will provide the men. May the Mother grant that it be soon enough.''

''Selah to that, Sire.''

''We need the cavalry. They need leadership, discipline, and a firm hand to guide them. They need someone who understands what has happened. In short, my Lord, they need you.'' Darius's eyes widened and he swallowed. This was the last thing that he had expected.

The Emperor watched him and smiled. ''Our cavalry,'' he said, ''is composed of arrogant, wellborn, self-centered glory hunters, but they are magnificent horsemen and brave to the point of folly.'' He cocked his head and raised his eyebrows. ''Will you tame them for us?''

''Your Imperial Majesty does me great and undeserved honor,'' Darius temporized. ''I misdoubt me, however, if those same hot, young, bloods would be willing to accept a foreign yoke.'' Neatly done, he thought and relaxed a little.

''On the contrary, it is the only yoke they would accept and the need is urgent.''

''What of the officers they have now, Sire?''

''The Colonel has been dismissed and exiled to his estates,'' Varodias said matter-of-factly. ''We were merciful, as is our wont. Three of his top officers were killed, and the fourth, the Adjutant, is a good man and loyal to us. He will obey our fiat. There is no problem there.''

Darius hesitated. He was tempted. Regimental command in the Umbrian army. They were magnificent fighters, and what better way to fulfill Arabella's mandate. This would bring him close to the Emperor and closer still to the action. Unless . . .

''Your Imperial Majesty is most persuasive, but there would have to be a condition.''

''Condition?'' It was Varodias's turn to be surprised.

''Yes, Sire. I cannot retrain your men unless I can lead them in battle.''

''Lead them in battle? In the field?''

''Aye, Sire. I cannot train men to face a death I cannot face myself. I should be asking them to do many new things. How would it look if I was not willing to trust my life to my tactics?''

Varodias sat back into the throne and stroked his chin. He looked speculatively at his guest. The silence stretched.

''It is nobly said, my friend, but we doubt that the Princess Regnant would countenance it. To assist us is one thing, to fight for us quite another.'' The Emperor made the statement reluctantly.

''I cannot do it else, Sire.''

''You speak to our heart, my Lord, but we shall have to think on this. We thank you for your counsel and for your offer of assistance.'' The Emperor pulled himself upright again and inclined his head. The audience was over.

Darius got to his feet and bowed. Had he offended the Emperor by making the demand? It was impossible to tell. The man just sat there with that sinister smile on his face. He bowed again and withdrew.

He padded back through the corridors with conflicting thoughts bombarding his mind. Varodias's motives ought to be his chief concern, but ideas for reorganizing the Regiment kept intruding. He bowed to the accompanying gentleman at the outer door to his apartment and let himself in. He slipped off his sash and was unhooking his jacket as he headed for the bedchamber. Otorin came forward to help him.

''How went the audience, my Lord?'' He took the jacket and brought it over to the press.

''Fairly well, I think,'' Darius said as nonchalantly as he could. ''He asked me to pull the cavalry together for him.''

''He did what?'' Otorin turned with satisfying surprise.

''He said they lacked leadership and discipline and asked me if I would do something about it.''

''I see. And what did you say?''

''What could I say? I told him that I was very flattered,'' Darius replied, knowing full well that he was drawing the story out. It was a rare opportunity to be ahead of his aide and he was enjoying it.

''But?''

''But that I could only accept if I could fight alongside them.'' He smiled at the look of horror on Otorin's face.

''You're joking. Tell me that you are joking.''

''I couldn't be more serious. It wouldn't work at all if the man telling them what to do, making them learn new ways of fighting, sent them off to battle and stayed safely up on the Causeway.''

"That's all very well, but what do you suppose our Princess is going to say if her representative and, supposedly, one of her better officers gets himself killed in an Umbrian battle?"

"The Emperor said much the same thing," Darius admitted unconcernedly, "but I wasn't thinking about the Princess when I made the offer. I wasn't expecting any of this, you know."

"I understand that, Sir, but I do think we ought to consult with Celador. This has no precedent and there are international questions to be considered." Otorin had rallied and was being calmly reasonable.

"A pox on international considerations!" Darius retorted. "The army's in trouble and I was asked for my help. I'm sure there would be international questions if the Umbrian forces got wiped out in the next battle."

"Very true, Sir, but, at the very least, we must keep Celador informed. I have a packet ready to send by cloudsteed. We'll simply add this report. Parchment is the only backplate armor we have in this assignment and it would be foolish not to protect ourselves back home."

"It will all probably come to nothing. The old raptor said that he would have to think about it. He probably won't offer it to me again." Darius pulled off a second boot and donned his slippers.

"I wouldn't be too sure of that, Sir." Otorin retrieved the boots and went and stood them next to the clothespress. "You know what the latest joke among the servants is? What's a Varodias victory? That's where the enemy loses all their machines and he loses all his men. My guess is that he can't find an Umbrian to do the job or that he plans to use you to discomfit someone."

"That's as may be." Darius started to pace. "The facts are that the cavalry is badly in need of reorganization. It isn't just a question of Umbria. Every army will have to make drastic changes to meet this new threat. If my ideas, and I do have some ideas, prove effective, they can be adapted to suit our own forces. Besides''—he turned and grinned sheepishly—''I rather hope he does ask me again. I'm bored, Otorin. I hate being cooped up in a palace.''

''I know that, Sir,'' Otorin said, with a return of his old humor. ''I do know that. In the meantime, let's go into the cabinet and compose a nice letter to our sovereign lady.'' He shot a sly look at Darius. ''By the way, how did the Formal mode go?''

''Well enough for him to offer me an important job. You can always make it fancier in the report if you want to. You're good at that. Now, let's get to it before I forget what was said.''

The following afternoon Otorin answered a thumping at the anteroom door. He returned with a packet that was secured by an oversized seal and handed it to Darius who sat propped up on the bed.

''This came for you, Sir. The old Imperial doesn't waste any time, does he?''

''Very grand.'' He turned the package in his hands. ''Fetch us a knife, there's a good lad. I'd like to keep the seal intact if I can.'' He looked up and grinned. ''I want to impress my daughter with it when I get home.''

''Best find out what's inside,'' Otorin replied and produced a hunting knife.

Darius slid it under the wax and gently pried the seal loose. He tugged out two pieces of vellum and looked them over.

''What are they? Are they what I think they are?''

''Um?'' Darius looked up. ''Oh, they're letters of marque. It seems that I have been appointed Colonel of the Regiment. Here, see for yourself.'' He handed them over. "Beautiful, aren't they? I'm glad they still do some things by hand here."

"They certainly are." Otorin held them up to the gaslight. "The calligraphy is very fine. Makes all the difference, good calligraphy." He looked over at his temporary master. "Do I take it that you intend to accept?"

"I do."

"Very well, Sir, but I must tell you that I think it better to wait until we hear from Celador. The Emperor will understand the protocol involved."

"Frankly, Otorin, I don't give a rap about protocol. The Emperor may be prepared to wait, but the Outlanders won't. Too much time has been wasted as it is. Arrange for horses and pack my practical clothes. I've an Adjutant Major to see and the sooner the better." He strode toward the door to the cabinet. He turned in the doorway. "She may forbid me, if she wishes to, and I shall obey, but until I hear from Celador I mean to do what I can."

chapter 5

The Adjutant Major in question stalked through the flaps of the tent that Darius had commandeered. He was a lean man with short, gray hair and a dark, trim moustache. His face was set, his back straight, and his legs bowed. He marched smartly up to the campaign desk and snapped his head down in salute.

"Adjutant Major Cortauld reporting as ordered, Sir."

"At ease, Adjutant Major, and thank you for coming so promptly." Darius rose and came around the desk. He would need this man's good will and he set out to get it. "Why don't we sit comfortably," he said, indicating a chair and pulling another over to face it. "We have much to talk about."

The Umbrian sat down, but remained taut. Darius followed suit and looked him over carefully. It would be easier if he knew more about the man. He should have made inquiries before he came charging down here, but he had wanted to give the Umbrian as little time as possible to prepare for him.

"I presume that the Emperor has been in communication and that you know why I am here."

"I got a message from the palace informing me of your appointment. It arrived barely an hour before you did." The reply was stiff. The wind-bronzed face was impassive.

"I can readily understand if you resent the imposition

of a foreigner over your head. Especially if there was no consultation. If I were in your britches, I'd feel the same. I'd like you to know that I did not seek this appointment and indeed I may very well get into trouble at home for letting his Imperial Majesty talk me into this. I would ask you to believe me when I say that the good, in fact the survival, of this splendid regiment was my sole consideration.

"I have no wish to usurp your authority. I am simply here to prepare the regiment for the next battle. Though the letters of marque do not say so, this is a purely temporary command." He looked across the barrier of space that separated them. The stony, polite attention had not moderated. He decided to change tack.

"This motherless war has finally changed, and if we don't change with it, this regiment will end up as a quaint, ceremonial relic. I've been a cavalryman all my life and I'm not willing to sit back and see that life become meaningless." He watched as some of the tension went out of the other man. Little signs; the uncurling of fingers and the slight shift of feet.

"The survival of this regiment as a fighting force, perhaps the survival of the Empire itself, depends on our ability to make changes and to make them before we have to face those slaughter wagons again. The Emperór thinks that the men will accept revolutionary concepts more easily from a foreigner than they would from one of their own. I seem to be the only foreigner available." He paused and waited for comment. None was forthcoming. He sighed.

"Am I going to have your support in this, or am I going to have to fight you too, Adjutant Major?" he asked.

"I am a loyal subject and liegeman," Cortauld replied. "I shall do as my Emperor bids me."

"Good enough," Darius said, with more assurance than

he felt. "His Imperial Majesty values your loyalty and he is right to do so."

"With your permission, Colonel, I have the list of officers that you asked for." He took them out of his belt pouch and passed them over. Darius ran an eye over successive sheets and looked up when he had completed the task.

"They are not all returned to active duty as yet, and the list is shorter than it was a few sennights ago," the adjutant remarked.

"It is still a remarkable set of names. I'm not that familiar with Umbrian society, but even I recognize some of them. That's another area in which you will have to help me. The Gwyndryths, mind, are the equal of any on Strand. We have been Holdmasters since the South was first settled. I, however, am a soldier, not a courtier. I've little patience with grand manners. There's no place for 'em on a battlefield and they cause too many unnecessary arguments off it.

"A lot of these"—he tapped the lists—"will laugh at me, more or less openly, for my foreign ways. I have no doubt that my accent will be mimicked in the mess tent. In short, I shall have need of a sympathetic interpreter."

"Regretfully, Colonel, I can't argue with you there." Cortauld permitted himself a smile.

"It's going to be hard on the men. Harder, I suspect, than you imagine. We are going to have to change a lot of ingrained habits, and we don't have the time to go about it gently. I'm afraid it is going to have to be shock tactics."

The Umbrian nodded slowly. "No more charging at protective suits and hacking away at air hoses," he agreed. "Soon it is going to be weapon against weapon; far apart. Guns against the flame chariots; no men at all."

"Odd though it may sound, I'm delighted to hear you

say so. I hope we shall be able to forestall that. In any case, I think the suits, if not the hoses, will be with us for a while yet. Those weapons are new and there aren't enough of them to do it all for either side. The Outlanders tried it and they lost. They'll use a combination next time, and that is where the Regiment comes in. They're the only ones capable of getting behind the crawlers to attack their footsoldiers. No more wild charges, however. It's a shame in a way, but that's the way it is going to have to be." Adjutant Major Cortauld nodded again, his lips pinched in. So far, so good, Darius thought. Now for the hard part.

"A couple of practical matters, Adjutant Major. I want a full-dress review day after tomorrow. Eleventh hour prompt. Please let the men know that anyone absent without leave will be dismissed from the Regiment."

"That is a little severe, don't you think, Colonel?" The Adjutant Major was clearly taken aback.

"Yes it is," Darius said blandly. "That's why I want everyone to be aware of the consequences in advance. Understand this, Adjutant Major, I intend to impose discipline as well as changes. Indeed, you can't bring about change without it. Life is going to be very different. If I had my druthers, I'd phase things in slowly, but we don't have the luxury of time."

"Just how different are things going to be, Colonel?" Cortauld's tone was defensive.

"For a start, the men will have to groom their own horses and no rank under Captain of Horse will be entitled to a batman."

The Adjutant Major's eyes were round and his mouth a tight line. "And just what do you propose to do with the grooms and the servants?" he asked.

"Have you replaced the men and the animals you lost?" Darius countered.

"We've enough horses, but good horsemen are harder to come by."

"Then we'll use the support personnel in the meanwhile. Since we'll be introducing new methods of fighting, they won't be at a disadvantage. In fact, they'll probably be easier to train than the regulars. Fewer habits to break."

"But, Colonel." The words exploded. Color had been creeping up the Adjutant's neck while Darius talked. Now his face had a purplish tinge.

Darius held his hand up and silenced him. "Let me guess," he said. "What I propose is completely out of the question. Those people may be excellent riders, but they aren't gentlemen. Right? No officer worth his spurs would fight side by side, on horseback, with a peasant from his estate." He looked at the man opposite and saw confirmation. "Thought so. Well, it isn't common practice in Arundel either, but I can think of one set of circumstances where it would happen readily anywhere on Strand. If your home Holding was being attacked, you'd use anyone who came to hand.

"Now, it may sound farfetched to say that we are in the same position here, but if we don't stop the Outlanders next time, they'll take the gate. No hoses, remember? Once they're past the Causeway, they can go anywhere they like."

"That's all very well, Colonel," the Adjutant protested, "but nobody's protecting their own demesne and no one thinks that the enemy will breach the gate."

"You were there, Cortauld," Darius said quietly. "You saw what those contraptions are capable of. Can you look me in the eye and honestly tell me that you don't think they could take the gate?" There was silence.

"We have to change and, unfortunately, we have to do it all at once. Of course it will be a wrench and of course it will engender resentment. That is why I shall dismiss the men who flout my authority by failing to attend the parade. I am well aware that it will make me even more unpopular, but a mutiny needs ringleaders and I'd rather weed them out at the beginning than try to contain them later.''

''Mutiny?'' Cortauld was shocked by the suggestion. ''I'll have you know, Colonel, that in all the long, glorious, history of this regiment there has never been a time, never even a suspicion . . .''

''I appreciate that, Adjutant Major. The Imperial Cavalry's reputation for loyalty to the throne is unimpeachable, but I am not the Emperor. There will probably be those who will consider opposition to me to be a patriotic duty.'' Darius gave a mirthless little smile. ''I intend to keep them too busy to act on their feelings.'' He looked over at the Umbrian again, but the man had himself well under control and his face revealed nothing.

''Now you can understand,'' Darius said in an attempt to lighten the mood, ''why the Emperor picked a foreigner to carry out the reforms he considers necessary. This foreigner,'' he continued, ''happens to agree with him wholeheartedly.'' There was a long silence and Darius waited, not knowing what else to say.

''I know that changes will have to be made,'' Cortauld said at length. ''I do wish, however, that they could be less drastic.''

''So do I, Adjutant Major. So do I. I don't relish this any more than you do. Believe me, I would not have accepted the Emperor's commission had I not thought that it was vital that I do so. In truth, there is no one else that the Emperor can call on.''

''Very well, Colonel. It seems that I have no choice. There are questions I should like to ask, but I need some time to think them through." Cortauld spoke evenly, but Darius was aware of the effort that it took.

"By all means." He rose to his feet and the Umbrian followed suit. "Feel free to come and see me at any time."

"Very good, Sir. Would the Colonel care to join me in my quarters for a glass before mess?"

"The Colonel would be delighted."

"Then I'll send someone to collect you. Very few of the officers dine in camp, but I'll introduce you to those who do." Darius inclined his head in thanks. "Will there be anything further, Sir?"

"Not for the moment, thank you, Adjutant Major."

"With the Colonel's permission." Cortauld drew himself up and saluted. He turned neatly on his heel and marched out. Darius watched the unyielding back until the tent flaps fell to behind it, and sighed again. This was going to be the toughest assignment that he'd ever had. Well, he'd wanted a little excitement in his life and it looked as if he were going to get his wish.

Darius recalled his sentiments on that first afternoon as he rode back to Angorn three sennights later. The trees were all dressed and the early brightness had faded from the leaves. It was one of those days that make men feel that all things are possible, but he was too tired for the seasonal magic to work on him. It was not that things had gone badly; they hadn't, they had gone unexpectedly well. It was fatigue. True to his creed, he had done everything he had asked the men to do. The sight of him cleaning his own boots and currying his charger had quietened a deal of the grumbling. He had demonstrated his exercises again and again and had practiced with each and every unit. The only problem was that they were twenty years younger and were already in fighting trim. They had been good, though, he had to admit that.

There had only been fifteen officers, other than those in the Wisewomen's care, who had failed to appear at the dress review. He had sent them home with letters to their families and dismissed them from his mind. He had received two letters pleading for reinstatement and several more demanding it, but there had been too much else to do for him to pay them much heed. It occurred to him, though, that he had better make sure that he still had the Emperor's backing and he had written to request an audience. Instead he had received an invitation to dine.

He rode through the outer gates and the little town to the palace. The only person who took notice of his return was the wardcorn, but his trumpet called forth no welcome. Darius stabled his horse and made his way to his apartment. He half expected to be waylaid in the corridor by some irate father, but no one he passed seemed to take much interest. He pushed the door open gratefully, and Otorin looked up from the breastplate he was polishing.

"Welcome back, my Lord," he said, setting the armor aside. "I had not expected you." He stood up and came to take Darius's cloak. "I was somewhat worried since I had not heard from you since you left." There was reproach in the voice.

"I'm sorry, Otorin. I should have kept you informed. There just wasn't time." He sat down heavily on the chair just vacated and put his right leg out. Otorin tugged obediently and then tackled the other boot.

"Thank you. Now that I'm here, I'll tell you all about it, but I'd dearly love to do it while I'm in the bath. Can you organize a tub and hot water?"

"Willingly, Sir. Are you hurt?"

"No, but I ache all over. Why do you ask?"

"Oh, it's just that I have received some visitors in your absence. They did not seem to be very happy with you, and I thought you might have met one of them."

"Probably relatives of some of the men I cashiered. Did they cause any problems?" Darius moved around to find a more comfortable position.

"I wouldn't say that, but it is unfortunate that, in the absence of the master, an angry man will vent his spleen on the servant." The words were accompanied by a wry smile.

"I'm sorry. I should have warned you. It just didn't occur to me."

"That's quite all right, Sir. It was really rather interesting. I learned several new expressions which I shall pass on to you as the occasion warrants. Some of the Umbrian aristocracy have very unrealistic expectations of the human body." He grinned and went off in search of hot water.

Darius lay, wrinkling slowly, with the steam curling up around him. Otorin was back at the breastplate. He looked up from his labors and asked, "Did you come back just for a good, hot soak, Sir, or is there something going on that I should know about?"

"I thought it would be a good idea if I saw the Emperor again. How is he taking all of this, by the way?"

"They say he's staying above it all, though there are constant rumors that he is inclining to this faction or the other. You hear it both ways."

"That doesn't sound too good," Darius said lazily. "I wondered why I wasn't granted a personal audience, but I suppose I should have expected it."

"He won't see you at all?" Otorin gave the gleaming metal a final buff and got up to put it away.

"I'll see him at dinner, but that's it. Get me a towel while you're up, will you?" He stood up, sloshing water over the tub's rim, and caught the towel that Otorin tossed to him.

''If the old boy deigns to show up,'' the squire remarked sourly.

''Oh, I think he will.'' Darius was out now and water was puddling round his feet. ''It was a formal invitation, after all. Better than nothing, I suppose.''

''A personal invitation to dine?''

''See for yourself. It's in my belt pouch.''

''Don't you see what this means?'' There was a rising note of excitement in Otorin's voice. ''You're not just invited to dinner in the Hall, you are going to enter with the Emperor. That's an honor usually reserved for visiting heads of state.'' He fished out the invitation and scanned it.

''Think so?'' The sound was muffled by the towel.

''Certain sure. It is the greatest mark of approval he could have given you. My oh my, but this will put the kit in the coop.'' Otorin's eyes were shining and he was grinning like a Dameschooler. ''I must get your clothes ready. We must have you looking your best.''

''Yes, there is that,'' Darius responded, sobered. ''On second thought, I'd rather have a nice quiet little audience.''

In the event, Otorin's handiwork was impeccable and the Lord Observor cut an impressive figure as he escorted the Empress to the table. The Elector of Estragoth gave him a welcoming smile as he returned to his accustomed place. The second gong sounded and babble broke out as the company took its seats. This time it brought Darius a feeling of satisfaction.

The Emperor talked earnestly with him during the first course, but made no reference to his new post. They talked instead of conditions in Arundel. It was all perfectly pleasant, but Darius turned to Estragoth with a measure of relief when the trumpets announced the second course.

"My condolences, my Lord. I could wish that I were seeing you again at a happier time."

"Thank you. Your concern is most kind and I am grateful for it." The words came out flatly, worn by repetition. The Umbrian looked up and Darius saw how much the experience had aged the man. The skin seemed slack on the bones and there were dark shadows under the eyes. "It is not easy for a man to bury a son who has survived to manhood," Phalastra continued, "but that has ever been the way of war." He stopped and made an effort to shake off his melancholy.

"I am told," he said, "that you also have been absent from Angorn." The eyes were brighter and not with tears.

"I have been trying to do a job for his Imperial Majesty," Darius acknowledged.

"So I have heard." Darius caught the ironic inflection and suddenly wondered which faction the man was allied with. Had he sent down the son of a close friend?"

"It is not difficult," Phalastra continued, "to form a clique in a place as filled with ambition as is this court, but to divide a government in absentia is quite a feat." The Elector was clearly amused.

"Surely, my Lord, you exaggerate."

"Surely I do not. When I returned, the galleries and the anterooms were abuzz. A motion was put before the Council seeking your expulsion." He paused for effect. "And there were a number among my fellow Councilors who had even more colorful suggestions. Are you aware that you threw the sons of six Electors out of that Regiment?"

"Not precisely, no. I knew they were all well connected, but your sons, especially the younger ones, have titles quite different from their fathers."

"Your actions have changed a couple of traditional alliances. Yes indeed, you have established a new kind of consanguinity." A little dry laugh escaped, but the eyes were serious.

"And what of the Emperor's family?" Darius inquired. "Do they not hold titles and estates? Have I avoided offense there? or," he added with a touch of venom that surprised Phalastra, "have I pleased his Imperial Majesty by humiliating one of his sons?"

Estragoth gave him a sideways look. "The Electorate of Anduin, in whose capital we sit," he replied slowly, "has provided most of our Emperors because it fronts our ancient enemy. 'Who controls Anduin, controls Empire' is a very old saying with us. Our illustrious Liege is not one to allow his offspring to establish a base of power beyond his control. You have seen two of his sons I think. They stay close to the throne; more out of fear than love, alas."

"I would have expected them to be major vassals in their own right once they reached majority."

"Their father keeps them on a very tight leash. He keeps his other son on an exceedingly long one."

"There is another son?" Darius tried to keep the question polite and perfunctory.

"He has a by-blow," Phalastra said matter-of-factly. "When he came of age, he was given lands far to the South. His name is never mentioned here. If divorce had been possible . . ." he let his voice trail away.

"Emperors may not divorce?"

"Oh, if there is a dynastic imperative, ways may be found, but this is a Maternite realm. A bastard will always be a bastard."

"But I thought that motherhood was the central theme of the religion?"

"Indeed it is," the Elector said with the weariness of the realist. "There is no stigma attached to the mother. It is simply transferred to the child."

"And the father does not acknowledge it? Interesting. It is the other way around with us. The child is acknowledged, though the legitimate children take precedence. It is the mother who is ostracized, at least in the countryside."

"So I had heard. Strange, is it not, how different two peoples can be? Two very similar peoples at heart. We must strive, you and I, to see to it that these differences do not divide us. That is why I welcome your visit among us. With contact comes knowledge and knowledge, I have always felt, feeds trust. And speaking of trust, may I be permitted a word of advice?"

"By all means. I can do with all the advice I can get."

"You would do well to isolate the men you brought with you from Celador. All those boys have friends—inside the Regiment and out."

"But the cloudsteedsmen have no part in this."

Phalastra smiled his patient smile. "You are being logical and that never works in this kind of situation."

"Yes, you're right. Thank you for the advice. I shall act upon it. It's a good example, though, of the one thing that's constant across the face of Strand. Human nature stays the same. I dare say that if our circumstances were reversed, I should be giving you similar council in Celador." Darius smiled ruefully.

"Do you think so, my Lord? I should like to think that centuries of looking at things differently would have led to more fundamental changes."

"Really? In what way?"

"Our two societies approach the world from very different points. Westerners look at things through the mind and the spirit and we of the East with the mind and the hands. It was what led the Scientists to band together and live apart in the first place. A man from the Magic Kingdoms confronts a problem and knows that it will either be solved by magic, which most of them do not understand, or by circumstances which they do not control. An Umbrian, confronted by a problem, knows that it can be solved by man. All that is necessary is greater knowledge and ingenuity. You believe in the gods of the odds and we believe that a man creates his own fortune."

Darius thought for a minute. "Well," he said, "it's certainly true that we believe that life is controlled by forces greater than we are, forces that we cannot fully understand. Nature has its own rules and we do best by adapting to them. Our Magicians can control the weather, but that is no guarantee that every year's harvest will be the same. Knowing that does not prevent us from trying to improve our yields. I am sure that the same instinct drives your yeomen despite the knowledge that all their endeavors, all their scientific husbandry, could be brought to dust by drought or washed away by flood. The circumstances may be very different, but the human instincts are the same."

"I am pleased to hear you say so, my Lord, for I have long felt that we have more to gain from mingling than from staying aloof. Unfortunately too few of my countrymen agree with me. They prefer to believe that the Magical Kingdoms are superstitious and backward." He laid a placating hand on Darius's sleeve. "Forgive me, my Lord. Those are not my opinions, but they are commonly held, even in Angorn."

Darius saw the earnestness of the accompanying look and smiled reassuringly. "Have no fear. I take no offense. In fact you have just proved my point, for there are many in Arundel who look upon the worship of the Great Mother as superstition and many in the Discipline, so my daughter tells me, who look upon Magic as a science."

He spotted a footman approaching and said, "The next course is upon us and that means that I must return to the Emperor."

"And I to the Imperial Astronomer, who, may the Mother be praised, has no kin in the cavalry." The Elector's smile came and went and, with a little bow toward Darius, he turned to his right.

Varodias was waiting and launched into an animated monologue about the war machines captured from the enemy. The Imperial "we" made it difficult to determine whether the Emperor had carried out the research singlehandedly or had headed a team of scientists. Either way, he seemed to know what he was talking about, though Darius found much of what he said incomprehensible. The Elector had said that he had little table conversation, but that certainly wasn't the case tonight.

"For the first time, the very first time," the Emperor crowed, "we know their words for 'on' and 'off.' Unless, mark you, they mean 'stop' and 'go.' "

"A most remarkable achievement, your Imperial Majesty," Darius said in a pause brought on by the need to eat.

"It is, is it not? It pleases us that you recognize that. We have felt in the past that some of our allies have not properly appreciated our achievements."

"I can assure your Imperial Majesty that the Princess Arabella has always had the liveliest regard for the ingenuity and expertise of the Empire. Your own knowledge and talents, of course, are the envy of Strand." Darius was rewarded with a wintery smile and cautioned himself not to be too effusive.

"You grow more diplomatic each time we meet, my Lord Observor." The eyes lit briefly with malicious humor. "She is a remarkable young woman, your sovereign, and a pretty one. Whom think you she will marry?"

"Who will she marry?" Darius repeated, caught off guard. "I really do not know. There are always rumors and she does not lack for suitors, but if she has a favorite, she does not show it. Still, as your Imperial Majesty pointed out, she is young yet."

"Clever, too. Two of my sons have tried for her hand and failed, but neither of them has an unkind word to say about her." Varodias gave a short bark of laughter that caused the Empress to look round in surprise. "That, my Lord Observor, takes supreme skill." Darius was nonplussed and said nothing.

"We hear," the Emperor continued, changing course abruptly, "that you have made remarkable progress with our cavalry. It appears that we were not mistaken in thinking that they would respond to a challenge."

Heard from whom? Darius wondered.. "They are most remarkable soldiers," he said earnestly. He looked at the Emperor and saw that more was needed. "I worked them very hard and I deliberately changed their habits, but they did not complain. Adjutant Major Cortauld has been invaluable. I could not do it without his help." Here comes the question about the men I sacked, Darius thought, but, instead:

"We are told that you yourself trained with them. That is not exactly the custom among our command officers."

He's playing with me, Darius thought. "Well, Sire, I was asking them to do things that they undoubtedly considered beneath them, and I do not ask my men to do anything that I am not prepared to do."

"And you banished the camp followers. Quite remarkable. Surely they objected to that?"

"I kept them too tired to think about sex, Majesty."

The Emperor tilted his head back and let go a high peal of laughter that silenced the upper part of the table. Then the noise resumed, louder than before.

"And do you still intend to ride your principles into battle?" the Emperor asked.

"That I do, Sire." The words were slow and careful.

"I cannot, in all conscience, change their entire way of fighting and leave them to it." He was saved from further comment by the Steward who came to remove the Emperor's plate.

"We have much more to say to you. We shall surrender you now, for form's sake, but do you inform my Lord of Estragoth that we shall keep you for both sweetmeats and savory." The Emperor inclined his head formally and turned, with resignation in the set of his shoulders, to his wife.

"Our beloved ruler in unwontedly talkative tonight," was Phalastra's opening comment.

"I thought as much. What's more, he asked me to tell you that he wants me for the rest of the meal."

"Indeed?" The Elector did not trouble to hide his surprise. "I think you will find that you have a bevy of new friends tomorrow."

"Does that mean that the, ah, commotion that my actions have caused will cease?"

"Hardly, but it will reduce your opposition. There are many who allied themselves with the disaffected families for purely political reasons. There were very few who thought that the Emperor would back a lone foreigner against so many of his most powerful vassals." He looked up slyly from his roast and his eyes twinkled. "It was to be expected that his Imperial Majesty would stay neutral and milk the situation for whatever advantage he could find. It is ever his way. There are clever men scattered along this table who must be sorely discomfited."

"What would you advise me to do, my Lord?"

"I should advise you to win the forthcoming battle, my friend. It would also be foolish of you to depend solely upon the protection of my esteemed Liegelord."

"And where do you stand?" Darius asked, emboldened by the man's frankness.

"One of the advantages of old age," Phalastra replied, "is that it gives you perspective. You can only be sure of your past and mine is long. I love this realm dearly, and I stand for what is in its best interest."

"And am I in its best interest?" Darius pressed.

"One can never be certain about the future, my Lord, but without you we may not have one." And with that Darius had to be content. "Apropos the future," the Elector continued, "there has been a battle at Stronta while we have both been gone. So far we have only had word by bunglebird, but it seems that the enemy used their new weapons there as well. They were only stopped by Magic, and after great slaughter. Including," he added, "the beheading of the Prince Naxus."

Darius shuddered despite the warmth in the Hall. "The Archmage's vision," he said quietly. "Was he . . . ?"

"On his horse; atop the Causeway," Phalastra finished.

"It's true then. The Archmage's vision is inescapable." There was resignation and regret in the pronouncement.

"Did you doubt it?"

"Not really. No, no, of course I didn't. I believe in the powers of the Talented—I've seen too many examples of it—but I hoped."

"As what sane man would not?"

The conversation was interrupted by applause from the lower end of the Hall, and they looked up to see a replica of the palace borne aloft.

"An apt reminder that it is time for you to return to the Emperor. Say nothing about Stronta. The information is not made public yet."

"I shall guard my tongue. And I thank you for your advice."

"Advice comes easy, my dear Gwyndryth, actions are another thing." The Elector raised his goblet in salutation and left Darius wondering.

The Emperor chatted amiably through the rest of the meal and continued to do so after the recessional had taken them out of the Hall. Darius did his best to pay attention, but a pall had been cast over what should have been his triumph. When he finally reached the tranquillity of his chambers, he felt as if he had been in a long, hard battle.

chapter 6

"How did it go, Sir?" Otorin caught the sash that Darius tossed at him. "By the looks of you, not too well."

"Oh, the dinner went well enough. Varodias talked nineteen to the dozen. He talked about Arundel, asked who the Princess would marry, went on and on about the crawlers, asked about the cavalry, threw some names at me of men who might be of help, and never even mentioned the cashiering—unless those names were on the list. I don't know. I really couldn't concentrate." He shrugged out of the jacket and started on the britches.

"Is the Emperor's favor so tedious, then?" Otorin asked quizzically.

"It's tedious not to be able to ask questions or speak unless addressed, but that wasn't it. There's bad news from Stronta. The Outlanders attacked and did as much damage there as here."

"They were stopped, though?"

"So it seems. You were at the Conclave, weren't you?"

"For my misdeeds."

"Prince Naxus, the King's brother, died just as we saw him die."

"Ah, yes. I see." There was a long silence, and Darius went on undressing. The soft bubbling of the gas globes became preternaturally loud.

"Don't go gossiping about it in the servants' quarters,"

Darius said at length, "it's privy information. Have you had any word from Celador?"

"Not as yet."

"Oh, and speaking of Celador, the Elector of Estragoth recommends that we take precautions against attack. He's afraid that there might be reprisals aimed at you and the cloudsteedsmen. See that they're alerted, will you, and watch yourself. Weapons may be outlawed in here, but a stiletto's easy to conceal."

"I'll see to it, Sir."

"I almost forgot. I'm bidden to a Council of War in the morning. The Emperor waited until after dinner to slip that one in on me. I expect that's where I'll get the tongue-lashing. He made it quite clear that my future depends on how well the Regiment does."

"There's nothing he could do to you," Otorin said reassuringly as he put the clothes away. "You're a citizen of Arundel and the Princess's special envoy."

"I wouldn't be too sure of that if I were you." Darius tugged his nightshirt over his head. "The Emperor's favor tedious? I don't think I'd call it that." He began to pace.

"I expect he's just playing games with you, though I'm surprised he didn't order you to take some of the men back. It would be good politics." Otorin's head moved from side to side as Darius prowled the floor.

"I don't know about the politics, but he's obviously having a right good time with all this. He enjoys seeing people discomfited, including me. It demonstrates the limits of their power, and this time he doesn't have to do anything directly. What the man is doing, in fact, is humiliating Electoral families by proxy, and I don't think he cares if they are supporters of his or not. I imagine I've served his purposes pretty well already."

"I must say, my Lord, you're getting shrewder as you get older."

"This place is aging me fast. And to think I complained of boredom!"

"What you need is a good stiff nightcap," Otorin said sympathetically. Darius stopped his pacing and nodded.

"Not a bad idea. What I'd really like is some well-fortified sack. Umbrian wines are too sweet for my taste, and they don't seem to have any cordials. Barbarous place."

"I just happen to have a skin put by," Otorin said with a smile, "though I had thought to save it for a meaningful seduction."

"Seduction? Then all the wenches must be in the servants' hall. A pretty girl would stand out like a good deed in a naughty world."

"The Emperor's subjects are loath to bring their families to Court for fear they'll be held hostage if the whim takes him."

"Go fetch that sack. It's too good to waste on kitchen slavies."

"As my Lord commands." Otorin gave a half bow and disappeared into the anteroom.

Darius climbed onto the bed. He was weary but wakeful. The news from Paladine was depressing, but if he was honest with himself, the evening could still be considered a triumph. Old Estragoth obviously thought it was. His mind turned to Otorin. The man was patently a knight. He was too old and too highborn to have snagged at squire's rank and yet he played the part to perfection. He gave a mental shrug. What difference did it make? His train of thought was interrupted by the man's return.

"Pull up a chair and join me. It's nice to talk to a friendly face for a change." Otorin poured him a cup and brought it over and then poked the fire before settling himself into a chair.

"What do you make of these people?" Darius asked after the first pull was down. "Is it what you expected?"

"Yes and no. Our intelligence has proved to be very accurate. Most of it comes from the Archmage, by the way, but I don't know how he gets it. Nothing quite prepares you for the reality, though. We knew that they were a highly mechanized society, but I never imagined anything like the armclocks they have."

"It's the attitudes they have that fascinate me," Darius remarked lazily. "They don't seem to have the same regard for human life as we do, at least not to hear the young officers talk, and the distinctions between the classes are far more sharply defined. None of them would share a bumper the way we are doing."

He hoped that Otorin would take the bait and explain his own position, but instead the "squire" jumped up and said, "Strange you should mention that. There's a minnesinger in the service of the Elector of Cantabria—Cantabria's mid-Empire and he hasn't been at court long." He grinned. "I find him an untainted source of information, and he can't get over the fact that a foreigner is interested in him.

"Anyway, there's a piece he's been practicing, and I asked him to copy it out for me. If you permit . . . ?"

Darius waved his leave and continued to sip until Otorin returned with the parchment.

"This isn't an original composition. It's attributed to someone called Bertrand of Born." He took a swig of sack and cleared his throat. "Here goes then.

" 'I love the gay Greening, which brings forth leaves and flowers, and I love the sound of birds echoing through the copse. But also I love to see, amidst the meadows, tents, and pavillions spread; and it gives me great joy to see, drawn up on the field, knights and horses in battle array; and it delights me when the scouts scatter people and herds in their path; and I love to see them followed by a great body of men-at-arms.

" 'My heart is filled with gladness when I see strong castles besieged and the stockades overwhelmed. Maces, swords, helms of different hue, shields that will be riven and shattered as soon as the fight begins: and many knights struck down together; and the horses of the dead and the wounded roving at random.

" 'I love to see men, great and small, go down on the grass; to see at last the dead, with the pennoned stumps of lances still in their sides. Greeningale is a happy time when Strand doth renew herself, but nought can make my heart leap so high as do these sacred sights.' "

The strong voice died away and the crepitations of the fire reclaimed the room.

"Is that the sort of thing you meant?" Otorin broke the silence.

"Yes, indeed. That's it exactly. The Born fellow's good. We should take him back with us."

"That would take some doing. He's been dead a long time."

"That reminds me, and don't ask me why, I'd best be lively tomorrow. I'd dearly love to have Cortauld second me at the Council. At least he'd know who the other people were."

"I wouldn't be too sure that he'd back you up," Otorin remarked as he rolled the ballad up.

"Don't be so hasty. He was all I could have hoped for."

"According to the kitchen, his nephew was one of the men you got rid of." Darius sat up, surprised.

"No! He never said a word. Which one?"

"Oxenburg. The Margrave Estivus Oxenburg. Sound familiar? If you'll forgive the pun."

"Yes, and I think that's one of the names the Emperor brought up."

"He's the one the kitchens talked about most. Seems he's something of a hero hereabouts."

"Quite extraordinary. Cortauld never mentioned the boy. And you doubted his support? The man's a thoroughgoing professional."

"Would you want me to ride to the camp and get him for you?" Otorin inquired. "What time's the Council meeting?"

"The eleventh hour."

"There's time."

"Do you mind?"

"Not at all. I'm the one who needs the exercise now."

"You're a good man, Otorin, and I'm grateful."

"Give you good night then, Sir." Otorin bowed, retrieved his depleted sackskin, and turned down the gas.

Darius was up early as usual. The gray light was too feeble to get beyond the embrasure, and he adjusted the gas globes with some trepidation. He got out his razor and began to strop it before he realized that, without Otorin, there would be no hot water. It was an automatic ritual and he let his mind wander.

Why hadn't Cortauld mentioned his nephew? You never knew with families. Bad blood between them? Was he happy to have the boy out of the Regiment? Family! He snorted to himself and put the razor down. He padded to the window. What did he know about family? His parents were dead, his wife was dead, dead all too young, and how much did he really know about his only child? He was always away at the war or busy with the Holding. Now he didn't even know where she was. He shook his head and peered out. Better to think about the Council of War.

Had Varodias lulled him, the better to throw him to the warcats this morning? The odds were heavily in favor of there being relatives of the men he had sent down on the

Council, and from all he had heard, it would be the Emperor's style. Yes, he could certainly do with Cortauld's help. On the other hand it might be dangerous to rely too heavily on a man he didn't know that well. All his instincts told him that Cortauld was a sound man, and he really had no choice.

There was a gentle knock on the door and Otorin backed in carrying a steaming bowl. He turned and started.

"Good morning, Sir. I wasn't expecting you to be up."

"And I wasn't expecting you back so soon. Is the Adjutant Major with you?"

"No. He'll be along later. After last night's warning I thought it best to get back as soon as possible." He put the bowl down next to the basin and pared soapwart into a fretted metal box. He swished it around in the water until he had a sudsy mix. "Would you like me to shave you this morning, Sir?"

"No, thank you. I'll manage. Why don't you get some rest? You must have ridden hard."

"We still have to go over last night's conversation."

Darius groaned. "If I must. Why don't you get us both some chai while I shave?"

"Very well, Sir. You'll find a uniform in the press. I took the liberty of having one made for you. Luckily your credit's good."

Darius stopped in mid-stroke. "What kind of uniform?" he asked suspiciously.

"Colonel of the Imperial Cavalry. It might be appropriate for the meeting."

"What's it look like?"

"Very smart. Black and silver with a lot of silver braid. It will make you look thinner." Otorin grinned mischievously.

"I'd get that chai if I were you, and you can wipe that smirk off your face."

"Yes, Sir. Right away, Sir." The grin was firmly in place.

The two men were working on a report for Celador when the Adjutant Major was announced. Sir Ombras Cortauld was immaculate and showed no signs of the ride or of the loss of sleep.

"Come in, Adjutant Major, come in." Darius rose. "You've met Otorin of Lissen, of course." Cortauld nodded politely, and Darius waved him to a chair.

"I should be obliged if you would rustle up another pot of chai and a cup for the Adjutant Major." Otorin bowed and left. "I'm sorry to have pulled you away from camp at such short notice, but I'm hoping that you'll be able to tell me something about the other men who will be at the Council of War before we get there."

"I am flattered that the Emperor would invite me. It is a high honor."

"Well, he didn't exactly invite you."

"Colonel?" Cortauld leaned forward.

"He invited me, or rather he told me to be there, and I decided that I needed you along."

"His Majesty is not expecting me?"

"Not yet, no. Is that a problem?"

"He is said not to like surprises." Cortauld was laconic. "We are very strict about protocol in this country."

"Yes, I know you are, but by rights you should be Regimental Colonel. I'm sure you will be when my tour of duty is over. There are all kinds of questions that you can answer that I can't."

"That is all very well, Colonel, but I'm not at all sure that my being there is a good idea."

"Do you feel awkward about being seen with me? I appear to be involved in some kind of factional battle and I don't know enough about your politics to understand what the ramifications are. I have no wish to embarrass you, politically, or socially."

"That's not it at all." Cortauld bridled as Darius had hoped he would.

"I'm glad to hear that. It's settled then. By the bye, I've decided to reinstate two of the officers. They presented some extenuating circumstances. Would you like me to readmit your nephew on the same grounds?"

If Cortauld was surprised, he did not show it. "Thank you, Colonel, but I've made it a policy not to interfere in family matters that do not directly concern me. That is a decision you must make without my help."

"But you have no objection?"

"None at all."

"Very well. Now, back to the Council. Do you know who's going to be there?"

"I suspect so."

"Know any of them well?"

"Grew up with most of them." The voice was dry, the delivery terse.

"Good. Then you can tell me what to expect and where the prejudices lie."

The talk was quiet, but intense, and lasted until the arrival of the Summoner. The Imperial official posed the first challenge to Darius's plan.

"My instructions are only that I must escort the Lord Observor. There was no mention of you, Sir Ombras." He was pompous and assured.

"Sir Ombras comes with me," Darius said flatly. "Now lead on." The Summoner opened his mouth. "Lead on!" Darius shouted and the man complied, his distaste plain.

They descended to the ground floor, crossed to the other keep, and climbed up to another of those paneled rooms on the third floor. As they crossed the threshold, the ward-corn on the roof blew his trumpet as if to signal their entrance. All eyes swiveled toward the Lord Observor and then slipped past him and fastened on Sir Ombras.

Varodias was seated at the head of a long table. The thin face with the gray and pointed beard was reflected accurately in its surface. He appeared to be wearing a leather surcoat with very full sleeves, but it was difficult to tell since most of him was hidden. No one moved.

''Give you good day, my Lord Observor.'' Gloved fingers drummed silently on the tabletop. The high, precise tones gave no indication of the Imperial mood.

''May the best of the day be before your Imperial Majesty.'' Darius completed the formula and bowed deeply. His obeisance as Regimental Colonel was far deeper than his bow as an envoy had been, and he hoped that Varodias noticed the distinction.

''We had not expected to see you, Sir Ombras. Do you dispute the Lord Observor's right to speak for the Regiment?''

''Indeed no, your Imperial Majesty.'' The Adjutant Major's voice cracked and he licked his lips. ''Your Imperial Majesty's choice is as wise as ever. I am here at the Colonel's behest.''

''Are you, indeed?''

''That is true, your Imperial Majesty.'' Darius was acutely aware that he was addressing royalty without being spoken to. If it offended Varodias, so be it. He was in trouble anyway. ''I, ah, humbly beg your indulgence, Sire. I lacked the time to ask for your permission, and I was not sure that Sir Ombras could get to the palace in time. Under the circumstances, I thought it best to bring him along.'' The explanation sounded lame even in his own ears.

The Emperor cocked his head to one side and the opposite eyebrow rose. The left hand danced with its reflection.

"How informal of you." The words were drawled softly, but the eyes bored up at him. "Dost deem it necessary to be seconded, my Lord Observor?"

Irony first, tongue-lashing later, Darius thought. He took a deep breath and looked down the table, past the eleven men standing along it. His voice was level and unhurried when he spoke.

"I am but newly come to this position, Sire." He indicated the frogging on the front of his uniform. "I am more than happy to discuss the new tactics that I intend to employ, but I do not feel competent to expound on the time-honored ways of the Imperial Cavalry. For that I must rely upon Adjutant Major Cortauld. I thought that it would be proper for him to be on hand to answer such questions should your Imperial Majesty care to pose them." He stood, hands hanging at his sides, willing his legs not to tremble, There was a silence and it stretched.

"We see. There may be something in what you say." The admission was grudging and was accompanied by one of the Emperor's mirthless smiles. "You are a stranger among us, my Lord Observor, and hence not fully conversant with our ways. We would suggest that, from now on, you bear in mind that we do not care for unauthorized surprises." Darius inclined his head in acknowledgment. "Now, gentlemen, leave us begin this meeting. Pray you be seated."

The two cavalry officers took the last two chairs, and Darius studied the group as casually as he could. None of them looked particularly friendly. Varodias called for reports, and it became apparent that, bad as the cavalry's losses had been, they were as nothing compared with those endured by the troops of the line.

The Emperor listened impassively until the turn came down to Darius. At that point he turned in his chair and said over his shoulder, "Scribe! When you have finished recording these proceedings you are to prepare letters requesting the swift delivery of reinforcements, armor, and provisions, in accordance with sworn obligation.'' The Emperor turned his attention back to the table.

''Colonel,'' he said to Darius, using his military title for the first time. ''It is your turn to render account. You will answer all questions, whether from ourself or from these our commanders, not as a representative of our Princess Cousin, but as an officer in our forces. Do we make ourselves plain?''

''Yes, Sire.''

''Very well. We know you to be sufficiently manned, though a trifle light when it comes to the upper echelons, so we shall dispense with that.'' The Emperor paused and looked directly at him. The hands were still.

That's right, you bastard, turn the screw, Darius thought, but he kept his face unrevealing.

''We have been told, Colonel, that you consider our tactics obsolete. We would have you tell the Council why you think so and what you propose to do about it.'' Varodias sat back and the hands transferred themselves to his lap.

There was an anticipatory rustling. Nibs were dipped and sheets of paper shuffled. One man, halfway down on the right-hand side, gave Darius an encouraging look. The Arundelian heard Cortauld's voice in his mind saying, ''You'll probably have an ally in old Bartold. He's the Elector of Caelgorn. Led a retainer's revolt against his lord when he was in his twenties and ended up with the title. He'll see the dismissals as a blow to hereditary privilege. He'd probably think differently if he had sons left.'' Darius wasn't sure the man was Caelgorn, but no one else looked remotely like an ally.

''When I said that tactics would have to be changed, your Imperial Majesty, I was not singling out the Imperial forces. Everyone is confronted by the same revolution. It matters not if you fight from a cloudsteed or beside a warcat; whether you fly a rotifer or handle a pike. The nature of warfare has changed for us all, but nowhere has it happened as swiftly as at Angorn. Our brave, mud-faced Farod would not know what to make of cannon or machines that fly. The new weapons have turned military strategy upside down.'' He looked around the table and saw muted interest, but no sympathy.

''Theoretically, gentlemen, there is no reason why the Outlanders could not bypass the Causeways completely and launch an attack from the Unknown Lands.'' He paused again and the sound of racing quills came into its own. Got 'em, he thought.

''We must stop thinking of the enemy formations in terms of convenient triangles and rectangles. Depending on the range of their new battle carts, they can do much as they please and—''

''There are those of us who have already given considerable thought to the matter,'' Varodias cut in. He had been sitting at his ease watching the effect that Darius's words were having, but now he sat up.

''We have been examining the captured vehicles most carefully, and we think it proper to tell you at this time that some very definite conclusions can be drawn.'' The man had come alive and there was pride and excitement in his voice.

''We have spent long hours with what our colleague from Arundel was pleased last night to call 'contraptions.' The fingers opened and splayed as if tossing the word into the air. ''We have found some answers; some very interesting answers. The fuel is liquid and carried in a tank at the rear. The engine has pistons, like our steam engines, though smaller. There is no trace of a boiler, however. We have not fathomed the nature of their armament, but we have found a chink in their armor.'' He stopped again, obviously pleased with himself. He looked around and his eyes were glittering. His audience stirred in their chairs and waited intently. He let them wait.

''Oh yes,'' he said, savoring his control, ''there is a weakness and we have found it.'' The corners of his mouth turned up as he did the round of the faces once more. Manipulative sod, Darius thought. Why don't you get on with it?

''The locomotive bands, my Lords, the locomotive bands.'' There was an uncomprehending silence. ''These strange war chariots have three wheels on each side,'' Varodias explained, drawing a diagram in the air with his finger. ''The wheels are connected by flexible belts. There are metal caparisons protecting the wheels, but there are gaps in the armor—at the back.

''We are not yet certain what function they perform, but they occur on all the captured vehicles. We have tested the fabric of the bands, however, and, while it is very durable, it can be cut. It seems to us that if a man could reach them, he would be able to damage them and thus disrupt the whole.'' The hands ceased their illustration and came to rest on the arms of the chair. Varodias sat back. ''Comments?''

The commanders looked at one another. To speak before one knew what the Emperor wanted to hear could be dangerous, but there was no guaranteed safety in silence. A broad man, with short gray hair and a puckered scar from ear to collar, spoke up.

''Clearly a job for the infantry, your Imperial Majesty.'' The voice was deep, rich and confident.

Lord Varnarek, Commander of the Infantry and a Marshal of the Imperial Army; uncle by marriage to one of the men I chucked out. Add personal animosity to military rivalry and you have an enemy. Darius was certain of the identification this time.

". . . exactly do you propose to get your men under the guns, if that is what we should call them?" Darius came back to the meeting and concentrated on what the Emperor was saying. "They will not sit there," the tenor voice continued, "and wait patiently for your people to run around them and dismantle them."

"I must take that under advisement, your Imperial Majesty."

"As ever, Sirrah. As ever. Do I hear other voices?"

Darius risked a look at Cortauld and the Umbrian shrugged faintly. The Emperor had asked him for his opinions once and then cut him off. He had made a shaky start at best, and he knew that the politic thing to do would be to keep his mouth shut, but this was important. The Emperor might well dismiss him, but there was a chance that someone in the room would remember his arguments and act on them in the coming months. Besides, the Umbrians were always looking for novelty, and if he could not get his ideas across here, what chance would he have in the Magical Kingdoms?

"Your Imperial Majesty?"

"Yes, Colonel. Are you proposing to volunteer the cavalry?" There was a mocking note in the reply that did not bode well.

"In a manner of speaking, Sire. Indeed"—he gathered his confidence—"I can see no other alternative. We can no longer be sure where the enemy will attack, and, with all due respect to Lord Varnarek, while I do not doubt the capability or the bravery of the infantry, a man on foot, encumbered with body armor, cannot get far enough fast enough. Your steam chariots might, but the terrain makes that impossible. Horsemen, acting in concert, but in small groups, could. In my opinion, quick response and tight discipline are the keys to victory."

"And do you seriously expect the cavalry to fight that way? My, but you are new around here." The remarks came from a middle-aged man with a bristling moustache that showed white around the edges. Darius smiled tightly as the laughter swelled. He glanced at the Adjutant Major and saw the color creeping up his neck. He ran his mental checklist. The Margrave Festin Manyas. Will inherit an Electorate: has no sons and is neutral. Doesn't sound so neutral to me, he thought, and allowed a cold note to come into his voice when he replied. The gauntlet was down.

"I do not expect discipline from my troops, Excellence, I demand it."

The Emperor intervened. "You have yet to tell us what you propose to do with this obedient band of men, Colonel."

"I intend to make them adaptable, Imperial Majesty. We are in the opening phases of a new game, and unfortunately, the Outlanders are devising the rules.

"Rotifers could attack the war wagons, but as far as I know, they have no teeth. The cannon have proved their worth, but they must wait for the enemy to come to them. Properly trained, the cavalry could reach the foe and, thanks to the discoveries of our illustrious Commander in Chief, immobilize them." Darius stopped speaking and glanced around. Every head save the Emperor's was bent. Varodias's lips were curled. His protégé had performed well.

"Comments?" he asked.

A throat was cleared and Varnarek's plummy voice rolled forth. "A lucid exposition, my Lord Observor." Darius inclined his head in thanks, aware of the use of his civilian title. "The only trouble with it," the infantryman continued, "is that it is completely speculative. 'If the enemy uses more vehicles; if they come thus or so; if I can get my men ready in time.' I too think the next attack will be different. It is my considered opinion that his Imperial Majesty has eradicated the threat of the new vehicles. If they had had more, they would have used them.

"I agree that the enemy has learned. They have learned that motorized assaults will not succeed. They will revert to their former tactics, and if we are so foolish as to change our successful formula, we shall hand them the victory." He sat back, looking complacent. There were supportive rumblings from several points around the table.

"The Lord Varnarek makes a good point, Sire," Darius countered quickly. "To second-guess the enemy is always a dangerous business. If the Outlanders were to launch a conventional attack, I should turn the regiment over to Sir Ombras Cortauld. He knows how the cavalry combines with your other units as I do not."

"If those boys 'combined' with another unit, the enemy would drop dead of surprise." The riposte came from a man on the Imperial left. Laughter erupted, and Darius turned questioningly to the Adjutant Major. He was staring straight ahead, his lips compressed. Darius sat back and waited for the chuckling to subside.

"The enemy's foot soldiers must be well rested," he said, "and it would make sense for their commander to use them, but I still think that it would be prudent to train my men to face this new threat. The enemy may try out a combination of suits and vehicles, and we should prepare a range of responses."

"Thank you, Colonel. Your point is well taken." A forefinger tapped the table and the Emperor glanced up at the clock on the mantel. "It grows late and we have a Court of Sessions to preside over. Are there any further questions?" Nobody was fool enough to raise one. "Very well, my Lords. We expect you to have your various commands up to strength with all due speed. We shall send messengers to various of our vassals to, ah, encourage them. For our part, the Imperial foundaries are working to improve the cannon, and we shall, of course, continue our research.'' He rose and the others hastily followed suit.

''May the beloved Mother grant us Her grace and permit us to meet here again. If She wills it otherwise, the Council will convene in our quarters at the Causeway.''

The military men, Darius among them, bowed deeply. They remained with their heads down as Varodias strode to the door, heels clacking on the rushless floor.

''I fear that I was of little help to you,'' Cortauld murmured as they came out of the obeisance.

''On the contrary, Adjutant Major, your presence was invaluable.'' Darius watched as the rest gathered in twos and threes, ignoring them. ''Will you join me in my apartments for a cup of wine?''

''Willingly, Sir. I am feeling somewhat chilled,'' Cortauld replied.

chapter 7

"How did it go, my Lords?" Otorin asked as he helped Darius out of his jacket.

"Bloody awful. Everyone had a good laugh at the expense of the cavalry."

"Oh, I didn't think it was that bad, Colonel. I thought you handled yourself rather well," Cortauld said. Darius harrumphed.

"Not that bad, eh? My staunch ally the Emperor, who was all smiles and honey last night, drips venom and allows his cavalry to be the butt of jokes. We have no battle plan because the rest of the army is understrength and because the head of the infantry is as open to change as a clothespress after a fortnight of rain. I can't take much comfort from that, I'm afraid.

"Have a seat, Adjutant Major, and don't mind my striding about. Otorin, pour us some wine, there's a good fellow."

"Varnarek could have been a lot more unpleasant," Cortauld said mildly as he settled into the chair.

"Then it's just as well he doesn't realize that we'll have to get the Regiment to fight out of the saddle."

"You intend to fight on foot?" Otorin stopped in mid-pour and then remembered himself and completed his duty.

"Have to. According to Varodias, the crawlers' only

weak spot is a narrow slot at the back. It may be susceptible to a lance thrust, but the odds are that the job'll have to be done on foot. I intend to see for myself before I go back to camp, and I think I'll ask his Majesty to devise a tool for it. That ought to appeal to the scientist in him." He turned from the window and caught Otorin's amused look. "I may be slow, old man, but I do learn."

"The men might do it if they thought it was one of your, um, unorthodox exercises, but they'll not do it on the battlefield in sight of the Causeway." Cortauld was blunt.

"I rather thought that would be the case." Darius started across the room again. "If they can be seen from the Causeway, we'll have been too slow, but they'll need an example set them. By someone they respect, so that rules me out. Tell me, Sir Ombras, how do you feel about fighting on your feet rather than your arse?"

Cortauld finished his wine and held his cup out for more before answering. "I'm an old soldier, Colonel. I believe in winning battles and staying alive."

Darius turned. "Thank you. I knew I could count on you, but I didn't want you to think I took it for granted. Now, what kind of terms are you on with that nephew of yours?"

The Adjutant Major's shoulders went back and his mouth set. The expression of leashed belligerence, coupled with the dark moustache, reminded Darius of a badgerdog he'd once owned.

"Now look here, Gwyndryth, you're not going to use me to get at my nephew."

"Easy, Adjutant Major, easy." Darius's tone was jovial. "All I want you to do is to arrange for us to meet."

"I'll see what I can do," the Umbrian replied guardedly. "I make no promises, mind."

"Fair enough. Let's have some more of that red, Otorin. Sir Ombras and I have just been ostracized by the entire High Command, and we could do with a little easement. Thank you, that'll do nicely.'' He sipped and then added, ''I don't know how I got into all this. All I wanted to do was tend my estates, marry off my daughter, and fight for my Princess. Instead, here I am, a game piece on a board I don't understand.'' He shook his head wonderingly.

''I don't think you realize quite how well you did today,'' Cortauld said, seemingly mollified.

''Come now, Sir Ombras. You don't have to play the courtier with me. I took you for a practical man.''

''And I took you for a good judge of character. The Emperor, may the Mother preserve him, always likes to have someone to hold up to ridicule. My former C.O. dreaded Councils of War. Candidly, I expected you to be the target. You can wager that when you showed up with me, without Imperial permission, the rest of them heaved sighs of relief. But the Emperor allowed me to stay and he let you have the last word with Varnarek. Do you wonder that the High Command closed its ranks?''

''That's kind of you,'' Darius said, ''but the final arbiters are out there beyond the Causeways. If I'm wrong about those bastards, it won't matter how many points I've scored with the Emperor.'' There was silence, and Darius started to pace again.

''Well,'' Cortauld said, ''thank you for the wine and for the opportunity to attend the Council of War. I'll try to track down my nephew before I head back to camp.'' He rose and handed his cup to Otorin.

''Thank you for your help,'' Darius said. ''It made all the difference. If I did as well as you say I did, it was due in great part to you.'' He held his palms out, and the two men touched fingertips briefly. Otorin went and held the door, and the Adjutant Major marched out.

''I'm glad that's over,'' Darius said when the door was

closed. "Good man that, but I still feel as if I'd been stretched on a rack."

"I'm sorry you don't feel your best, Sir. There's a cloudsteedsman waiting in the cabinet. He's brought a reply from Princess Arabella, but I kept him here because he was at Stronta when the enemy attacked. I thought you'd like to hear the story firsthand."

"Quite right. Show him in. By the way, do you know what the reply was?"

"Of course, Sir." Otorin's grin flashed out. "She approves the appointment, but bids you swear no oaths of fealty to the Emperor."

"I hadn't thought of that, though I suppose, technically, he is entitled to one. Perhaps he won't think of it." Darius took the chair that Sir Ombras had vacated.

The man who followed his squire out of the cabinet was young, but he had the look of a cloudsteedsman about him; the bowed legs and an air of indefinable superiority. He saluted briskly.

"Wingman Destran reporting as ordered, Sir."

"At ease, Wingman, and welcome to Angorn, though the palace is not as hospitable a place at the moment as it might be. Did my aide brief you on the precautions and protocol needed?" He paused and the man nodded.

"Good enough. See you obey them, and under no circumstances, no matter what the provocation, are you to raise your voice, let alone your fists, against an Umbrian. Clear?"

"Yes, Sir."

"Right, then. Be seated." Darius waited until the young man obeyed. "I hear," he went on, "that you were at the battle at Stronta. What can you tell me about it?"

The self-assurance was gone in an instant. Memory stripped away the veneer of sophistication, and the cloudsteedsman looked even younger. Probably his first major engagement, Darius concluded.

"It was terrible, Sir." The voice was low, the words hesitant. "I've never seen anything like it. It wasn't anything like the things we'd been trained for." He swallowed.

"Fetch him some wine, Otorin," Darius ordered. "Take your time, son. I know it's difficult. You lose comrades?"

The 'steedsman nodded and took the proffered cup with a mumble of thanks. He took a drink and it seemed to steady him.

"I didn't see it all," he said, "but what I did manage to see was bad enough. They cut the Paladinian army to pieces, burned them to pieces, rather." He took another drink.

"Start at the beginning, son, it'll make it easier."

"Well, Sir, we were on patrol. Word had come down from the King, from Robarth Strongsword, that there was an attack coming. I suspect the Magicians must have told him, because there was no sign of anything unusual going on. I'd been up the day before, and it was as quiet as could be. Anyway, the Paladinians were all deployed North of the Causeways in battle formation. The weather was clear with a strong South wind to keep the Others' atmosphere at bay." He broke off and looked up at Darius.

"Is it true, Sir, that they can't control the weather here?"

"Quite true. They don't hold with Magic here, and that means no weatherwards."

"I'd heard that, but I didn't really believe it." He caught Darius's eye. "Sorry, Sir. I'll get on with it.

"We were making a pass across the front, right over the barrier zone, when they broke out. I'm too junior to have been at the Conclave at Celador, but I knew what they were right away. Crawling boxes came out of the fog.'' He gave a little shudder at the recollection. ''There must have been twenty of them. There was a cavalry unit off to our left and they just''—he hesitated—''they burned them away.'' He took a gulp of the wine.

''We turned and flew back to alert the army. It never occurred to me that we were in any danger. We were aloft and the cloudsteeds were faster than they were, but as we pulled away, they started shooting at us. They got the cloudsteed next to me and the Wing Sergeant—tumbled them right out of the sky. It panicked the rest of the 'steeds. We were over the Causeway before I could get mine back under control. Luckily the herd instinct kept them together.

''We banked right and I could see Prince Naxus—I didn't know who it was then, but they told me later—riding up and down waving a sword. The boxes were still coming, burning everything in their way. We circled for landing, and the Prince was cantering up and down, up and down. Then he had no head. The horse bolted and he . . . and he—'' The youngster stopped and groped for words.

''Don't worry, son,'' Darius said kindly. ''I know what happened. I saw it at the Conclave. Give him some more wine, Otorin, and give me a refill while you're at it. Carry on when you feel up to it, Wingman. I'm sorry to press you about something so unpleasant, but what happened at Stronta affects what may happen here. I have to know.''

''I'm sorry, Sir. I'm not usually like this.'' The boy pulled himself together with an effort and sat up straighter.

''What happened next?''

''We circled to the East of the Place of Power. That's a large ring of giant stones with two huge pillars in the middle. We can't fly over it. The cloudsteeds won't do it. It's very old. They say it was there before we were. The Great Maze to the South of it is full of very old Magic too, but somehow that doesn't bother the cloudsteeds.'' The youngster's tongue was unlocked now. Everything was tumbling out.

''I could see three Magicians on top of the tallest pillar. It's all black. Anyway, there were two old men and a woman and they were wearing robes. The men were standing and the woman was sitting in front of them. I don't know exactly what they were doing, but, all of a sudden, thunderheads raced up. It had been clear as water, not a cloud in the sky, and then there was a full-blown storm right overhead. The eerie thing was that once they were there, they stopped moving, the clouds that is. It was . . . frightening. It was so unnatural.

''There was thunder and wind; peals of thunder and stock-still clouds. Then one of the Magicians raised something. I guessed that it was the Mage and that it had to be his Staff. The moment he did it, bolts of lightning started coming down. We were gliding in for landing, but I could still see the other side of the Causeway. The lightning was attacking the boxes. That's the only place it was landing. I swear that the old man was doing it. I know it sounds crazy. There was no way he could see through the wall, but I swear he was aiming at them.'' He looked at Darius, his eyes pleading for belief, and Darius nodded encouragingly.

''The air was prickly. My skin itched and my cloud-steed's mane was crackling. I looked at the Place of Power, and the Magicians' hair was standing straight up. Their clothes were flapping, but the hair didn't move.'' He took another sip of wine and licked his lips.

''We landed as close to the Place of Power as we dared. The Wing Leader said that he reckoned that if the Others got through the gate, we ought to protect the Magicians. They were the only hope we had. There was all sorts of rushing around behind the wall, but I knew the real battle was going on up on the pillar.'' He fell silent. It was as if the spells had reached out and quenched him.

The gas gargled softly, and the light from the window seemed to dim. Clouds going over, Darius told himself, but he glanced at Otorin nevertheless. The squire stood motionless, wineskin in hand, caught by the tale. Darius cleared his throat to break the tension, and the 'steedsman roused himself and glanced over apologetically.

''The Magician in the middle, the one I thought was the Mage,'' he resumed, ''kept that Staff pointing up, but the other one collapsed. He just seemed to crumple up, and after that it started to rain. I've never known rain like that, never. It was as if the clouds were angry, growling and flashing and hurling rain down. I had to tuck myself under my 'steed's wing. I tried to see out, but it was no use. The rain was coming down so hard, bouncing up so high, that it seemed to be raining upward. It went on and on. There seemed to be no end to it.''

''Then what?'' Darius prompted.

''It eased off eventually and I crawled out. I looked over at the Place of Power, but I couldn't see the Magicians. They said afterward that one of them died, but I don't know for sure. All I saw was those old stones sitting there and brooding as if nothing had happened. We were all anxious to get away. The weather was still too unsettled for flying, so we had to walk back to the stables, and that was no easy thing to do.

''The ground was all standing water and sticky mud. It clotted up on my boots and we had to keep stopping to clean it off the hooves. They reckon that's what stopped the boxes. No one knows for sure. By the time things got organized the enemy had come up and dragged them away. We were on alert for a fortnight, but they didn't come back.'' The voice ran down and the sound petered out.

''Well, we can thank the gods of the odds for Magic,''

Darius said briskly. "We could have done with some of it here. I can't see the scientists agreeing to it, but if things get any worse, they may have to." He stared at the fireplace, shook his head slowly, and then came back to the visitor.

"Thank you, Wingman. You have been a great help, and I know you must be tired after your journey. Otorin will take you to your quarters. Remember what I told you about the Umbrians and keep out of trouble." He heaved himself out of his chair and returned the man's salute.

He watched them leave and poured himself some more wine. The news was worse than he had expected. He had known that the casualties would be heavy, but the fact that the Outlanders had retrieved their crawlers was a bad blow. If the lightning had not damaged them badly and it had indeed been the rain that bogged them down, they could be back in action soon.

A knocking at the outer door stopped him in mid-stride. What now? he thought as he went into the antechamber. Another summons from Varodias? He really wasn't up to another session with the Emperor. He opened the door and tensed at the sight of the man who stood in the corridor. This was no Imperial flunky.

He was a good height for an Umbrian, well over the normal six feet, though several, reassuring, inches shorter than Darius. He had thick, straight brown hair which framed the face and covered the ears. From the top of the forehead to the end of the nose was a straight line, as was the mouth beneath it. The posture was erect and the build impressive. The clothes were quiet, but expensive, and, though impeccably made, seemed somehow too tight. Darius braced himself. If this one had come to avenge himself, or some relative, the encounter was likely to be painful.

"Yes?" Darius said gruffly.

"I hight Estivus, Margrave of Oxenburg, and I seek audience with the noble Lord Observor from Arundel." The voice was as deep as a Songean's, but the tone was that of a petitioner, and Darius relaxed.

"I answer to that."

Surprise flitted briefly over the unlined face and was suppressed. Didn't expect me to be answering my own door, Darius guessed.

"I am expecting you. Enter and be welcome." He stood aside.

"You are expecting me, Sir?" The surprise was back.

"I did ask your uncle, the most esteemed Sir Ombras, to contact you. Be you seated, my Lord." Oxenburg selected a plain wooden bench, and Darius took one of the chairs by the wall and brought it over.

"I was not aware that you were seeking me out." The Margrave sounded apologetic.

"Indeed? In that case, to what do I owe the honor of this visit? And can we drop the Formal?"

"Willingly. I take it you share my distaste for high language?"

"I find it something of a strain," Darius admitted. "Now, what brings you here?"

The man hesitated, and Darius realized that, for all his considerable physical presence, he was nervous.

"Out with it, lad. I'll not eat you."

"I've made a bad mistake, Sir. I acted on impulse when I stayed away from the dress review. I didn't stop to ask why or to give you a chance to explain. If a subaltern of mine did that in the field, I'd have his epaulettes." The words had come out in a rush. The young soldier stopped and drew breath. "I'm sorry, Sir," he said ruefully. "I'm not being very clear. I'm not used to this kind of thing, and I'm not finding it easy. I had a whole speech worked out, but it's of no use now." A ghost of a smile appeared.

"And all in the Formal mode." He looked up under his brows at Darius and was relieved to see an answering smile.

"Are you by any chance asking for reinstatement?"

"Yes, Sir. I am."

"Good. Because that's precisely why I asked your uncle to contact you."

"Then you'll take me back?" He betrayed his youth in his eagerness.

"I'm prepared to," Darius replied judiciously, "but there are certain conditions."

"Name them, Sir. There's another battle coming. I can feel it in my bones, and I can't just sit back and do nothing." The voice rumbled with sincerity.

"Very well, but I warn you, you won't like it. However, I shall expect you to obey me in this as you would in any other case."

"I pledge you my service, my Lord," Oxenburg said without hesitation. "Save where it concerns my oaths to my Emperor and to the Elector, my father."

"I'm glad you said that, son." Darius leaned back until only the back legs of the chair touched the ground. "What I want you to do is to help me train the Regiment to fight on foot."

"On foot?" Oxenburg was incredulous.

"Oh, not completely. They'll have to ride to the target, but then they'll have to dismount to attack it. I've no desire to make the horse obsolete. That I leave to the Emperor and his steam machines. However"—he paused for effect—"you met the future in your last battle and it beat the mother's milk out of you. If the cavalry is to survive, it must adapt.

"The Emperor tells me that the enemy machines have one vulnerable spot—above the rear wheels. To get to it, we'll have to dismount. Clear so far?"

"Yes, Sir."

"Good. Now, you and I both know that the idea will meet with, um, a certain amount of resistance, but if they see that you and I and the Adjutant Major are prepared to leap from the saddle and attack on foot, they will at least give it a try."

Oxenburg sat back, and the settle creaked under him. He said nothing, lost in thought, and then he resurfaced.

"All right, Sir. I'll do as you ask. When do you want me to report?"

Darius breathed a sigh of relief. The boy was key to the success of his plan. There was no guarantee, even with his support, that the hidebound regiment would go along with his tactics, but without him, the idea was doomed. He was about to answer when the anteroom door opened. Otorin summed up the situation in a rapid glance, bowed, and went directly to the bedchamber, leaving the door ajar.

"I suggest you ride back to camp with me. I've got some paperwork to do before I leave, more's the pity. Will two hours give you enough time to make your farewells?"

"Sooner if you like."

"Two hours will do nicely. I want to have a look at the crawlers if I can. You can meet me at the stables; oh, and no retainers."

Oxenburg smiled. "I'd heard about that order, Sir."

"Welcome back to the Regiment, Margrave."

Both men rose, and Darius returned Oxenburg's salute. He escorted him to the door.

"I'll see you in two hours, then."

"I'll be there, Sir. And thank you, Colonel."

Darius clapped him on the arm. "I'm counting on you." He closed the door and turned toward the bedchamber. "Otorin!"

"Sir." The squire was in the room in a trice.

"Know who that was?"

"I can guess. Impressive-looking specimen, isn't he?"

"He's rejoining the Regiment. We'll be riding back together."

"I told you that last night's appearance would set the hedgehoppers twittering. He obviously saw which way the vane was pointing."

"I don't think that's why he came, but it makes no difference. I need the man."

"You are a marvel, my Lord," Otorin said slyly. "Last night you enter the Hall as the Emperor's personal guest, and today you ride out with the renowned Margrave. You are become the most cunning and successful of maneuverers in this whole intrigue-ridden court. My cap is doffed, Sir."

"That's quite enough of your sarcasm. If you want to get a report out of me, you'd best keep a civil tongue in your head."

"As your Lordship commands," Otorin replied with mock humility.

chapter 8

The road went straight South through the Imperial Forests, league after league of massive trees whose names Darius did not know. Dark clouds scudded low and the light was flat and gray. Greeningale was no more than a sennight away, but there was none of the lift, none of the quickening anticipation of the festival that Darius usually felt at this time of year. He made a mental note to ask Sir Ombras whether the Regiment had any traditional ways of celebrating the day. He could tamper with the way they fought, but festivals were another thing entirely.

A pair of grice started up from the side of the road, but the horse paid them no mind. It was battle-trained and used to louder noises than that. Darius's eyes followed the birds until they were lost in the trees. The drab light made the new green of the leaves look sallow. It matched his jaundiced outlook.

If Otorin was to be believed, he had scored a spectacular series of coups, but he didn't feel victorious. What the Council meeting had brought home most forcefully was the extent to which he had exceeded his original mandate. It was good to have Varodias's backing, but bad to need it. Oxenburg ought to be a trump card, but he was an unknown quantity. He could turn out to be the Jester. Rain began to patter down, and he pulled up the hood of his cloak. It increased his sense of isolation.

The Margrave had ridden beside him for the first couple of leagues, and Darius had outlined his theories. The man had listened attentively and had asked intelligent questions, but he had shown no marked enthusiasm. When Darius had run down, they rode on together in companionable silence for about another league and then the Margrave had dropped back. He had stayed three lengths to the rear ever since. Was it done as a mark of respect? Or was he symbolically putting a distance between himself and his new commander?

Estivus, Margrave of Oxenburg. Darius rolled the name around. It had a nice ring to it, and the lad fitted it well. He'd liked the youngster instinctively, but he knew from experience that that wasn't the surest ground for judgment. Still, he seemed a very sound chap. Bit too much of a romantic, perhaps? He'd noticed when they were mounting that Oxenburg's uniform bore no insignia of rank. The gesture was probably quite genuine, but it was a touch theatrical.

The real trouble was that it was Varodias who had brought the name up, and Varodias was the least impulsive man Darius had ever met. Had the Margrave returned at the Emperor's request to spy on him? Probably, Darius conceded, but he had more to gain than to lose from it. He turned in the saddle and looked back. Oxenburg gave an 'all's well' sign, which Darius returned. Well, he thought, no good brooding over things you can't do anything about. There's too much else to do.

Events belied Darius's pragmatic pessimism. The three officers were reintegrated without fuss, and Sir Ombras greeted the return of his nephew with apparent equanimity. There were the expected grumbles over the new maneuvers that Darius introduced, but the sight of the foreign Colonel, the Adjutant, and the Margrave throwing themselves out of the saddle and attacking the back of a mocked-up crawler provoked much greater comment. When the trio started explaining and demonstrating the new tactic, criticism was stilled.

After a particularly arduous morning, Sir Ombras stood panting beside Darius. "I haven't been this fit since I was a subaltern, but I'm getting too old for this sort of thing."

"Only one more day, then we can sit back and supervise," Darius said, wiping the back of his neck with a kerchief. "We'll give 'em a sennight at it here and then I want to move 'em North of the Causeway. By the time we're finished, they'll be too tired to care where they are. Battle will come as a relief."

"I'll get it organized. Shall we take full equipment?"

"We won't be coming back here before the fight, if that's what you mean, so take all the support troops and the spare mounts. Light body armor only, though. Mobility's going to be the key. You can't do what we've just been through in full regalia."

"I don't mean to sound disloyal to you," the Adjutant Major said, kneading the small of his back, "nor to the Emperor, but aren't you putting an inordinate amount of faith in his Imperial Majesty's discovery?"

Darius looked at him and laughed. "It would seem so, wouldn't it? But I took the precaution of having Otorin bribe one of his friends in the palace to sneak me in to where the crawlers are kept. His Imperial Majesty was right. That's the only weak point. If we can't disable them, we're done for."

"I hope you're right. You know, of course, that the men are going to curse you either way."

"So long as they wait until the battle's over."

It was a pious hope, but it was dashed the moment they bivouacked beyond the Giants' Causeway. There were complaints, there was some malingering, but, above all, there was an explosion of ribald stories featuring "the flying Colonel,'' a reference to Darius's arrival at Angorn. Darius countered by ordering up his cloudsteed and watching over the exercises from the air.

Just when things were beginning to look organized, braying trumpets from behind the Upper Causeway announced the arrival of the Commander in Chief. When there was rain in the offing, the enormous wall did nothing to impede sound, and Darius had been aware for some time that the army was mustering on the other side. If Varodias had joined them, he must think that an attack was imminent. The cavalry was not ready to fight yet. They all knew what to do, but most of them were still painfully slow.

He wondered if he should go and pay his respects or wait until he was summoned. He had sent word back to Angorn before they had broken camp, so the Emperor knew where he was, but that might not satisfy etiquette. He wavered and did nothing until his question was answered by an Imperial Runner with orders for him to attend the Emperor at yet another Council of War.

The morning specified dawned clear, windy, and unseasonably cold. The fledgling sun found Colonel Gwyndryth going over his notes. Little prickling sensations were running through his mid-region. He paced up and down rehearsing answers under his breath until he forced himself to go and bathe and change into full regimentals.

There was still time to kill, so he decided to survey his command from the air. He called for his cloudsteed and donned the padded jacket over the frogged one. He gathered up his gloves and went out. He felt better once he was in the air, and he was pleased by what he saw below. From here, at least, the Regiment looked orderly and cohesive. It was exhilarating to skim above the world, even though the wind bit at his face. In a rush of bravado, he decided to fly the cloudmare to the Council. Best to put on a bold face if you are going to advocate the unorthodox. He turned her head to the South.

Once past the Causeways, the Imperial Army lay spread beneath him. Canvas villages had sprung up since the Regiment had ridden through. There had been hillocks of coal then, there was a great mound of it now. Beyond it, the Imperial compound stood out, as much for the profusion of flags flying as for the size of the Emperor's tent. He looked down for a suitable place to land, but the square of brown earth at the center of the compound drew him. As well be hung for a sheep as a lamb, he thought, and circled in over it.

Darius needed no wardcorn to announce his arrival. There were necks enough craned back, and the effect of the cloudsteed on the neighboring tents was considerable. Fabric ballooned and snapped and guy ropes thrummed beneath the beating of the powerful wings. There were two grooms waiting by the time they landed. The cloudmare knelt and he swung off and slid down. He handed the reins to one of the grooms and looked round, seeing with dismay that the cloudsteed had left deep gouges in the parade ground.

"See that she has a good drink and some fresh hay," he said as he stripped off his gloves and unbuttoned the jacket.

There were faces around three sides of the square. They stared at him. He ignored them and worked his way out of the coat. A figure detached itself from the crowd and moved cautiously across the intervening space. The skirts of his robe were lifted clear, which, combined with the hunch of the shoulders and the delicacy with which the feet were placed, gave an impression of effeteness to his progress. Darius stood his ground.

"Give you good day, my Lord Observor," Phalastra of

Estragoth said and dropped the folds of his robe. He held his palms out.

''May the best of the day be before you, most noble Elector.'' Darius touched hands firmly and felt that he was meeting an old friend. ''I seem to have caused a bit of a commotion. I hope his Imperial Majesty was not disturbed.''

Phalastra looked up under a cocked eyebrow and said caustically, ''You will certainly be made aware of it if he was.'' He immediately took the sting out of the words with a smile. ''Despite your mode of arrival, or perhaps because of it, you are commendably punctual. In fact''—he glanced at his armclock—''we are not due for twenty minutes. Come take some chai with me. We can go over to the meeting together.''

''Chai sounds good, especially after an hour in the air.''

They crossed the open stretch, and the watchers melted away.

''Here we are,'' Phalastra said, pointing to a tent of the same burgundy and blue that he had been wearing on the day of his son's death.

It proved to be richly appointed. The walls were insulated with trailing tapestries and the floor flowed with the warm colors of Isphardi carpets. There was a brazier at each corner and, in the center, a ring of chairs surrounded a larger one. There were small octagonal, inlaid tables between the chairs. It was hot in there after the chill of the skies and Darius willingly handed his flying gear over to a servant.

''An old man enjoys warmth whenever he can,'' Phalastra said, as if reading his mind. He moved to the chairs and held his hands out to the glowing metal basket. He ordered the chai and then gestured for his guest to be seated.

"I've been told that you are not having too easy a time of it." The old voice was light, pleasant, and unjudging.

"It's very difficult not to ruffle feathers when you are trying to do something new. There's been some grumbling, and I've acquired a lot of nicknames that I'm not supposed to know about, but the men have trained very hard." I wonder who he's getting his information from? Darius thought.

"I'm delighted to hear it. How are you getting along with the Cortauld clan?"

"Very well, the gods be thanked. I couldn't do any of it without them."

"So I had heard." The phrase was accompanied by an enigmatic smile. "A very staunch family. Ah, here we go. Thank you, Barsan." He turned to Darius. "Would you like a spot of something in yours?"

"Thank you, but no. I want all my wits about me this morning. We can't go on as we have, and we can no longer afford to make mistakes."

"I agree. Do you think you can handle it?"

"If this were Arundel, I would have no problem. Here, however . . ." He let the sentence trail off.

"My friend, there is no difference between military politics here and military politics elsewhere. They are simply a matter of power and survival. Even our beloved Emperor is unsure of his own survival. That is what makes him so dangerous." He sounded approving. "Mind you," he continued, "the politics work to your advantage in some ways." The disturbing smile flicked on again.

"In what ways?" Darius asked suspiciously.

"Your advent has deflected the wrath of the traditionalists from the newer branches of the Imperial Forces. You would do well to cultivate them." He put down his cup. "Now, if you have finished your chai, we should be going. It would be a shame to spoil the effect of your earlier entrance by being late.'' He looked up sideways, bright and curious as a hedgehopper.

''I'm glad you'll be there this time,'' Darius said as he got to his feet. ''Tell me, does the Court see this Council of War as a confrontation?''

''The Court,'' Phalastra replied, ''does not know what to think of you. You must remember that we are not accustomed to foreigners. The only outsiders most people see are Isphardis in their garish silks or an occasional Songean chief who doesn't know a knife from a fork.'' There was lively contempt in his voice. He broke off to wave away a servant who had brought a cloak and Darius's jacket. ''It is but a short way and we could not wear them at the meeting,'' he explained.

He ushered his guest to the tent flap. ''One of these days,'' he resumed as they emerged, ''I'll beguile an hour recounting some of the motives that have been attributed to you.'' He laughed and led off along the duckboards that edged the parade ground.

''Did you come to greet me as a sign to those watching that I was not in disfavor—yet?'' Darius inquired. ''Have I been talking to the Emperor in the person of his Chief Counselor?''

''Oh, you are too generous,'' Phalastra said and linked his arm through Darius's. ''His Imperial Majesty does me the honor, upon occasion, of listening to me. Am I acting in an official capacity? No. Are you in disfavor? I cannot honestly say. I do know that the cashierings caused no undue Imperial eruptions. That surprised and confused a lot of people.'' He looked up. ''Our being seen together in such outward amity''—and he joggled their arms—''will cause tongues to clack, of course.''

Darius chuckled at the artificial ingenuousness of the man. ''I rather suspect that the Emperor is an apt pupil of yours.''

"This is where the meeting will be held," Phalastra said, changing the subject. He withdrew his arm and shook his robe out. "By the way, I'll answer the question you didn't ask. I came out to meet you because I wanted to greet a friend. I was not unaware"—he shot Darius a sly look—"that my behavior would be liberally misinterpreted." He gave his dry little laugh.

Darius smiled at him, relieved somehow. "I'm very grateful for the friendship," he said, and peered into the tent.

It was very large and made to look larger by the sparseness of the furnishings. There were no tapestries and no carpets. Fresh rushes had been strewn and there was a subtle aroma of crushed herbs. The throne dominated the space and, despite the size of the area, was out of scale. It sat atop a small flight of stairs, and above it the headcloth with the Imperial arms stretched to the roofpole.

There was a raptor perch by the right arm, vacant for the moment, and the obligatory braziers flanked it. A semicircle of chairs was ranged in front of it with another brazier in the middle. Darius counted the chairs. There were nine of them. The closer you get to the fighting, the smaller the group gets, he thought.

"Here we go," Phalastra said quietly and sailed into the tent, leaving Darius to trail him. "My Lords, give you all good day." He waved cheerfully to the two groups of men who were waiting. Darius noticed that the Elector was the only one not wearing a uniform.

"My timepiece says that it is but five minutes short of the tenth hour; shall we be seated?" Phalastra lifted his hem clear of the rushes and moved firmly to the last chair on the right, the one closest to the throne and the brazier beside it. Darius was swept along in his wake and took the chair next to him.

As he sat down, he saw that the stocky Varnarek was

appropriating the chair opposite Phalastra. Next came the Imperial Provisioner. He had had dealings with the man over a new tool to use on the crawlers. The heat rising from the fire between them blurred Bartold of Caelgorn's features. Still friendly? Darius wondered, but his scrutiny was interrupted by a a fanfare. He rose to his feet with the rest and came to attention.

Varodias strode through them, wearing a dark blue and silver uniform, followed by a scribe. He walked with quick steps, and Darius noticed how high the heels on his boots were. The Emperor mounted the four stairs and turned. His short cape swirled around and the silver lining glinted. He looked them over for a moment and then settled into his throne.

"At ease, my Lords," the distinctive voice said. He waited for the creakings and shufflings to die. "Air Commander Nizeram, the head of our Rotifer Corps"—Varodias paused and nodded briefly in the direction of the youngest man in the room—"informs us that there is considerable turbulence in the Others' atmosphere. He opines that the enemy is about to attack in force.

"It seems probable to us that we shall face more of their new war chariots. We cannot know how many, nor the manner of their use, but we must be ready for them." He looked around the curve of faces, and Darius felt the back of his neck begin to crawl. He plays us like an instrument, he thought, and he is exceedingly good at it.

"We shall dispose of our troops thusly." The words were curt and decisive. "My Lord Varnarek, do you station your men forward the Angorn Gate in their habitual formations. Colonel Gwyndryth, do you remain on either wing as at present.

"My Lord Jessup"—he looked directly at the commander of the newly formed Imperial Cannonry—"you will divide your command and act in concert with the cavalry. Any new cannon that our foundry can deliver will be stationed on the Upper Causeway to control the approaches to the gate.'' He ticked off his decisions on the fingers of his left hand.

He turned to his right. ''How are the new recruits coming along, Marshal?'' he asked Varnarek.

''As well as can be expected, Sire, especially when you consider how late some of them were in getting here. We are still not up to full strength, but the infantry will give a good account of itself.''

''We rely upon it, Marshal, we rely upon it.'' He had already dismissed Varnarek and was looking at Darius. ''Tell us, Colonel, have you carried out any regular, traditional drills of late?'' He underscored ''traditional.''

''No, your Imperial Majesty,'' Darius said. It was a question he had not expected and he experienced a pang of anxiety. ''There hasn't been time,'' he concluded lamely.

''Think you not, Sirrah, that at least part of your command would benefit from having the rust rubbed off them in case the enemy does attack in the conventional manner?'' The sarcasm was evident.

''Absolutely, Sire. You are most wise,'' Darius replied. The Imperial gaze lingered and the corners of the mouth twitched up. Then, to Darius's relief, his attention moved on.

''You are to keep the rotifers aloft, Air Commander, and you are to keep us informed.''

''As your Imperial Majesty decrees.''

''My Lord Provisioner.''

''Yes, your Imperial Majesty.''

''Do you provide long glasses for all our senior officers in the field. It occurs to us that events are apt to move too fast to rely entirely upon information from the Causeway.'' The Provisioner raised his arm. ''You may speak.''

"May I just ask these Lords, since we are all gathered together, to have a list of their requirements in my tent by the ninth hour of the morrow?" They're all the same, Darius thought. The army may change, but the type never does.

"Is that all, Tarban?"

"That is all, an it please your Imperial Majesty."

"Then let us get down to cases. We require a blacked board. We want no errors committed out of ignorance or misunderstanding." He clapped his hands, and three soldiers appeared with the board. "My Lord Varnarek, do you take the chalk first."

It took another hour to hammer out the overall strategy, and whenever there was disagreement, which there frequently was, the combination of Darius, Nizeram, Jessup, and Caelgorn managed to circumvent Varnarek's objections. The Emperor remained aloof until the arguments began to stale, then injected himself into the proceedings once more. The sharp voice cut across the basso rumblings that filled the tent.

"It seems perfectly clear to us. We shall abide by the battle plan that is on the board. Is there anyone who does not thoroughly understand the part their troops are to play?" He looked at each one in turn. "In that case, we declare this session of our Council of War closed. May the Mother, in Her infinite mercy, grant us victory." He rose and the Council rose with him. The scribe gathered his papers and his utensils and followed his master out. The trumpets sounded again.

"That was very neatly done, my Lord," Phalastra said as he came out of his reverence. "I was impressed by the way you handled old Varnarek." The eyes twinkled. "Though I shall, of course, deny it if asked. Tell me"—he took Darius's arm and steered him toward the exit—

"are you planning to leave right away, or will you take a jar of wine with me?"

"I think the Regiment's safe for a couple of hours, and it wouldn't hurt my political standing, would it?"

"You grow cynical, my Lord." He let go of Darius's arm and turned to place a hand on Varnarek's sleeve. "I think you did splendidly this morning, Marshal. It was good to hear our ways so cogently defended."

That, thought Darius, is downright brazen. He doesn't care if I see how he works it. He does it and I smile to myself; the Emperor does it and I sweat.

"Colonel . . ." The voice broke into Darius's musings, and he looked down to see Nizeram at his elbow. "Thought I'd introduce myself. Wanted to tell you I like the way you think. Anytime you want to take a ride in one of my ships, just you let me know."

Darius smiled at him and said, "I appreciated your support and I appreciate the offer, but, tell me, are you by any chance angling for a ride on my cloudsteed?" The younger man's face lit up, but Bartold of Caelgorn joined them before he had a chance to reply.

Thus it was that the throng that dawdled around the Imperial enclosure saw the Council of War emerge from the meeting in amiable discourse. The rumors would be good, which was precisely what Phalastra of Estragoth intended.

chapter 9

The Lord Observor was in a good mood the following morning. He sent his requests in to the Lord Provisioner and saddled up the cloudmare. She rose into the Southerly winds and beat her way across toward the gate where the vanguard of the Umbrian army was emerging unquietly. Most of them looked up when her shadow passed over them. The men on the ground stood out clearly; little creatures with diminutive weapons. He wheeled the 'steed and headed North toward the Outland atmosphere.

He put her into a climbing spiral, preferring to gain altitude while still well clear of the oily brown curtain. The sight of it always spooked him, and today he was going to try something that he had never thought to do. He was going to fly over the muck itself. He had flown as high before on this winged courser, but he had looked down at a distance. Nizeram had told him the day before that his men flew regular patrols over the atmosphere, so there ought not to be any noxious fumes. Still, he was acutely aware that if anything did happen to his mount, it would be certain death in the corrosive fumes below.

The cloudsteed leveled off and resumed her stroking Northward. The cloak that shielded the Others and all their doings was below him and ahead. He was crossing barrier land; soil that had once been covered by the murk. Territory surrendered by the foe was dangerous. It had to lie fallow for generations before it could be reclaimed. To enter too early was to invite mutations—some beneficial, he had to admit that. The barrier lands had created the ancestors of the beast he flew, had given them the warcat and the now extinct skywhales. Could the air above the fog do the same?

Too late to worry now. They were over it. He tugged on the left rein and tapped the left flank with his heel. The cloudmare turned obediently Westward. He looked to his left. Home and wholesomeness were there. The other way was an unnervingly endless stretch of heaving brown. He saw picket lines; Cortauld's command, Oxenburg had the Eastern wing. He looked down, his stomach tightening as he did so. The upper layers of the Outland atmosphere began to quiver, as if roiled by his glance. He braced himself for fetid odors of decay, but his nose gave his imagination the lie.

He forced himself to stare down past the rippling shoulder. The turbulence was more intense than it had seemed from over clean ground, its area larger. More machines? Preparing for an attack? Was it his mind playing tricks, or was it warmer up here than it should be? He swallowed. He leaned forward and pressed on the arched neck. The cloudmare responded instantly and went into a glide that brought them closer.

There was movement. No doubt about it. A tongue was protruding West. Manufacturing sheds did not behave like that. Crawlers then, moving in single file. They were outflanking Cortauld, whether they knew he was there or not. Oh, to be a Magician with lightning in my fists, he thought. Better yet, to be able to see through this brackish murk. Seeing into the future was all very well, but gaining some sort of knowledge about the Outlanders would be infinitely more valuable.

He swung the cloudmare left and let her fly well beyond

the interface before he turned her into the sun. It was easy to look down now. There was the reassuring green of life below him and then the vigorous ants that were the cavalry. He pressed down on the mane and tweaked the right rein. The cloudsteed spiraled down for a landing.

A welcoming party emerged and rounded the guy ropes of the Adjutant Major's tent just as Darius unrolled the ladder down the cloudmare's side. He moved nimbly down and gave the reins to a trooper.

"Give you good morrow, Colonel. What brings you hither?" Cortauld was brisk and cordial.

"Best of the day, Adjutant Major, gentlemen. A word with you if I may, Sir Ombras." The two men walked away from the rest, and when Darius was sure they were out of earshot, he said, "They're up to something, Ombras. I've just done a flyover and they're on the move."

"Back toward the Angorn Gate."

"No. The other way."

"Farther West?"

"Just so. They're not moving very fast, but I don't want to take any chances."

"Think they're trying to draw us away from the gate?"

"Who knows? Are they aware that we're here? Do they think we can see them? One thing I do know, we can't afford to be outflanked." Darius took off his gloves and unbuttoned the jacket. "If they catch us napping, they'll roll us up and the cannon will have no protection. If the enemy catches them before they have a full head of steam up, it will be all over. D'you see what I mean?"

Cortauld gave a harsh laugh. "I think so, Colonel. All you want me to do is to cover the whole line, stop the enemy as it comes out, and, above all, stop them from turning my flank."

"Knew I could count on you, Ombras." Darius grinned

at him. "Now that we've taken care of things on this wing, I'd best see what's going on on the other side."

"Don't expect to see my nephew. You ordered him to take the reserve units on the old exercises." He shook his head. "Never thought I'd ever call them that. You still want me to do it tomorrow?"

"Too risky. We'll just have to depend on their battle reflexes. By the way, is the artillery around? Have you spoken with Lord Jessup?"

"Artillery's South of here, close to the Giants' Causeway. Haven't seen Jessup yet. I've been dealing with a very pleasant Bombardier. Odd-sounding rank, isn't it? Still, there you are."

"Better tell him what you're up to. Let me know what his plans are. I'll be back as soon as I can." Their walk around had brought them back to the cloudsteed, and Darius retrieved the flying reins. He climbed back up to the saddle and settled himself in. He looked down at the Adjutant. "Don't you polish them all off before I get back. I've a mind to get my hands dirty."

"I'll try and save one for you, Colonel, but I make no promises." Sir Ombras ducked his head in salute, and Darius answered it.

There were more troops deployed below him now as he approached the gate. He felt like a boy again with a toy army set up ready and waiting for him to move the pieces. The dispositions they had talked out at the Council were taking shape. They were no more real than they had been on the blacked board, merely more realistic. The three forward battalions were already in place, and the three second-line ones were on their way. If the attack came now, they would be in no position to retaliate.

The East wing of his command came into view and he set course for the Outland once more. They made the long, tight climb and then glided down the wind and over the spadiceous fog. It was no easier on his stomach this time than it had been the first time, but what he saw below gave no room in thought for that. Once again there was a central pool of moil, but this time two ribbons extruded, one East, one West. He turned the mare to the right and followed the column that moved away from the gate.

He came to the head of the line and circled. Nothing seemed to be happening. He put the cloudsteed into another turn. No movement: they had stopped. He applied both heels to her flanks and she sped South, away from the enemy, away from the malefic brew. He brought her down abreast of the Regiment and waited as she stood, head hanging, flanks heaving. Finally, she sank to her knees, and he hopped off as she rolled to her side. He uncinched her and rubbed her belly fondly. She whickered at him.

He went in search of something with which to mark the place so that the troops, when they came, would know where the enemy had stopped. Nothing grew in that desolate expanse. Armies had tramped the life out of it, and chariot wheels had scored its unproductive skin. There was wood, but it was broken pike staffs and spear hafts. It took him twenty minutes to assemble a decent-sized cairn. The cloudmare lay where he had left her and got to her feet with a very human-sounding groan when he prodded her. He climbed up to the saddle and walked her round into the wind.

Darius was surprised to find Oxenburg waiting for him when he landed. The young officer followed him as he led the cloudmare away and helped him rub her down.

"The disadvantage of having a cloudsteed," Darius remarked, "is that there's twice as much of them to curry."

"You wouldn't have to worry about it if a certain Colonel, who shall remain nameless, hadn't taken it into his head that everybody had to care for their own animal,'' Oxenburg said from the other side of the 'steed.

''I thought you were supposed to be drilling the reserves.''

''I did, but they didn't really need it. It's hard to forget one's early training.''

''Well, I'm glad you're back, because you're going to have to ride out and soon. The bastards have moved again. The end of their line is about a mile East. I've set up a marker on the plain. I'll need a couple of men on fast horses. One will go to Angorn and get hold of Wing Captain Cipton; he's the head of my cloudsteed escort. He's to get his men out here as fast as possible. I want to use them for reconnaissance. The other message is for Flight Commander Nizeram. He offered me a ride in a rotifer, and I mean to take him up on it. I'll ride over to H.Q., and I'd like to be picked up there.'' He straightened up and arched backward to ease his tired muscles.

''Deploy the units at intervals in a staggered line from here to the marker and get in touch with your artillery contingent so that they can back you up,'' he continued as they walked toward the tents. ''I'll take command of the reserves if they're needed.''

''You're not going to fight, are you?''

''Don't look so surprised, Brigadier. I may be old enough to be your father, but I'm not decrepit yet.''

''It's not that at all, Sir. I just thought that diplomatically—''

''Diplomacy be damned. There's a job to be done.''

''I swear you're as stubborn as my old man.'' Oxenburg was clearly amused.

''Don't swear, pray. You're a believer. Pray for a little more time. I flew over the infantry on my way here. They're nowhere near ready. By the way, I'll have to borrow a horse: the cloudsteed's too tired to fly again today. You might have someone walk her over to H.Q. later."

"No problem, Sir."

Darius looked down at the helmet of shining hair and patted Oxenburg on the shoulder. "You're a good man, Estivus. If those prayers of yours work, I'll be back to discuss final tactics with you. If not, good hunting."

"I'll get the messengers off and see to a charger for you. Then I'll get the command moved out." Oxenburg ducked his head in a salute and wheeled smartly away. Darius stood by the tent and watched the erect back with a mixture of emotions that surprised him. If he'd had a son, he would have wanted him to turn out like the Margrave.

The daymoon was already on the downslide when the rotifer arrived. It came in a whirl of wind and almost drowned out the terrified neighing of the horses. Darius crouched defensively until it had rocked to a standstill. He waited until the vanes had slowed to a stop before he stood up.

It was an awkward square with the corners rounded off. There was a humped roof with an unlikely crest of metal feathers drooping from a central shaft. There were windows across the front and a right-angled pipe that puffed out balls of white smoke. There was a tail that ended in a circle of smaller feathers. The whole was painted a dull gray. Darius regarded it suspiciously. He was going to have to entrust himself to this machine. At least with a cloudsteed there was the illusion of being in control.

He chided himself for this superstition and strode forward as a door opened and a short rope ladder fell down. He climbed up awkwardly and kept his head down as he went through the low opening. He was in a small chamber. The metal wall to his left had a door in it and a metal bench along it. The windows he had seen from the outside were to his right. In front of them were two chairs, separated by a binnacle. One, set on a single leg, had a semicircle of pedals and levers in front of it. The other had gauges and a wheel. Both were occupied by young men with cropped hair wearing blue shirts without sleeves, blue trousers, and black boots. A third was standing. He saluted.

"Welcome aboard, Sir. It is a privilege to fly with the illustrious Observor from Arundel. I am to convey greetings from the Air Commander and to say that he looks forward to his half of the bargain."

"At ease. My thanks to you for coming so promptly. What's your rank, lad?"

"Navigator, Sir. Gaitan's the name."

"What are your orders, Navigator?"

"We are supposed to patrol the edgeline and report on any movement, unless you wish it otherwise."

"No. That's precisely what I want to do. I should like to be set down as close to my Western command as possible."

"Very good, Sir," Gaitan replied. "You'd best sit down during lifting." He motioned to the bench.

Darius did as he was bidden. Sound rose around them and assumed a definite rythmn. Darius found himself gripping the edge of the bench and staring fixedly at the ceiling. The wall at his back felt warm, the seat started to vibrate, and his scrotum tingled. He felt that this preposterous appliance was alive and straining to be gone. It was an artificial bunglebird preparing to stagger into flight. The wall grew warmer and the floor tatooed against the soles of his boots. Then, abruptly, the furious, tiny motions were gone, submerged in the greater movement of the lifting.

He watched the roofpoint of his tent slide from view,

and his ears began to clog up as they did when he went up on the cloudsteed. He held his nose and blew gently as he had been taught.

"You've been up in one of these before then, Sir." The Navigator had turned from his charts and was watching him.

"No, but I ride a cloudsteed and the same thing happens," Darius shouted back.

"Air pressure."

"Whatever. Am I going to have to stay back here?" Darius was beginning to feel cooped up.

"You can come forward once we've reached cruising altitude. Just make sure that you hold on to one of the straps." Gaitan pointed to the leather loops attached to the ceiling. "You can never trust the wind."

"What happens back there?" Darius jerked his thumb toward the wall.

"That's where the works are. The boiler's in there with the water and the coal. There's an engineer and two stokers, and when you begin to think it's too hot in here, just remember it's far worse back there." He smiled with the mischievous arrogance of an insider toward a neophyte elder. He turned and looked out the window, then said, "You can come and have a look now if you like. We're flying horizontally."

"Is that why the floor is tipping down, or am I imagining it?"

"No. There's a forward tilt. Just be sure to hang on to the straps."

Thus it was that Darius of Gwyndryth, last direct male descendant of one of the oldest houses on Strand, found himself peering down, meaty hands in leather straps. The curling patterns of the Outland atmosphere were mesmerizing. The heat and the steady throbbing were making him drowsy, and his thoughts kept slipping away. Off to Marianna and her impossible search; off to the remarkable fact that a lad from the Marches was flying over the enemy for the third time in a single day, let alone in a contraption like this. Machines, he thought, weren't frightening once you got used to them. They were just noisy. His wool-gathering stopped the moment he saw planned movement in the clouds below.

"There they are. The bastards are still on the move," he yelled. "Which direction are they heading?"

"Due East, Sir. Moving slow; no more than a league an hour."

"Thank you, Navigator. Is that the head of the column coming up?"

"'Far as I can tell, Sir. There doesn't seem to be anything happening farther West."

"Can we backtrack, please? I'd like to see how far they've moved toward the gate." His throat was beginning to feel raw.

"Back it is, Sir." Gaitan translated the request into Umbrian and the rotifer banked. The sun slid across the windows as it turned. Darius clung to the straps and, when they were level again, wiped the sweat from his eyes.

"I know," he said, "I know. It's hotter for the men back there." He stared down at the telltale band of churn.

There wasn't much doubt about it. The enemy was getting into position. They would come charging out in an extended line. This was going to be a battle like no other. He felt a quickening of excitement.

"I've seen enough, thank you. Can we go back and land at my Western command post?"

"Anything you say, Sir." The Navigator sounded jaunty. He translated at the top of his lungs, and the airship yawed again. This time Darius's stomach reacted, and he clenched his teeth together. He was not going to embarrass himself in front of these boys. He concentrated on the ground so far below and was rewarded with a zigzag line of mounted units. A tiny speck of blue and white caught his eye.

"See that tent down there?" he asked. "I'd like to land as close to that as possible."

"Right you are, Sir. I think it would be best if you sat down until we're on the ground."

His trepidation returned when the craft began to judder anew, but he tried to look calm and collected even though the sweat was streaming down his face. The flight had been an experience, but not one that he cared to repeat. He had expected a jolt as they landed, but it was the diminution of sound that convinced him that they were down. He rose and thanked the men and backed down the ladder, relieved to be out in the fresh air again. When he turned, he saw the craft was surrounded, at a prudent distance, by cavalrymen. He spotted Cortauld and moved to meet him.

"Well, Colonel," the Adjutant Major said, "you certainly pick spectacular ways to visit your troops. I hesitate to think what you'll do to top this one." They waited until the rotifer had chuffed its way aloft before turning and entering the tent.

"You are to be congratulated, Ombras," Darius said, accepting a cup of wine. "I flew all the way out here to check on the Outlanders' position for you, only to find that you are perfectly positioned. How did you know how far they'd gone?"

"Blind luck."

"Don't say that. You'll destroy my illusions." He took a drink and found that he was thirsty.

"Oh, there was method. The luck was in stumbling over it."

"You can tell what's going on in that fog?" Darius was alert.

"If you get close enough to the curtain, you can hear the engines. When they move, the ground vibrates." The Adjutant sounded diffident, but Darius knew that he was pleased.

"Excellent, Ombras, just excellent."

"One of our scouts reported it while we were moving Westward." Sir Ombras made it sound perfectly ordinary.

"Promote him."

"If you insist, but I'd rather not." Darius's eyebrows rose in question. "Young pup had no business being that close."

"I see your point," Darius said slowly, "but you must remember that I've taken a lot of the dash and daring away. They're spirited young men. You must do as you think best, of course. Now, let's discuss tactics, but first . . ." He drained the cup and held it out for a refill. "That rotifer flight has made me very thirsty. It's very hot in there and you sweat as much as you do in a Belengar brothel. Ah, thank you." He took a long pull before he put the cup aside.

"Still, you get a bloody good view from up there. Our friends behind the curtain have got machines in place from here to the gate. I'm not inclined to let them loose on the infantry, so I've decided to take the reserve and move them out in front of Varnarek's positions. That'll leave you without reinforcements. Think you can handle it?"

"That's not the point. That isn't what was decided at the Council," Cortauld objected.

"I'm very well aware of that. I'll take the precaution of informing the Emperor. I don't think that the enemy will wait for Varnarek's objections."

"What if they break through us?"

"You've got Jessup's guns behind you. Besides, the enemy's strung out pretty thin. If I were their commander, I'd sweep round both wings and hit hard in the center. I'll wager they think they've outflanked us."

"If they think the way we do," Cortauld said sceptically.

"I know, but what else can we do? We must keep a sharp watch, twenty-six hours a day. I've sent for my cloudsteedsmen. I'll send them aloft with red and green flags. Red for crawlers, green for suits. Keep an eye out for them."

"Will do. You going to stay and eat with us?"

"Kind of you, but there's too much to do. I'll need a horse though."

"I've earmarked the biggest charger we have. It's not the fastest animal in the world, but then it's going to be carrying a lot of weight." Cortauld suppressed a smile and did it badly.

"I can see that you're the kind of soldier who gets jollier as battle approaches," Darius said. "I seem to be going the other way. I was full of optimism this morning."

"Cheer up, Colonel. Just think, if you've guessed wrong, Lord Varnarek will have you drawn and quartered in front of the whole army."

"Very funny, Ombras. Let's get that horse before you come up with any more jovial notions," he said and finished off his wine.

chapter 10

There are days when a man has to gallop at full tilt just to keep up with the hounds. The day following his ascent in the rotifer was just such a one for Darius. The cloudsteed escort arrived and were given flags and patrol schedules. Messengers arrived from all quarters. The Lord Provisioner's man smoothly regretted his master's inability to provide extra glasses. Varnarek's envoy didn't bother to keep the original sarcasm out of his voice while asking the Marshal's question. "Is this the last move, or is constant change part of the new strategy?" The Imperial Herald was deferential. Darius wrote a reply for the Emperor, cursed the Lord Provisioner under his breath, and sent verbal assurances to Varnarek.

His feeling of riding full tilt on a rocking horse contrasted in his mind with the unexpected quiescence of the enemy. They should have attacked by now. Instead, his cloudsteedsmen reported that activity had concentrated into three areas and then that the turbulence had stopped completely. Like a pot being taken off the fire, as one of them put it. He didn't like the sound of it, and he took his worries to an early bed.

He woke up all at once out of a dreamless sleep. When he had lain down, the white stripes in the canvas had been suffused with pink. Now they were pale lines against the night. The lantern was idiosyncratic, but yielded a grudging pool of light after the fifth spark. Darius swung off the cot and donned his mail. He put his uniform on over it, then put a baldric over his shoulder and adjusted his sword to his left hip. Slinging his cloak over his shoulders, he ducked out into the nightmoonlight.

He went down to the picket line in search of his black stallion. It was tethered at the far end, a little distance from the others, and whinnied as he came up with a saddle on his hip. The sleek hide seemed to absorb the light and only its eyes and its teeth marked it off from the night that surrounded it. Darius spoke to it soothingly and reached out and stroked the heavy neck. The charger allowed itself to be tacked up and did not protest when the girth was cinched.

There were fires gleaming in the night, and their reds and oranges made the sleeping men huddled around them both vivid and obscure. The fires talked to themselves as they fell inward, and the men muttered and snored. Beyond the firelight the world was black and silver, and shadows grew like soot. Stars twinkled in unfamiliar patterns overhead. Wonderful weather for crawlers, Darius thought. What we need are a couple of good Magicians to bring us rain.

The wind had dropped, and he drew the cloak around him as he rode around the sentry posts with a word of appreciation or robust cheer for every man that he encountered. No one slept on their watch, though flasks had doubtless been hidden at his approach. He rode out toward the advance scouts well pleased, a big, dark figure on a great black horse stalking through the nightmoonlight like a portent.

Darius let his mind wander over the past few days. He had reached the point where he had done everything he could to ensure victory. From now on the vagaries of chance and the performance of men under pressure would come into play. The outcome would be determined by the gods of the odds. Was there anything he had missed? Trenches, he thought. Trenches across the front lines to stop, or at least to slow, the crawlers. Why hadn't he thought of it before? It was so simple.

Not in Umbria, he reminded himself. To dig them would be to admit that they were on the defensive, and if Varodias had declared the last battle a victory, he would never permit trenches to be dug. There probably wouldn't be time anyway. He urged the stallion into a canter to get the blood moving for both of them. He kept him at it until the fog bank detached itself from the background of the night. It hung there, eddying and swirling softly, made almost beautiful by the nightshine. A lethal beauty, to be sure. He rode as close to it as he dared, feeling exposed in the icy light. His nerves fibrillated.

He rode Eastward in the direction of the Margrave's men with honed alertness. A thin red beam parted the darkness ahead, shocking the eye and sending fear screeing reflexively through the body. The charger dug his forehooves in, and Darius leaned back automatically. They sat and waited. The horse's ears were forward, and Darius scanned ahead through the scarlet beads that danced across his sight. A breeze ruffled the interface in a brief squall and was gone. Darius shivered.

Somewhere a machine coughed and whined into life. It was joined by others, and the air was filled with the awakening of war. Darius slid off the horse, and as soon as his boots touched the ground, he felt the trembling. The warhorse began to prance as it doubted its footing. He pulled the head down and got a foot into the stirrup. He hopped around as the animal moved nervously and then swung himself back up into the saddle. He turned the head toward the Upper Causeway and had no need to urge the beast into a gallop.

They pulled up in front of Darius's tent, the noise of their arrival bringing the camp to life. Darius was already giving orders as his mount was led off. The Regimental Trumpeter was in appalling form, but he got the men moving. Adramet, the Regimental Standard Bearer, trotted over and retrieved the flag. Both Company Commanders arrived, one already in armor, the other engaged in a final struggle with his mail.

"Good morning, gentlemen." Darius was all brisk authority. Confidence was evident in his unhurried movements. "The enemy, with total lack of consideration, is about to attack. Their machines are active; I heard them. They've got their weapons loaded, too. I saw a flash out about a mile East. One of them put his finger in the wrong place—if they have fingers.

"I want you to take the men forward," he said to the commander of the reserves. "I want them ready and waiting for the motherless bastards, and I want every misbegotten contraption they send against us stopped." He started to pace, hands clasped behind his back.

"Cortauld and Oxenburg are going to let them advance a ways before they attack. They want them immobilized within range of the cannon. We, on the other hand, only have the infantry behind us, and if we let the whoresons get close to them, they'll be roasted like chickens on a spit. We've got to stop 'em and we've got to stop 'em fast.

"I'll stay here with the Headquarters unit, at least until I see how the battle is shaping up. Send all messages here; they'll be redirected if necessary. Questions?" He looked from one to the other. "Right, off you go then. And good hunting." They exchanged salutes, and he watched them as they mounted and rode off.

The map table arrived and the charts were unrolled and pinned. Runners and their mounts congregated at a distance and waited for employment. Camp stools appeared, and hot coals were shoveled into perforated drums. Links were lit and light flared as the resin caught and sputtered. Beneath the noise of horses and the jingle of bits was a rising hum that the ear discounted and kept rediscovering. Darius needed no messenger to tell him that the attack was launched.

Lord Varnarek's envoy found him leaning over the table. He hesitated for several minutes before he dared to break into that concentration to ask what was happening.

"The enemy is attacking. We are stopping them," Darius answered preoccupiedly, thereby adding to the stock of stories that had begun to circulate about him.

They saw the stabbing red streaks first, and then the screams of wounded horses overrode the soft predawn wind. A lathered horse raced up and a trooper flung himself from the saddle to report the first statistics. Twenty crawlers, line abreast, a dozen or so yards apart and killing from two hundred feet away. The young soldier stood at attention, trying not to tremble. The only color in his face was donated by the torches. Darius's questions were slow and calm.

"Casualties, son?"

"Difficult to say, Colonel. More horses than men, I think." His breathing was coming back under control.

"Have we stopped any of them?"

"Two of them collided. They're still firing, but they're stuck."

"Are our men attacking the way we did in practice?"

"Far as I could see, Sir." Someone handed the youngster a mug of chai, and his teeth rattled briefly on the rim as he gulped it down.

"Any suits following up?"

"No, Sir."

"All right, Trooper, go and get yourself something from the mess tent while it's still up, then report back to your unit. Tell your commander to keep a sharp watch for their regular troops. I can't think they'll make the same mistake again. Tell him to keep me posted. I'd as soon not have the bastards in my tent before I've trimmed my beard. Off with you now."

Darius stood in the leap of linklight giving quiet orders, hearing reports, radiating confidence. He was enjoying the unraveling of the tensions that inaction had brought on. He was clearheaded and somehow remote from himself. Part of him was sitting back and assessing his performance even as his hand went out and redrew the patterns on his charts. He updated the maps as the riders came in. The parchment became crowded as he added arrows for the flank attacks. He looked up at the sky and it told him even more.

Flittering red scarred the heavens like lightning bolting upward. Nature had reversed itself, and the earth blazed while the skies stood still. Riderless horses with manic eyes trotted aimlessly away from terror, and the sound of rending metal came as sweet music. The detached part of his brain told him that from the top of the Upper Causeway, the whole affair must look like a theater spectacle with special lighting effects at the back of the stage. The backdrop of the Outland atmosphere probably looked opalescent in the weapons' glare. Death could be quite beautiful if it was far enough away.

The course of action in this huge arena had come clear early on, but he continued to pace and plot and discard charts. Between eighty and a hundred crawlers were engaged, depending on the reports, in three simultaneous thrusts. The cavalry had slowed them dramatically, but were giving ground. The cost was heavy. Whenever an enemy vehicle was stopped the arrow that had represented it became an inked square, but an hour before dawn, Darius could only count twenty-seven of them.

The hubbub of command that swirled around the calm vortex that was the Regimental Colonel could not blur out the nearing sounds of conflict. Metal rang on metal and curses became comprehensible. A fleeing horse broke through, dragging its rider. Darius hoped that he was dead. It snapped him into action.

"To horse! To horse! Trumpeter! Where are you when I need you? Blow, boy! Blow! Get 'em mounted." He himself raced for the black stallion and swung up easily into the saddle. He leaned over and plucked up a lance. He walked the horse over to a weapons table and leaned down and retrieved two of the spikes that the Emperor had designed. He balanced the lance butt on his toe and turned his mount toward his tent. As he did so, the night went charnal red and the tent puffed itself into flame. It became a dancing square, silhouetting the men who were mounting and riding toward him. He looked to the North and, in the distant gloom, saw a metal box with a thin, questing snout.

There was no time for caution now. This was war and survival. This was what he had been born to do. To drive the hated foe back was an atavistic need and a pleasurable compulsion.

"Rally to me the cavalry! Rally to me!" His deep voice carried as well as any trumpet. "Come on, lads. Look sharp. How many are we, then?" He stood in the stirrups and counted heads, oblivious of the target he presented.

"Where's Commander Cromford?"

"Here, Colonel."

"Good. You take this lot. Yes, the twelve of you over there, Commander Cromford will be in charge of you. Cromford, take 'em and skirt that thing. If there are any more of them coming, I want them stopped.

"Right. The rest of you, close in on me!" He waited while the ten remaining horsemen drew in. "Everybody got their spikes? Good. We're about to have the pleasure of taking that mother out. You all know the drill.

"Adramet." He nodded to the Standard Bearer. "Put that thing down. You're going to take these five and come in from the Southeast. The rest of you men come with me. We'll approach it from the West. It can only take on one group at a time. Remember, keep low. The only safe place is in close. Let's get moving, then. I'll hold the horses on the first pass."

The crawler did not appear to have moved, but the snout swung. It spat a lizardlike tongue of red which exploded into flame when it touched the mess tent. Darius kicked the charger into a canter, moving diagonally across the field of fire, his face pressed into the flying mane. He looked sideways at the slow, grinding process of the war chariot. The deadly trunk swung lazily in his direction. He swerved toward it in a race to get by it before it sighted him. He saw it move down on him and then it was past. He tugged on the reins and switched grips on the lance. The wagon was so close that he could smell the heat of it.

He raised himself gingerly and glanced around. He was the only one through so far, and the crawler's crew was occupied farther ahead. He twitched on the right rein and the stallion responded immediately. They trotted after the vehicle as it rumbled and groaned over the broken terrain. He could feel the earth shaking as they came up with it. The charger trod daintily; it neighed in protest and he spoke soft words that were drowned out. Something registered, though, because the horse quieted. Darius hefted the lance and let it dip into position. He took aim at the darkness of the opening, so much smaller than he remembered, and spurred forward.

The long wood was snatched from his grasp, and the crawler seemed to hesitate. The haft snapped and the tip was splintered as it was ingested. The metal beast ploughed on and spat death again. Darius blinked rapidly to clear his eyes. He climbed out of the saddle and stumbled after the machine, groping for the spikes in his belt. He skipped sideways, keeping pace with it, and sacrificed first one and then the other to the little rectangular oubliette. They made no mark, and he pounded on the side in frustration. He became aware of a man beside him and yielded his place, ducking aside to retrieve his mount. He tasted the sourness of failure as he collected reins and watched while his men squirmed around the back of the crawler like pups in search of a teat.

The box coughed again and was rewarded with a howl that dwindled to a bubbling whimper. Men began to peel away and reclaim their mounts, and still the crawler advanced.

"Stay close and keep low," Darius admonished them. "We don't have guns to finish the bastard off, so we'll have to do it ourselves." They milled around him in nervous obedience. He ignored his own advice and sat tall in the saddle trying to think of something to do that would stop the juggernaut.

The crawler hesitated again and something caught deep inside it, some piece of metal carried relentlessly toward an unprotected vital. This time it was the crawler that screamed. It slewed and wrenched itself to a lopsided standstill. A ragged cheer broke from dry throats as it whirred impotently amid the ruins of the mess tent. Puffs of ash billowed. The turret swiveled in search of vengeance, and Darius noticed that the sky beyond it was beginning to pale.

"Ware the cannon," he bawled and the five remaining horsemen circled first one way and then the other with the respect of survivors.

"Someone get me one of those long-handled hammers

from the picket line," he called over his shoulder. "I'm going in."

He slipped off the charger's back and turned him loose before sprinting across the space that separated him from the crawler. He leaned nonchalantly against the vibrating metal and grinned in the waxing light. His blood was up. The turret creaked above him as it turned, and he was jolted to his knees by the recoil when it fired. The air around him was acrid and smelled singed. He checked himself swiftly, but only his pride was injured.

Adramet, the Standard Bearer, came around the corner of the craft. He was doubled over, smiling perversely and carrying a sledge.

"Sorry I took so long, Sir. It took a potshot at me, so I did some crawling of my own."

"Nice going, lad. I'm glad you kept your wits and the hammer about you." Darius's voice was lively. The exhilaration of battle was taking over. "We're going to take that motherless gun out, you and I. I'm going up top and you're going to hand that sledge to me."

"Want to hear my report first? This thing isn't going anywhere."

"What? Oh, sorry, yes of course." Darius felt somewhat chagrined that he had let his physical pleasure in the release of combat take him away from the details of command, but the need to hit back at the enemy grew nevertheless. "Carry on, Adramet."

"This bastard got four of my five." The Standard Bearer kicked the crawler. "As far as I could see, Cromford's squad stopped one, but there's another as got through."

"Send a runner to warn Varnarek. You can slip away and organize that while I'm distracting this one."

"Sorry, Sir. You don't get rid of me that fast. I took the liberty of doing that already."

Darius looked at him with surprise and respect. "Nice

work, lad. Nice work. You're going to go far in this regiment." He grinned at the man. "Providing we can deal with this contraption. You ready?"

"Sir!"

"Right then, hand that thing up to me when I turn for it."

Darius looked up to spot the position of the gun and then heaved himself nimbly up onto the body of the crawler. He turned for the hammer and, edging round to position himself, climbed onto the flat turret top. It stopped turning upon the instant, and he got to his feet, a tall figure against the cold, clear dawn. He braced himself, lifted the hammer high above his head, and brought it down resoundingly against the side of turret.

There was a dull clang as metal injured metal. The superstructure shuddered under the impact of the blow. Darius's spirits were roused, and with an access of fury, he pounded the machine as if he were wielding a two-handed broadsword. It quivered and rang and deep dents appeared. He was an antic giant, a towering ebony silhouette possessed by destruction.

The sides and edges of the turret crumpled, but remained sealed. He paused, surveyed his handiwork, and was not satisfied. All the difficulties, the doubtings, the frustrations of tackling the unfamiliar welled up in him, and he turned on the lethal tube that had burned away so many with an outpouring of rage that left it bent and useless. Then he stopped. He stood on trembling legs, his shoulders aching and sweat running down his face and body. He canted forward and leaned on the long handle, his head hanging and his lungs bellowing for breath. When, at last, he raised his head, his eyes had the look of madness spent.

He was brought back by cheering and the sound of boots

scrabbling on the sides of the crawler. Someone took his hammer away, and hands helped him down.

"Get away from it," he croaked, but the voice seemed to him to come from far away and he wasn't sure they had heard. He tried again.

"Get away. They may blow themselves up." It was as if he were listening to someone else talk, but the words had the desired effect. Darius shook himself as the adrenaline in his body subsided and the euphoria of effort ebbed. Time to get back to work with what was left of the staff.

"Cromford! Commander Cromford? Anyone seen the Commander?"

"Crawler got him." The statement was blunt and anonymous. Darius sighed and turned to Adramet.

"Well, son, it seems as if you've got a field promotion."

"Thank you, Colonel."

"First thing you can do is round me up a table and see if you can find some charts." He cocked an ear downwind. "Seems to have quietened down. See if you can get some food rustled up for the survivors—if the cooks haven't run away. I'm going to try to clean up a bit and get something to drink. Banging away at that thing has given me a bloody great thirst. I'll be back to help you reorganize as fast as I can. I doubt they'll give us too much of a breathing space. Oh, and pass the word that I'm mighty proud of the men."

"Take your time, Colonel. I'll get things going here." Adramet turned and began giving precise, rapid orders. Darius watched him appreciatively and then went off in search of water.

The new commander was as good as his word, and when Darius returned, refreshed but not much neater, the map table was in operation again. Messengers from Cortauld and Oxenburg had already been questioned, and the charts were well marked. Darius studied them carefully, the course of battle made plain and impersonal.

Three crawlers had broken through his defenses. One he had battered into submission, one the luckless Cromford had dealt with, and the last one was behind them somewhere. The assault on the wings had been heavier and the enemy's success greater. A dozen of the war chariots had got by Oxenburg's forces and ten had broken through on the West. The artillery had proved itself, but it had been well and truly blooded. Twelve of the twenty field pieces had been reduced to flowing metal. The broken masonry of the Giants' Causeway had been a reef to most of the remaining intruders. They had torn the bottoms out of their vehicles in the dark.

Wisewomen's helpers began to move forward past the command post. With them came reports of the infantry's losses from the three crawlers that came at them out of the night. They had proved impervious to pikes and were halted only when they bogged down in a human mire. They sat now like obscene spiders at the center of red webs, though the filaments were turning a crusted brown as the flies fed. They made spasmodic attempts to move, but only sank deeper. There would be no way to count the number of victims that it had taken to stop them. From time to time, fire would spray forth from this turret or that to keep the Umbrians away, but both sides knew that only one outcome was possible.

Darius rubbed his eyes wearily as the aftermath of the fighting took its toll on his body and his spirit. He sent the cloudsteedsmen aloft, refusing to believe it was all over. Laden bodyslings and litters were making their way back toward the gate. It was time to revert to the battleplan drawn up at the Council of War. There was no sign yet of the enemy's foot soldiers, but they would not be long in coming.

He recalled the survivors of the forward force, combined them with the Headquarter's staff, and sent the lot of them to the rear. They had earned the rest. He walked slowly over to the smoldering remnants of his tent and looked in vain for his flying gloves. He took their loss as a personal affront, a new coal for the kernel of hate he needed to fight well. He wheeled and called to the last of the runners. He directed the man to take the black stallion over to the Margrave's lines. That done, he went back to the crawler and walked around it warily.

Little eruptions of ash accompanied every footfall. He moved in close and tapped it with his knuckles; lightly, ever so lightly. He spread his hand and laid it flat against the machine. It was warm. He placed his other hand on it and tried to imagine the occupants as they faced a slow death. No image came and he could summon no compassion for their plight. He'd lost too many good men for that. He patted the machine and walked off to saddle his cloudmare.

chapter 11

Darius flew over the ground his men had contested. The alien armament stood out clearly against the chewed-up earth. It had felt good to go up against that crawler, and he tried to resummon the joy the realization that he could tackle something new and best it had brought. It was a pale echo of the original elation, but it cheered him. From now on he would have to abide by his word and hand over command of the Regiment. Tired though he was, he did not relish the thought of being sidelined.

He was jolted abruptly out of his self-absorption by a burst of brilliance. He clung to the high pommel as the cloudmare threw herself into a shearing dive. The ground swung dizzyingly as she pulled back out of it. He was too busy trying to stay in the saddle to see where the shot had come from, but he hoped devoutly that it was from one of the stranded vehicles rather than from the brown bank that shielded the enemy. If it presaged another attack with fresh crawlers, it could mark the end of the Umbrian army as a fighting force.

They skimmed low over the battered remnants of the Outland assault, and Darius was relieved to see that there was nothing to fear from them. They had been target practice for Jessup's cannon and sagged like garden furniture left out for too many Winters. Small figures moved among them. None of them looked up or waved as their shadow passed over. As he came closer to the Adjutant Major's camp, he saw exhausted soldiers lying, corpselike, around cooking fires. Those who were still up were moving with the overcautious deliberation of the drunk. Tiredness, he told himself. He tried to count the remaining men as they came in for a landing, but wasn't quick enough. All he knew was that there were not enough of them.

He led the cloudsteed over to the line of spent horses and tethered her before fetching a bucket of water. Then he went in search of Cortauld. The Adjutant was in the familiar blue and white striped tent, sitting at a table, his head swathed in a turban of bandages. As the Colonel stooped his way in, he started to rise to the salute.

"Sit down," Darius growled, shocked at the gray tinge to the normally ruddy skin. "You look like an old-time Magician."

"Our friends from the fog decided to give me a haircut," Cortauld said with an attempt at levity. "If I'd have known, I'd have taken my mail hood off. My left ear got the worst of it. Hot metal. I can't hear a thing on this side for the moment."

"Anybody look at it?"

"Yes. A Wisewoman gave it the once-over. If the drum escaped damage, I'll probably hear again." He stated the fact simply, without trying to evoke sympathy.

"I'll keep my fingers crossed," Darius said. "How about the other casualties?"

The Adjutant Major's eyes went distant at the question and he was silent. "Bad," he said at length. "Very bad. We lost a lot of good men. They just kept on coming out into the nightmoonlight." The voice was so quiet that Darius had to strain to hear. "You were right about them starting at the far end and about their seeing better in the dark. They saw well enough to pick off half my men. By the Mother, but they were fast." The voice got lost somewhere. Darius waited, wondering about the extent of the damage to his friend, but there was no more.

"You did very well," he said, "and the men fought the way we had hoped they would. What matters is that we stopped them. The few that did manage to get past us caused absolute havoc among the infantry. If we hadn't done what we did, made the sacrifices that we made, the enemy would own the Angorn Gate by now." He watched the other man closely.

The Adjutant gave a tired smile and rubbed his neck where the bandages chafed. "You're right. It must be a sign of old age. It's just that I've seen too many brave young men die in the past month or so." The color of a lifetime in the open air sat unnaturally on his cheeks. It looked as if it had been carelessly painted on. The moustache stood out in too great a contrast.

"Do you feel all right?" Darius inquired. "You look as if you could do with some rest. I can fill in for a while if you like." He wasn't prepared for the fierce glitter that he saw in Cortauld's eyes. "A suggestion, Ombras; merely a suggestion," he added hastily.

The Umbrian looked up at him with a wry smile. "Look that bad, do I?"

"Not really," Darius lied, "I'm just not sure how advisable it is for you to ride into battle with your head ringing."

"Well, Colonel, I'll give you points for consideration, but if you think you're going to finagle your way into my command again . . ." He spoke with mock ferocity, but Darius had no doubt that, beneath it, the man was completely serious.

He allowed himself to smile broadly. "No, Ombras, no." He patted the Umbrian on the shoulder. "I'm off to join that good-for-nothing nephew of yours. I'll not edge him out, either. I'll be a good lad and mind my place. He did well, by the way, but I expect you've already heard."

"Let a couple more get through than we did, if the messengers are to be trusted."

"Then we've heard the same figures." Darius finally committed himself to a chair and found it too small for comfort. "How long do you suppose we've got before they attack again?"

"You're still convinced they'll come?"

"You know I am," Darius said, weariness finally coming through.

"So am I. If I were them, I'd have done it already."

"Me, too. I can only think that they weren't expecting to be opposed so close to their own lines, or for us to be able to get behind the crawlers."

"Think we scared them off?"

"I'd like to." Darius abandoned the chair and started to pace. "How are you off for equipment?"

"Fine. There are more than enough of the heavier lances to go around. It's more men I could do with."

"You'll be getting half of the reserves—of what's left of the reserves. They fought well. In fact," he said, looking slyly sideways, "our success rate was better than yours."

"Yes," Cortauld replied dryly, "I understand that the enemy made a token feint at the center." The two men smiled.

"Speaking of that, I'd better get Jessup to put the one that got by us out of commission."

"You mean you didn't put them all out with your trusty hammer?"

"Oho, so that story's making the rounds, is it?"

"I don't know what happens in Arundel, my dear Gwyndryth, but there's no way of keeping a thing like that quiet in the Umbrian army."

"There certainly doesn't seem to be anything that I can

tell you. Maybe one thing. There ought to be hot food by the Giants' Causeway at midday if my orders get obeyed."

"Now that's what I call news."

"That head wound's making you caustic. Anything you want to tell me?"

"I'm letting as many of the men as I can rest, but I've got patrols out."

"Perhaps they're waiting for nightfall. Since we don't have any Magicians to fix the weather, you might have a word with the Mother and ask her for a nice, bright night-moon."

"You've picked the wrong man, I'm afraid. She hasn't had any reason to listen to me for years."

"The men are lucky to have you anyway," Darius said. "If anyone can take the Regiment into the future, the Cortauld family can." He walked over to the Adjutant and patted him on the shoulder once more. "Take care of that head of yours. We can't afford to lose you, the Regiment and I. Now, don't you dare get up. I can see myself out."

"Colonel."

"Yes, Ombras?"

"It was bad, but if it hadn't been for you and your ridiculous ideas, it would have been much worse."

"Thank you, Ombras."

It was almost midday when Darius touched down on the Eastern Wing, and Oxenburg was waiting for him. The dark blue eyes lit up as Darius climbed slowly down, and the scar on his cheek was compressed by his grin.

"Here comes the flying Colonel," he said as he came out of his salute. "The single-handed slayer of war wagons. We are honored, Sir." The men around him smiled as he performed a deep bow.

No wonder his men adore him, Darius thought. "A little more respect for your elders and betters, young man."

''As the Colonel orders.'' The brown hair bounced as he snapped into another salute.

''You're as bad as your uncle, who sends his regards. You're not as lucky as he is though. He only got wounded, but I decided to fight on your wing.''

''Yes, Sir. What are your orders, Sir?'' The man was instantly professional, all levity banished. ''My uncle was wounded?'' The question popped through.

''At ease, Brigadier. Your uncle has a scalp wound. He looks fetching in a turban, but he's very much in command, as you are here. I'm simply reporting for duty. You put me where you want me and tell me what you want me to do.''

''Any preferences?''

''A meal first and then some sleep.''

''Ah, I see you mean to make yourself useful. You can use my tent. I'll have some food sent to you and I'll have you woken if anything happens. I'd offer you a change of clothes, but I doubt we have anything that would fit.''

''You're very kind, but I don't feel like dressing up for the enemy. By the way, did that black animal of mine show up?''

''Yes, he's here. He's been fed and watered. We had to hobble him away from the other horses: he was getting a bit obstreperous.''

''Thank you for that. Now, point me to that tent.''

Darius was shaken awake before his body was ready for it and emerged stupefied, not knowing where he was. He yawned as things fell into place. His head was muzzy and he resented being woken up so soon. He had barely closed his eyes.

''Brigadier Oxenburg's compliments, Colonel, but something's up. He thinks you'd best get dressed.''

''What's happening?'' Darius asked as he swung his legs

slowly off the bed. "Pass me my jacket, there's a good chap. Thank you."

"I don't rightly know, Sir," the trooper replied, "but one of your flying horses came in, and things have been buzzing ever since."

"I see. What time is it?"

"Mid-afternoon, Sir. You've been out over three hours."

"That so? Feels like much less. Still, it gives us a decent stretch of light. What's the weather like?"

"Starting to cloud up, Sir."

"Pity." Darius stood up and yawned prodigiously. "I've a piece of advice for you," he said, the first part of the sentence blurred by the last of the yawn. "No matter how tired you are, never, never sleep in your mail. I don't care how well padded your gambesons are." He moved his shoulders and winced. He shook one leg and then the other. After slipping his baldric over his head, he adjusted his sword. Then he put his cloak on and turned to the young cavalryman.

"Take me to the latrines and then to the Brigadier."

He waited while the Margrave conferred with his officers and then moved up when they dispersed to their units. Oxenburg looked up and handed him a long glass. Darius tugged it open and then played with the eyepiece until the distant Causeway came into focus. There were three little dots of green, and as he swung the glass, a fourth popped up. Red for crawlers, green for suits, he thought.

"When did it start?" he asked.

"About fifteen minutes ago. Your 'steedsman tells me that the artillery started pounding away at the crawlers you left. Seems someone on the other side doesn't like it."

"Did my man say how they were suited, or how they were armed?"

"Hoseless, as we expected, and using some sort of hand

cannon. Same kind of flame as the big ones, but nowhere near the range."

"That's something to be grateful for. And what are you going to do about it?"

"Nothing for the moment, except to get into position to do something when the time comes."

"Nothing?"

"We have to let Varnarek have first crack," Oxenburg said, smiling. "War wouldn't be worth winning if we didn't."

"I see your point. Then what?"

The Margrave shrugged. "Then we either fend off a flank attack, or, if the enemy pushes the infantry back too far, we'll go in and attack them from the rear. We've been over all this before," he added with a trace of impatience.

Darius recognized the insecurity behind the tone and ignored it. "Where are you most shorthanded after last night?" he asked.

"Front-line officers." There was a hint of challenge beneath the statement, even though the voice was level.

Darius smiled to himself and allowed himself to rise to the implied bait. "Want me to take a squadron?"

"Are you allowed?" The question was studied.

"You going to report me?" Darius's attempted jocularity sounded a trifle forced.

"I probably should."

Darius moved to break the growing tension. He put an arm round the other man's shoulders and wheeled them both into his familiar pace.

"Oh, come on now, laddie," he said, humor bubbling through, "would you deny all those foot soldiers the chance to gloat if I came a cropper?"

"Well, there is that," Oxenburg admitted as he succumbed to the ploy.

Darius withdrew his arm and came to an abrupt halt.

"Brigadier!" The voice was suddenly curt and commanding.

"Sir!" Oxenburg's response was automatic.

"I order you, in the Emperor's name, to give me command of a squadron."

"Yes, Sir." The Margrave was at attention, but a smile crept up the corners of his mouth.

"May I ask, Brigadier, what you find so amusing?" Darius was every inch the parade-ground martinet.

"Oh, nothing really, Colonel. I was just contemplating the list of duties to which I could assign that squadron of yours."

"Oh, no you don't, young man." Darius dropped his pose immediately. "My squadron is not about to fortify the rear, dig latrines, or protect the kitchen detail. We're strictly fighting men; clear?"

"If I didn't know you better, Colonel, I'd say you were being insubordinate." The twinkle in the large eyes belied the words.

"I'll do anything you tell me to," Darius said seriously. "I owe you a great deal and I wouldn't deny you this chance for the world." The two men stood facing each other, and Oxenburg looked straight up into the taller man's face.

"I think the eighth squad will do you best," he said. "They've been combined from other units that have been hit too badly to be cohesive. They're good men, but they're a bit demoralized. It'll do them good to have you fighting with them."

"Thank you, Estivus. I appreciate it, and I'll do my best not to turn up embarrassingly dead."

"I shall expect no less." Oxenburg smiled and slapped the other on the arm. "Your lot should be sleeping around, let's see, around the fifth fire down."

"I'm grateful," Darius said. "We shan't let you down, but you'd better brief me, just to be on the safe side."

The newly commissioned Squadron Leader retrieved his charger fifteen minutes later and rode it along the clusters of cloaked cocoons until he came to fire number 5. He sat back in the saddle, looked down at the shapes that were now his responsibility, and was obscurely glad that he would never have time to get to know them as individuals. There were advantages, he reflected, when one was ignorant of the wives, the children, and the problems. Soon, all too soon, these shrouded, embryo warriors would emerge from their woolen chrysalides and assume human guise, complete with endearing traits that would make their eventual loss unbearable.

He dismounted and led the stallion to the tether line. He was loath to wake the men before he had to. Leave them dream while they still could. Brass blared and shattered the fragile peace. He moved reluctantly to the fire and launched into the age-old litany. The curses of the Eighth Squadron, Second Battalion, died aborning as the members recognized who was rousting them.

The Eighth was to horse with remarkable alacrity, and all seventeen of them reacted in their various ways to the unexpected advent of the Colonel. It straightened the backs of most of them. A runner came galloping down the line and drew in sharply in front of the black horse.

"Brigadier Oxenburg sends his compliments, Sir, and General Varnarek has called for a flank attack from us. All units to muster line abreast and ride to the charge."

"Thank you, Cornet. The Eighth Squadron reports ready." Darius pivoted in the saddle and called to his men. His voice assumed the traditional cadence of the drill square. "Aaaayth Squaad! Lehhft face! At a walk, forwaaard. Watch it there. Keep the line. Easy as it goes."

The line of horsemen maneuvered and jockeyed into

position, their horses prancing. The trumpet spoke and the equine wave rolled into a trot, then curled into a canter. One of the regimental standards accelerated past Darius to assume a front position, and the colors swept down in salute as they passed him. He dipped the guidon on his new lance in acknowledgment and couched it against his right side.

The saddle rocked beneath him in the comfort of the canter, and above him, the clouds began to striate in the sunlight. The pennons that had survived the night's encounters streamed out aslant. Ahead, the tracery of the opposition's weapons stood out like the welts left by a whiptail. The familiar fatalism of imminent combat came over Darius, but that didn't stop his stomach clenching as he leaned forward.

The black charger stretched out and moved effortlessly into the vanguard. Darius pulled back on the reins with his left hand in an effort to hold him back, but the horse would have none of it. He threw back his head and laughed into the rush of air. He had started the day in command of a regiment and now he couldn't even control his mount. Abandoning himself to the elixir of danger, he forgot his tiredness and aches. Behind him, the trumpet sang hoarsely and lances came down as the Eastern Wing of the Imperial Cavalry leaned into the climax of the charge.

The unreliable sun flashed intermittently off their helms as they rode toward history. The omnipotent image of the knight was about to be reduced to the repetitive fantasies of troubadors, but they were shielded from the knowledge. Elation surged up in them as the enemy's flank drew near. They were mounted warriors about to ride down the despised footmen of the foe. Immune to the judgment of minstrels, they crouched in anticipation of the shock of lance striking home. They rode in battle-stained bravery, frayed banners wind-whipping away, in the confident exultation of tradition restored. They thundered down in a heedless gallantry that would succeed only in part and then only because the Outlanders were elsewhere engaged.

The bloated shapes of their opponents turned with seeming slowness to meet the new challenge. Filaments of red sprang out and Darius heard bones snap behind him as stricken horses crashed. Momentum carried the rest on, and the ululating horde careened into the enemy. Darius impaled a suited Outlander as his charger breasted on. Without conscious thought, he found his sword in his right hand and struck downward as the surrounded stallion reared up and dealt havoc with its sharpened forehooves.

He rose in the stirrups and laid about him, countering thrusts from the blades that had appeared now that the battle was in the middle of close encounter. The charger reared again, and Darius's practiced body responded easily as it lunged forward, clearing the way deeper into the enemy ranks. He dropped the reins and stood up again, wielding the sword to left and right. Man and animal worked together as one. They were welded together by training and instinct and laid about in bloodless slaughter. Nothing but spurting brown smoke issued from the rents and fissures they opened. It burned the skin and made the eyes water as it eddied around them. The world was reduced to reflex, and there was no time for fear.

Darius hacked and dodged, snatching glances to try to locate his men. His clothes stuck to him and his arms began to ache again. Tears flowed from his stinging eyes. The saddle canted under him as the warhorse rose again, and he thrust and turned and thrust. He chopped down at a white shape to his left and an incandescent pain excoriated his blind side. His flesh had been conditioned of old and had been braced for hurt, but this blow twisted him with shock and outrage. He heard himself scream. The charger, as it had been trained to do, reared at the sound, and the long blade was torn from the grasp of its wielder. Darius looked down and saw the incongruous point poking through the front of his tunic. The bile rose in his throat.

The horse's legs came down unevenly on the suits of fallen opponents, and pain sang through Darius's side. Then it went mercifully numb. He tried to push the metal down and out, but it grated along his ribs and his head swam. He groped at the stallion's neck for the reins while his infinitely tired right arm cut feebly at an assailant. His consciousness lurched, surprising him and sending fear racing through his veins. His plucking fingers found the reins, and he tried to turn the charger. He was surrounded by milling combat. He tried to force a way through the press to clear ground. His vision clouded, but he had no hand free to swab his eyes. Things seemed to ebb and flow around him in time to the pounding of his heart, a pounding that was a sudden insistence in his head.

He spurred his mount and laid about him in a blaze of anger and disbelief. He knew that his arm was failing, that he himself was failing, but rejected the knowledge fiercely. The way opened before his onslaught, and he clapped his heels to the bloody flanks. The black charger sprang forward at his urging and bugled its defiance.

The sound was cut off suddenly as the creature was jarred to a halt, and Darius felt himself fly forward. Time stopped for him and showed him courtesy. His fall felt endless and graceful. His last emotion was one of profound annoyance, and his last image was of his daughter, aged six, holding a hawk up with both hands to keep it from falling. From falling.

chapter 12

The Master of Gwyndryth was submerged in an ocean without currents, sunk deep in mindless calm, without antecedents or future. He drifted in an enforced tranquillity imposed by his body as it tried to knit sinew and tendon within the riven flesh. He needed no mandragore to make him torpid. Death had approached and touched him, had beckoned with the inexorable finger from which all the meat had long since sloughed off, but he had refused to follow. His spirit lay in shards, incapable of resistance, but his stubborn body would not surrender him to the perpetual dark. Now it went about its business without regard to logic or precedence.

The Margrave of Oxenburg shared the long hours of vigil beside the living effigy with Otorin of Lissen. From time to time, the silence and the pressures within him forced the young Umbrian to speak. He spoke about the battle and the Regiment, of his uncle and the funerals, of the Emperor and of his hopes for the future. His intention was to bring the Colonel closer to the surface, to claim back one life from the growing list of the lost, but what he reclaimed in that unshriven apartment where Darius lay ghastly in the gaslight was his own wholeness.

For his unresponsive listener there came a day when the sound became an enigma that settled into organ music. The preoccupied visitor never noticed the fluttering of the eyelids. There was a brief moment when Darius knew that he was alive, and then the music closed in again. Then it faded and was gone.

The next time Darius surfaced he was dosed by the formidable bulk of Sophrinda, the Emperor's personal Wisewoman. She held his hand until he was asleep again and then closed him in with bedcurtains. Otorin wove his way in and out of the Holdmaster's imaginings as well, bearing cool towels and, occasionally, broth. He dreamed that he was visited by illustrious men; the Elector of Estragoth with a mien as long as Winter and the Emperor in hunting clothes. Gradually, his body released him, and there were times of pain, some not borne as nobly as he would have liked. In those times Sophrinda always seemed to be there to bring him a measure of relief.

There were days when he floated high on a hot wave of clarity, and then it was he who was impelled to speak. Those who attended him said later that he was delirious and made little sense. He, when he emerged at the far shore, felt that he had been privy to great revelations. Their precise meanings raveled away as he gained strength, but the conviction persisted. He pulled himself clear of the tides of illness, exhausted, emaciated, and purged. Livid puckers bracketed his rib cage. He tried to call back the memory of the particular battle that had placed them there, but his efforts at recollection ended in sleep.

Darius woke once more with an uneasy head and a clear memory of where he was and what had happened up until the time he was wounded. He did not know the outcome of the battle, but he was in Angorn, so the Outlanders must have been turned back. But what of his new friends? What had happened to the Regiment? He sat up slowly and looked around the hangings for the bell pull. There was sunlight on the floor and the flickering on the ceiling probably meant that the fire was lit. A broad ribbon of embroidered cloth presented itself to his questing fingers and he tugged on it.

He peered round the curtains for a remembered mechanical clock. It was afternoon. He lay back and waited until Otorin came skidding around the door, concern and alarm writ clear across him.

''Where's Sophrinda?'' Darius growled. It was by no means up to his best growls, but he was pleased with it.

Otorin grinned with relief as he came to an ungraceful stop. ''So, you're feeling better. Welcome back, Sir. There were a couple of times when we weren't entirely sure . . .'' His voice trailed off, leaving a strong residue of emotion in the air.

''Never mind that.'' Darius cut through it with a rumble. ''Where's the old woman?''

''Back at her usual duties, I presume. She said she'd be back from time to time to check on you.''

''She left of her own accord?'' Darius was sharply suspicious.

''Not entirely.'' Otorin spaced the two words.

''Meaning?''

''I''—a hesitation—''asked her to leave.''

''And why did you take it upon yourself to do that? Was she unskilled?'' Darius heaved himself up to glare, but was caught by the pain that skewered him.

Otorin was beside him in an instant, easing him back against the bolster. ''My Lord, you must not excite yourself so. Terrible wounds like yours are slow to heal.''

''What happened?'' Darius's face was gray with pain and his eyes were watering. The voice was low and husky.

''You were wounded in the side. One of their 'old-fashioned' blades went through your side. It missed your lungs and your vitals, but you lost a lot of blood. It was a long time before they pulled you out of there.''

''Not that.''

"With Sophrinda? You were delirious and talking non-stop. She was the only one with you most of the time, and she's the Emperor's trusted confidante."

"Does she speak Arunic?" Darius inquired sarcastically.

"Of course, Sir. All Umbrian Wisewomen are trained in the West. In fact, she was born in Arundel."

"No matter." Darius waved the subject away irritably. "What happened in the battle?"

"Ah yes, that." Otorin smoothed the bolster and re-adjusted the blankets. "The battle." He stepped back and straightened up. "What do I tell you about the battle? Do you remember anything about it?"

"I remember the crawler attack and the cavalry charge. I remember the fighting and that great black horse rearing and striking." Darius paused. "What a magnificent fighter he is."

"Was."

"Ah." There was hurt in the exhalation.

"I am told that he was tremendous. You were unhorsed and down, but he kept them off you. He stayed astride you and kept them off you for half of an hour. They burned him to pieces eventually and you could hear him clear to the Causeways. He was quite terrible." There was a long silence while the sun and the fire made the room inappropriately cheerful.

"Ay me." It was a long phrase. "What did we ever do to deserve their devotion? I shall not ride his like again." Darius was silent again. "What of the battle?" he asked at length.

"It is generally conceded that the cavalry saved the day."

"And the Regiment?"

"Not too good, I'm afraid." The aide paused and a shadow crossed his face.

"Well? Go on, man," Darius rasped.

"There are not . . . not very many left." He put his hand out as Darius moaned hoarsely, but he dared not touch him. The broad body contorted with grief. The lips drew back across the teeth and the breath came and went raggedly. Finally, Darius rolled onto his side with his back to Otorin and drew up his knees. The squire waited until the breathing lengthened and evened out, and then he tiptoed away.

Darius retreated into fever again and Sophrinda returned to his bedside. When he came back again it was as a skin-clad last upon which a proper body might be built. He lay, silent and open-eyed, and allowed himself to be fed broth like a child, by the spoonful. He received no visitors. Otorin made an attempt to invade the sanctuary, but he was bested by the impregnable authority of a Wisewoman in the performance of her duty. He was further rebuffed when the first person summoned to the sickroom was the Margrave of Oxenburg.

The soldier was shocked by what he saw when he limped in on his cane. The room was all warmth and firelight, and the gas globes poppled drowsily, but what held him was the blanket-bundled figure by the hearth. For an instant the man looked like an Umbrian to him, too small to be an Arundelian. Before he could move, Sophrinda swept down on him.

"You're not to tire him, d'you hear me, young man? I'll be back in a quarter of the hour." She shot him a loaded glance as she passed. "You bide me and behave yourself," she said as she let herself out.

Oxenburg checked his uniform as best he could with his left arm in a sling and the cane in his right hand. He limped over to the dreaming figure in the dark chair and drew himself up. "Brigadier Oxenburg reporting as ordered, Colonel." His head dropped in salute.

"Are you real, or am I imagining you again?" The seated figure did not turn its head. The voice was soft and distant.

"Quite real, Sir—what's left of me."

"The last time I dreamed you, you told me that I was as much of a nuisance alive as dead. You were wrong, you know. I'd be much less of a nuisance, especially to myself, if I were dead."

"You mustn't talk like that, Colonel, and anyway, you didn't dream me the first time. I was trying to make a joke. I didn't even think you could hear me."

Darius's head emerged from the woolen shroud and turned to look at the visitor for the first time. Oxenburg was unable to keep the shock off his face. The shrunken visage that confronted him was a jarring mixture of youth and age. The clear planes of the bones looked ageless, and the hollows from which the eyes glistened hid the lines. The hair and beard were long and white, as if his illness had consumed their color. The death's head smiled at him, and the muscles that brought it about did their work in plain view.

"You don't look that good yourself," Darius said, and Oxenburg let his breath out in audible relief.

"I didn't know what to think," he said with an answering smile.

As soon as it had been reciprocated, the smile on Darius's face died. It was as if he were rationing all his movements. "Sit down, lad. I've been told that we won. I've also been told that there's almost nothing left of the Regiment." He paused as he spoke, like an actor delivering lines. "Sophrinda won't answer any questions. She's worse than a Sergeant Major. I need to know what happened, son. My imagination is getting too vivid in my old age."

"I'm not supposed to upset you. That old battle-ax will have me stretched and tanned if I do."

"I think I've the strength to take it. I may not be strong enough to tackle a Wisewoman yet, but I've never flinched from a battle report."

"Perhaps it would be better if we put it off for the next time, Sir."

"I assume that I still have my commission, Brigadier?" The voice was silken, and it made the Margrave's sense of danger bristle.

"Of course you do, Colonel," he said quickly.

"Then let us make that an order, shall we, Brigadier?"

"Yes, Sir." Oxenburg automatically straightened up and winced as the weight shifted on his hip.

"At ease, lad. There's no need for that." It was Darius's turn to be embarrassed.

"Mind if I unbutton my jacket, Sir? It's a little close in here for me."

"Of course, of course. I seem to have turned into an Umbrian, forever huddling over a fire. Here, let me take the cane." He held out a hand, and Oxenburg was appalled at how clawlike it had become. This time he tried not to show it.

"Thank you, Sir," he said as he handed it over. "There, that does it." He leaned forward and took back the cane. He settled himself gingerly, his back still parade-straight, and began in the monotonous cadence that betokens an official report.

"On the eighth of Thoden, the Imperial Cavalry reorganized into two wings on the order of the Regimental Colonel—"

"Hey, hey, hey, that's quite enough of that, Estivus. I know what I look like, that pier glass is merciless, but there's no need to treat me like the Mother's Messenger. I don't want the record, I want to know what happened, before that woman chases you out of here with her pestle."

"Oh, in that case," Oxenburg said with a shadow of his former grin. "I've been told that a certain Colonel led the East Wing's charge slap into the middle of the enemy, just like a glory-hunting younger son in his first battle."

"Ha!" Darius snorted. "They probably also say that his charger ran away with him."

"Not yet, but I'm sure they will." They smiled at each other.

"Be serious, lad. We haven't that much time. She's like a wild warcat with young."

"Right you are. The charge you led smashed the enemy line. They turned too late to withstand us, and Varnarek's men hit them from the other side once they realized that the tide had turned. Same thing happened on the other side of the field. The enemy fought bravely, I'll give them that. They did us grave harm, but the losses would have been acceptable, save for one little thing." His posture had relaxed and the shoulders had curved forward. Beads of perspiration formed at the base of his throat and purled out of sight.

"They had more of those godless machines in reserve," he said slowly. "They came out behind the West Wing and burned them to a crisp before they knew what was happening."

"All of them?" Darius's whisper was rough with horror.

"All of them. Uncle Ombras, the lot. Not a man or horse left alive, and few of them recognizable. I know. I saw them."

The silence stretched, and into it came Sophrinda, ready for combat. She stopped and looked with surprise at the seated and unspeaking men.

"Well," she said approvingly, "you two have been good, but I'm afraid you'll have to go now, Margrave. Perhaps you can come back and see him again tomorrow.

Mustn't try to do too much too soon." She bustled over to rearrange the Lord Observor's blankets while Oxenburg struggled awkwardly to his feet. He straightened his shoulders and ducked his head.

"Colonel." He waited to be dismissed, but the figure in the wing chair did not move or acknowledge him in any way. He turned and, with a nod to the Wisewoman, made his way painfully out of the apartments.

Darius sat on, staring into the fire with unseeing eyes. He shrank in on himself. His mind insulated itself against madness by withdrawing and allowing him no coherent thought. Sophrinda put him to bed, and it was a while before she would let him have visitors again.

In due time the shock became manageable and the pace of recovery picked up. Otorin replaced Sophrinda once more as Darius regained appetite and strength. The shadows and the silences, however, remained unchanged. The hair and beard were trimmed by the Court barber. Their whiteness added to the impression of age, but it was the eyes that were the oldest of all.

Darius had decided to return to the world, to abandon the comfortable drifting, divorced from memory, in which he had taken refuge. The return of knowledge caused him pain, like blood returning to a limb long asleep. He allowed the immediate past into his ken as slowly as he could and faced it as honestly as he was able. He had been given the Regiment and it had been destroyed under his hand. Angorn was still here, he reminded himself, but it gave him scant comfort. As his body acquired flesh, his mind learned to accept what he could not change.

He became restive, and the apartments began to feel like a prison. He tried on his clothes and found them all too large, so he asked Otorin to find him a robe that would let him move easily and keep him warm. Then, early one morning, before the Court was up, he emerged into the corridor leaning on Otorin's shoulder and a stout staff. His appearance caused consternation among the servants and the squires. Some great, gaunt prophet had dropped into their midst and was stalking the galleries of the keep. They avoided his shadow and made a variety of warding gestures as he passed.

As the word of his recovery spread, scrolls, flowers, invitations, and gifts accumulated in the antechamber. Otorin dealt with the correspondence and politely refused all invitations. He protected Darius as fiercely as Sophrinda ever had. People began to wait in the passageways for a sight of the Lord Observor, though none dared confront his person. For his part, Darius seemed unaware of them. When, as was inevitable, his early-morning habits became general knowledge, throngs defied palace convention and rose early to stand and stare as he passed.

On those occasions silence ran before him like a bow wave and whispering broke out behind. It was rumored that the Emperor himself, disguised as a steward, had gone to witness the strange progress of the tall, thin man in the long robe: a man who was girt in the unassailable dignity of obliviousness.

When his charge, as Otorin had come to think of him, asked to be taken riding, he knew that another corner had been turned, and when he was asked to finish the account of the battle, he felt that complete recovery was at hand. He was careful, however, to keep the account bare and factual. Of the thousand men that Darius had commanded, three hundred and forty-seven survived, most of them from the support units. Sixteen of the cannon had been destroyed, and fully a third of the infantry had been mown down. Three of the cloudsteeds had been tumbled from the sky and their riders lost. On the enemy side, all of the first wave of crawlers had been disabled, but six of the ten that had destroyed the Adjutant Major and his command had escaped back to safety. It had been hailed as a great victory. The Emperor had held a triumph. Lord Varnarek was a hero, as were Sir Ombras Cortauld and his nephew.

"And what think they of me?" Darius inquired tiredly. Otorin looked up quickly, surprised by the use of the formal mode. "What think they of the foreigner who took the flower of their youth, the hope of their future, and flung it into the flames like a funeral wreath? What say the people of Umbria to the High Priest who has no gods, but sacrificed their sons anyway?"

"They hold you in awe, Lord," Otorin replied gravely and in like mode. "For their sakes you have gone beyond the threshold. You have come back, but you are mightily changed. They look at you and they know fear. It is said that you have saved the Empire. The legend is growing. There are songs."

"I can imagine," Darius said, reverting to the informal.

"Well, they're still a bit tentative, but they'll get more certain as they get further from the truth," Otorin said, matching the dryness, relieved that the depression had eased. "By the way, there's a service of thanksgiving to the Mother that's awaiting your recovery."

"In that case I shall have a relapse. Preferably one that gets me sent home immediately."

"Sorry, Sir; not a chance. It's set for a sennight from yesterday. The Chamberlain has offered to have you carried in on a litter if need be. Come to think of it, it would make for a rather dramatic entrance."

"You can stop right there, my friend. They'll have me make a speech—you know they will. I don't care what anyone says, I'm not a Maternite and I'm not participating. Once was interesting. Twice would be unbearable." Darius's voice had taken on the high, fractious note of an overtired child. Otorin, well versed in the small signs, persuaded him to lie down and rest. It took three more days to jockey him into attending the service, but Otorin had to promise that there would be no speech.

Darius became moody and difficult. He submitted his resignation to Varodias, with a copy to the Princess Arabella. Varodias refused to accept it and countered by making him a Knight of the Imperial Cross and promoting him to the rank of General. The Lord Observor declined public investiture for either honor. He terrified the Court tailor when the man tried to fit him for a new uniform. Considering the barrage of sarcasm the man had to endure, the result was a tribute to his patience and integrity.

Otorin was braced for trouble on the morning of the ceremony, but Darius was quiet and seemingly at peace with himself. He had no trouble dressing him, though he could not convince him to wear all his decorations. They settled on the new cross in deference to the Emperor, and Otorin stepped back with an approving look after he had hung it around Darius's neck. The black tunic and trousers with silver piping and star of rank below the left clavicle made him look even taller and thinner. The hair was short and the beard had been cut to an elegant point. Otorin knelt and gave the calf-high black boots a final buffing.

"There, that should do it," he said as he got to his feet. "I must say, you look very grand."

"I won't wear that absurd hat," Darius said sulkily, pointing to the black tricorn with a white plume that sat on top of the chest.

"Don't worry"—Otorin was soothing—"you won't have to. All you have to do is carry it. But don't forget to put your gloves on before you go to the Chapel."

"Lot of nonsense, all this dressing up.'

"Well, it's not going to be for very long," Otorin reminded him, "and you don't have to do anything except sit there. You don't have to stand or kneel—in deference to your terrible wounds." He allowed himself a small smile. He glanced over at the clock. "Well, time to get going." He crossed the room and retrieved the offending hat. "Here you are. And don't forget to put the gloves on."

Otorin left him at the Chapel door with the rest of the notables and went in to join the congregation. Darius nodded to the Mother Supreme, who was wearing a cloth-of-gold gown for the occasion, caught up, as always, to suggest pregnancy. The Emperor and Empress were cordial and Phalastra of Estragoth was warm and welcoming. To his credit, Lord Varnarek came over and was civil. Darius did not find the talking easy.

Trumpets sounded, and as they processed in, the orchestra and choir burst into a hymn of praise to the Mother. They walked slowly up the aisle and seated themselves in tiered state on either side of the High Altar. The Mother Supreme's marble throne was at the apex on one side, and Varodias's more ornate version dominated the other. Varnarek and Jessup sat below the Priestess, and Darius, belatedly pulling on his gloves, sat with the Empress below her husband's throne.

The Mother Supreme rose, and with her the congregation, all save Darius. He sat unmoving through her a cappella introit and their responses. His face remained impassive throughout the Elector of Estragoth's limpid eulogy for the fallen, but those who occupied the front pews saw the tears. When he finally rose for the recessional, the haunted mask was seen by everyone. There were few who forgot it.

The service bolstered Darius's resolve to leave. He sent the remaining cloudsteedsman to Celador with a request that he be recalled. He began to go flying on the cloudmare again. By the time his letter of release arrived, he felt strong enough to make the long journey back to

Gwyndryth. Otorin was far from convinced, but knew his man well enough to know that protest would be unavailing. Darius sent his recommendation that the Margrave of Oxenburg replace him as Regimental Colonel to Varodias and requested an audience.

He was prepared for delaying tactics and was surprised when the audience was scheduled within the sennight. He was prepared for Varodias to raise objections. The appointment was, after all, at his Imperial Majesty's pleasure. Instead, Varodias made a suitable speech of regret and aquiesced with considerable charm. Darius backed from the presence in pleased bewilderment, a state that lasted until Otorin explained that the Emperor was only too glad to see him leave. His status as a folk hero was making it hard for Varodias to claim the victory as his own. The Emperor was not a man to suffer overshadowment gladly.

It was in fact Otorin who delayed him. The squire's insistance that the diplomatic niceties be observed was adamantine. The Princess Arabella had sent monies for a farewell banquet to be hosted by the Lord Observor. The honor and dignity of the throne demanded it. The Emperor countered with a State Banquet in his honor. Both events were considered great successes. Darius hated them both equally.

Not all of it was irksome. Phalastra of Estragoth demonstrated his knowledge of human nature by taking him out for a day of hunting and by insisting that Otorin accompany them as his guest. There was a farewell dinner with the Margrave which was more affecting than he had expected. The new Regimental Colonel had healed well, though he still walked with a limp. His new responsibilities seemed to have routed his melancholia and Darius envied him for his youthful resilience.

There was one final argument with Otorin and one final

ceremony. The argument was the only one that fortnight that Darius won. Otorin was set on accompanying him back to Gwyndryth and then flying on to Celador. Darius would have none of it. The ceremony, which immediately preceeded his departure, was mercifully brief. The Emperor and all the chief men and women of the Court came to see him off. There were people on the walls and on rooftops, and they cheered him to the mounting block.

He climbed into the saddle, waved at the throng, and checked to see that they had left the cloudsteed enough room in which to take off. They cheered him through the canter and the launch and they were still waving and cheering as he circled in the updraft from the twin keeps. He looked down and saw the people in the town hanging out of windows and crowded into the streets. The whole of Angorn is craning to see the last of me, he thought as they came out of the spiral and headed due South West.

The cloudmare was far more heavily laden than when they had flown in, but her wings beat true and strong. Now that he was finally away, he found that his mood was curiously flat. Well, what do you expect? he asked himself. Perhaps it would have been more politic to go to Celador and make his report to Arabella, but he had earned the right to rest. Celador be damned, he thought. A wounded man goes home to heal, goes back to the peace and quiet of his own demesne. That is the right way, the traditional way.

chapter 13

Belengar lay dreaming in the late Summer heat. Shops were shuttered and market stalls were empty. Buyers and sellers snoozed in the relative cool brought by thick walls and marble floors. The air was moist and humid and sat heavy as a house kit on a sleeper's chest. The streets were deserted. Strays lay in the shadowed alleyways and twitched with dreams or fleas, or both. The ubiquitous water was still lively as it fell down fountains, flowed through the gutters, and plashed up against docks and ships. It was the only busy thing in the slow season.

As Darius flew over the Magic Kingdoms, men and women toiled in the fields to bring the harvest in, winnowers repaired their flails, and millers trued their stones. Kina lowed and munched on the fading grass, ignorant of the pens that waited and the slaughtering that lay beyond them. Puffy flocks of sheep grazed on the hillsides, flax retted in the ponds, and in the nearby sheds, looms were being overhauled. It was everybody's busy season.

Darius sailed above it all, oblivious to most of it. He was content to be aloft again, happier to be going home. It would be tranquil, and there would be only such ceremony as he would countenance. He would stroll slowly among the vines and supervise the pressing. He would ride around the fields and encourage the gleaning hands. He would preside over the festivities when all the gathering was done, and eat and drink of the provender of his own lands as a knight should.

He conjured up pictures as he flew. Perhaps his errant daughter would be there; if she was back from her search; if she was unharmed. There would be no unicorn, of course. That had been nothing but the groping of the Council of Magic after the shock of the Archmage's vision; the old army adage "When in doubt look busy." Well, he'd gone along with it. He'd honored the oath of fealty beyond the bounds of contract. That was family principle. He smiled high above the clouds. The girl was a Gwyndryth, no doubt of that.

If the gods of the odds still favored him, Marianna would be safe and whole and not too disappointed. Then, the fates willing, but doubtless not his daughter, there could soon be another ceremony. It was past time that she was married, and with her great adventure behind her, she should be ready to settle down.

The clouds opened up and suddenly the Melnikons were ahead. They were insignificant when compared to the mountains he had flown past on the Empire's border, but they had their own, well-loved, beauty. At their feet lay the speck that was Gwyndryth and the flashing ribbon of the river. He was almost home. He felt a surge of affection for the old place with its tidy fields and strategic coppices, with the fishing village at the river bend and the rows of vines strung across the hillsides. He put the cloudmare into a broad circle so that he could savor the unusual view.

The Hold drowsed in a slant of sunlight, its blockiness disguised by foreshortening and its lines softened by creepers and the greens and russets of long-established lichen. They swung lower, and he caught the gleam of Oracle Lake to the South. What held his attention, though, was the activity around the Hold. The bunglebird he'd sent from Angorn must have arrived late, and they were preparing a welcome. He peered down and frowned. There were cloudsteeds down there. A tic of anxiety began to build. There should be no cloudsteeds.

He came in for a landing in the main court and braced himself as they skimmed the walls. The wings cupped back, and before he could worry about his form they were down. He backed stiffly down the rope ladder and tossed the reins to an unfamiliar groom. He looked around. There were people scurrying, bent on errands, and not a one of them payed him the slightest mind. So much for the welcome. He stopped a passing page and sent him off to find Lord Obray, his Senechal. The boy was deferential, but showed no sign of recognizing him. Had Obray heard rumors of his death and decided to usurp the hold? No! Not Sir Amyas. It was an unworthy thought bred of his recent sickness.

He decided to stand his ground and wait for the Senechal. Time was when he'd have been up the steps to the main door two at a time. He allowed himself a twisted little smile. He would also have been bellowing. Now Obray would have to come to him. He squared his shoulders and walked around a little to ease his legs. The small door set in the right-hand half of the main portal opened, and a figure ran down the steps toward him.

She was hugging him before he fully realized that it was Marianna. He bent and kissed the top of her head and wished that she wouldn't squeeze so hard. He pushed her away to look at her and was surprised by what he saw. The dark red hair was short and uneven, the face and hands were deeply tanned, and the nails were cracked. The eyes had tears in them, but the smile was as he remembered it.

Marianna linked her arm through his and walked him back to the house, talking nineteen to the dozen. It took him a while to understand that the High Council of Magic was under his roof, but he wasn't clear why. In fact, nothing was very clear. He stumbled on the bottom step. Marianna stopped and looked closely at him, then hustled him up the remaining stairs past a startled Sir Amyas Obray and put him to bed.

He spent a day with shadows before Marianna's image solidified beside the four-poster. He watched her for a while and saw her as a stranger might. She had changed. The wild, coltish beauty of the willow years was gone. A young woman of character and considerable good looks sat reading. Despite the peasant tan, she was the spit and image of her mother, though the mouth and determined chin were his. A paradox. He took it with him into sleep.

She was still there when he woke, or there again, and this time she was waiting for him.

"Welcome back, Father. How are you feeling?" She rose and put a cool hand on his brow.

"Better, thank you. The journey must have tired me more than I realized."

"Well," she said, removing her hand, "you don't seem to have a fever."

Darius hoisted himself into a sitting position and supressed the grimace that the twinge of pain prompted. "How long have I been asleep?" he asked.

"You landed two days ago."

"Two days?"

"Yes, and the bunglebirds you sent from Angorn got in yesterday."

"Bloody stupid birds."

"It doesn't matter. This place is such a madhouse that most of the people don't know that you're here."

"I don't understand," he said. It sounded querulous.

"Do you remember anything I told you when you arrived?"

"I'm rather vague about my arrival."

"In that case," she said with what he considered an inappropriate smile, "I have a great deal to tell you."

"First things first," he interrupted. "Are you," he hesitated, "are you all right?"

"Of course I'm all right."

"Oh naturally," he said sarcastically. "You go off into the wilderness with a man I'm not even allowed to meet, looking for a creature that doesn't exist, and I'm not supposed to worry?"

The smile brightened. "Oh, but they do exist."

He looked at her suspiciously. "You found the unicorn?"

"A whole family of them." Her teeth gleamed in the brown face, but he could tell that she was not joking.

"A whole family of unicorns?" he said wonderingly. "That is a truly splendid achievement."

"And they're here, here at Gwyndryth," she rushed on. "Only nobody but the Mages and Sir Amyas is supposed to know. Jarrod knows, of course," she added.

"Wait a minute," Darius said. "Did you tell me something about the High Council of Magic being here?"

"So you do remember."

"That accounts for the cloudsteeds then."

"I beg your pardon?"

He looked up. "Doesn't matter." He smiled at her and reached out and squeezed her hand. "I am really proud of you. You are a true Gwyndryth." Marianna colored with pleasure at the compliment. "Well, you better tell me the whole thing again from the beginning." He leaned back against the bolster and listened intently while she told her story.

"That was quite an adventure," he said when she was finished. "And now they're here, in the caverns?"

"They certainly are. Jarrod and I are feeding them."

She giggled unexpectedly. "I'm getting very good at stealing hay and apples."

"What's he like, this Jarrod?" he asked as casually as he could.

"What can I tell you that I haven't said already?"

"You've told me what the two of you did. You haven't told me what he's like."

"He's not a bad sort—for a Magician. He's very young, of course, and hopelessly juvenile, but, all in all, he was a good companion."

"And he never tried to—"

"Never." She cut him off with the half-truth.

"And when can I see these wonders?" Darius asked, changing the subject.

"As soon as you're strong enough."

"In that case," he said, pushing the covers back, "the sooner the better."

"Not so fast." She leaned forward and put a hand on his chest. "You've been badly wounded. Oh, don't bother to deny it. Who d'you think has been changing the dressing? You'll stay here until I say you're strong enough to get up."

"You're no Wisewoman, and I say that I'm more than ready to get up."

"Not today," Marianna replied with irritating authority. "If your fever doesn't come back tonight, you can get out of bed for a bit tomorrow."

"Perhaps these unicorns of yours could make me whole," he said pettishly. This was not how he imagined his homecoming.

She took him seriously. "Perhaps they can. All right, up with you then."

"Now?" He hadn't expected this.

"Yes, now. Let's see how well you walk. It's a long way down to the caverns."

Darius tried for her, and still more for his own pride and dignity. He failed, and it was two more days before she would let him make the trip. Even then, he had to lean on her down the final part. He did not object when his daughter usurped his prerogative and operated the hidden lever. He stood in front of the gaping black entrance, breathing a little more heavily than he would have liked, trying to imagine what it was that he was expecting.

A spicy smell with a sweet afterscent teased him. Not remotely like the smell of byred horses. Closer to a cloud-steed, but not that, either. Marianna moved forward into the darkness, and he followed reluctantly.

"What is it that I smell?" he asked, more to reassure himself than for information.

"The unicorns, I expect." Her shoe scraped on the brick floor. There was the tick of struck flint. It was repeated several times, and then erratic light flared as she lit a torch.

Darius strained his eyes looking for something he was not quite sure of. "They're like great big beautiful horses, only that doesn't come close to it," had been Marianna's inadequate description. He couldn't see anything beyond the dazzle. The torch retreated and lit another and then another. The barrel-vaulted space came to flickering life. Something gleamed beyond the reach of the linklight. Another circle of rust brick bloomed, and into it came a large, glossy white shape. It seemed to absorb the colors around it and became pink, shot through with white satin. A unicorn.

The horn compelled his eyes, a whorl of soft nacre tapering to a wicked point. He put a hand out to steady himself, and the texture of the wall was reassuringly rough on his palm. This was no fever dream. The creature was plain before him. He had no more defenses against it, and his knees began to tremble. He willed them to stop, but they ignored him. He was aware of noise, and two more of them trotted into the light. The closed world of the caverns began to waver.

"It's all right, Father. They mean no harm." Her hands on his arm steadied him, and he took a deep breath to clear his head.

"Perhaps I am not as far recovered as I had thought," he said weakly.

"I should have warned you. They have that effect on everybody, even old Ragnor, I'm told, but I doubt that he'd admit it."

There were four of them now, and they seemed to hem him in. The first he had seen was the largest, but not by much. That must be the dam. What had Marianna said about the colts? Two males and one female; then the young female would be the smallest one. He stood and stared. They stared back.

They were exquisite, though that was the wrong word for animals of such obvious strength. The bunched muscles showed under the hide. The heads were fine-boned and clean of line, the eyes large and blue and fringed with lashes. The manes and tails had gold in them, though perhaps that was a trick of the light, and ended in curls. The hooves looked to be made of silver. And then there were those riveting horns, made of who knew what. He had secretly expected to be disappointed, to see some freak that could be mistaken for a legend at a distance, but there could be no doubting, not in the presence of these magisterial beasts.

Marianna walked over, reached up and stroked the dam's neck. "This is Amarine, Father. Amarine, this is my father." The girl was radiant, and Darius knew her well enough to know that it was not borrowed from the light.

The big unicorn paced forward slowly and extended her head. She snuffled at his doublet and then took another step and put her jaw on his shoulder. He didn't flinch, but it took all his control to hold still. Her cheek settled against his and he was surprised at its softness. His eyes flicked to the long, spiraling horn that seemed to burst from the forehead.

"I've never seen her do that before." Marianna's voice was almost an interruption. "She must really like you."

"I expect that she is extending her friendship because I am related to you," Darius said and heard the tremor in his voice. The unicorn may have heard it too, for she withdrew her head. He wanted to stroke her, but did not dare.

Amarine took a step backward and shook her head. The mane whipped about. She wheeled delicately, brushed Marianna's hair with her muzzle, and walked back into the darkness in an echoing clatter of hooves. The colts, curious to the last, lingered and then followed her. Darius watched them fade away with regret and continued to stare even though he knew that there was nothing more to see. Marianna waited on him.

"They are quite something," he said at last. "I really didn't know what to expect, but they are so much"—he hesitated—"bigger, bigger in every way, than anything I had imagined."

"They even overawe the Mages," Marianna said as she began to extinguish the torches. "Trip the lever for me, please, Father."

Darius complied. The wall opened and the vague light of the cellars filled the entryway. "I may be imagining things," he said, "but I feel much stronger."

She doused the last torch and the brickwork disappeared. There was no sound from the unicorns. Only the spicy tang that hung in the air told Darius that he had not imagined the whole thing. That and his renewed vitality.

"Thank you for letting me see them. It was a privilege." He stood aside to let her precede him. "You know,'' he said as the wall closed behind them, ''I think I'll attend Hall tonight. I've yet to greet my guests.''

Marianna smiled in the gloom. ''I'm glad that you feel up to it, but I wouldn't tell them the source of your sudden improvement if I were you. I didn't get permission to bring you down here.''

''Why should you need permission?'' he asked as he followed her up the stairs. ''This is your home and you found them, after all.''

''I agree.'' He noticed the edge in her voice. ''But the Mages have taken them over.''

''Well, I suppose that's to be expected. What's going to happen to them? They're welcome to stay in the caverns as long as they need to, though I should think they would be happier in the open air.''

''I know. Nobody knows what to do with them. They are obviously here for a reason, but not one of those powerful people upstairs knows what it is. I know one thing, though,'' she added. ''I'm going anywhere they take Amarine.''

She was fierce in her declaration, and Darius knew better to comment.

''I'll keep a bridle on my tongue,'' was all he said.

Darius's confidence had evaporated by the time he took his traditional place at the head of the table. He was flanked by Arabella of Arundel and Naxania, Princess of Paladine. The Archmage stood next to Arabella, and Greylock, the Paladinian Mage, was to the left of Naxania. It was the most impressive group of people to be under this roof for better than four hundred years.

He felt proud, though, as he looked down the table. Gwyndryth would live forever in legend as the place where the great Mages first saw the unicorns. Marianna had undoubtedly brought great renown to the name—if they ever allowed the news to get out. He looked around the Hall, royalty on either side of him and his vassals gathered at his table.

Lady Obray had done a fine job. The aroma of trodden herbs rose subtly; the wood, where it was visible, gleamed darkly under his best plate. There was more plate displayed at the sides of the room where his stewards waited. It should all be making him feel secure and confident, but he had yet to face his ruler. He smiled nervously at Arabella. She returned the smile.

"The Princess Regnant is most welcome in my humble abode," he said with a bow. "As is your Royal Highness of Paladine." Another bow.

"We are exceeding pleased to be here and to have this chance to welcome you home after your mission on our behalf," Arabella replied as she took her seat.

"I know that this is not the proper time for it, Ma'am," he said, "but I am ready to make report upon my embassy whenever it should please you."

She gave him a long, unnerving look, and the hollow place in his chest filled with feathers. "We have had report of you, my Lord Holdmaster. Our Cousin Varodias has written to us." She paused and let him dangle. Her face gave nothing away. He reached for his spoon, feeling as if his features had frozen in place. "He is most generous in his praise. Indeed, news of your exploits preceded you." She released him.

Darius bowed his head to hide his relief. Princes are the same the world over, he thought. They play with us.

"When you are recovered from your wounds," she continued, "we would have you come to Celador. We shall have need of you. For the moment, though, we judge that you should enjoy some well-earned rest."

"Your Royal Highness is most benevolent, and I am fortunate to serve so gracious a sovereign," he said, and inclined his head again. A quick trill of laughter brought it up.

''La, Sir. You do us too much honor.'' She dabbed at her mouth with a piece of lace. ''Do you not know that there are broadsheets telling of your exploits tacked to every village pole? No, we see by your face that you do not. Forgive our laughter then, it was misplaced. We have been too cloistered in Celador to see much of true humility and worth.''

''You are kind, Ma'am,'' he replied, wondering what she was really trying to say.

''Now, tell us of Umbria and our Imperial Cousin.''

He started cautiously, but had hit his stride when the Chief Steward arrived with the second course. Arabella held up a hand.

''We would fain hear you to the end, my Lord, but we must attend to the Archmage. Let us continue anon.'' She nodded and moved her attention to Ragnor. Darius turned obediently to his left and found himself under the scrutiny of flecked, bluish-green eyes. The Princess Naxania was ready for him.

He inclined. ''Your Royal Highness does my house honor by your presence.''

''It is we who are honored to be the guest of such a remarkable family. The father rescues an empire, and the daughter''—she checked herself as a servingman passed behind her—''the daughter is remarkable in her own right.'' She held his eyes and smiled at him.

It produced a feeling not unlike the one he had experienced in the caverns. He was suddenly acutely conscious of his white hair. He had seen the Princess before at Celador, but only from the back of the Great Hall. He had thought her young and striking, but he had not realized how beautiful she was. He was well aware of it now. The raven hair and the porcelain skin made Arabella's pale handsomeness seem insipid by comparison. He really ought not to be thinking along these lines, he chided himself. She was a King's daughter. The thoughts persisted.

"We long to hear of Angorn," she said, and the husky voice seemed surrounded by echoes; as if something had gone wrong with his hearing. "We have never been invited to Umbria, though my father and the Emperor get along well together." The disturbing eyes were wide.

Darius took a deep breath and launched into his recital again. It was easier this time. She hung on his words, but he put that down to royal good manners. He found that he was enjoying himself and was sorry when he had to turn back to Arabella. The meal that he had looked forward to as an ordeal passed more quickly than he wanted it to.

The next day he called for all his best clothes and fretted over the fact that they were too big on him. He selected a robe that he had last worn as a young man and ordered the tailor to alter the rest of his things. He should set an example to his household, he told himself. Part of a Lord's duty was to maintain state. Before he went down to dinner he dabbed himself with civet oil, a thing he had not done for more years than he cared to remember. He told himself that he was an old fool, but that did not stop the coursing of his blood.

Darius spent the days riding around the estates with Sir Amyas. This was what he had planned to do, was the chiefest pleasure that he had anticipated on the long flight home. All was as it should have been. The Senechal's stewardship had been exemplary. Grain nodded in the fields, fruit ripened in the orchards, roads and bridges were in good repair, and fish jumped in the hot stillness of the afternoons. His lands were fertile and beautiful. He tried to concentrate on Sir Amyas's running commentary, but his mind kept slipping off. The smell of new-mown hay conjured up images of young couples lying together on a rick. The white flash of a deer's tail in the woods reminded him that rutting season would soon begin.

Most of his chief vassals were away at the war, but he visited their wives and inquired about their sons. Marianna would need a husband capable of defending the Hold once he was gone. With her looks she ought to be able to make a better match than a local one, but one never knew. She was dissatisfied at the moment, that much was clear from the little that he got to see of her, and it didn't seem like an auspicious time to broach the subject. He knew that he ought to try to find out what was really bothering her. When she was little she had always brought her problems to him, but now she was holding herself aloof. He didn't know what to say to her.

Events conspired to make it easy to postpone such things. Greylock of Paladine was taken mysteriously ill, carried up from the cellars on a litter. Then the unicorns emerged from the caverns, and the routines of the Hold were entirely disrupted. Darius meant to talk to the Courtak boy, to thank him for taking care of Marianna (though to hear her tell it, it was the other way around), but he was always with the unicorns or with his Mage.

Darius caught rare glimpses of him and conned him carefully when he got the chance. He didn't look as young as Darius had thought he would. He was the tall, stringy type, but he had none of the softness that Darius associated with boys. "Hopelessly juvenile" was what Marianna had said, but that was not the way he seemed to her father. He wondered again if anything had happened between them on the quest. He hoped not: it would be a most unsuitable match. Then he remembered the unicorns and took heart. If the unicorns were here, they must both still be virgins.

He was greatly flattered when the Princess Naxania sought him out. She professed great interest in Gwyndryth and its history and asked to be shown the points of interest. There was nothing in the least provocative in these meetings, and they were never alone together, but it gave him reason for hope. He was in that state where happiness can be bestowed with a look and ecstasy evoked by a casual touch.

Marianna grew more moody, despite the adulation that attached to her as the story of the unicorns circulated. On the brief occasions when they met, she always managed to prick the bubble of his contentment. He found that he was relieved when she left to go on one of her innumerable errands. Then one day she announced, in a peremptory way, that she had to go to Stronta with the unicorns; just a flat statement, no asking his permission. He did not like the idea of her going away again so soon, but she was a person of importance now and he felt petty for wanting her to stay home.

The Hold was abustle with preparations and departures. Darius sat alone in his study feeling sorry for himself. Then the note came. The Princess Naxania was asking if she could impose on his hospitality for a while longer. Suddenly the idea of his daughter going to Stronta while the Princess of Paladine stayed at Gwyndryth seemed an excellent one. He told himself that he was a foolish old man, but he felt like a very young one.

The Holdfolk were in a holiday mood, he could sense it as he went about, and he felt at one with them. The great ones would soon be gone and the small army of temporary retainers would go home with coins from his strongroom to liven their Winter. The old saying that it never rains on a Mage had proved true, and that meant that the interrupted harvest could be brought in with little loss. It was going to be a good year for the Holding.

It was a rare season when all things ran together. They had much to be thankful for, these men and women. They were proud of their Holding and that pride had been enhanced by the visit of these illustrious guests. They had the shared satisfaction of labor well performed. It was as if they had staged a pageant and brought it off. And with what a cast; and with what wonderous effects.

Beautiful Princesses and mighty wizards paraded for them. There was the mystery of the unicorns and the greater mystery when they disappeared from the middle of the South meadow, taking the young mistress and her Magician with them. There was comedy provided by the Archmage as he was strapped to his cloudsteed and, Darius hoped, there might even be romance. There would certainly be enough good gossip to take them clear through the Season of the Moons. Oh yes, it would be a year to remember.

chapter 14

The day after the last dignitary but one had taken to the skies Darius and the Princess went hunting. She had an excellent seat and was in on most of the kills. They took no bucks this close to the rut, but returned with enough venison to restock the larder. It was a long and satisfying day, and Darius was feeling pleased with his stamina.

"Do we have to dine in state tonight?" Naxania asked as her horse was led away.

"Of course not, your Highness." Darius was concerned. "It was thoughtless of me to keep us out so long. My fondness for the hunt sometimes makes me heedless. I am sorry. I should have realized that your Highness was tired."

"Don't flatter yourself," she said informally. "I suspect that I have more energy left than you do. I should simply prefer not to be on display tonight."

"I understand, Ma'am." Darius persevered with the formal mode. "If you wish to dine in your apartments, it is easily arranged."

"I prefer to dine in your apartments," she said, and looked directly at him.

He felt a palpable thrill, an arrow of sensation that left him tingling. He stared at her and no words came. Her eyes widened and she nodded confirmation. "I shall be most honored,'' he said, finding his tongue. ''Sir Amyas can take my place at Hall.''

''The twentieth hour, then? And I think it would be best if the service was discreet.'' She gave him a most unregal smile and his heart seemed to do something awkward.

''I shall be there, your Highness.'' As he bowed he realized how stupid that sounded, but she didn't appear to have noticed. He offered his arm and escorted her to the foot of the main staircase.

''Until this evening, then,'' she said, and gave him that smile again.

He stood and watched her until she was out of sight, and then he took the stairs to his own room two at a time.

The next few days were the happiest that Darius could remember. He had been in love before, but, back then, he had not been so close to death. Love now was a renewal, an affirmation of the joy of life. They took unattended expeditions to different parts of his land and made love in unlikely places. The Princess behaved like a lusty country wench and Darius was hard put to it to satisfy her pliant demands. He felt like a young squire again, and when she finally left him, as he knew that she must, he ached at her loss and chided himself for being no better than a love-struck page.

The sennights after Naxania's departure were difficult ones for Darius. The depths of his unhappiness matched the light-headed elation he had felt before. The Hold was suddenly very empty. Both the women in his life were at Stronta, and he heard nothing from either of them. He paced and fretted, rode and worried.

The Others had already attacked Stronta once this year, but they had attacked Angorn twice. Women should be safe enough at Stronta, he thought. It was a modern fortress, and Robarth Strongsword was a believer in old-fashioned precautions. Still, there was cause for anxiety, and all he could do was sit and wait for a summons to Celador. That would be better than nothing. At least there he would have some idea of the progress of the war.

He must let go of his longing for Naxania, that he knew. For her their brief affair had been a dalliance, an opportunity seized far from the prying eyes of her Court. And yet . . . She had been ardent, but she had also been quiet and tender. There had been genuine affection, he was certain of that. What difference did that make? he asked himself bitterly: she was a Princess.

There was hope, nevertheless, though he told himself that he was being foolish, and when word came that a bunglebird had arrived from Stronta, he raced up the stairs to the cote and arrived out of breath. The message was from Naxania, but it was cool and impersonal. Appropriate royal thanks for his hospitality. He was disappointed and upbraided himself for having expected anything else. Still, there might have been something more that she had said. Bungle birds were unreliable. Perhaps it had forgotten.

The next messenger from Stronta rode in. Darius watched from a window as he crossed the courtyard. From the look of the mount, the man had ridden hard. The impression was confirmed when the man presented himself. He had spruced himself up and his clothes had been brushed, but his exhaustion was evident. Darius accepted the letters that he brought and sent him away to eat and sleep.

Why that sort of haste? Darius wondered as he stood turning the packets over in his hands. One was addressed to him in Marianna's copperplate hand and the other bore the seal of Paladine. Why had the messenger pushed himself so hard? It couldn't be good news. He hesitated and then opened his daughter's letter.

It was brief and hastily penned. She had been in a battle, but she was all right, she said, without giving details. She had discovered a great truth, she said, without explaining. Could he please send her maid to Stronta with some purple dresses as the Court was in mourning for Robarth Strongsword and there was no purple cloth to be had. She said that she missed him and sent her love. It was not a reassuring letter. He decided to wait until he had spoken to the messenger before he opened the other packet.

The man was still gaunt and hollow-eyed the next time he was shown into the withdrawing room, but he was steady on his legs and his skin no longer looked pallid. Darius sat him down and poured him a cup of wine.

"Are they looking after you properly?" he asked as he helped himself from the jar. "Getting everything you need?"

"Yes, thank you, Sir."

"Good. Sir Amyas tells me that your name is Reffred Gorse. That right?"

"Yes, Sir. I'm one of his, I should say her, Majesty's Royal Messengers."

"So I gathered. I also understand that there has been a battle and that the King of Paladine is dead. Can you tell me what's happened?"

Gorse looked at him and the weariness was back in his eyes. "Have you seen any fighting recently, Sir?" he asked.

"I've seen one battle and fought in another this past year."

"Ah, well then, you probably know how it is. Did they use the fire weapons and the battle wagons?"

"That they did."

"Well, Greylock, he's the Mage of Paladine, came up with a spell that deflected the fire from their weapons, but something went wrong. We messengers always wait behind the Stronta Gate ready to ride wherever the King sends us, so I didn't see what happened at the beginning of the battle, but they routed us beyond the Causeways.

"Soldiers came streaming back through the gate. Eventually they had to bring the portcullis down and close the doors. There were a lot of good men trapped on the other side. That was bad enough, but it was just the beginning. The Outlanders burned the gate down."

"No!" The monosyllable exploded from Darius.

" 'Fraid so, Sir. There was nothing anyone could do about it. We held them at the gate for a bit, but they got through. There was hand-to-hand fighting for the barracks, but we got pushed out in the end. Things got a bit panicky. It was a mess." It was as if he were describing a domestic upheaval at somebody else's house. The numbing haste of the ride seemed to have bleached the emotion out of him.

"There were men running around, officers yelling, trumpets sounding; absolute bedlam. I stayed close to the King for as long as I could in case I was needed. He was in a terrible temper." The messenger paused and took a drink.

Darius didn't press him. He was trying to assimilate the news. His worst fears had come true. The Paladinians hadn't adapted their defense and the Outlanders had got through the Causeway. He swallow some of his wine without tasting it.

"Two things saved us at that point," Gorse resumed. "Two people I should say. Greylock got his spell working again and that gave us the time to regroup. The King was just magnificent." A little color came back in the voice. "He stood up in the stirrups and whirled that sword of his over his head. He yelled at the soldiers, called them cowards, told 'em to remember their oath and to think of their loved ones. There was no denying him. The emotion was creeping back.

"He got them organized—all the mounted men in front,

infantry behind them. Sent me to the rear. I saw him riding up and down the lines making a speech. I don't know what he said, but whatever it was, it worked. Even the unicorn joined the counterattack."

"The unicorns joined the battle?" Darius broke in.

"Just the big one."

"I have been in a battle," she had written. Fear twisted in his gut. "Go on," he said.

"It was quite a sight. There was a curtain of light reaching up to the sky and our side was riding toward it, then it was gone. Fighting started then, and we seemed to be doing pretty well. Suddenly there was another curtain. It was fire this time." He stopped and drank deeply.

"Go on, man, what happened then?"

The messenger swallowed. "It came down and burned them all up. It was so sudden. No one stood a chance. And it kept coming. It was headed straight for us and getting bigger all the time and then it veered off toward the Place of Power. There were two Magicians on top of one of the pillars, I could see that much. I suppose that one of them was Greylock. Anyway, this sheet of flame is rolling down on the Place of Power and then there is a gigantic clap of thunder. My horse reared and almost threw me, and by the time I had him under control again, the fire was racing back the way it came. It burned up all the Outlanders who were on our side of the Causeway."

"What happened next?" Darius asked.

"Next? Nothing. We waited, but no new suits appeared. Reinforcements were eventually sent forward, but the Outlanders had gone. It was unreal." The man's voice quavered. "It was like a nightmare."

All gone, even Marianna's unicorn. It was a catastrophe. Even if the Stronta Gate had been rescued, the Alliance was maimed. And with Robarth dead . . . "Prince Justinex was also killed in the battle?" Darius asked.

"Aye, my Lord."

"And the King's brother was killed earlier in the year, so who rules in Paladine now?"

"Queen Naxania, Sir. Your letter was from her."

"Yes, I see," Darius said. That was that then. Princesses might dally and flirt, but a Queen could not. "This must have been a sore blow to your country. The King, the Prince, the army, to say nothing of the unicorn."

"Funny thing about that, Sir. The unicorn turned up safe and sound in her stable. Not a mark on her, and I know she was in the battle. I saw it myself."

"They do say that unicorns are miraculous beasts," Darius said, feeling a relief that had little to do with unicorns. "Well, thank you, Mr. Gorse, for bringing me the news. This is a terrible loss for Paladine and for the Alliance. We have all lost a great leader. For myself, I own that I am glad to hear that my daughter is safe—and that the unicorn was unharmed.

"You must stay as long as you like. I shall make sure that you are well provisioned for the journey back, and there will be a purse to go along with the provisions."

"Your Lordship is most kind," the messenger said, getting up. He bowed and retired.

When he was gone, Darius went and fetched Naxania's letter. He had not wanted to read it before he knew the context in which it had been written. There was no reason for delay now. He broke the seal and pushed back the flap. The first thing that came out was a royal commission in the Paladinian army; it was for the rank of General. The letter that accompanied it was only a page long. He must come to her aid; the Kingdom needed him; she needed him. She had written to Arabella and was certain that she would agree. He must hurry. She signed it simply, Naxania.

He stood looking down at it. There was hope after all.

Of course he would go, he must start making preparations immediately. Otorin would advise him to wait until he had heard from the Princess Regnant, but Otorin wasn't here. Naxania needed him. It was unseemly to feel happy about such terrible news, but he couldn't help it. He was going to Stronta and Marianna would get her dresses.

He circled over the great star fort and saw that Naxania's messenger had not exaggerated. The thrusting stone points were as formidable as ever, but their outlines were blurred by the ripple of tents that he assumed contained the wounded. The Upper Causeway cut across the landscape as it had for more than a hundred years, but now there was a great swath of black along it. He dipped down over the walls and came in for a landing. No one challenged him, no trumpet blew and no groom turned out to assist him. Bad times indeed, he thought.

Since he had arrived without squire or manservant, he had to lug his own bags to the Lord Chamberlain's office. He was kept waiting in the anteroom while his credential were checked and then was treated with obsequious deference and assigned a servant. He was shown to an ornate suite of rooms and scowled at the doors as they closed. His temporary manservant looked apprehensive.

A brief tour revealed a bedchamber with chairs around the fireplace and side tables against the walls, a private privy and a cabinet stocked with quills, ink and paper. While the man unpacked, Darius sat down to write the Queen a letter. It was difficult to think of the young woman he had held as a queen. He sighed and dipped a quill. This was going to be a peculiar assignment. He wondered idly what the man would think when he came upon a houndbag full of dresses.

He heard a sound behind him and turned, prepared to explain, but instead of the servant, Naxania stood in the doorway. He was out of the chair in a trice and down on one knee.

"You must not kneel to me, my Lord; not now." She advanced and held out her hands. "I have too great a need to lean on someone for a while."

He rose and kissed her hand. She was dressed in mourning and her face showed the strain she was going through. His eyes flicked to the doorway behind her.

"I sent your servant on an errand," she said, as if reading his mind. She smiled at him, though her eyes were misty. "I'm so glad that you came."

He bent down and kissed her on the mouth, his arms going around and holding her. She responded, and then broke off and pushed herself back.

"You understand," she said, "that there can be no suspicion of romantic involvement on my part. My subjects would not tolerate it so soon after, so soon after . . ."

"I understand, my darling," he said hastily, trying to forestall the tears. "I shall not presume. I am just grateful that you did not forget me."

"I did try," she said, and turned toward the bedchamber. "I was reared on the duties of royalty, especially female royalty." She gave a hard, little smile and started for the door with Darius behind her. "Our value to the realm is our marriageability. I am young and now I am a queen, but I have had no chance to live. I shall never have that freedom."

He steered her to the bed, and went and fetched a chair for himself. "This is a very difficult time for you," he said as he sat down. He reached for her hand. "You have gone through so much, and now, of a sudden, all the responsibility for Paladine rests on those lovely shoulders. I shall do everything I can to make the burden easier for you. You have but to command me."

"I know you will. That is why I sent for you. There are

so few who understand, but I feel that I can depend on you, and I have need of you, both as a woman and as Queen.'' She squeezed his hand and then drew hers away.

''The army is in a desperate state. So many killed, so many wounded. And it's not just men.'' Her voice was choppy. ''When those evil creatures threw the fire at us, it consumed everything; horses, saddles, pikes, longbows, everything.''

She looked up at him and her eyes were moist again. Her hands twisted in her lap. ''I saw it all, you know. I was at Greylock's windows directing the weather and I saw it all. I saw the lights in the sky and the fire. It rolled out of the barracks and grew until it was twice the height of a man on horseback. They didn't stand a chance; not a one of them. It was so hot that all that was left were charred bones and metal.'' Her voice had gone high and bloodless. The horror was held in on a tight rein.

She cocked her head slightly and he saw that the tears were gone. ''My brother never believed in Magic,'' she said quietly. ''He said it was a lot of rubbish I'd invented to make myself important. He said it didn't make sense, but he was destroyed by something that couldn't happen.

''Daddy, poor dear Daddy, he believed in me. He was always amazed that I was Talented, but he believed in me. It made no difference. I couldn't help him. Magic couldn't save him.'' Her face was tight and shiny, and she sucked in her bottom lip.

''But Magic did defeat the fire, didn't it?'' His tone was earnest and gentle. ''It was your rainstorms that put the fires out.''

''Oh yes,'' she said with a hollow little laugh, ''but only after it was too late.''

''You mustn't blame yourself. Nothing could have saved them.''

She drew herself up. ''I'm not blaming myself. That

isn't what I meant at all.'' Her mood had changed. ''Greylock and that protégé of his were the ones who stopped the fire.'' Her voice hardened. ''Cost them dearly, too. The Place of Power has disappeared, all but the central block. Greylock's body is on top of that. We can't even move him. I've tried to rouse him, but I have had no success. The unicorns were about the only things to escape, though no thanks to your daughter, I might add.''

''And what about the boy?'' Darius asked to steer things away from Marianna.

''Oh, he's all right. He managed to come out of it a hero, or so the Archmage thinks. He's gone and made him Acting Mage of Paladine.'' Her face darkened at the thought. She gave Darius a speculative look.

''I'd keep an eye on him if I were you. He's turning into a rather formidable young man and the unicorns give him a, how shall I put this?—a rather unique rapport with your daughter.''

Darius looked at her questioningly.

''Oh, I don't think you have to worry in that regard,'' Naxania said, not unhappy to see the doubt implanted. ''He's still very young, immature in lots of ways. No, if anyone makes the first move it'll probably be your daughter. She made a very favorable impression on my father. Did she tell you that he had decorated her? No? How surprising. You must get her to tell you all about it.'' There was a dry quality to her delivery that made Darius uneasy.

''She is well then?'' he asked.

''As far as I know. We see little of her. She is always off on that unicorn of hers.''

''That's a relief then. She did mention in her letter something about being in a battle, but I'm sure she was exaggerating.''

''I doubt it. She was with the troops at the Stronta Gate when it fell and she was in the vanguard of the charge with my father and brother. Her escape was quite miraculous,'' Naxania's tone was openly hostile, ''and since it remains unexplained, fantastical rumors circulate.''

''I'm sure that there's some perfectly ordinary explanation,'' Darius said placatingly. ''I shall have to ask her about it when I see her. She doesn't even know that I am here, unless the Chamberlain's office informed her.''

''He made no mention of it when he told me of your arrival.'' A malicious, little smile grew. ''Like most of my Court functionaries, the Chamberlain does little without instruction. He is uncertain of his standing now that the old regime, with its complex web of alliances, is gone. Oh yes, they're all guessing now.

''There used to be a King's faction and an Heir's faction, but the Princess never had a faction.'' There was a sour undertone to the pronouncement. ''That used to make the Princess very unhappy. Her father's love was her only ally, her only protection, but that love could be used to advantage.'' She spoke of herself as if she were describing someone else, someone remote.

''If a coming man, desirous of her father's ear, saw her as a conduit to favor, she allowed him to use her, and thereby amuse her. There would be riding expeditions and presents, until he realized that, while her father loved her dearly, he paid her no heed.''

She was calm and ironic, but the romantic girl who had been bruised into cynicism showed in the set of the eyes and the unsureness of the mouth. Darius felt that she was vulnerable after all, and that pleased him.

''Am I boring you?'' she asked suddenly.

''No, my love, though you sadden me.''

''Well, then, let me see if I can be more cheerful.'' The mood had shifted again. ''There is a happy outcome to the story. There were a few, a very few, who took a liking to the lonely little girl and continued to visit her, even after their hopes had been dashed. Now she will be able to reward them.

"Most of those who tried to use me are dead, lamented, no doubt, by some, but not by me. Those that survive sit and search uneasy consciences. It is past time that they suffered." The last was delivered defiantly.

She sat, straightbacked and composed, against the bolster, avoiding his gaze. There are too many hurts held in, he thought; too much bitterness. He was not too good with words, but he recognized the distress beneath the mask and his heart went out to her. He moved to the bed and put his arms round her. He held her as the tears began in small snatches of breath and ended in long shuddering exhalations.

He looked down at the tumble of black hair against his doublet. She was so very young, and so very much alone. She needed someone steady to protect her and guide her through the difficulties to come. He would take care of the army for her and be there when she needed his support. She probably wouldn't make it easy for him. He was in love with a very powerful and complex young woman, and the next few months were going to call for a great deal more than military expertise and a good way with the men.

He fished in his sleeve for a kerchief and handed it to her.

"You'd best dry your eyes before the servant gets back. It would not be good if the rumor spread that I had bullied the Queen on my first day here."

She gave him a wan smile and blew her nose obediently. "This is not exactly the way I intended to greet you," she said, husky-voiced. "Grown men and Queens are not supposed to cry."

"More's the pity," he said, getting up. "If I can find the ewer and basin, I'll pour some water so you can wash your face."

"I'm so glad you came, though the job I'm handing you is not an enviable one." She got up, walked over to him and took his sleeve. "Promise me that you won't be one of the ones that walks away?"

He kissed her on the forehead. "I promise."

Things were moving too fast. He wasn't in control any more. Well, he decided, with a rush of confidence engendered by her smile, he was still young enough to be flexible.

chapter 15

"You're here. You really are here." Marianna had burst into the anteroom scant minutes after the Queen had left. "The Chamberlain said that you'd arrived unexpectedly, but I didn't altogether trust him. He doesn't approve of me."

"Back up and let me look at you. They told me that you were still alive and in one piece." Darius took in the high color and the sparkling eyes. His gaze traveled up and his heart caught. Her hair was held back by a gold circlet that had belonged to her mother.

"I hear that congratulations are in order," he said.

"For what?"

"I hear that King Robarth Strongsword decorated you personally."

"Oh, that," she said dismissively.

"Oh, that," he mimicked, and grinned. "My, but haven't we become grand." She grinned back sheepishly. "What I don't understand," he said seriously, "is how the King could have allowed you near the front lines."

"He didn't really. Amarine and I became something of a good-luck symbol for the troops." She was talking rapidly, and Darius recognized the tactic. "I was with the Headquarters' group by the Gate, but things happened too fast."

There were questions that Darius wanted to ask, but he

decided to let them go for the moment. He took her arm. ''They've assigned me a squire since I couldn't bring a man with me. He should be around here somewhere. I'll send him for some wine, and you can tell me what's been happening. Your letter wasn't very clear.'' He went to the door and yelled. He dispatched the man to the cellars and returned.

''You've got a far grander set of rooms than I have,'' Marianna remarked as he lowered himself into a chair.

''Rank has its privileges,'' he replied. ''I'm a General now, or rather, I'm a General again.''

''Congratulations. That's wonderful. Not that you don't deserve it after what you did in Umbria.'' The accompanying smile turned into a puzzled frown. ''If you've been promoted, what are you doing here? Did you get leave? Is this the last I'm going to see of you for months?''

''Oh, no.'' He looked pleased with himself. ''In fact, you are going to be seeing a great deal of me; at least I hope you will. I am a General in the Paladinian army.''

''Oh.''

''Well, you might look a little happier. I have been seconded to her Paladinian Majesty's Armed Forces to help them reorganize after the defeat.''

''It wasn't a defeat,'' she contradicted. ''It was a total victory, a costly one, I'll admit, but no less a victory for that. The Outlanders who got through the gate were completely wiped out, and the rest of them have pulled back way beyond where they started from. They've yielded leagues of ground.''

''Have they indeed? I hadn't heard that. Still, if the accounts I have received so far are accurate, I find it hard to describe the battle as a victory. The Stronta Gate was burned, the barracks severely damaged, and the army decimated, including almost all of its high command. If it hadn't been for your Magician friend, it would have been a lot worse." He kept his tone light and reasonable.

"That's as may be," she said defensively, "but everybody else thinks it's a victory. Even the enemy does, or they wouldn't have withdrawn. Greylock and Jarrod are big heroes."

"People need heroes," he cautioned, "especially when times are bad, and as far as I'm concerned, these times could hardly be worse."

"Oh, but you're wrong, Papa." The sparkle was back in her eyes. "In one way they couldn't be better." Her smile was triumphant. "The war is finally over."

"Young lady, I've had a long journey and I'm not in the mood for bad jokes."

"I'm very serious, Father. There's a lot that I have to tell you. Now that I think about it, your being appointed head of the army is a wonderful stroke of luck. People will listen to you where they might not listen to Jarrod and me."

There was a gleam in her eye that Darius distrusted. "What will they listen to me about?" he asked warily.

"This is going to require an open mind on your part."

"I was afraid of that." He broke off. "Ah, here's the lad with the wine. The timing couldn't be better. A toast will undoubtedly open my mind." He took the proffered goblet and waited until Marianna had hers. He lifted it.

"To the Gwyndryths and their new honors," he said.

"To us," she replied.

"Now," Darius said as the man withdrew, "tell me how you got into the battle and how you got yourself out of it."

Marianna settled herself in her chair and took a sip of the wine. "I was with the Headquarters' unit in front of the Stronta Gate," she began. "The enemy was attacking and messengers were riding in and riding out. I kept out of the way as best I could, but one minute there was order and the next it was a madhouse of fleeing troops.

"Prince Justinex and I wanted to organize a counterattack, but we were overruled. Then King Robarth gave the order to retreat behind the Causeway and close the gates." She stopped and shook her head at the memory. "D'you know how long it's been since those gates were last closed?" she asked.

"It'll go back a ways."

"A hundred years at least," she said, and an emotion that Darius could not catalogue made her pull in her lips and widen her eyes. "Knowing that people were being shut out and condemned to die," she continued, "was bad. Seeing those gates burn down was worse. I mean, we've always thought of the Upper Causeway as being impregnable; at least I have. If things went really badly, we could always close the gates and be safe." She looked up and gave a weak smile. He nodded his understanding.

"I was disappointed when we trotted under the portcullis, I really was," she went on. "I was so close to action, so close to all the things that you and what you called 'the young hounds' always talked about, and I wasn't going to get any closer. Part of me, though, was glad that the portcullis was behind us." Her eyes slid away.

"Every thinking man is afraid at one point or another in a battle," he said kindly. He was on familiar ground here, though he had never thought to be on this particular ground with his daughter.

"You never made it sound like fun, Papa. It was always a job to you. Some men, like Sir Amyas, manage estates, you manage soldiers. But the boys, the young hounds, made it sound exciting and glorious." She pushed herself back on the banquette as if to put distance between them. "Well, I've seen it for myself now. A battle isn't tidy and it isn't fun. I saw some very brave people, but I didn't see anything glorious.

"It's a brutal, dangerous job," Darius agreed, "but consider the alternative. The only way I cope with war is to see it as something I have to do. The more knowledgeable I become, the more skillful in battle, the greater chance I have of surviving and, more importantly, of ensuring that others survive."

"It's wonderful to have you here, Papa," she said impulsively, sitting forward again. "There isn't anyone else in the world I could talk to about this." She smiled up at him.

He had never been able to resist that smile, and all thoughts of reprimanding her melted. "What happened South of the Causeway?" he asked. "I need to know as much as possible if I am to do the work the Queen expects of me."

"Robarth was superb," she replied. "When the inner gates began to burn there was still a lot of confusion. There were dazed soldiers wandering around looking for their units and getting in the way of the reserves. I was riding backward and forward, trying to rally them. They were edgy as horses before a storm. I felt that they wanted to break and run. Nothing was said, but men looked over their shoulders too much, too often, and there was a lot of muttering. Do you know what I mean?"

"Unfortunately, I do."

"The King got them together, though. We fought. Some of us did," she corrected herself. "I got sent to the rear. Amarine was at a disadvantage among the buildings in the barracks complex, was what they said, and I couldn't deny the logic of that.

"The enemy eventually pushed them out of the barracks. They lost of lot of men doing it, but, in the end, we had to pull back. That's when Greylock gave us a respite.'' She stopped and sighed and rubbed her temples. ''I'm sorry. This is more difficult than I thought it would be.''

''It's all right. Take your time.''

''Everybody's dead.'' The words were so quiet that Darius leaned forward to hear. ''I know it. I saw it, but it doesn't seem real. I don't know why I'm alive. If it hadn't been for Amarine, I wouldn't be. What have I ever done to merit exemption?''

''Welcome to the ranks of the warrior,'' Darius said. ''The world that does not fight regards us as a necessary evil, and it suits them to think of us as unaffected by death. We are, though. Every time I've lost a young man entrusted to my command, it's hurt.

''I thought I was untouchable when I was young—until I was wounded for the first time. I spent almost a year recuperating at home. That was when I started to see the things I had always taken for granted clearly. That was when I started to court your mother.'' He paused and his face softened.

''That brush with death and the year that followed made me realize that all the things I was sworn to defend were worth the risk to life and limb. Then your mother gave me something worth surviving for. She gave me you.'' He smiled at her. ''Survival's a matter of luck and skill, and one's as important as the other. One can train, plan, and devise strategies, but when the fighting comes down to the press, getting out alive is the prime goal. There is no way in which you should feel guilty for being alive.''

''You always did know how to make me feel better about things,'' Marianna said and it warmed him.

''You're my daughter and I love you. Besides,'' he added with a touch of self-righteousness, ''that's my job too.'' She let it go. ''So, what happened next?''

''Where was I?''

"Greylock had given you breathing room."

"Oh yes. He and Jarrod put up a screen of sorts. It stopped the fire weapons. That's when Robarth was at his best. The troops were in full retreat, screen or no screen, but Robarth stopped them. He gave them their confidence back." She took a sip of the wine.

"It was a very peculiar time. The skies were dark and there were occasional flashes of lightning. Greylock's shield was intercepting the enemy's fire and glowing like the Western Lights. It was eerie and exciting. I didn't know what to do. If Amarine and I had ridden away, it could have started a rout, but I didn't have a unit to join. I stuck to the royal party and waited to be told what to do." She was deep in her memories now.

"Nobody said anything to me. The army advanced and I went with them. I just pretended that I knew what I was doing. That walk forward seemed to take forever. Then, suddenly, we were charging, and then there was fighting all around. I didn't have time to be afraid, but puncturing suits wasn't as satisfying as I had thought it would be.

"There was a moment, though, when I was sure that we were winning. It was weird. It wasn't particularly obvious from where I was, but somehow I knew that we were winning. Then, all at once, there was a halt, like one of those awful silences at parties. I looked up and I saw that roll of flame. It didn't look that impressive at first. In fact, I thought they had set fire to the barracks. But it kept coming and it grew.

"The horses were the first to know. They turned and bolted, and just like that, a victorious thrust became a pell-mell rout. Amarine stood her ground, and I saw the fire rear up and engulf the vanguard. That's when Amarine took me away."

Marianna stopped and took a deep breath. She let it out slowly and then drank some wine. Darius waited for her.

She looked over at him as if weighing how much more to tell him.

"I explained about Interim to you, didn't I?" Darius nodded. "And you watched when Jarrod and I left Gwyndryth, so you know what I mean."

"Let's see if I've got it right. When the unicorns want to go somewhere, they concentrate on it and then they're there."

"That's more or less it, though it's far more complicated. One of the family, or an ancestor of theirs, has to have visited the place." She looked over at him again. "Strand isn't the only place they can go," she added.

"I'm not sure that I follow you."

"I know. It's hard to explain. You're just going to have to trust me." She took another sip. "There are other worlds besides this one," she said carefully, "thousands of them. They are all connected by what Amarine calls 'the lines of force,' and the unicorns use those lines to get from one place to another."

"Just a minute. I'm prepared to accept this if you tell me so, but how do you know?"

"Well, you know that Jarrod can talk with the colts . . ."

"Oh, I see. They told him and he told you."

"Yes and no. He explained part of it to me, but Amarine told me the rest," Marianna said.

"You never told me you could talk with her."

"I couldn't. I think you'd better let me tell the story and then you can ask questions." Darius nodded and settled back to listen.

"When Amarine felt threatened, she went into Interim. I blacked out right away. She went back to the place she had come from. It's in the middle of everything and all the lines of force radiate out from it. That's about as much as I know. I wasn't there long enough to get much of an idea of what it's like. Anyway, while I was recovering from the effects of Interim, Amarine started talking to me. Not out loud; in my head. I knew then that I had died. It took Amarine a while to convince me that we had escaped and longer to explain where we were. I was numb from the trip and I couldn't take anything in. She finally had to let me see into their family Memory to convince me."

"I confess that I am having a hard time myself."

"Unicorn families share a common Memory that goes back for as long as there have been unicorns. I don't know how they find what they're looking for, but Amarine had no trouble showing me what she wanted me to see. Are you with me so far?" Marianna inquired.

"Just about."

"Good, because it gets weirder. The reason I said that the war is over is that the unicorns' Memory says quite clearly that the Others were the first on Strand." She straightened her back and watched his face carefully. It was unrevealing.

"You sure?"

"Absolutely."

"Well, that's certainly interesting, but I don't see what that leads to."

"You don't believe me, do you?" she asked, stung by his lack of enthusiasm.

"If you tell me that they were already established here when we came across the Inner Sea, I'll believe you."

"Not just here. All over Strand. This was their world."

"How were we created, then?" he asked reasonably. "We can't survive in their atmosphere."

"I don't know, Papa. Maybe we started off in their atmosphere and then moved out. Sea serpents come ashore every year to lay their eggs and rear their young. Maybe we're like them, except we can't go back anymore. Maybe

Magic has something to do with it. After all, they think they bring the sun up every day.''

''And what does your unicorn say?''

''There's nothing in the Memory about how we started, but Amarine says that we have been expanding our area for centuries. I don't understand the connection, but she says that that's why we're so keen on growing things, why green is considered a lucky color.''

Darius's eyebrows were raised. ''It's quite a story,'' he said cautiously, ''but I still don't see how it can help us win the war.''

Marianna clicked her tongue impatiently. ''I didn't say anything about winning the war, I just said that the war is over.''

''And how do you come to that?'' he asked, watching her face carefully in his turn.

''Well, it's obvious. Once people know the Outlanders are only trying to defend themselves, that we are the real aggressors, there won't be any reason to go on fighting. We've got more than enough land.''

''Aren't you forgetting something? They are the ones who do the attacking. Did the Paladinians do anything to provoke the attack on Stronta? I very much doubt it. We never even knew they were there at the beginning, not until they started killing people. All the ballads say so.''

''Of course our ballads say so. What else would you expect? I wonder what their ballads say?''

''If they have ballads.''

''Don't you see, Papa? The reason they've pulled back all up and down the Causeway is to send us a message.'' She leaned forward in her earnestness. ''They've proved that they can hurt us badly, but instead of following up, they've withdrawn. Would you do that?''

''That would depend on the circumstances, naturally, but for Paladine's sake I hope you are right.''

"You think I'm making the whole thing up, don't you?" she challenged.

"No," he replied judiciously. "I'm sure that you believe it. I'm just a little concerned that the unicorn may have misled you. Not intentionally, of course: you may have misunderstood."

"Unicorns don't lie, Father. They don't even have a concept for untruth." She spoke heatedly and sat back as if she felt that her attempt to convince had failed.

Darius recognized the storm signals. "Have you spoken to anyone else about this?" he inquired.

"Just Jarrod." She was curt.

"And what did he have to say?"

"The colts were there to back me up. There wasn't anything he had to say."

"The trouble is, you're expecting the rest of the world to believe the unsupported theories of Jarrod and yourself. Granted that you have some stature as the discoverers of the unicorns, but you are both very young. Your only 'proof' is the word of the unicorns, and no one else can talk to them except the two of you. A lot of people are going to be skeptical. You must expect that."

"Not everyone on Strand has the same vested interest in warfare that you have," Marianna retorted nastily.

"Ah, the idealism of the young." He raised his hands in mock resignation.

"You're doing what you used to do when I was a girl. You're going to humor me until I grow out of this phase." He winced inwardly at her acuity. "Well, this isn't a phase and I'm not going to grow out of it. You can't treat me like a child anymore."

"I'm not treating you like a child," he said defensively. "But you've got to face the facts. I believe you, but you can't expect people to change their way of thinking overnight. People don't like to think that they are oppressors.

Consider all of the people who have lost husbands, brothers, sons, and friends. There's scarcely a family on Strand that hasn't suffered some kind of loss. That's bad enough when you think that the sacrifice is in a noble cause. You're asking them to believe that their loved ones were lost in some meaningless expansion and that, on top of that, they were morally in the wrong. Centuries of tradition are not lightly overthrown."

"You're hateful, you know that?" She took another sip of her wine, and Darius saw that her hand was shaking. "I thought that at least my father would understand how important this is and would try to help me. It seems that I was wrong." There were tears in her eyes now. "I've always depended on you. I've always looked up to you, but I suppose I shall have to manage on my own from now on." She looked over at him defiantly. "I'm disappointed in you, Father, I can't deny that. I had counted on your help, but this is too important for me to lay it down just because some people won't accept the truth." She put her wine down and stood up.

"I think I'd better leave now, Father, before I say something that I shall regret."

"Now hold on a minute. There's no need to rush off. All I'm trying to do—"

"I know what you're trying to do," she cut in, "and I resent it. I don't know exactly how I'm going to get the truth out, but I'm going to do it whether you like it or not. Goodbye, Father." She turned and half ran from the room, slamming the door behind her.

Darius had started from his chair and now stood staring at the door. He was shocked more than angry. She had thrown some ferocious tantrums when she was little, but she hadn't done anything like this in a very long time. All he'd done was try to warn her not to get her hopes up too high. If she went ahead with this nonsense, she'd only end up getting hurt. Couldn't she see that, even if she was right, it wouldn't make any difference? No one would want to believe her, unicorns or no unicorns.

He should have done a better job of explaining it to her. Her knowledge of human nature was limited. She'd led a sheltered life, had very little experience of the real world. She'd grown up a lot in the past two years, she wasn't his little girl anymore, but she was still so very young. He rubbed his forehead and then picked up his goblet and began to pace.

This was the last thing he needed. Naxania had given him the task of creating an army virtually from scratch, and here was his daughter, who claimed to be the good-luck symbol of the troops, about to go around telling people that the war was over. That would never do. Paladine could not afford to drop its guard, least of all when it was so vulnerable.

He should have told her to keep the story to herself. He shook his head. No, that would never have worked; not with his Marianna. If he'd said that, she was quite capable of jumping up on the High Table during Hall and making a public announcement. He smiled in spite of himself. She was a handful, there was no-denying that, and she was his responsibility.

The smile faded. Naxania would not take kindly to having her father's reputation as a valiant warrior diminished while his candles were still burning. He already had enough problems where Naxania was concerned. At Gwyndryth he had had her all to himself. There were younger men here, higher in rank, wealthier certainly, and unencumbered with difficult daughters. He sighed. Women, he told himself, were born to complicate a man's life, and here at Stronta, he had two prime examples. He sighed again.

chapter 16

There was a clatter of hooves outside the loose box where Jarrod was grooming the unicorns. Amarine's ears went up, but Jarrod didn't notice. His concentration was divided between the task at hand and the interplay of the colt's minds. He was aware that they were slowing things down so that he could follow. There was no condescension in it, but the effort was apparent. He was both grateful and chagrined.

How fast they've grown, Jarrod thought and was instantly dowsed in their sense of humor. He swatted the nearest rump in reply. When he had first encountered them, he reminded them, they had been small and furry. Now they dwarfed him and were getting fat. A tail caught him in the middle of the back. He had known that it was coming, but the implementation was too swift for him to dodge.

They had never been childlike, there was nothing remotely human about them, but, back then, such a short time ago, they had been juvenile. He had felt that he had known more than they did. Now they were treating him with the patience shown by adults to bright children. Their chorus of agreement was cut short by the appearance of Marianna.

''Father's here,'' she said without ceremony, and went over to stroke Amarine. Jarrod watched her, uncertain of her mood. So much had changed since they had returned from the Anvil of the Gods. The red hair was controlled by gold now, she wore dresses and wore them well, and the scent she used seemed out of place in a stable. She was more appealing than ever. She turned back to him.

"Naxania's asked him to rebuild and reorganize the army. He's been made a General." She was matter-of-fact.

"That's a big job," he said neutrally.

"Of course it is. That's why she summoned him. I mean, look what he did for the Umbrian Cavalry."

"Oh, I agree. Paladine is lucky to have him, and it'll be nice for you to have him around as well."

"I suppose so."

"Is anything the matter, Marianna?"

"Matter? Why should anything be the matter?" She was abristle in an instant.

"No reason. I just thought you'd be glad to see your father again. You really didn't spend very much time at home."

"I am. Of course I am." She looked at him and her shoulders suddenly slumped. "I told him about the Island at the Center."

"And he didn't believe you," Jarrod finished for her.

"No. He believed me, or at least he said he did. No, it's worse than that. I could understand that, but what he said was that it didn't make any difference."

"No difference?"

"No. The Outlanders attacked us first, remember? All the ballads say so:-

'Along across the Bascombe Swale
The young Sir Swythin rode that day.
In heedless hunger of his youth,
He coursed the conies down the trail

And knew not that he was the prey.' " she quoted. "Surely they taught you that at the Collegium."

"In Dameschool, actually," he replied, nettled by her sarcasm. "But that's not the point; from what we know now, it's obvious that the Outlanders were forced to attack. They had no choice."

"Not obvious enough apparently. My own father . . ." She shook her head fiercely. "Oh, I suppose I should have expected it. He's fairly old, and he's spent all his life fighting the Others."

"I wonder why there's so much about us in the Memory?" Jarrod asked, trying for less emotional ground. He knew the answer before the sentence was complete. It arrived in the familiar plait.

The earliest ancestor was sent here. That was Beldun. Jarrod somehow heard his thoughts as a bass continuo, even though there was no sound. *This was one of the first reference points in the Memory, so his descendants tended to visit.* The legato was unmistakably Pellia. *My ancestors didn't think much of yours.* Nastrus.

If I carry through the musical metaphor, Jarrod thought, Nastrus is a reed instrument. He was aware that Nastrus heard him and didn't understand the allusion. The colt had decided to take umbrage anyway and his mental posture made Jarrod grin inwardly. Nastrus was not amused.

'This world fell out of fashion for a while,' Pellia interjected. *'When the next ancestor came here, your kind had multiplied and moved to this continent. The fighting started soon after that. None of our kind returned until Mam decided to foal here.'*

'How do you know that the Outlanders were here first?' Jarrod asked.

'When the first ancestor came here they were already many and you were few. He could not see them, of course, but he heard them as we hear you. Neither your kind nor

theirs could hear him,' Pellia added. *'The Memory is sure,'* Beldun contributed. As far as he was concerned no further explanation was necessary.

'Can you hear them?' Jarrod's question was urgent.

'I heard them when we were at the Force Point.' Nastrus. *'If they are close enough.'* Beldun. *'We cannot enter their breathing clouds,'* Pellia cautioned, one step ahead as always.

"Marianna!"

"I know, Jarrod. I know. Amarine heard them and I hear her."

"D'you know what this means?"

"I can guess what it might mean." She was calm and in control.

"It's the reason for the verse. It must be." Jarrod was becoming increasingly excited. "Don't you see? Everybody's been asking why the unicorns were sent to us. Well, what have we been lacking all these centuries?"

"The Great Spell?" She was being sarcastic.

"That, of course," he said, taking her seriously. "No, what we've never been able to do is to communicate with the enemy."

"We still can't."

"We can now."

"How?"

"Through them. You heard them—well, you heard Amarine. You know what I mean."

"I think so, but if I do, you're wrong."

"Why? They can hear what the Others are thinking."

"Yes, but it doesn't work the other way around."

"How do you know?"

"Amarine says that the Memory is clear. There was never any reciprocal understanding. Sorry—that's how it translates."

''Up until about a year ago, the Memory would have said exactly the same about us.''

'There was some contact,' Nastrus interjected. *'That's where you got your ridiculous preconceptions about us.'*

''What's your point?'' Marianna asked.

''My point is that you and I communicate with the unicorns, so why shouldn't there be someone on the other side who can?''

''There might be something to that, though I don't know how we're going to get them close enough and keep them safe. D'you think you could explain that to my father?''

''I don't even want to try.''

''But we have to try, Jarrod. This whole thing is far too important. It may be why we were chosen.''

''I know that. It's just that you have to go about something like this gradually.''

''Gradually?'' She drew the word out. ''How many more lives is gradually?'' Her temper was rising again and her eyes had regained their customary snap. Jarrod groaned inwardly. She was going to be difficult and she was going to want her own way.

''I agree with you. I agree,'' he said placatingly, ''but we can't just go out and get up on a tree stump and lecture the troops. We have to do things properly. You know how easily rumors spread. If the wrong faction got hold of this and twisted it—''

''Faction?''

''Yes, faction; where there are courts there are factions.'' Jarrod's voice took on the slightly condescending tone of a town cousin. ''There are always noblemen who think that they could do a better job than the royal house. Why do you think my family never comes to Stronta?

''My grandfather challenged Robarth Strongsword when he first came to the throne. My father was one of the young King's companions and he stayed loyal. My family lost, and they never forgave him.'' He was trying to be casual and his voice sounded all the bleaker for it. The colts were very still.

''All right.'' Marianna broke the silence. ''I admit that I hadn't thought about that. So, what do you propose that we do? Anyway,'' she went on without waiting for an answer, ''I don't see why you couldn't get up on a stump and say anything you wanted. You're a Mage now and people will believe anything you tell them and this happens to be the truth.'' The challenge was back.

''I'm only temporary, an Acting Mage. Greylock's still alive,'' Jarrod replied.

''Mage, Acting Mage, what's the difference? You're supposed to be a big hero, but you're afraid to go out there and tell them the truth.''

''It's not that simple, Marianna, really it's not,'' he protested.

''It seems simple enough to me.''

''You can't just go and shake up people's beliefs.'' He felt infinitely older than she was. She was right, he couldn't deny that she was right, but she was so naïve when it came to the real world. ''People just get angry and stop listening.''

''You're the one who's not listening. I may not be as sophisticated as you are. You've spent all your life around Magic and capitals, and I'm only a little country vole, but we're not talking about etiquette. We are talking about peace. We are talking about no more fighting, no more strips left fallow because the farmer never came back.

''Doesn't that stir something in you? Doesn't the idea of not having to raise a son to be a soldier if he isn't suited to it mean anything? No.'' She waved a hand back and forth. ''Forget that. Why should that mean anything to you? How can I phrase it so that it penetrates?'' Marianna paused rhetorically and looked him up and down.

"Can you imagine," she asked, "how much genuinely beneficial Magic could be developed if you didn't have to spend so much of your life thinking of ways to keep the enemy at bay? Just think how much good you could do if you didn't have a war to fight."

"You're the last person I would have expected to be a pacifist," Jarrod retorted.

"I'm not a pacifist, you boob, I'm a woman. We see things more clearly. We're not so caught up with our toys."

"Wait a minute!" he said, and smiled at her. He reached for her hands and, after a hesitation, she surrendered them. "I think that we should try to stop the war. I just think it should be done in a sensible way that doesn't cause any major disruptions." The touch of her seemed to burn him, and he tried to keep his fingers from trembling.

"You're just afraid of making a few temporary enemies," Marianna said, deflating his ardor. "As soon as the facts are evident, they'll fall into line."

"That's the problem. The truth is never going to be evident. Our only proof lies in the unicorns' Memory." He shook her hands for emphasis. "The rest of the world has to take us on trust."

"And why shouldn't they?" she inquired.

"There are people," Jarrod explained wearily, "who will believe anything we tell them. If they could worship the unicorns, they probably would. Then there are people who will believe nothing we say. We're freaks. Haven't you realized that yet?"

She extracted her hands from his grasp and walked away a few paces. "You're clouding the issue, and I don't in the least feel like a freak. A woman of my station is always being stared at. That's natural. What isn't natural is this war. It's a hideous mistake, and we are the only ones who know it. It's up to us to see that it stops. With something this important, there can't be any buts."

"No," he said sadly, "that's where you're wrong. I agree that we are going to have to try to stop the war, but there are going to be a vast number of buts."

"So you're not even going to try."

"That isn't what I said. I'm just not too optimistic about the outcome. I don't want you to get your hopes up too high. Going directly to the people is far too dangerous. It's not going to help if we set off riots against the ruling houses. We have to start at the top. If we can convince the people who direct the war, it'll go much faster."

"I tried with my father," Marianna said sourly, "and you can see how far that got me. Do you think you can do better with Ragnor?"

"With the Archmage?" Jarrod was taken aback.

"You've cast yourself as the strategist, can you see this working unless we have the Archmage behind us?"

"No, I suppose not," he admitted.

"You suppose not?" She had regained the initiative. "Of course not. You are going to have to convince him and the sooner the better."

There was a sinking feeling in the pit of Jarrod's stomach. He had been in a cocoon of healing for a long time. Diadra had nursed him, and Agar Thorden, Greylock's longtime second-in-command, had seen to the orderly running of the Outpost and had taken care of the network of village Magicians and weatherwards. Now the outside world had invaded his haven, using Marianna as a stalking horse. He kicked the bale he was leaning against and pushed himself upright.

"I'll ride to Celador as soon as Diadra says I'm fit enough."

"Diadra? Wisewoman to the Mages? Let her prized invalid go? You'll be too old to make it by then."

"She may be a little protective," Jarrod admitted with a smile, "but she knows what she's talking about."

''You look fit enough to me,'' Marianna said, looking him over. ''Your hair still has some gray in it, but not that much, and almost all the lines are gone. You're still a bit thin, but then you always were built like a Greeningale weed.'' She dodged his playful lunge.

''Now, don't you go exerting yourself,'' she teased. ''You need to conserve your strength for the ride to Celador.''

''And you have to ride back to change for Hall. Ah, the glamour of palace life!''

''If you think it's that glamorous, you can always put on your Magical finery and join us,'' she retorted. ''Your chair sits there empty.''

''It's not my chair, it's Greylock's.'' All his humor had vanished.

''I'm sorry,'' she said, instantly contrite. ''I didn't really mean to be flippant. I know how much Greylock means to you and how hard it must be for you to have him stuck out there . . .''

He shied at her choice of words. ''That's something that I have to attend to,'' he said deliberately.

''You're going to get him down?''

''I have to try. The problem is that the Princess, I mean the Queen, tried to free him and failed.''

''You're a better Magician than she is, aren't you?''

''That's not the point. If I make the attempt, she's likely to construe it as a criticism of her powers.''

''Poor Jarrod. Nothing's simple anymore, is it? Still, you can't just leave Greylock sleeping on top of that rock. Will it be dangerous—apart from the Queen?''

''Magic is always dangerous,'' he said sanctimoniously.

''You will be careful then?''

''I want to get Greylock back, not to join him,'' Jarrod said, delighted that she cared enough to caution him. ''Now, you'd best say goodbye to Amarine or you'll be late, and I'll wager that Naxania doesn't care to be kept waiting."

"Her Majesty insists on her royal prerogative," Marianna agreed with a small shake of the head to denote bemusement or disgust, Jarrod wasn't sure which. "She's been very nice to me lately and that worries me." She went over and put her arms around Amarine's neck, and Jarrod made his own farewells to the colts.

'Your emotions are very strange,' Beldun remarked. *'Confusing, but entertaining,'* Nastrus concurred. *'Ignore them,'* Pellia advised.

chapter 17

Darius let himself into his rooms. He was tired and depressed and the good-for-nothing squire they had assigned him was nowhere to be seen. He unhooked his doublet and poured himself some sack. It had been a disheartening day, in fact it had been a disheartening sennight. He had visited all the installations, and the cumulative evidence of disaster was overwhelming. The ruin of the gate gaped like an accusation, the barracks were badly damaged, and the ground was a gummy black after the rain. The ashy skeletons of trees and buildings only served to point up the desolation.

He shucked the doublet and tossed it onto the back of a chair. Naxania had set him an impossible task. There was no command structure left. He had to carry his commission from the Queen with him and explain himself every time he wanted to see something. There weren't enough healthy men to stave off another attack, and most of the equipment was gone. He had been reduced to setting men to scavenge the plain for metal.

There was a light tapping at the door, and it opened before he could respond. A cloaked figure slipped around it, closed it, and locked it.

"Who the blazes are you and what are you doing in my rooms?" he demanded.

The figure turned and put back the hood. Naxania

smiled gleefully at him and was in his arms before he could bow.

"You startled me," he said when his mouth was his own again.

"It was a bit dramatic, wasn't it? Your squire has the afternoon off. I wanted to make sure the coast would be clear."

"I'm glad you came," he said. "It's been a very frustrating sennight. Do you know how difficult it is to be in a room with you and not be able to touch you? To see you presiding at Hall and not be able to talk to you?"

"I hope it is agony," she said teasingly, and kissed him again.

"Does my beard bother you?" he said as they disengaged. "I never thought to ask."

She laughed. "My mother always used to say that kissing a man without a beard was like eating a boiled egg without salt. No, I don't mind it at all, and it makes you look very handsome."

"I think that's my cue to escort you to the bedchamber," he said and picked her up in his arms.

She gave a surprised little squeal of pleasure. "Put me down, you impulsive bear. We've some business to discuss before you drag me to your den." He put her down reluctantly. "That's better. Now go and sit over there. I don't want you too close. I want to be able to concentrate for a little while.

"First of all, have you had a chance to evaluate the military situation yet?"

He retrieved his wine and went and sat down. "It isn't good, but you knew that already. The first two things that have to be done are to rebuild the Stronta Gate and to put all the able-bodied men in the palace under arms. Jobs will have to be arranged so that they can drill regularly. These are only stopgap measures, but they must be put into effect immediately. I can take care of the gates, but the palace muster will require an order from you.

"I don't have all the facts yet, but I've toured most of the installations and the Wisewomen's tents, and I've talked to as many people as I could. About the only important witness I haven't interviewed is the Courtak boy, though I suppose I shouldn't call him that now." He paused. "I didn't get a chance to do more than greet him at Gwyndryth. You've known him for a long time, what's he like?"

"That little whippersnapper? I made him what he is today. Without my verse he would still be an apprentice at the Collegium. I even helped to create his Staff. Helped him? I had to do it almost single-handed. Greylock was too tired and Courtak was too inexperienced to be of much use. In spite of all of that, does the little wretch so much as pay a condolence call? He does not."

"I have heard that he was very ill," Darius said diplomatically, wishing that he had never brought the name up.

She was not mollified. "Ill? If he is too ill to make it through the Great Maze to pay his respects to his monarch, then why is he fit enough to go riding on unicorns?"

"He's scarcely more than a boy, my love," Darius said, taken aback by the vehemence, "and his illness came from his efforts against the enemy."

"Whose side are you on?" She was clearly angry. "I tell you that the 'boy' is lacking in respect and you make excuses for him. Am I not worthy of respect?"

Darius looked across the room at the unfamiliar virago. She was talking about the Magician almost as if he were a rival for Darius's affections. He had asked a simple question and been answered with a tirade.

"Of course you are, my darling," he said soothingly. "You are the Queen."

"Yes, I am," she agreed, relaxing slightly, "and that young man better realize that. Without me he is nothing."

The thought seemed to calm her. ''Greylock always had a soft spot for him,'' she said. ''I felt that his interest was more than a little unhealthy, but no matter. There must be something about him that escapes me. The Archmage seems to have fallen under whatever spell it is he casts.''

''He seems a nice enough lad,'' Darius ventured.

''That's just the problem. He's so ordinary. That kind of raw power ought to have some kind of outward sign, it should set him apart, but all we get is a lumping great boy.''

''He is very tall,'' Darius said, relieved at the direction the conversation was taking.

''All the Talented are tall, or almost all of them. Arabella's undersized. I must admit, though, that he's turning into a good-looking young man.''

''Oh, I wouldn't say that,'' he demurred.

''That's because your daughter's half in love with him,'' she countered.

''I wouldn't say that either.'' Darius drew himself up in the chair a little. ''I've talked with her about him and I didn't get that impression at all.''

''Yes, quite,'' Naxania said dismissively.

''Well, he seems to be quite a hero with the troops, and the army, what's left of it, is badly in need of heroes.''

''And what, pray, is wrong with my father?'' The voice was rimed.

He had said the wrong thing again and hastened to make amends. ''Of course your father is a hero and the troops revere his memory. He was a hero for as long as I can remember. He was one of the greatest fighting men that Strand has ever seen. 'While the memory lasts, the spirit shall survive,' he said, quoting from the Book of the Dead. ''Your father's death was a huge blow, not just to Paladine, but to all of Strand. That is why it is so important for the survivors to have some hope to hold on to.''

''And what of me?'' The voice was no warmer.

He was not doing well. He shifted in his chair. ''My visits have also shown me how much faith and love resides in the hearts of her subjects for Paladine's beautiful,'' he got up and crossed to her, ''young,'' he took her hands and kissed the left one, ''Queen''. He kissed her other hand.

She smiled up at him and rose. She leaned her head against his chest and put her arms around him. ''I don't relish giving that young man another decoration, but I suppose it would be politic.'' She brightened. ''I can't hold any investitures until after the official period of mourning is over. If I did it then, it would coincide with the coronation and would be seen as a gesture of largesse.'' She turned her face up and he kissed it. The kiss held until she pushed at him.

''I have to breathe from time to time,'' she said. ''Oh, and before I forget, I've found a way for us to be together for a couple of days.''

''You clever wench.'' He tightened his hold.

''Let me explain before you kiss me again. A bunglebird arrived earlier this evening. The Chief Warlock of Talisman is dead and the Archmage bids me attend the funeral. The High Council will convene at Fortress Talisman to confirm his successor, so I cannot refuse. I want you to come with me.''

''Going to a funeral is not exactly my idea of a romantic interlude. Besides, I'm not sure it such a good idea. We have been to so much trouble to be discreet.''

''I have no intention of going with you on my arm, but we must take advantage of whatever opportunities fate presents us with. I can't take you with me as part of my official entourage; you're an Arundelian.'' She moved out of his embrace.

''It's all very tricky,'' she said. ''If I confine myself to the Talented, it will be said that the Queen is surrounding herself with Magicians, but any courtier I select will be viewed as an object of favor, worse, he'll see himself that way.'' She clicked her tongue. ''I just wish that old fool had hung on until I was properly established. It is enormously difficult being Queen and Talented.

''What makes it worse is that my brother was openly against the Discipline. The inevitable clique that gathers around the Heir Apparent followed his lead. They all become Maternites when he did, and tinkering with machinery became fashionable.'' She paused. ''They did not give me an easy time of it, those friends of his,'' she said with deliberation. ''Now they are afraid. Fear immobilizes, but it also breeds plots. The Chief Warlock's death plays straight into their hands.''

''How so?''

''I am a member of the High Council of Magic. I cannot refuse this invitation. If I go accompanied by Courtak and Thorden, those who were my brother's men will conclude that they have no hope of offices. That can push them into revolt. If I make it a mixed delegation, those same men will whisper that I am trying to give undue weight to what should be of concern only to the Discipline.'' She looked at him and her changeable eyes for once looked beseeching. ''So you see, my most dear,'' she concluded, ''I shall have need of a friendly face and of impartial advice.''

''What possible pretext could I have for being in Talisman when there is so much for me to do here?''

''The cloudsteed Wings sustained considerable losses, did they not?''

''You know they did.''

''And where are cloudsteeds raised and trained for battle?''

"Very ingenious. I shall have to acquire new cloud-steeds and arrange for new riders to be trained."

"A trip to the Commander of Fortress Talisman is indicated, don't you think?"

"Undoubtedly, but isn't the timing a little obvious?"

"Not at Stronta. This is a Magical matter. The Cote Warden and I are the only ones who know about it, and it would be worth his life for him to divulge a message to anyone other than the person it was intended for. I can delay the announcement for a couple of days. If you made your arrangements immediately, you could be gone before I brought the matter to my advisors."

"You will make a splendid Queen," he said admiringly. "One other thing, though . . ."

"Speak."

"I am going to need an assistant here."

"That seems reasonable."

"I should like to try to get Otorin of Lissen. He was with me in Umbria, and I trust him."

"I'm not sure that appointing another Arundelian would be a politic move, besides, the man's a spy."

"You know that?"

"Of course I do. You don't suppose that Arundel is the only country to collect information about its neighbors, do you?"

"I suppose not, but I can promise you that he will be strictly under my command. I'll make that a condition. There's no need to give him a rank. He would report directly to me. Unless, that is, you think that I am a spy, too."

"The thought had crossed my mind," she admitted.

He moved away from her. "Is there no one you trust?" He was shocked and it showed.

"I trust you, my sweet man, a great deal more than I trust myself."

"I'm not sure that I find that comforting," he said grumpily.

"You mustn't be angry with me." She ran a finger around the edge of his beard. "I have to think of such things. It's a responsibility that comes with the Crown."

"I'm sorry," he said, not quite sure what he was apologizing for. "I really do need an aide, though."

"I'll think about it," she said, pressing herself against him. "In the meanwhile, let us take advantage of this time I have stolen. I don't trust my ladies-in-waiting. Lettuce Greenly is probably too stupid to spy on me, but one can't be sure." She backed away and reached behind her to unlace her dress. "And perhaps," she added with a sensual, almost baritone drawl, "you can convince me about that aide in a most undiplomatic way."

Morning found Darius asleep, alone in the big bed. He was sprawled out and his expression was peaceful. Jarrod, by contrast, had left the cot he had slept on since he was a boy well before dawn. He had Made the Day and was preparing for an hour of exercise with his friend Tokamo. Marianna's comment about his weight had stung. There was a knock on the door and he straightened up. Tokamo's portly figure came through the door without waiting for permission. He was puffing slightly from the effort of the stairs.

"A bunglebird came in from Celador last night. From the Archmage."

"I don't suppose you happen to know what it said?"

"The Chief Warlock is dead and you're to go to the funeral," Tokamo replied blandly.

"Did it say when?"

"The funeral's in a sennight, but you're to be at Fortress Talisman two days earlier. You're to take the unicorns."

"Good," Jarrod said with satisfaction. "That means that Marianna will have to go."

"It didn't say anything about her."

"It didn't have to. Anywhere Amarine goes, she goes. Did it say anything about a new Chief Warlock?"

"No. Got any ideas?"

"Not really," Jarrod said. "It doesn't have to be a Talismani. It usually works out that the Mage is a native of the country, but there's no rule about it."

"Know what that could mean?"

"No, Tok. You tell me. You had a year more of the Collegium."

"Funny you should mention it. Dean Sumner could be the next Chief Warlock."

Jarrod groaned. "Spare me. He never did like me."

"That was only because you were such a rotten student." Tokamo chuckled.

"What's so funny?"

"It just struck me that you must have become an object of veneration for the lazy and the not-so-bright." He laughed again.

"I think you had better explain that."

"Oh, it's just that for generations to come they'll be saying, 'Jarrod Courtak never matriculated and he got to be an Acting Mage.' "

"Very amusing. I think it's time we went out and took us a little exercise. It might wipe that silly smile off your face and give you a sense of respect for your betters. I think we'll start with a nice brisk run."

It was Tokamo's turn to groan.

chapter 18

It was one of those clear, crisp mornings that lift the spirits. The sun was too young to dispel the chill, but the air was as tangy as a winesap and the early bulbs were out. Hooves rang cleanly as the royal party gathered. It was an insignificant gathering as far as the numbers went. A coach, four wagons, a handful of servants, a small delegation from the Outpost, led by the Acting Mage, and two dozen of the Household Cavalry formed the bulk of it. The uniqueness was provided by the Queen, who was handed into the coach by her lady-in-waiting, and by the unicorns.

The Queen was in mourning purple and heavily veiled. Marianna was up on Amarine, cursing under her breath at having to ride sidesaddle. Jarrod rode Beldun, and the other two colts flanked them. A trumpet crowed and the Royal Standard was unfurled. The Standard Bearer dipped the flag to his sovereign and then rode off to the head of the column. They moved out under the arch of the West gate and into the long shadow cast by the starpoint.

The tents with the wounded were quiet, but the woods that cradled the palace were alive with birdsong. Jarrod knew that the colts were glad to be out, eager for new things to see. He felt the urge to canter that came from them.

'We have to keep our pace the same as the coach,' he cautioned.

'All the time?'

'Yes, Nastrus, all the time. We're on display, whether we like it or not, and I want you to behave. Humans who don't know you as well as I do think that you are wonderful, so I'd like you to try not to destroy their illusions.'

'Is that an example of human humor?' Beldun asked.

'We are going to represent Paladine and Magic at a solemn occasion. We have to act accordingly.'

'Watch out,' Nastrus warned, *'he's going to stamp his useless hooves and have one of those emotional disturbances.'*

'That's enough out of you.' Jarrod made no attempt to hide his irritation. It wouldn't have helped if he had. Nastrus ignored him and quickened his pace.

The road emerged from the woods and raised itself above the paddy fields that spread over the bottomlands. They were an even brown at this time of year, and there was skim ice on the canals. The cavalry broke into a canter, and the colts needed no urging to follow suit.

There was noise which, as they came closer, resolved itself into cheering. Jarrod stood in the stirrups to try to see what was happening, but the ceremonial plumes ahead made an effective screen. A knot of workers came into view suddenly, and the cheering died. It picked up again after the unicorns had passed. Jarrod knew the colts' incomprehension and disappointment. Their puzzled hurt tugged his spirits down.

'You are too rare and special for mere applause,' he explained hurriedly. *'These are country people who have probably never heard of you. Humans cheer for things that they understand, and you are entirely beyond their ken.'* The colts were not convinced.

From their vantage point on the roadway, they could see

a long way over the flat landscape. They could also be seen. The clusters of people became more frequent and it soon became evident to the colts that the general amazement was tempered by pleasure and awe. Jarrod sensed that they were reaching for the emotion and savoring it.

Word of the cortege's coming spread as if borne by the wind. The chance for a glimpse of the new Queen would have pulled all but the most indebted hands from the fields, but the rumor of the unicorns brought the country gentry and their families to the borders of the road as well. Naxania basked in this demonstration of her people's love.

The classes mingled easily, as they would on a state occasion, linked by the excitement. For some it was a reason for having stayed alive so long in a difficult world, for others something to boast and gossip about. Most came out of curiosity, but all would be marked by it. Being among the first to see the unicorns would keep for them the specialness that often fades with the bloom of youth.

The colts preened, their self-esteem quite restored. Their keen awareness of being the cynosures transmitted itself to Jarrod, and his spine straightened automatically. He surveyed the pageant on either side; ladies waving lace kerchiefs, red-faced laborers, old women with rough, loud voices honed by years of calling men in to meals. He smiled at them all. What had started as a journey toward death had turned into a patriotic progress.

''Did you ever think—'' Marianna's voice broke into the circle of enjoyment that Jarrod and the colts shared—''when we came down this road to Stronta about a year ago, that we would be riding back like this?''

He turned in the saddle so that he could look at her. ''I wasn't even capable of imagining it.''

''It seems such a long time ago,'' she said. ''I can see that girl, all dressed up like a page, not knowing what was going to happen and trying to pretend that it didn't matter.

I see her quite clearly and I know her well, but she isn't me.''

''I'm the other way around,'' Jarrod commented.

''I don't understand.'' She turned away and waved to her left.

''It's as if I were a bird again. I'm circling up there, looking down at all of this. I'm the same as I was then: it's the fellow on the unicorn who isn't real.''

Marianna leaned forward and took a bunch of flowers held out imploringly by a small boy. ''Well, I agree with one thing. The Magician riding beside me is the same oaf I met at Celador.'' She flashed him a wicked grin and offered the flowers to Amarine.

''Thank you very much. You are as charming now as you were then. Speaking of which, you still owe me a dance.''

''Only if you've been practicing.''

''With whom, pray?''

''Tokamo, perhaps?'' She laughed. ''And who knows what you get up to with Diadra when nobody's around.''

''Diadra?'' The idea of the Mage's personal Wisewoman took him by surprise, and he whooped at the image of the old dragon dancing. The colts caught the idea and magnified it until Jarrod was clinging helplessly to Beldun's neck, sides heaving and hurting. He begged them to stop and, when he had mastered himself, pushed himself weakly back into the saddle and wiped his eyes.

'Whatever must those people think?' Pellia asked teasingly.

'I want you to behave,' Nastrus quoted. *'We are on display, whether we want to be or not.'*

''Welcome back,'' Marianna said. ''That was quite a performance. I didn't think it was that funny.''

''Unfortunately, the colts did.'' Jarrod massaged his ribs.

''Shame on you, Jarrod Courtak, trying to shift the blame to innocent young creatures.''

''Innocent?'' He rose to the bait as she had known he would. ''They're a conniving set of ne'er-do-wells.'' He took a number of deep breaths. ''Where were we?''

''Dancing, I think, but I rather doubt that a grand ball will be part of the funeral services.''

''True.'' He followed Marianna's example and waved to the crowd.

''I wish old King Sig could be here,'' she said, raising her voice to be heard. ''He would love all of this. It would be like becoming one of his legends.''

''Is that what you think is happening to us?''

''In a way. I know that it's all due to the unicorns, but they don't.'' She gestured toward the people and was rewarded with another cheer.

''I wonder if the old boy made it through the Season of the Moons,'' Jarrod said, changing the subject back again.

''Of course he has.'' She was decisive. ''He's a tough old raptor, and he's lived in the mountains all his life.''

''We left him with plenty of wood and plenty of game,'' Jarrod agreed. ''I don't know how well he'll fare next Winter, though, with no one to help him stock up.''

''He can take care of himself. He just got us to do the work for him. Still, it would be nice to see him one more time. Who knows? With these beauties''—and she leaned forward and patted Amarine's neck—''anything is possible.''

She sat back up and started to wave again. Jarrod hoped for more conversation, but in that he was disappointed.

The night was cold and starry. The snow-capped mountains of Talisman shone in the nightmoonlight, and the wind that came down from them had a keen edge on it. The royal party was surrounded by the glowing lines of protection that the Magicians had laid down, but they generated no heat. Jarrod, swaddled in his cloak, lay awake. The afternoon's conversation ran through his mind.

So much had changed since that trip from Celador to Stronta, but the basic things were still the same. He was still cold, sleeping out in the open while Naxania was protected from the wind by a tent. Marianna was somewhere out there in the darkness, as she had been the year before, and she still had the ability to turn him inside out. If you start thinking about her, he told himself, you'll never get to sleep, but he thought of her until he slept.

Marianna was no more talkative the next day, and Jarrod had plenty of time to admire the scenery. The landscape changed as they neared the border. The plain undulated into foothills. There were meadows filled with black and white kina, and, beyond them, miles of vineyards interspersed with fruit trees. The white pockmarks of old quarries began to assume a pattern on the mountainside ahead.

There were no more crowds once they had crossed the border. The distant flocks, browsing on the slopes, seemed to mirror the clouds. It was orderly and peaceful. Jarrod was glad not to have people reaching out toward them, but the colts clearly missed the adulation. They attracted attention, but the first hay crop was being brought in. Men and women would stop work and lean on their scythes or their crooks and stare until the foreigners had gone by, but, unicorns or no unicorns, they were back to work before the party was out of sight.

'There is something troubling you,' Amarine remarked as she plodded around a hairpin turn. *'The weather is fine. You should be enjoying the outing more.'*

'Nothing's troubling me,' Marianna thought back and brushed dust out of the creases in her skirt.

'I feel the things that are upsetting you,' Amarine re-

plied, unperturbed, *'but I do not understand them. There seem to be two different themes, but they get tangled up. One concerns the Magician. He worries you. He worries me, too.'*

'Jarrod? He worries you?'

'He has a great deal of influence with my offspring. It makes me uneasy.'

'Oh, I don't think it should. Jarrod would never do anything to hurt the colts. He feels about them the same way that I feel about you. If anyone tried to hurt the colts, he would die defending them.'

'I am aware of that. There is great love and trust between them, as there is between us, but you are human and we are unicorn. It is an experience I cannot deny my foals, but still I worry. It is not natural.'

'It feels natural,' Marianna objected.

'That is the danger, but I do not mean to let you evade the question. I need to understand as much as I can. What is it that is causing this undercurrent of discontent?'

'I don't understand most of it myself.'

'I sense great love for your sire and anger toward him. I see pleasure in you at being away from your home and great longing to be back there. There is much tenderness for the Magician and a strong desire to be rid of him. There is much that does not make sense.'

'I know,' Marianna admitted, *'but that's the way it is. Everything's muddled up these days, and it used to be so simple.'*

'Go on,' Amarine prompted.

'I like Jarrod, I really do. He's sweet and decent and he does his best, but he can be so . . . Oh, I don't know how to put it. It's as if he were two people. One of him does these incredible things, which, when you think about them, are terrifying. The other one is this gormless, Dame-schoolboy moping around behind me,' Marianna replied.

'But you are attracted to him.' It was a statement.

'Sometimes.' The admission was grudging.

'Mating is a natural urge. It is not meant to be curbed.' Amarine said.

'We are supposed to be able to control it. I am going to have to marry a man who can better the fortunes of Gwyndryth.'

'You will root yourself to one spot? That is not natural either.'

'Not for our men, but it is for almost all women.' Marianna thought back tartly.

'Does the Magician know of your feelings?'

'I certainly hope not.'

'But the female always initiates mating.' Amarine was puzzled.

'That may be, but on this world it doesn't pay to let that be seen. Men, for all their muscles, are fragile creatures. They look as sturdy as ripe peaches and they bruise as easily.'

'You sound very experienced.'

Marianna acknowledged the humor that lay behind the thought. *'I've good eyes and ears,'* she admitted, *'and I pretend well.'*

'This is all very difficult,' Amarine confessed. *'What of the thread that concerns your sire?'*

'I'm angry at him. You know that.'

'Why?'

'You can see that, too. He says he believes me, but he won't help us.'

'Not that. There is mating trouble here, too.'

They trotted past windbreaks of fluttering cinder trees, but Marianna was oblivious to the scenery, lost in a wash of hostile feelings.

'My father's having an affair with the Queen. I know he is.' It was an angry declaration.

'And should he not?'

'Not with her. She's just using him, and when she's bored she'll throw him away like fruit peel.'

'And if she does not?'

'She will. She's a Queen and he's far too old for her.'

'Troubling,' Amarine thought, and left it at that.

Jarrod rode beside them, unaware of the colloquy that was going on. If the colts were privy to it, they did not pass it on. He was, in any case, as close to shutting them out as he could be. His self-absorption was intense, and yet his preoccupation paralleled Marianna's. Love was making him miserable. It was torture not knowing how Marianna felt about him, but he did not have the courage to ask her. What if she laughed at him? He glanced over at her. She looked so elegant in the long skirt as she moved effortlessly to the rythmn of the trot. If he had any hope of capturing her affection, he would have to convince Ragnor that the war must stop. It was a daunting prospect, and the Archmage had a withering tongue if he had a mind to use it; so had Marianna. He wasn't looking forward to the next few days.

The expected summons from Ragnor came only hours after their arrival at Fortress Talisman, and it made Jarrod as nervous as he had thought it would. Now that he was in the presence, matters were no better. He had knocked and been told to enter, but the room was dark and the Archmage nowhere to be seen.

"Ah, there you are." The voice made Jarrod jump. He looked around for the source.

"Forgive me if I don't get up, this chair is too good at keeping the drafts out, and I'm too old and comfortable to stand for ceremony." Jarrod located the chair beside the fire. The high wings obscured the occupant.

"Help yourself to a cup of wine on the way over," Ragnor continued. "There's a decanter on the table."

Jarrod complied and had a quick drink before taking a chair from against the wall and carrying it over to the hearth. The wine was warming and the firelight was cheerful. He looked at the Archmage and tried to gauge his mood, but the old face was unreadable in the flickering light.

"Good evening, Sir."

"Evening, son. I'm sorry I wasn't with the welcoming party, but I always think it's best to leave that sort of thing to the locals. You all settled in?"

"Yes, Sir. They gave me a very comfortable room across the court."

"They're hospitable people. I usually enjoy my visits here, but not this time. Funerals make me bad-tempered these days. If I'm not presiding, I'm in attendance in some capacity or another. More often than not, I'm saying the obsequies of a friend. Ardoin of Talisman is, was, the last of my contemporaries. It's getting lonely up here." He paused and scrunched down in the chair. "We were never that close, but, with him gone, I feel like a walking anachronism. I know exactly how the last of the skywhales must have felt."

The Archmage picked up a tankard from the small table beside him and took a pull. "Funny how things turn out." He obviously intended to do the talking and Jarrod settled back, relieved. "Ardoin was a couple of years ahead of me at the Collegium and the most popular boy there. He was good at anything he turned his hand to." Ragnor gave a rheumy chuckle. "Later on, if he wanted to turn his hand to your girl, you didn't stand a chance. If envy is a sin, as the Maternites hold, I was a very sinful young man. In fact, I qualified on more than one of their counts." Ragnor stopped and smiled to himself. He looked at Jarrod.

"I know that it is impossible for you to imagine that

we creaking ancients were once full of sap and sass, but we were. Ah yes, indeed we were." The voice faded away, but the smile remained.

"Bah," he resumed with a return to his usual manner, "you are so young that I find it hard to resist the temptation to shock you." He pushed himself back up.

"I can't believe that, Sir," Jarrod said, straight-faced.

"Can't believe that I'd say something just to shock you?"

Jarrod mustered his courage. "Oh, I believe that, Sir. I don't believe that you'd resist the temptation."

There was an agonizing moment of silence and then Ragnor laughed.

"You surprise me, son. I didn't think you had it in you."

"I've been around the colts too long," Jarrod said. "Well, one colt in particular," he amended.

"They are well, I trust."

"Flourishing. The exercise of the ride here did them good. They are endlessly curious about us, and the trip was good on that count as well. People turned out and lined the road and cheered us. They enjoyed that part of it best of all."

"I'm glad it went well. I was feeling a little exploitive. I wanted them here to show them off and to dress up the funeral. Ardoin was much loved. He's the only Chief Warlock most of these people have ever known. He'd hate all the pomp, but pageantry is an important part of what both Magic and royalty provide for the people.

"The Discipline has few public rituals. That is why those we do have must be lavish and impressive. They should be inspiring and mysterious without being intimidating. They should generate a feeling of veneration and pride, but not of worship."

The voice had risen and was exquisitely pitched, and

Jarrod realized that he was hearing a quotation from a speech. It was compelling nonetheless.

"You have, of course, brought your Staff and a suitable gown?" Ragnor was back in the present.

"The Staff is here, but I have no special gown."

"Surely you could have borrowed one of Greylock's?"

"To wear at a funeral? With my Lord Mage lying bound to what remains of the Place of Power?" Jarrod couldn't hide his surprise.

"I hadn't thought about that. You're quite right. The funeral's tomorrow, so there isn't even time to have something made up. What do you have with you?"

"A clean Magician's robe—and my Staff."

"I've heard about the Staff. Greylock's report said that it was very powerful, and he is not given to hyperbole. It was not damaged in the battle?"

"When I first saw it," Jarrod replied, "after the Magic was done, it was dull and unresponsive and the runes were blackened." He hesitated. "All I could think of was that I had ruined the Princess Naxania's pet artifact."

"I think I can understand that," Ragnor said, and smiled.

"Fortunately for me, my Staff recovered."

"At the same rate that you did?" Ragnor hazarded.

"I don't know, Sir. Greylock's Wisewoman refused to bring it to me at first. When I did get to see it, it was quite restored, which was more than could have been said for me."

"Good enough. A plain gown and the Staff it shall be. Be sure the robe is ironed. You can get away without it if there's a lot of embroidery, but not if it's plain. I had thought of using you as one of the coffin bearers, but you're a bit too tall for the rest of them. I think it would be best if you took care of the Candles of Remembrance. I don't have to tell you to use your Talent to keep them alight until they are installed in his pavilion. I'm sure that you can see what a shock it would be to this nation if the Candles are snuffed out before their appointed time." Jarrod nodded.

"You'll be on the dais." Ragnor's bony hand made an indeterminate gesture. "A page will come and escort you up to your chair. Keep your shoulders back and pace slowly. Place the Staff firmly every time. It's a short ceremony, in keeping with Ardoin's wishes, so you won't get to sit. The chair's more of a place marker than anything else. Got that?"

"Yes, Sir. Will I be required to do anything during the ceremony?"

"Just make sure that the candles stay alight. You'll remain behind with them while the body is taken to the Burning Ground. Once the coffin is consumed, there will be a procession back to the Hall. Arabella, Naxania, and I shall each take a candle, and you will escort us to the pavilion and make sure that they don't go out. Clear?" Jarrod nodded again.

"Good. Now let's discuss the unicorns. Will they do what you tell them to do?"

"Within limits. It's more of a partnership."

"I'd like them in the Great Hall for the service, but I'll settle for having them in the procession to the Burning Ground and at the Installation of the Candles. Think you can do it?" Ragnor took a drink and looked across the firelight.

Jarrod followed suit. "They know why we came here," he said, "and, in truth, they are rather looking forward to the funeral."

"Looking forward to it?"

"I haven't had any deep, philosophical conversations with them yet, but they don't look on death the same way that we do. It may be because all their actions are preserved in the Memory." Was this the time to broach the subject of the war? Not in the middle of discussing funeral arrangements, he decided. That would be unseemly.

"D'you think they're here to study us?"

The question startled Jarrod. The Archmage was still slumped comfortably in his chair, cradling his wine, but Jarrod felt the hairs on the nape of his neck crawl.

"I don't think anyone sent them here to spy on us," he said, weighing his words. "As far as I can gather, the dam decided to give birth in a pleasant, secure place. The Anvil of the Gods is certainly that. The colts were born here, and this is a fascinating experience for them. They have a chance of providing their communal Memory with some new material. They are certainly studying us, but that's the reason. After so many generations, it's a challenge to find something new."

"I'll have to trust your instincts. I just wish I knew what they were here for."

"Well, Sir, the Lady Marianna and I—"

"Speaking of her," the Archmage said, cutting him off, "I assume that she will accompany the unicorns?"

"I'm sure she will. But, if I may suggest, Sir, it would be best if someone went and consulted her about it."

"I'll trust your instincts on that, too. There will be no Hall tonight, for obvious reasons. They'll serve us a meal in our rooms fairly soon. Get an early night if you can. Someone will come for you about an hour after the Making of the Day. Be sure that you are ready. And remember to have that robe ironed." Jarrod recognized his cue and rose. "I'll see to it, Archmage. Good night, Sir."

"Good night, son. I'll see you tomorrow. Don't worry about the service. All you have to do is stand there and look dignified."

"Yes, Sir. Thank you, Sir." He drained his cup hastily

and withdrew. There had been no chance to bring up the war.

"Oh, one other thing." The soft voice froze Jarrod on the way to the door. "There will be a meeting of the High Council of Magic tomorrow afternoon. As an Acting Mage, you are expected to attend. We'll hold it here—sixteenth hour." The Archmage paused. There were questions he ought to have asked, questions about Paladine, about the unicorns, but he didn't feel up to it. Not tonight.

Jarrod waited for something more, but nothing was forthcoming. He crossed to the door and turned. He couldn't see Ragnor anymore. The Archmage was lost in his chair by the fire.

"Good night, Sir," he said. There was no reply.

chapter 19

Jarrod stood on the steps that led up to the Banqueting Hall and watched the procession turn into Main Court. First came musicians, mounted on cloudsteeds, playing a doleful thednody. They were followed by a company of hackbutmen in disconcertingly gay ceremonial uniforms. Next, the crystal carriage, purple plumes at the four corners, drawn by four black horses in purple caparisons. The harnesses were black and silver. The coachman and attendant footmen wore midnight blue with silver trim, the whole topped off with black tricorn hats, their purple streamers fluttering in the light breeze. As the coach drew abreast, Jarrod saw the simple coffin resting on the raised, draped platform.

The two royal ladies rode behind in an open brougham. Both were heavily veiled and Arabella wore a tiny pillbox hat to anchor hers. The matched pair of white horses that drew them were made funeral-decent by unrelieved black harnesses and caparisons. A company of warcats and their warriors surrounded the Thane, who walked, bareheaded, at the rear. There were no cheers from the onlookers pressed against the railings. It would have been inappropriate, and besides, it was not the Talismani style to show emotion. Time to go inside and take up my place, Jarrod thought.

The massive, rustically carved sutler's screen blocked his view of the Banqueting Hall when he made his way in from the kitchens, but the hum of the assembled mourners, the creak of benches, and the waft of incense conjured up the picture. The coffin and the notables had already gone in through the main doors, but there was a little while yet before the participants need enter.

The line was headed by Marianna and the unicorns, and Jarrod knew that a special enclosure had been built for them hard by the dais. He had heard the hammering in the night. He moved forward toward Marianna. She was standing by Amarine's head wearing a long-sleeved, high-necked gown of soft purple, edged with black. She looks as if she has just stepped out of a portrait, he thought. It was a concept that the colts didn't understand. They moved restlessly, and he worried about their patience with human rituals.

That idea was greeted with condescension. *'This is a new experience for us,'* came the strand of thought that was Pellia. *'For you, too,'* Beldun added. *'Of course we shall be respectful,'* said Nastrus, penetrating to a deeper level of anxiety.

Jarrod glanced around. The colts had been impeccably groomed, and their silver hooves shone in the candlelight. He felt proud of them. In fact everybody looked impressive. He was the only exception. His gown had been pressed, but he felt out of place among all the somber elegance. His hand tightened on the Staff. That at least could not be diminished.

'This is the first time we have come across a human death that has been peaceful,' Beldun remarked in Jarrod's mind.

'There have been many deaths on the battlefield of late,' Jarrod acknowledged, *'but it's not like that usually. These are especially perilous times.'*

'The atmosphere is very different.' 'There's nothing about your death rites in the Memory,' Pellia and Nastrus said simultaneously.

'We do honor to the memory of the dead,' Jarrod answered them both, *'and by remembering we give them life.'*

'Mam says it's time to go,' Beldun cut in, *'and she says you're to stay in step this time, Nastrus.'*

'Remember, this is a solemn occasion,' Jarrod admonished, before turning and making his way back down the line to his proper place. He heard the combined intake of breath as the unicorns entered the main hall and enjoyed the effect his charges had and their pleasure in it.

He positioned himself behind Dean Sumner and picked up the stately pace. He followed the embroidered black gown and was momentarily dazzled as they rounded the screen and moved from relative gloom into the light of a hundred candles. They glittered on chandeliers, shone from sconces, and lined the central aisle. At the back of the dais, three lighted pillars of wax stood out. Those were the Chief Warlock's Candles of Remembrance and they were Jarrod's responsibility. He concentrated on them and committed their simple pattern to memory.

He heard the colts before he got a good look at them. He couldn't follow what they were thinking, but a lively discussion was going on. They were standing on either side of a large wooden armchair. Marianna stood in front of it. He watched her curtsy as Arabella of Arundel passed her and again for Naxania of Paladine. She made no move for Dean Sumner and only gave Jarrod a faint smile. Respect for royalty, but none for Magic, Jarrod thought. He grasped the front of his gown with his left hand and lifted it to negotiate the steps up to the dais.

A page detached himself from a line at the side of the stage and led him to a high-backed soskiawood chair with a cloth of estate above it. Wrong chair, he thought, and then realized that he now merited the emblem. The colts were in his mind, distracting him with their curiosity. He bowed to the page, planted his Staff, and swung around to face the people. The Hall was packed and everyone was standing. Most were staring at the unicorns.

Deep-voiced horns sounded from the minstrels' gallery and prompted a short, double file of Apprentice Magicians to emerge from behind the screen, swinging censers. They processed up the aisle, peeling off as they reached the steps, and formed a line with their backs to the dais. The music swelled to a crescendo and died, the incense hung heavy, and into the ensuing silence and smoke came the Archmage. It was a magnificent entrance but only those on the dais facing the congregation saw it.

Jarrod had seen the Archmage in full panoply once before, at the Conclave at Celador, but there had been too much going on for him to have appreciated the impact of the regalia. Here at Fortress Tailsman, Ragnor was the embodiment of the maxims he had laid down the previous day. The white hair and beard set off the long, seamed face. The sapphire biretta, denoting the Magedom of Arundel, sparkled in the candlelight. The heavy Chain of the Archmages swung gently against the rune-stitched gown. Aromatic mist curled up from the censers and Ragnor seemed to float through it. The heel of his Staff tapped through the hush, as inexorable as the coming of death.

He made his way up the stairs to the stage and moved with solid grace to the midpoint of the apron. As he passed Jarrod, the Paladinian saw that the tired, cold old man of the night before had metamorphosed into a presence of great force and dignity. In the execution of his office, the great Magus was ageless and invincible.

Ragnor turned and faced the assembly. He raised his Staff slowly. If hovered for a long moment and then came down thrice upon the boards. The hollow dais amplified the sound.

"Our friend is gone, but not forgotten. He has removed the light of his countenance from us, but the sweetness of his smile remains.'' The words fell, clean and strong, into the quiet.

''Eshkalon Ardoin was my brother in Magic, and I remember him as he was. He was greatly gifted and became greatly loved . . .''

The practiced voice rolled on, but Jarrod let it drift away and concentrated on the three candles burning behind him. No change as yet in the pattern, but he decided that he had best keep part of his awareness on them. Eshkalon Ardoin, the other part of him mused, I never knew he had a second name. I wonder if Greylock has another name. Strange knowing a man all these years and not knowing something as simple as that. There was much that he wanted to know when Greylock came back. If Greylock comes back.

''The body decays, but the memory is green.'' Ragnor's voice organed out. He was moving into the final phase of the ceremony, and Jarrod came back to it with a guilty start. Nastrus was a smug presence in his mind.

''The body decays no matter how worthy the spirit,'' the mourners intoned in response.

''While memory is green, the spirit survives,'' Ragnor asserted.

''The spirit survives until memory fades,'' the assembly agreed.

Ragnor waited until the echoes had lost themselves in the sooty rafters. ''May the memory of Eshkalon Ardoin outlive us as we outlive him.'' He raised his Staff again and brought it down three times more. The soundings were a closing knell.

The people bowed their heads and remained still until the choir announced itself with an a cappella recessional. That brought on a brief flurry of activity, and Jarrod wondered what was happening. Then he realized. The coffin had lain at the front of the Hall, out of sight of the dais, and now they were going to carry it to the Burning Ground.

Once the simple box was hoisted and steady, the Archmage made his way slowly to the stairs and went down to take his place behind the coffin. Arabella and Naxania followed him. Dean Sumner and Magister Handrom brought up the rear, leaving Jarrod alone on the dais.

'Yes, you follow them, and you have to go slowly,' he replied in response to a query from Pellia.

'This is all very interesting,' Nastrus chimed in. *'We have more concepts in common than I had realized. Although, of course—'*

'Not now, Nastrus, Jarrod cut in. *'I have to concentrate.'*

He was just in time. The doors in the middle of the side wall were thrown open. The chandeliers swung and the candles guttered and went out as the fresh air swept in. People turned back toward the dais, and there was an audible sigh of relief when they saw that the Candles of Remembrance burned on. The cortege slow-marched out, and the rest of them crowded in its wake. There was a milling pause, and Jarrod knew that the procession was being joined by fourscore young men in white tunics, one for every year of the Chief Warlock's life. They were soon assimilated and the exodus began anew.

Jarrod put his Staff carefully by his chair and sat down. There was no reason why he couldn't shield the candles and be comfortable. He reached with his mind for the colts and found them entering the Burning Ground. He saw the pyre through their eyes and noted that the coffin was already in place atop it. Marianna's back was just ahead and then she turned off to one side. The colts did not follow her and neither did Amarine.

This was not what had been planned. *To the right,* he thought out at them. *Follow Marianna!* They either did not hear him, or ignored him. A decision had been taken and he wasn't aware of it. He didn't know what to expect, and it made him anxious.

The colts paced on, and Jarrod was aware of the consternation they were causing. He was aware of it because they were aware of it, but there was no hesitation on their part. Amarine continued to the far end of the pyre, and the colts took up stations on the other three sides. Jarrod was confused by the three different views superimposed one on the other. What now? he wondered. Whatever it was, he had no control over it. He hoped they wouldn't do anything that would give offense.

Jarrod was subliminally aware that people were pressing in through the gates. He caught the smell of incense and the unicorns' distaste of it. He felt momentarily disoriented. One part of him was concentrating on the candles behind him, and the rest of him seemed to be at the Burning Ground; all over the Burning Ground.

He could hear Ragnor, though none of his viewpoints gave him a sight of the man. He could not understand the sounds because they were being filtered through the unicorns, but the emotions registered clearly. The Archmage must be delivering the eulogy. The colts were quiet and attentive. The tone rounded and the volume began to build. A note of hope came into the delivery, and Jarrod knew that the speech was coming to an end.

There was a moment of silence and then, without warning, a surge of energy pulsed out of the unicorns' minds, Jarrod was caught off guard and recoiled. He checked the Candles hastily and then returned to the colts. The kindling at the base of the pyre was ablaze and he watched as the whole thing caught. How did they do that? he wondered. Nastrus had tried to light a torch at Gwyndryth and hadn't been able to do it.

'*What happens now*?' Beldun's question in his mind

startled Jarrod, but he was relieved that full contact had been re-established.

'They will come back here and escort the Candles of Remembrance to a special pavilion. It's my job to ensure that the candles stay alight until they are installed. They represent our memory of him.'

'What happens to the body?' Pellia inquired.

'It's reduced to ashes.'

'She means after that.' Nastrus was being patient with him.

'When all the ashes have cooled, in about two days, they are collected together and there is another procession to the pavilion. They are dug into the soil in front of the door and a tree is planted to represent the continual rebirth of the Chief Warlock's spirit. We are supposed to think about the person whenever we see their tree.'

'It is a pretty conceit,' Pellia commented. *'Even unpleasing humans can, at the last, produce beauty.'*

'When we die, Beldun remarked, *we live on in the Memory. Everything we do and see and think is there.'*

'We both cherish the memory of our dead,' Jarrod said.

'Yes, but your memories are so short,' Nastrus objected.

'Mam says that it's time to go.' Pellia ended the colloquy firmly.

'Follow Marianna and take your cue from her,' Jarrod advised.

'She has already communicated with Mam,' Pellia informed him. *'We are to walk back to where you are, but we do not go to the pavilion with you.'*

The colts turned their attention elsewhere, and Jarrod sat waiting in the Great Hall. The page reappeared and asked him to stand in front of the tall candles. He collected his Staff and did as he was told. They took away his chair and left him in solitary state upon the dais. The three points of flame burned steadily.

chapter 20

The Installation of the Candles had gone without a hitch, and the somewhat awkward funeral feast was over. Everyone else seemed to be retiring to their rooms, but Jarrod went to check on the unicorns. He half expected Marianna to follow him and kept looking over his shoulder, pretending to be examining the buildings. Indeed, he was not immune to the excitement of a new place. By Paladinian standards he was very well traveled, but he felt more like a small town bumpkin.

The unicorns, when he found them, were munching placidly on fresh hay. The large loosebox was spotless and it was obvious that they had been brushed down. Their coats gleamed. They were pleased with themselves, but he could feel the tiredness. Their display at the Burning Ground had taken a lot out of them. When he started to question them about it, they simply said that it had been Amarine's idea. They did it to show respect and the people had liked it.

Being with you has taught us much about fire, was Natrus cryptic offering, and Jarrod decided not to pursue the matter.

With one unsatisfactory encounter behind him, he entered the Archmage's withdrawing room with trepidation. Ragnor was already seated at the head of a large table, going through papers. The other four people were grouped around the fireplace and had their backs to him. Dean Sumner, his former Headmaster, and Sumner's deputy, Magister Handrom, were talking earnestly to the two royal ladies. Jarrod was tempted to turn around and walk out before anyone noticed him.

"Ah, there you are. Come on in, son." Jarrod moved forward reluctantly. "You know everyone of course," Ragnor said and gestured toward the fire. Jarrod bowed.

"There's a lot to be discussed, so I propose we get down to it." The Archmage looked at them and beamed as they moved in and took their chairs. "The first order of business is relatively pleasant. We have a newcomer." He nodded down the table at Jarrod. "And three of our regular members are undergoing changes of estate. Naxania of Paladine returns to us a Queen." He bowed his head briefly to her. "My old friend Sumner has relinquished his position as Dean of the Collegium and will, subject to the confirmation of this Council, assume the title of Chief Warlock of Talisman. If there be any who challenge his right, let them speak." He glanced around. "Good. Congratulations, Chief Warlock.

"Sommas Handrom will succeed him as Dean. Does anyone say him no? Capital, congratulations, Sommas. I'm sure the old school will prosper under your hand. Lastly, Jarrod Courtak has been appointed Acting Mage of Paladine and is entitled to a seat until our brother Greylock is restored to us." Ragnor was being the consummate chairman.

Jarrod sat very straight and his eyes flicked from one face to the other. No one paid him any special mind. All he had to do, he reassured himself, was sit there and keep his mouth shut. They certainly wouldn't be looking to him for advice.

"Now that the vacancies on the Council have been filled, we can proceed." The meeting was firmly in Ragnor's hands. "This is the first time since Celador that a full quorum has met, and conditions have changed radically since then. Then we faced the extinction of our race. That is no longer true. I know that is a strange thing to say after the terrible losses so recently suffered by both Paladine and the Empire, but I believe it to be so."

He knows about the origins of the Outlanders, Jarrod thought, but the Archmage's next words disabused him.

"A series of extraordinary events, completely unforeseen by me, has changed the fabric of my vision. Strandkind is by no means safe, but we have bought time. Since that is so, we must not neglect our more parochial problems. The Discipline now has one problem that could destroy it even if the enemy disappeared tomorrow." He sat back and steepled his fingers.

"We are a tiny, powerful minority, we're even taller than the rest of the population, but we've never been persecuted. Ever wonder about that?" He looked out over his fingertips. "One of the reasons is that people are afraid of us. We take great pains not to frighten them, and they know that we have always used our powers for the general good, but it's common sense to stay on the good side of someone you feel, deep down, could turn you into a loathsome, hopping thing if they felt like it.

"Fear alone can't account for our good fortune, though, and we certainly don't hold the people in thrall. No, we've been safe so far because ninety percent of the Magic performed is small, useful Magic at the local level. Our control of the weather, while not perfect, is a daily boon. But, above all, Magic has survived all these centuries because it has been for all the people. It is used, impartially, for good. 'Impartially' is the key word." He paused and took a sip of water.

What's the old man getting at? Jarrod wondered. The

only danger to Magic that he could think of was the disappearance of the Place of Power.

"If Magic and the Monarchy," the Archmage resumed, "ever get interlaced in the public mind, both institutions will suffer. The Discipline will suffer the more. We are as exposed as the monarchies and far more vulnerable. Our men and women labor, for the most part, unprotected and alone.

"When I became Regent of Arundel, I was always careful to keep my roles as Mage and President of the Council of Regency separate. Decisions were always made by the full Council and announced in its name. Mind you"—he smiled reminiscently—"I was tolerably good at getting my own way." Arabella gave a little laugh and Ragnor's smile grew.

"When the Princess Arabella was young," he said, "there was no evidence that she was touched by the Talent. She was fair-haired and her eyes were blue and she was no taller than she should have been. Her Talent, when it emerged, was unlike any other. It was limited entirely to healing, and the Arundelians only loved her the more for it.

"Now, however, we have two rulers on the High Council of Magic. Both of you sit here, not because of your powers temporal, but because you are necromancers of unusual skill and sophistication. You are sovereigns nonetheless. You are both young and you are both women.

"We live in a warrior's world, and warriors have always made the mistake of thinking that strength is purely physical. It never ceases to amaze me," he said, appearing to digress, "how men who spend so much time preparing for fighting, fighting, and recovering from fighting can have the time or energy left to cause internal trouble, but I remember full well that they do. Ambition and energy seem to go together.'' He nodded as if some memory confirmed the thought.

''It has always been harder for women and minors to hold the throne. Children grow up, but you''—he glanced left and right—''will always be women. And there will always be ambitious men. My present information assures me that neither of you has any need to worry at the moment. The Princess Regnant is more popular now than at any time since her sixteenth birthday.'' He grinned at her unexpectedly and then became serious as he turned to Naxania.

''And you, my dear,'' he said, covering her hand briefly with his long, spotted one, ''are insulated by the tragic losses your nation has suffered.'' He sat back again and turned his attention down the table.

''Neither condition will last indefinitely,'' he said dispassionately. ''You can both look forward to challenges to your authority, some disguised as offers of marriage. Ordinarily, the Discipline would not be overly concerned. It takes no sides and knows that, whatever the outcome, it is indispensable.

''Now, however, there are living links between both thrones and the Discipline. If you become unpopular, for whatever reason, the hostility may spread to include all Magicians. That is one problem and the other is related.

''Power, if allied to some measure of competence, is habit-forming. It is hard to share and harder still to lose. If there comes a time when it seems likely that the throne will be taken from you, it will be difficult to resist the temptation to use your powers for what you would undoubtedly tell yourself was 'the good of the country.' It would be even harder if your sons were in peril. It simply must not happen.'' The Archmage spaced the last four words out and rapped on the table to emphasize each one.

There was, Jarrod noted, no deference to temporal rank

in the Archmage's words or his behavior. He wasn't even talking among equals. He had barely raised his voice and was wearing none of the accoutrements of his office, but he was clearly telling subordinates how he expected them to behave. Jarrod remembered Greylock's admonition that a successful Mage had to be a monarch's indispensable counselor, and marveled at the way the Archmage was handling the two women. The Archmage confounded him again by standing up abruptly.

"Arabella of Arundel and Naxania of Paladine, I speak as your Father in Magic. I require you now, before this Council of your peers here assembled and in loving memory of our departed brother, to renew the Oath of Apprenticeship." He looked from one to the other. The two sat unmoving, as if stunned. "I must also warn you, before this gathering, that should you become forsworn, you will be disowned by the Discipline."

Jarrod found that he had been holding his breath, and he let it out slowly and quietly. He watched the two women. They were sitting erect and stock-still. Arabella was pale and her mouth was slightly open. Two spots of color burned in Naxania's cheeks, but her mouth was a tight, bloodless line.

Ragnor pressed on. "Do you, Arabella, Princess Regnant of Arundel, swear before your peers here assembled that you will never use the Talent that you have inherited frivolously or selfishly, in your own behalf or in that of others?" The old formula rang out.

"I do so swear." Arabella's voice was even and her face revealed nothing.

The Archmage repeated the question to Naxania. Her response was clipped and cold.

"Thank you both," Ragnor said, and sat down again. "I'm sorry that I had to spring that on you, but I'm sure you understand the need." He looked benignly at the two women. They did not appear to be warmed. ''Now that that's over,'' he continued obliviously, ''I think we might discuss—'' An urgent rapping silenced him.

Jarrod looked over his shoulder as the door opened and a military man entered. He closed the door carefully behind him and saluted.

''The Commander's apologies for disturbing your Excellencies, but he bids me report that the Outlanders have attacked and taken Fort Bandor.''

''Bandor? That's impossible!'' Sumner's voice was shrill with disbelief.

''The garrison managed to get off two bunglebirds, or at least two reached Isphardel. Others, doubtless, were sent to Angorn.''

''When did it happen?'' Naxania was sharp and peremptory.

''It is difficult to say, your Majesty. The weather in that part of the world is uncontrolled. Storms could have delayed the birds and then the message was relayed through Stronta. I would think at least a fortnight ago.''

''Thank you, Wing Leader.'' Ragnor asserted himself. ''You may tell Commander Yadan that we thank him for keeping us informed.'' The 'steedsman saluted, turned on his heel, and left.

''It's a mistake,'' Jarrod blurted out as the door closed. He regretted it instantly.

Ragnor looked up, surprised by the outburst. ''Bunglebirds are notorious for getting things wrong,'' he said judiciously, ''but that young man seemed quite certain of his facts.''

Jarrod was committed now. This was the last place he would have chosen to make his case, but he had no choice. ''You don't understand,'' he said, gathering his courage. ''The Outlanders wouldn't attack us; not now.''

"Does this have anything to do with the Lady Marianna and the unicorn?" Naxania asked.

"You know?" This was totally unexpected.

"Her father told me," Naxania replied noncommitally.

"I think somebody had better explain," Ragnor said, looking back and forth.

"Very well," Naxania said. "The Holdmaster of Gwyndryth, whom our Cousin of Arundel has graciously loaned to us to help rebuild the Paladinian army, came to me and told me that his daughter had learned to communicate with the big unicorn. The unicorn had told her that the original inhabitants of this world were the Outlanders and that we developed later. It is her contention that we are driving them out of their ancestral lands."

"Preposterous," Sumner interjected.

Typical, Jarrod thought. He was bad enough at the Collegium; with this new title, he'll be impossible.

"It does seem improbable, Dean, I beg your pardon, Chief Warlock," Naxania agreed, "but the child's father assures me that she is not normally given to, ah, fantasies."

"This true, Courtak?" Ragnor asked.

"The colts have access to the same Memory and they confirm it," Jarrod said stiffly.

"Are you trying to say that we and not they were the original aggressors?" Handrom used the tone of ironic surprise that Jarrod remembered from school.

"The Others must certainly think so, Sir."

"And how do you arrive at that conclusion?" Handrom pressed. Jarrod bristled and opened his mouth to reply.

"This is a radical notion," Ragnor cut in decisively. "Until we understand the ramifications, I want you all to promise me that not one word of this leaves the room. Do I have your word?" He looked around the table. "Good.

Now, what does all this have to do with Fort Bandor?" Naxania shrugged.

"The Lady Marianna and I felt that it explained the enemy's recent behavior," Jarrod said before anyone else could cut in. "They have come out with these deadly new weapons and inflicted great losses. They almost got to the Angorn Gate, and they actually got through the Stronta Gate. Then they withdrew, even though they must have known that we were no threat to them for the moment. Think what that means. They have actually given up ground of their own free will. I don't think that has ever happened before. It seemed clear to us that they were trying to send us a message. They were saying, "You know that we can defeat you, but if you leave us alone, we will leave you alone."

"And they underline this so-called message by seizing a key fortress. I don't remember that happening before, either." Sumner's high, dry voice demolished the theory effortlessly.

"They could have been provoked," Jarrod countered.

"Across all those leagues of contaminated ground?" The new Chief Warlock was poised for the kill. "I think not. Nobody would be fool enough to risk mutation by crossing it before it had greened."

"Magic can cover leagues without touching the ground," Jarrod retorted, "and the Umbrians manufacture surprises daily." He was amazed at himself. Part of him was insisting on caution, but his dislike of Sumner was too strong.

"Be that as it may." Ragnor took control again. "There is nothing we can do about Fort Bandor. It's a military matter."

"Not entirely, Archmage."

"Begging the Queen's pardon?"

"We do not know as yet if bunglebirds reached the Empire, but, since the garrison was Umbrian, we must suppose so. It would be advantageous, however, if the Kingdoms, with the support of the Discipline, could effect the recapture. At the very least, in a matter of such magnitude, we should take part.'' Everyone sat back, and Naxania allowed herself a small smile.

''A very good point, my dear,'' Ragnor acknowledged.

''Fortunately,'' Naxania added. ''everybody needed to make the decision is here in Talisman. By happy coincidence, the Holdmaster of Gwyndryth is in this country to negotiate the loan of cloudsteed units to Paladine. He would seem to me to be an excellent choice to lead the expedition. He's a proven soldier, he's Arundelian, seconded to Paladine, and, should liaison with the Umbrians become necessary, he has better credentials than anyone. He is, after all, a hero to the Umbrians.''

''Are you sure that you can spare him?'' Arabella inquired sweetly.

''You are considerate, Cousin,'' Naxania replied, deadpan, ''but in an emergency like this, my country's need must come second.''

Jarrod's ear detected the insincerity of the exchange and it puzzled him.

''These matters had best be discussed with the Thane and the Commander, to say nothing of the good Holdmaster,'' the Archmage said firmly.

''But we already know what we want to do,'' Naxania protested.

''That is precisely when it is best to consult with people. If you know how to get in touch with Gwyndryth, I suggest that you do so. The rest of you, hold yourselves ready. Yes, Courtak.''

Jarrod had raised his hand. He swallowed. ''I know that this does not look good, but please bear in mind what I said. The revelation about the Outlanders might be the reason that the unicorns were sent to us. They may well be agents of conciliation."

"We'll keep it in mind, son," Ragnor said as he got to his feet. "Speaking personally, I'd as soon not trust the Outlanders. They've shown themselves capable of some nasty surprises of late. Now they've breached the Causeway somehow and taken a castle that's supposed to be impregnable. Doesn't sound like a gesture of conciliation to me." He paused and sniffed. "I'll be in touch with all of you later."

Chairs scraped, and Jarrod's first High Council meeting was over. He'd survived, but he hadn't made any converts. Ragnor, obviously, wasn't going to take their side. Well, he'd done his best. Marianna couldn't say he hadn't tried.

That night Jarrod was summoned once again. He knocked, and when there was no reply, he walked in confidently. Or at any rate as confidently as he could when he didn't know why the Archmage wanted to see him. He paused to let his eyes become accustomed to the gloom. The chair by the fire emerged. There was a bright corner of a comforter over the arm. He advanced.

"Good evening, Archmage. You sent for me?"

"What?" The slumped figure in the chair did not move.

"I said good evening, Sir."

"Oh. Oh, yes. Courtak. Yes, good of you to come." Ragnor struggled up and rearranged the comforter over his lap. "Get yourself some wine and pour me some. Pull up a chair. Might as well put a couple of logs on the fire while you're at it . . . Ah. Thank you . . . Yes, that's much better." He took a healthy swig of his wine and then hunched toward the fire. Jarrod sat himself down and waited.

Slowly, the head, skull-like in the firelight, came around and the eyes looked at him; into him.

"How are you feeling?"

"Well, I thank you, Sir."

"You are completely recovered from your, ah, travails at Stronta?"

"As far as I can tell, Sir."

"Good." The Archmage sipped from the horn cup that Jarrod had given him. "I have a job for you," he said.

Not again, Jarrod thought with a sinking feeling in the pit of his stomach. Haven't I done enough? He kept his thoughts to himself.

"You were at the meeting," Ragnor continued, "so you know what's going on. The Holdmaster of Gwyndryth will be taking charge of the expedition, unless I miss my guess. I think it would be a good idea if you went with him. You've had experience in mountain terrain, and you'll make an excellent representative of the Discipline."

"But," Jarrod began.

"No buts, I'm afraid. We need someone with power who's adaptable. Both Arabella and Naxania are needed by their countrymen; I'm too old; Sumner has to have time to settle into his new post; and Handrom will be running the Collegium. Our friend Greylock is unavailable.

"You, on the other hand, are young and strong, and you look as if you could hold your own with a sword. You've got the Thorden feller to handle the day-to-day business in Paladine and Naxania for the ceremonial part, should that become necessary. There really is no one else to whom I can entrust this sort of mission." Ragnor looked at the boy, confident that he had overwhelmed him.

"What about the unicorns?" Jarrod asked.

"Oh, I should imagine that the Gwnydryth girl is quite capable of looking after them."

Jarrod cast about for another excuse, but could find no way of escaping Ragnor's logic. It looked as if he were off into the unknown again. The old man probably expected him to perform miracles.

"When do I have to leave?" he asked.

"As soon as the expedition is ready. Speed is of the essence. No more than two days, I should think. The Talismanis will provide you with suitable clothing, and I'll help you with powders and simples."

"What will I have to do?"

"Haven't the slightest idea," Ragnor said cheerfully. "Weather control, I should imagine, and whatever else you can do to help the Holdmaster recapture the fort. You'll have to talk it over with him."

The boy would like to balk, but he doesn't dare, Ragnor thought. He's developing a mind of his own and that could be troublesome. I'll have to keep an eye on him and see that I make an ally of him. My knowledge and his power could make for a formidable combination.

"We must talk more about the Outlanders when you get back," he said. "You made some very interesting points this morning." Play him gently, he thought. "Funny how things work out, isn't it? If Ardoin hadn't died precisely when he did, we shouldn't all have been together when the news came. Now, if you have any questions, don't hesitate to come and see me. My door is always open to you."

"Yes, Sir. Thank you, Sir." Jarrod drank some of his wine and stood up.

"This is all coming very fast for you, isn't it?" Ragnor remarked cannily.

"I never seem to be in the same place for very long these days," Jarrod admitted.

"I'm sorry, lad. I should have preferred to bring you along more slowly, let you grow into your responsibilities, but the times dictate otherwise. However." He stopped and looked up, then held out his cup for a refill. "You'll do well, I know that, and the experience of acting on your own, Magically speaking, will be invaluable."

The voice followed Jarrod round the room as he put his

cup away and fetched the flagon. Easy for the old man to say, he thought as he poured the wine. He's not going to be out there. And with Marianna's father of all people.

"Anything else I can do, Sir?" he inquired.

"No, thank you, lad. You go and get a good night's sleep. I'll ring for the Duty Boy if I want anything. Come and see me tomorrow and we'll go through my spell chest. I take it wherever I go."

"Thank you, Sir. I'll be round in the morning."

"Good night, son, and don't worry, you'll do us proud."

Jarrod let himself out and made his way back to his room in a resentful frame of mind. Just that morning he'd explained why he thought that the Outlanders should be left alone, and now he was being sent off to fight them. Nothing in this whole mess made sense.

chapter 21

Darius was pacing. The Battle Room of Fortress Talisman was an unnerving place for the uninitiated. It jutted out over the plain, and the Upper Causeway hugged the mountainside below. He had never been in a room like this. The roof and walls of the front third were made out of panes of clear glass; imported from Umbria, no doubt. The web of leading that held them looked scarcely more substantial. It was not unlike being in the nose of an Umbrian rotifer. He did not care to stand there too long.

Very strange place, this Talisman, he thought. The people were quiet and practical, farmers mostly, rooted in family, fields, and livestock. Yet they were capable of building something like this and of devoting themselves to cloudsteeds and warcats. Their ancestors had been firebrands who preferred to tame an unpromising mountain range than live in vassalage, but the present day Talismanis were as slow to anger as they were to smile. And then there was that precious vote of theirs. He shook his head and circled the room again.

Strange people, he thought. Borr Sarad has been Thane for nigh on twenty years and performed right yarely, yet every six years he goes abegging, attending village meeting and defending his leadership. It was entirely unnatural. Imagine having to go around the Holding explaining oneself to the freeholders. A noise behind him broke his train of thought.

The Archmage, tall and stooped, strode into the room, hands clasped behind his back. He stopped and looked up. Darius felt the surprised stare as if it were a physical touch. Then the wrinkles began to deepen and Ragnor smiled. He showed his palms.

"My Lord of Gwyndryth, what a signal pleasure to see you again. I must confess that I did not recognize you. You have filled out nicely since I was your guest." Ragnor was all smooth graciousness as he moved forward. Darius automatically fell into step beside him as he headed toward the windows. "Had it not been for the Umbrian cut of your beard, I should probably still be at a loss."

"Your Excellency is kind to remember me."

Ragnor looked over to see if any irony was intended, but the man looked sincere. "Are you quite recovered from your wounds?" he asked.

"The rest of me is too old to say that anything is like new anymore," Darius said ruefully, "but I am fit enough to fight again. There are still twinges when the weather is damp."

"I know exactly how that is," Ragnor commiserated. He drew up and gazed at the abnormally distant horizon. "My trouble is that I was born too late. I should have been Archmage when things were based in the South. You must find it very difficult to leave that beautiful Holding of yours."

"It is a wrench," Darius admitted.

"And speaking of beautiful Southern sights, how's your daughter? I saw her at the services, but I haven't had an opportunity to talk with her."

"Then we are equals, Excellency. A mere father cannot compete with unicorns." The two men exchanged smiles.

"You have made considerable sacrifices for the good of

Strand and for the cause of Magic. On the other hand, your line has achieved an immortality that few can match."

"Yes, I am becoming enured to the fact that I shall be remembered, no matter what I do, as 'the father of the girl who found the unicorns.' "

"Oh, she's a credit to you, no doubt about that. Of course, by the time the songs are all written, she will have manifested miraculous prowess at a very young age, indications of the great things to come. Did you have any reason to think that she was unusual?"

"We used to say that she was better outdoors than indoors. She rode at a very early age and loved to visit different parts of the estate—expeditions she called them. Nothing exceptional, though."

"With her mother dead and you away so much of the time, she must have been alone quite a lot when she was growing up. Did she have a vivid imagination? So many children in those circumstances seem to develop them." The Archmage put the question casually.

"She was too busy hunting with the boys," Darius replied with a short laugh.

"Ah, now that will provide ample fodder for the fabulists. By the way, did Naxania tell you why we are having this meeting?"

"Bandor's fallen and an expedition has to be mounted to recapture it."

"Just so. Did she say anything about its composition?"

"I thought that was what we were here to decide."

"It is, indeed, and here come the rest of them now."

They turned, and Darius watched as the women entered with the Thane and the Commander of Fortress Talisman behind them, Darius's pulse quickened at the sight of Naxania, and he bowed low lest he give himself away. There were introductions and endless minutes of aimless conversation as pages set steaming tankards of cider around what was normally the planning table. The pages departed, but the pleasantries continued. They don't know what the protocol is, he thought.

"Borr, my old friend." The Archmage's voice cut across the buzz. "You are host here. Do you dispose of us according to your whim. The skeins of precedence are too tangled to admit of protocol." He backed up his words by moving to the table and standing behind a middle chair.

Borr Sarad ushered the ladies to chairs on either side of the head of the table, took the chief seat himself, and let the other two sit where they wanted. "We all know why we are here," he said after they were seated. "We have to decide what, if anything, we are to do about Bandor."

"It must be retaken immediately." Naxania's tone brooked no dissent, but she was not at home in Stronta.

"Granted, Majesty," the Fortress Commander said boldly. "The question is how?"

"Let us not forget," Sarad added, "that the garrison was Umbrian, paid for by the Isphardis. Apart from a few Songean tribes, the Isphardis are the only ones who are threatened. Why should we concern ourselves?"

"Oh, dear me, lots of reasons," Ragnor said, and took a pull at his cider. "I shan't give you a speech about the spirit of the Alliance, but if you'll permit me to don my temporal hat, I'll point out a couple of things. The Isphardis, as the Thane pointed out, have the most to lose. Let us not forget that the news came to us from Belengar. You may be certain that the city is in an uproar. Nothing stays secret in Belengar.

"The Oligarchs control most of the trade in the world. Just think how grateful they will be to the party that rescues them from peril and, more importantly, resecures the land routes. Would you rather they be even more beholden to the Empire than they are now? Or would you like to redress the balance in favor of our economies?"

Shrewd old man, Darius said to himself. Not one word about Magic.

"A point well taken, Archmage," Naxania said quickly. "I think we are agreed that our three countries should recapture the Fort."

I wonder what her game is? Darius thought. She's very determined about this.

"Easier said than done, Majesty." It was the Commander again.

"If your Excellencies permit?" Darius's voice rumbled out and brought silence. Wrong title, he thought. "The only way we can transport a sufficient force, fast enough, is by cloudsteed. By coincidence, Commander Yadan and I have just concluded an agreement whereby a full squadron will be made available to Paladine. The squadron is international in makeup, but it will be stationed at Stronta. They are ready to fly." Naxania smiled her approval and it warmed him more than the cider.

"How many men do you think it would take, General?" It was Sarad.

Darius felt easy, despite the company and the surroundings. This was his kind of discussion. "Surprise, mobility, flexibility—those are the keys. The attack will have to come from the South. The Fort's impregnable, or at least it was, from the North. Besides, if the enemy has decided to occupy instead of raze and retreat, they'll want to keep their lines of supply and communications open from the North. That'll make it hard for the Umbrians to get to the Fort. My best bet, however, would be that it was a hit-and-destroy raid."

"I don't think that we can afford to wager at this point." Ragnor said. "What I don't understand is what could have prompted the attack in the first place. And at such an impropable target. It makes no sense."

Something nagged at the back of Darius's mind, something to do with the windows. Then it came clear. ''There is one way that it might make sense, Excellency.''

Ragnor swiveled in his chair. ''Go on, my Lord.''

Darius stroked his beard while he put his thoughts in order. ''While I was in Umbria I saw their new flying machines, the same ones we all saw in your vision. I even went up in one. They can fly over the Other's atmosphere. If they set up forward depots of coal and water, and if they thought that the metal casing of the rotifer would protect them over the new Barrier Lands . . .'' He let the thought hang.

''So it could have been retaliation,'' the Thane concluded, ''but why Bandor?''

''I would have to guess that the Outlanders aren't prepared to take on the main Umbrian forces. Bandor is isolated. They wouldn't have to commit too much in the way of men and material. They obviously had the element of surprise going for them.''

''That's certain. I imagine the garrison Commander went into shock when he realized what was happening. A posting to Bandor is like taking a sabbatical. I wonder how the bastards, begging your Majesties' pardon, got over the Causeway.'

''Perhaps, my Lord Thane, they did not.'' Arabella spoke softly.

''I'm afraid I don't follow, Ma'am.''

''There was a part in that cloud of the future that we witnessed at Celador where the Upper Causeway was being attacked by slime and appeared to be crumbling. The Outlanders have used all the other new weapons that the vision revealed.'' There was an uneasy silence when she finished.

Commander Yadan broke it. ''All the more reason to go and take a looksee. How many 'steeds do you reckon, General?''

"Two Wings," Darius said. "If we can recruit any of the Central Range clans, so much the better."

"Are we agreed, then?" Naxania asked.

"It would seem so, my dear," Ragnor answered her. "There is, however, one suggestion that I should like to make. I think it is important that the Discipline be represented in this undertaking." He looked blandly around at the suddenly guarded faces of the men. "Well"—he was all innocence—"the weather in Songuard is uncontrolled, and cloudsteeds are more constrained by weather conditions that most creatures . . ."

"I don't suppose that you have anyone in mind, Excellence?" The Thane of Talisman was bleakly humorous.

"As a matter of fact I have an excellent candidate," Ragnor said, beaming around, letting them all in on the joke and allowing them to make him the butt. "A young man who knows the mountains of Songuard at first hand, is a considerable Magician, and has proved that he can withstand adverse circumstances."

"And the name of this paragon?" the Thane asked.

"Jarrod Courtak. He's the Acting Mage of Paladine. He handled the Candles of Remembrance."

"The one with the unicorns?" The question came from Commander Yadan.

"That's the one," Ragnor agreed.

"Bandor's that important to you then?" The Talismani's eyes were bright and knowing.

"To us all, Fortress Commander; to us all."

"Well now, that seems to be it," Borr Sarad said from his seat at the head of the table.

"Not quite, I think," Arabella said, abandoning the royal "we" for the first time in Darius's hearing. "There is still the matter of the man to lead the expedition."

"Your Forgiveness, Ma'am"—Sarad was deferential—"but I had thought that that was a foregone conclusion.

Speed and, I assume, secrecy are vital, so we have no time to go searching. The Cloud Wings are coming from here and the Magician is Paladinian, so I presumed that the leader would be an Arundelian. Since we have such a man here, a man, moreover, who knows more about the Umbrians than any of us, I assumed that my Lord of Gwyndryth''—he made a gesture in Darius's direction—''would be going.'' He gave the Holdmaster a crooked little smile. So that's the way the wind's blowing, Darius thought. I should have guessed.

''A capital choice,'' Ragnor said before Darius had a chance to open his mouth. ''That's settled then.'' He rubbed his hands together.

The very picture of the benign partriarch, Darius thought. He's much too pleased with himself. I wonder what the old rogue's up to.

''Dear Ladies,'' Ragnor continued, pushing back from the table and getting stiffly to his feet. ''I suggest that we leave the military men to work out the details. I'll brief the Acting Mage of Paladine.''

Naxania and Arabella followed his lead and the three soldiers rose and bowed. This is rich, Darius thought, as he watched Naxania leave. I came to this meeting more to get a sight of her than anything else, and now I'm committed to go off and leave her for who knows how long. Gods, but things move fast at this level. One, two, three, and off he goes. It had obviously been decided beforehand. He wondered if she had made any effort to keep him during the backstage maneuvering.

He saw her again at Hall that night, but he was seated a long way down the table. He was in the same withdrawing room with her after the meal, but she gave no indication that she wanted to speak to him. He resigned himself to an early bed and retired to his room. He was finishing his nightcap, feeling sorry for himself, when the summons came.

"Did her Majesty say what she wanted to see me about?" he asked the lady-in-waiting, willing her to walk faster.

"No, my Lord. All she said was, 'Letty, my compliments to the General, and he's to present himself forthwith.' "

"Is her Majesty in a good mood tonight, Lady Greenly?"

"La, Sir." Blond ringlets bounced as she turned a pert face to him. "What a question. Her Majesty is renowned for the sweetness of her nature and the eveness of her temperament. How, then, should she be otherwise than in a good humor?" The corners of the mouth, a very attractive mouth Darius thought, compressed and threatened to move up.

"How, indeed?" he said. The little minx, he thought, if she had a fan in her hand, she'd be flirting.

The young woman stood aside and ushered him into the Queen's antechamber. She gestured for him to remain and disappeared through another door. She was back quickly and led him into the sitting room. Naxania was standing by the fire in what looked like a quilted dressing gown, holding her hands to the blaze. She turned.

"General Gwyndryth, your Majesty," Lady Greenly said, and sank into a curtsy. Naxania caught Darius's eye and he bowed forthwith.

"Thank you for attending us so promptly, my Lord. Letty, you may go."

They watched as the lady-in-waiting backed from the presence, and waited for the door to close. She was in his arms as the latch clicked and her mouth was demanding. They held the kiss and then he pushed her gently away.

"Gods, but it's been a long time."

"Only a sennight, impatient man." She moved back into his embrace. They complcted the kiss and it was she who moved away. "Get yourself some wine and come and sit down before I forget what it is that I want to say." He obeyed and joined her by the fire.

"Sit over there," she said.

"You could always sit on my knee, or, better yet, we could lie down together on the rug."

"You've the mind of a bolting stallion. Now sit down and behave. We'll be leaving tomorrow and you can ride back with us."

Darius eased himself into the chair and took a sip of the wine. "Oh, I think not, my love." he said carefully.

"Really?" It was a warning more than a question.

"The expedition will be leaving from here, and since you were all kind enough to volunteer me, I shall leave with it."

"Surely they could fly to Stronta and you could join them there?"

"I'm afraid not. There isn't time for dalliance."

She pouted. "You sound angry with me."

"Well, you seemed happy enough to have me go off and fight again."

"It's the best possible thing that could happen," she said.

"I think you're going to have to explain that to me." There was a dangerous rumble to his delivery that sent a quick thrill through her belly.

She leaned back and shook her hair. "It's quite simple. Neither of us likes the constraints on our meetings. As matters stand, I cannot change them. If I kept you close by me at Stronta, it would cause resentment. You are a newcomer to Court and you are a foreigner. You may be a hero in your own country, but you are scarcely known in mine. You will, however, be going to Bandor as a Paladinian General. You told me that my subjects have a need for heros. When you return in triumph, you will be a national hero. What could be more natural than for the Queen to look to you for advice? It will also make your work with my army a great deal easier." She smiled with satisfaction.

"You are amazing," he said with some asperity. "You had this all worked out in advance, didn't you?"

She grinned at him. "I also have an excellent reason now for bringing your friend Otorin onto the staff. He will be reporting to Stronta in a fortnight. Who else is there who knows of your advances in cavalry tactics? I arranged it with Arabella while the three of you were discussing strategy, or whatever it was that you did after we left."

He laughed and got up and crossed over to her. He bent down and kissed her. "I don't know what I'm going to do with you," he said.

"You could show me your gratitude."

"You've seen it before, but it's more than ready to demonstrate again."

"Then let us not keep it waiting," she said, and rose from the chair. She took his hand and led him toward the bedchamber. "We must make use of what little time we have."

How easy men are to manipulate, she thought as she placed his arm around her waist and smiled up at him. How beautiful she is, and how sensual, he thought as he moved his hand toward her breast.

The lovemaking was urgent and hungry the first time, and slow and languid the second. The fire had burned low by the time they were spent. Naxania lay in the crook of Darius's heavily muscled sword arm, eyes closed, smiling contentedly. "You know what the best part of that is for me?" she asked.

"I wouldn't dare to guess," he replied sleepily.

"While it's happening, I can't think of anything but us and our bodies."

"What sort of things don't you want to think about?" he asked lazily, more to humor her than out of curiosity.

"Oh, your daughter, for instance."

"I should hope not; not then."

"You know perfectly well what I mean. She's a clever little thing. We may be able to keep this from the Court, but you won't be able to fool her. I think she suspects already."

"I certainly haven't said anything to her, and we waited until after she left Gwyndryth."

"You wouldn't have to say anything. If what you've told me is true, I'm the first woman you have taken a serious interest in since your wife died."

"Of course it's true," Darius protested with more vehemence than accuracy.

"Exactly. She's had you all to herself for as long as she can remember. Now she's afraid she's going to lose you. Daughters don't take kindly to their father's mistresses. That knowledge comes firsthand." She gave a little bark of mirthless laughter and shifted her position slightly.

"If she's anything like I was, she'll try to make you feel that you're defiling her mother's memory. I tried it on my father and at first I thought it worked. I became a past master of the wounded look, and the women never lasted long. When I got a little older I realized that I had nothing to do with it. He just got bored with them. I hated him then and I was glad that my mother had died when she did."

Darius felt her body stiffen during the recital. Poor darling, he thought, she's still bitter.

"It makes me wonder about that story of hers," Naxania said, switching directions.

"What story is that?"

"Your daughter's story about the Outlanders."

"You think Marianna made it up to punish me?" he asked, and reached behind him to adjust the bolster.

"It would be a very shrewd double blow. She puts you, as a soldier anyway, in the wrong morally, and if she turns out to be right about the motive behind the Outlanders' pullback, there goes your principal occupation. It has been her only successful rival, and without it you would spend your time with her at Gwyndryth. Mind you, I don't expect she sees it quite that way."

"It's an ingenious theory, my darling, but there is one flaw in your logic. She couldn't have invented it. The unicorns back her up."

"And how can we be sure of that?"

"She got it directly from the big one."

"So she says. Unfortunately, the only one who can verify that is our young Acting Mage, and the two of them are as close as cutpurses. Do you really think that he would give her the lie?"

"I don't know. I don't know the boy that well."

"I do." Her inflection was enigmatic. "Has it ever occurred to you that she may be telling the truth, but that the unicorn lied to her?"

"Naxania!"

"Oh, stop it." She sat up in the big bed and pulled the sheet up. "Everybody falls over themselves at the thought of the unicorns, but what do we really know about them? All we have to go on is the assertions of children."

"You're not much older than they are, my love," he remonstrated gently.

"Maybe not chronologically, but in every other respect they are puling infants."

He smiled tolerantly at her and stroked her hair. "You were the one who foretold the whole thing," he reminded her. "Surely the unicorns are here for our benefit. They were, after all, summoned by Magic."

"That's just it, nobody summoned them. That verse came out of nowhere. I certainly didn't ask for it. Everybody assumes that because the verse was forced on me in the middle of a High Council meeting, it is a blessed revelation. All I can tell you is that it was extremely unpleasant to be taken over and used like that."

"I can understand that, but they have been a blessing, haven't they?"

"Have they? What exactly have they done for us since they first appeared?"

"They probably saved Stronta."

"They probably killed my father," she retorted. The long black hair swung down like a curtain between them.

Darius sighed inwardly. He had been looking forward to this reunion. Here they were, naked and in bed, and they were arguing about unicorns.

"They didn't do too good a job of protecting the Place of Power, did they?" She pressed her point.

"From all reports, they did all they could to help us," he said placatingly.

"Who knows." She was not mollified. "They could be another of the enemy's new weapons."

"Oh, come now; that's going too far. You've seen them. You've been up close. You really can't think that the Outlanders could create anything that extraordinary."

"We don't know what the Outlanders are capable of. How can we be? Before you saw the Archmage's vision, would you have believed that they could attack us without air hoses? How about the death boxes and the wall of fire?"

"Those are mechanical inventions; the unicorns are flesh and blood."

"I don't know," she said tiredly, abandoning the argument. "I don't know what to think anymore. There are times when I envy your daughter and Jarrod Courtak the simplicity of their idealism. They believe that the rest of the world would think the way they do if only they could be made to understand the truth.

"The truth! Poor ninnies. Whose truth? If they could see things from the top, as I do now, they'd realize that anything important comes trailing lots of different truths and several kinds of justice." She pushed her hair back.

"Poor darling," Darius said, admiring the sway of her breasts, "being Queen isn't much fun, is it?"

"It's a lot of hard work," she admitted, shifting position and leaning against him. "I never realized how much there was to do, how many important decisions to make. Everyone expects me to be an expert on everything.

"Oh, Darius, it's such a big country. There's no way I can keep it all in my head. Too much goes on: things change so quickly. I can't keep up." She looked down at him and there were tears in her eyes.

He surged up protectively and held her. "So many problems," he said into her hair. She nestled against him. "You know I'll always be there to help you. I run my Holding well and I've had charge of a regiment that I'm proud of for a dozen years. I know that's nothing when compared to a kingdom, but I could be of some use." He held her away and looked at her with serious eyes. "Half the battle is knowing that you can't do everything yourself. The other half is delegating responsibility to people you can trust. If they are competent, so much the better.

"Once you've picked them, watch them like a raptor. Circle above them so that they are aware of your shadow. If you're satisfied with them, be sure you keep them." The eyes lost their intensity, and he pulled her back into a tender hug.

"So wise; so strong," she said into his shoulder. "You

I shall keep.'' She tightened her arms for a long beat and then leaned back. ''But not tonight. It would not be seemly, nor would it be politic, for you to be seen leaving my chambers at a compromising hour.''

Darius groaned. ''There are distinct disadvantages to being in love with a Queen, especially one as beautiful as you.''

''Why,'' she asked with a return to good humor, ''do I believe you when I automatically suspect everyone else?''

''Because''—he flipped backed the sheet and swung his legs off the mattress—''my intentions are nakedly dishonorable.''

chapter 22

Jarrod stood in front of the long panel of polished tin and tugged at the cloudsteedsman's uniform they had given him to wear. He felt warm in the quilted jacket and found the tight-closing collar awkward. Other than that, it was a fairly good fit. At least it makes me look less thin, he thought as he started to unhook the front. He stared at himself, long legs apart, jacket open, hands on hips. It was rare to find a mirror in which he could see all of himself. A thirty-year-old man stared back at him. Every inch the dashing warrior, he thought cynically.

He ran a hand through the curly hair. No gray left, he noted thankfully. He turned his head from one side to the other. When he was this thin, his nose looked far too big.

"Gods, but I look old," he said aloud. "The only women who would be interested in you are old enough to be your mother." A Talented girl might understand, he thought, but there seemed to be so few of them. He cocked his head to the side and made a face at himself.

I look mature enough for Marianna, but it doesn't make any difference. She really doesn't see me anymore. She still thinks I'm the boy I was when we met. Oh, what's the use? She's never going to fall in love with me.

He was still staring at the mirror, but he was no longer aware of his image. How old am I going to look after the next time? he wondered. How long before the string breaks and the ball doesn't return to the cup? He reached up and touched his face, focusing on the looking glass once more. Perhaps he wouldn't have to perform any Magic at Bandor. Everybody seemed to think that the Others would be gone by the time they got there. Or they'd be dead; they couldn't last forever in those suits. He nodded and his reflection copied him.

He turned away and began taking the uniform off. His mind ran on. For someone who hadn't known many girls until recently, he had certainly come into contact with a remarkable range of women lately. Princesses, a royal mistress, Marianna, of course, and then there was the little whore in Belengar. He remembered the tiny room with the big bed and the girl with the long hair. She was even younger than he was. He smiled and folded the clothes up carefully, so they would keep their creases.

He remembered having to prove that he was a Magician by taking off her clothes without touching her, and he recalled the roundness of her eyes while he did it. It was the first time he had ever seen a female naked, though he pretended that it wasn't, and, amazingly, she hadn't minded that he wasn't allowed to have sex. He'd go back and find her one day, after this Bandor business was over. No, he reminded himself, not while the unicorns were here. Time to go to the stables and time to put the girl from Belengar out of his mind. It wouldn't do to face Nastrus in this condition.

He managed to banish the girl, but his underlying frustrations were still there when he strolled through the gate of Stable Court. They were swamped by the surge of affection that greeted him. The colts were eager for exercise. Their dam had already been taken out by Marianna, and they were impatient. He couldn't blame Marianna for starting off without him, but he was disappointed nevertheless. He began to saddle up Beldun.

'Your urge to procreate is quite understandable,' Nastrus remarked in his inner ear. *'However, when it comes into contact with the Marianna female, it become unintelligible.'* There was agreement from the other two.

'Don't ask me to explain,' Jarrod replied ungraciously. He put a knee against Beldun's belly and cinched the girth strap. He adjusted the stirrups and then swung up. *'It would be difficult enough without you, but with you here, it becomes impossible.'*

'I cannot follow your logic,' Pellia complained.

'There is no logic, I'm in love.' His humor was Wintery.

'This is a concept we do not have,' she said, puzzled.

'You're very lucky. I'd be better off without it, too.'

'What has this to do with us?' Nastrus inquired.

'As long as you and your mother stay on Strand, I can't—what was your term?—procreate.'

'Ah, and it's your rutting season,' Beldun concluded before Jarrod could finish the thought.

'Why must you refrain from rut because of us?' Nastrus asked half a beat behind his brother.

'Because the only people you are supposed to trust are virgins.'

'Not true.' Beldun. *'Ridiculous.'* Nastrus. *'Only in the case of an unmounted human female,'* from Pellia.

'One at a time, please,' Jarrod thought out firmly. *'Now, let me see if I understand this. You don't care whether I'm a virgin or not?'* Amusement filled his mind.

'The only human we have ever run away from is you, and you have been at pains to refrain from mating,' Beldun remarked as if it had been obvious.

'Then why does Marianna have this special bond with your mother—right from the beginning?'

'Because she is unmounted,' Beldun explained patiently.

'Ever since there were unicorns,' Pellia elaborated,

'there has been the duty to protect unmounted human females. Once she has mated there is a human male to protect her, so she has no further need of us.'

'How can you tell the difference?' Jarrod asked, and waved to a group that had stopped to watch the unicorns. He tried on a smile, but it felt artificial.

'You smell different. Didn't you know?' Nastrus was genuinely surprised.

'We smell different?' So was Jarrod.

'You do to us,' Beldun confirmed.

'Before is more pleasant than after,' Pellia added. *'It is one of the reasons we prefer—what was your word?—virgins?'*

'I see. So it really doesn't matter.' He startled the bystanders by throwing his head back and roaring with laughter. He urged Beldun into a trot and went chuckling down the broad avenue toward the gate. Then he stopped laughing as a thought struck him.

'What about Marianna?' he asked. *'Will she lose the ability to talk to your mother after she . . . if she . . . ?'*

'There is nothing in the Memory,' Nastrus reported. *'None of our line has ever shared thoughts with humans before. Our family is the very first.'* There was evident pride in the statement and Jarrod was grinning again as they passed under the gateway.

Beldun broke into a canter down the straight road South. His ideograph said clearly, *'If you do what is in your mind to do, and Marianna does not, she will be very angry with you. I know that is not logical, but, from my observation, it is very human.'* The others agreed. Jarrod felt himself blushing and clapped his heels to Beldun's flanks. He surrendered to the sensations of the gallop.

His new knowledge made his next meeting with Marianna even more difficult than it would have been. She came storming into his room. Her eyes were gray-green and snapping.

"How did you wangle your way into this one?" she demanded.

"Wangle my way into what? What are you so angry about?" He was on the defensive already.

"Don't try to play the innocent with me. There's an expedition to Fort Bandor, I'm told. You are going, I'm told, and I am to trot quietly back to Stronta with the unicorns. That's what I mean."

"I didn't have anything to do with it," Jarrod protested. "Ragnor just ordered me to go. I don't even know what I'm supposed to do when we get there."

"Why you? Why does it always have to be you?" she yelled. "I know as much about Songuard as you do and I'm a damned sight better in the wild than you are."

"The unicorns can't go," Jarrod said weakly. "There's nothing about Bandor in the Memory. Someone has to look after them."

"Old Lazla will do it beautifully."

"Yes, but they have to get back to Stronta. Besides, we are the only two people in the world who can talk to them. They couldn't risk both of us. Don't you see?"

"They wouldn't have to risk both of us. Why don't you stay home and look after them?"

"It could be very danger—"

"Don't you dare start with that." She cut him off.

"They need a Magician," he said patiently. He hated it when she was in this kind of mood.

"Oh, that again." Her disgust was plain. "You and your precious Magic. That's always your excuse. You just won't admit, will you, that they'd rather trust a callow boy than send a woman. You're all the same, you know that? It makes me so angry!" She glared at him. "Oh, what's the use?" She threw up her hands, gave him a final glare, and swung on her heel and stalked out. She slammed the door.

Jarrod was shaken, but his nascent resentment at the unfairness of the attack had been undercut by the glimpse of tears in her eyes when she turned. He went and sat on the bed and put his head in his hands. Why does it always have to end like this? he wondered. I hoped she would wish me well, might even miss me while I was gone. Instead, everything's my fault.

He sat, brooding. Nothing he ever did was right with her. She was never satisfied. She was already famous for having discovered the unicorns, but that wasn't enough. And it wasn't as if he wanted to go on this bloody expedition. Nothing was going right. Why, of all people, did her father have to be the leader? On the other hand, his mind ran on, she and her father were very close. If he managed to make a good impression on Lord Darius . . . There he went again, making plans.

He was still upset when he went to take the colts out for exercise. He expected to be ragged about it, but they were surprisingly sympathetic.

'You are not the one she is angry at,' Pellia advised him. *'Mam says that she is unhappy because the males in her life are going off to war and leaving her behind.'*

'Poor Marianna,' Jarrod thought back sarcastically, *'she has to stay in Stronta with you, while I have to go off into the back of nowhere and fight Outlanders.'*

'Pay him no mind,' Nastrus told his sister, *'it's probably a rutting effect.'*

'Are we going to stand here all day, or are we going to gallop?' Beldun interposed. *'A gallop is good for ill humors.'*

Jarrod shook his head and went to get his saddle.

'Do humans pine for their females when they are separated?' Nastrus asked as they were riding out.

'I wouldn't know, I've never had a female. Why do you ask?'

'Curiosity. Rutting and emotion have nothing in common for us, but they seem to with you. Dams and their offspring are linked, but sires and dams are not.'

'Your way is probably better,' Jarrod thought.

The next couple of days did little to improve Jarrod's disposition. There were instructions and meetings with other members of the expedition. There were farewells and a new uniform to try on. There was too little time and too many new people. He found Wing Commander Oster Dahn, Darius's second-in-command, daunting. On the morning of the third day he found himself, Staff in hand, peering anxiously through the linklight-broken dark at a confusion of preparations. Three pages stood behind him relaxing gratefully, the baggage they were carrying scattered at their feet. Jarrod was wondering what to do next when Dahn materialized at his side.

The man was so bowlegged that he walked with a slight roll. He wasn't very tall and he had the kind of face in which a smile would be an aberration. Despite his size, he exuded authority.

"Morning, Excellency. I trust you slept well." He spoke in Common, but his Arundelian accent gave it flavor.

Jarrod was nervous. "Vigils of preparation and purification are rarely restful, Commander," he said, trying to establish his own authority.

Dahn was unimpressed. "Oh, you shouldn't have gone to all that trouble, Excellency. The flight there will be quite routine. So that's the famous Staff, is it? I'd heard that it was big, but I underestimated the size. Never mind, there'll be no problem stowing it. It'll go where the lances usually do; just over the right wing. Do you want to strap it on or should we do it?"

"Your people would be much better at doing that than I," Jarrod answered, "but I think that I should be the one to approach the cloudsteed with it."

"I couldn't agree more. In fact, I'd not have it any other way. We've picked a good, steady mare for you. She's over there." He gestured into the darkness.

The boys picked up the luggage reluctantly and followed the Mage. He'd been a bit of a disappointment to them. He didn't look like a Mage, just like a very tall 'steedsman. The Staff was big all right, but it didn't do anything. At the very least, it ought to have glowed in the dark. The whole thing was a colossal letdown not worth losing the sleep over.

Jarrod walked slowly in the direction Dahn had indicated, and the Staff clinked on the frosty ground as if it were iron-shod. The shape of the cloudmare loomed up. All eyes were on her as the party approached, but she stood there, solid and unmoving. Jarrod reached her and stopped. White clouds of breath hung in the air; twin jets of steam came from the animal's nostrils. The Staff moved out gently and came to rest against the broad flank, but she paid it no mind.

The tableau broke and there was a scurry of activity as the Staff and the luggage were positioned and strapped down.

"Ever ridden one of these?" Dahn inquired as the helpers withdrew.

"I've ridden horses and unicorns, but I've never been aloft," Jarrod admitted.

"The principle's the same. The stirrups work a little differently and the saddle's a damned sight more comfortable. You don't use the stirrup to get astride. You either use a mounting block or the rope ladder attached to the saddle. When you're installed you haul it up and secure it.

"Now, see that loop up there?" He pointed. "You put your whole leg through there. Same for the other leg on the other side. They hold your thighs parallel. There's a thong as goes up to that ring binder on the saddle. See it?" Jarrod nodded. "Then it comes down again to the stirrup iron, right? You put the balls of your feet on the bars and clamp the boots tight. There's a small wheel on the outside. You turn it toward you to tighten and away to release. Clear?" Jarrod nodded again.

"Good. That gets you set in the saddle. It cups you so there's no danger of your falling off. If you want to lean forward of the wings, you knock the saddlebow outward with the heel of your hand. It's hinged, though you can't see that from here." He gave Jarrod's arm a reasuring pat.

"That's important to remember," he continued. "You can't stand up in the saddle half a mile up the way you can down here. If there's any kind of gap between you and the saddle, the wind will simply pluck you off and have you hanging by the bootsoles. If you want to stand, you stamp down on both stirrups at once—a good, hard stamp, mind. The ring binders open and the extra loops come down and lengthen the stirrups. That gives you more thrust and stability and keeps you firmly in the saddle. A lot of flyers ride at full extend all the time. Like me to run through that again?"

"Thank you, but that won't be necessary. I couldn't forget if I wanted." He hadn't meant to, but he knew he sounded irritable. "I'm sorry," he said, "I didn't mean to snap. I'm just nervous."

"Be something wrong with you if you weren't. I was sure I was going to vomit on my maiden flight, but it goes away as soon as you're up there. Once you're properly astride there's nothing more you need do. Dapple, that's her name by the way, will do everything else. She's one of the best we've got. Been with us a long time."

"D'you want me to climb up there?"

"Yes, please, Excellency, but I'd put on the helmet and the gloves first. You'll be wearing them all the time that you are aloft."

Jarrod took the proffered leather hood and turned it round in his hands. It looked sinister in the erratic light. He slipped it over his head and pulled the skirt down over the collar of his uniform. There were eyeholes that mewed in the corners of his vision. There were two slits for the nose and a thin gash for the mouth. Breathing was easy.

"Comfortable?" There was little muffling of the voice.

"Fits nicely," Jarrod replied as he pulled on the gloves.

"You won't even know you're wearing it after a while. You ready?"

"Not really, but I've no good reason to delay."

"Up you go, then. I'll come up behind you and get you settled in."

Jarrod went through the routine faultlessly and without reminders. "Anything else I should know?" he asked when he was sitting comfortably.

"Ever done any jumping?"

"A couple of times out hunting. Nothing voluntary."

"You sit into the takeoff and back on landing, same as you would with a horse. You lean into the climb and sit back on descent. That's all there is to it. All set?"

"Yes, thank you, and thank you for showing me what to do."

"You'll do just fine. I'll see you after we land."

"I shall look forward to that, Wing Commander."

Dahn climbed down and Jarrod found himself with nothing to do but wait. The light had come quickly and now the horizon was aflame. What would the Songeans make of that as a portent? he wondered. The scene blurred and for an instant the wall of fire was bearing down on him again. He shook his head to clear it and the clouds came back. He reached down and patted the Staff with his gloved hand.

The shapes ahead were black against the dawn. Cloud-steeds stood patiently while their riders checked buckles and gear. His view to either side was partially blinkered by the upthrust triangles of Dapple's folded wings. He twisted in the saddle. There was one last line of 'steeds behind them. Better take stock of the equipment while there's still time, he thought.

The squared-off pommel rose comfortingly to mid-torso, cradling him in tooled leather. The saddleback was curved at the sides and came up to just below the shoulder blades. Dahn had been right about how it felt. He leaned back appreciatively and looked over his shoulder. The three bags that had given the pages so much trouble looked inconsequential on the massive back.

He was aware of no signal, but the comfortable bulk beneath him moved and, within paces, was into a trot. Jarrod resisted the urge to post. If one of the stirrups lengthened now, he'd never be able to get it back up again in time. He clamped his knees in and his stomach clenched as well. His mount quickened her pace, and the whoosh and snap of the wings unfurling startled him.

The spotted shoulders heaved in front of him as if they were being driven by the ground. The long wings curved up and pulled back down. Jarrod could feel the immense strength bracketed between his thighs, and fear was transformed into excitement. He loosened his grip on the reins. He leaned forward into the wind and peered through the whipping gray mane. It was as exhilarating as hunting, though it could not compare to a gallop with the colts.

The forward 'steeds started to rise, line after line of them, and then the one directly in front of them was off the ground. He saw cinder trees at the end of the field. He was poised for the lift-off, every muscle tense, but the steady, old girl they had given him kept pounding along. He glanced hastily left and right. Empty.

The trees were close now. She wasn't going to make it, and there was no way that he could pull her up in time. His maiden flight was going to end in ignominy or injury, or both. He was yelling. In what he knew was a gallant and futile effort, the cloudmare gathered herself and leaped. His body surged against the pommel and he was briefly terrified that it would give. It held.

His eyes took in the pewter flutter of underleaves in an updraft. They were miraculously clear. He pushed himself back with his elbows and forced himself to unclench his hands as the cloudmare took them upward in a wide, circling climb. She came out of it in exact position and headed into the rising sun with the rest of the flight. Jarrod let out a long breath.

He settled into the saddle and went through his body, muscle by muscle, willing himself to relax. He became aware of the silence. The saddle creaked occasionally, but that was all. It was strangely pure. He felt as if all his problems and frustrations had been left behind, down there with the toy trees and the kerchief-sized fields. Up here he was an anonymous member of an elite group. Both adjectives pleased him. He leaned down and ran a hand affectionately over the rippling skin as the wings swept on relentlessly.

chapter 23

They had been flying for a goodly number of days and this was the best part of the expedition as far as Darius was concerned. He set himself to enjoy it. The mere fact of sailing through the skies without effort was just as thrilling as it had been at Angorn and the scenery unspooling beneath him far more interesting. The fuzz of the first green shoots was about as far from the brown boil of the Outland atmosphere as you could get.

He had no responsibilities up here. Even if he fell asleep in the saddle, it wouldn't make any difference. The big, white cloudstallion he was riding needed no help from him. He breathed deeply, feeling the bite of the cold air in his mouth. His mind, free to wander, took him back to Fortress Talisman and Naxania.

She of the long, black hair and the long, white limbs; a wonderful contradiction of a girl, though there was nothing girlish about her mind or her performance between the sheets. He moved on to their last meeting. She had been especially passionate and more than usually demanding. She lay afterward with her head on his shoulder, hair spreading down and covering his belly.

"I shall certainly miss this," she said, rubbing her cheek against him.

"You don't have to send me away."

"Of course I do. Everything is set."

"Send someone else. It's liable to be a waste of effort anyway. They'll have put the fort out of commission and gone home. It'll probably be a cleanup and burial detail at best."

"If they keep it, they have a perfect base from which to attack Isphardel," she countered.

"No they don't. It's too far away. It would secure a vital supply route if they launched a major offensive in the region, but that's about it."

"It comes to the same thing. Do you realize what this has done to trade already? The Oligarchs are paralyzed. Nothing is happening in Belengar. Merchants are too busy moving their families and their capital out of the country to be bothered with letters of marque and bills of lading. I have reports that our wool trade is at a standstill. It couldn't come at a worse time. I need to raise taxes to reequip the armed forces. It really is most inconvenient."

"I hadn't thought of it in those terms, but I still don't see why you don't leave it to the Umbrians. I doubt that Varodias will think well of this. Besides, they are far better equipped to mount a siege, if it comes to that."

"Mechanical devices are limited," she pointed out. "They break down in bad weather. There's no weather control there and Winter lasts clear through Greeningale. Besides, I need you to come back a hero."

"Oh, so I'm not good enough as I am, is that it?" he grumbled sleepily.

"You just proved yourself more than worthy," she said, and tweaked his beard, "but the Court will be somewhat harder to convince."

"We're not back to that again, are we?" Darius rolled away from her and lumbered out of bed to douse his face. "I have men to lead. I can't be thinking about being a hero."

"Just retake the fort. Leave the rest to me. Your being

a foreigner will become an advantage,'' she said, following him out of the bed, ''and,'' she added, taking advantage of the fact that his face was swathed in a towel to pluck a white hair from his chest, ''your age will serve their vanity as proof that there can be nothing between us. Poor, shallow fools, what do they know of real men?''

He captured her hands and drew her in for a kiss. ''I'll come back,'' he said when it was done, ''and, hero or not, I'll do my best to put your army back into fighting shape. I love you dearly, but I am not suited to a life of intrigue. I'll not skulk in corridors. It's not my style.''

''Of course you shan't, my darling.'' She pressed herself against him. ''It's just that if you came back a hero, my obvious admiration of you would seem natural.''

''If you don't stop moving like that, my admiration will become obvious.''

Darius smiled to himself beneath his flying helmet. It had ended up being a sweet leave-taking. And he still had to come back a hero. The cloudsteed banked into a turn and brought Darius back to the present. There were mountains ahead and a river running North toward the Causeways. The Assaras, white to the shoulders, and the Jodderon River with a thin, dark line of moving water between its icebound banks.

The cloudstallion was gaining altitude over the foothills. Other 'steeds were circling up around them. Down below, fields, bare terraces, and the filigree of Winter woodlands replaced each other as they swung. The white 'steed leveled off below the peaks and stroked Eastward toward Umbria.

The air was still in the lee of the mountains, and the crags and ravines stood out clearly. Fireblanket trees were splashes of crimson against the snow. He was close enough to make out the spoor of some large animal that had floundered its way across a scarp. He felt elated with an underlying thread of caution. It was a good feeling; the way he felt when he was riding into battle.

The thought was no sooner in his mind than the problems were back. If the Others were still at Bandor, what in creation was he going to do? There hadn't been a siege since the first year of Robarth Strongsword's reign. It was a problem he'd never had to face. As far as Darius knew, the only sure ways of taking a well-fortified castle were by treachery or starvation. Neither option would be open to him at Bandor.

The way he saw it, he had only two things going for him. One was surprise and the other was Magic, and he had no idea what kinds of Magic the Courtak boy—the Acting Mage, he amended—could perform. He'd have to have a talk with him. He'd put it off too long as it was. Truth was that he was uneasy around the boy. He looked over his shoulder to see if he could spot the young Magician, but he was too far back in the formation.

The double Wing came in to land, as the sun dipped toward the horizon behind them, and trotted to a halt. The cloudsteeds stood and relaxed while the riders went about the task of setting up the camp. When they had cooled off they were taken to the picket line and rubbed down, then they were watered and after that they were fed. The daymoon had the sky to himself by the time the 'steeds were blanketed, and only then did the men turn toward their own comforts.

Jarrod found himself standing behind Darius in the food line. The long leagues in the sky had given him ample opportunity for thinking, and he had come up with some ideas. This was his opportunity to talk to the man. He hesitated and then tapped the Holdmaster on the shoulder.

"D'you think I could have a word with you after supper?" he asked.

"Certainly, Excellency," Darius replied. "As a matter

of fact, I'd been meaning to talk to you. Is anything wrong?''

''No, no, nothing's wrong,'' Jarrod said hastily. He was nervous. ''It's just that we'll be getting to the Gorodontion Mountains in a couple of days, and after that the weather will be uncontrolled and we might not have the time.''

''Let's eat together. No need to wait until after supper to talk.''

'Willingly, Sir, though I must confess that at the moment, I'm more interested in food than talk.'' There, he thought, that sounded better. ''I lost my lunch,'' he added by way of explanation.

''You get 'steedsick?''

''Oh, no. I love it up there. It's just that I was about to sink my teeth into the bread and cheese when we hit one of those empty spots. My mare went down, my stomach went up, and I don't know where the bread and cheese went.''

''Unnerving when that happens, isn't it?'' Darius commiserated, and held out his plate for food.

They collected mugs of chai and found themselves a spot by the fire. They ate in silence, neither one willing to start the conversation. Finally Darius looked up and said, ''We'll have to do some hunting when we get to Bandor. I'm getting tired of dried meat and boiled marioc, and my teeth could do with a rest.''

''I didn't bring a bow with me,'' Jarrod said, ''but if I could borrow one I'd be happy to go out. I did most of the hunting when we were looking for the unicorns.'' Listen to yourself, he thought; currying favor again. Try to remember that you're a Mage now.

''Kind of you to offer, Excellency,'' Darius replied as he put his plate to one side, ''but I expect that we'll have more important things for you to do.''

He looked the lad over. The first thing you noticed was

that he was tall even when he was sitting down. There was no mistaking this one as anything but a Magician. Both Marianna and Naxania had made disparaging remarks about his age, but if he had to go by looks alone, he'd have said that Jarrod was in his early thirties. Naxania was right about one thing, he wasn't a bad-looking young man.

"What was it that you wanted to talk to me about?" he asked.

Jarrod put his mug down. "I was wondering what you were going to do when we got to Bandor." He was pleased with the way he had put it; polite but professional.

"So am I," Darius said bluntly. "Everything depends on what we find when we get there."

"Do you know what you want me to do if the enemy is still there?" It was getting easier.

"I don't even know what you can do. My daughter tells me that you threw a wall of fire at them as Stronta; could you do it again?"

"No. They manufactured the fire. I just turned it back. Besides, I had the colts to help me then." And my Staff and Greylock and the spirits of the Place of Power. Anxiety stabbed at him unexpectedly. Now there was just himself and the Staff. What had Ragnor said? "On your own, Magically speaking."

"Pity. I've never had to invest a castle before, and we obviously lack siege machines. We'll just have to wait till we get there and then develop a strategy based on what we find. It's quite possible that the Umbrians will be back in residence, in which case I'll have a deal of diplomatic dancing to do."

"I have one practical suggestion," Jarrod said, and moved round until he was facing Darius.

"Let's have it. I can do with all the help I can get."

"Well, it seems to me that surprise is our best bet."

"It's about our only bet."

"You'll be sending a scout ahead to fly over the fort?"

"Yes, indeed."

"If the Outworlders are still in Bandor, they'll be expecting some kind of counterattack eventually. They know that we ride cloudsteeds and they'll be keeping an eye out."

"What's your point?

Jarrod finished his chai before replying. His confidence was growing. "If your scout was spotted and downed, you'd lose valuable time and the element of surprise would be gone."

"True. What do you propose?"

"If a cloudsteed can be saddled up to take two people, I could fly with the scout. One of the things that I can do is to make things invisible. It's frowned upon at the Collegium because there's such a temptation to abuse it, but this is an exceptional circumstance. I'd make us both invisible.

"There are wild cloudsteeds in Songuard, I've seen them myself. If the enemy saw a solitary, riderless cloudsteed, they might not think anything about it. Of course, if they are jumpy and quick to loose . . . But even if they shot the cloudsteed down, they wouldn't know that there were men in the area. You'd still have the element of surprise." He clasped his hands around his knees and rocked back gently. That had come out well.

"Why not make the 'steed invisible?"

"Because I can't see both wings at the same time. It wouldn't matter if they were at rest, but I can't hold the pattern if they're moving all the time."

Darius grunted and gave him a long, weighing look. It had never occurred to him to risk the young man. He had assumed that whatever Magic was needed could be performed from a safe distance. He couldn't allow the fellow to put himself in jeopardy. He was a Mage and, on top of that, he was a hero to his people. They'd suffered enough loss for the time being.

Still, it was a good idea and he couldn't just turn the boy down cold. Marianna might have a low opinion of him, or might pretend that she did, he amended, but he had moved up awfully fast. What should he say? Best be frank, he decided.

"It's a very good idea, Excellency," he said slowly.

"I'd really rather you didn't call me Excellency," Jarrod cut in. "I don't feel like an Excellency."

Darius smiled. "I know what you mean. People call me General and I look round to see who I should be saluting. As I said, it's a good idea. In fact, it's the Excellency part that's the problem. You're an important man and I can't risk your getting hurt. Paladine's in a bad way just now and they already have one Mage out of action."

Jarrod winced. It was a low blow. He felt his anger kindle. "Then you should have left me at home, but you didn't. I'm here and I have no intention of standing at the side of the tilting ground and cheering you on."

The lad certainly has guts, Darius thought, and he's a lot younger than he looks. That's eighteen talking. "I understand how you feel," he said, "believe me I do, but you have to take the longer view. For reasons of state that I do not fully comprehend, we are, if at all possible, to retake Fort Bandor before the Umbrians. It is also important, I am told, that I involve Magic in some way. I fully intend to use you in any way that I can, but if I returned without you, the expedition would be rated a failure even if we ousted the Others and beat the Umbrians to it by a month. Now I don't think that would serve either Paladine or Magic."

"I have no intention of getting myself killed," Jarrod said stiffly. "What you don't seem to understand is that

Magic constantly entails taking risks. Making Magic is far more likely to be the death of me than the Outlanders.''

''I don't know very much about Magic, Sir Jarrod. I don't understand it and I'm perfectly prepared to believe that it's dangerous. But I have no control over that. When it comes to Magic, you are responsible entirely to yourself. I am, however, the leader of this expedition and I am responsible for your physical well-being. I mean no disrespect to your office, but I'll pull rank if I have to.''

There was a brief pause while both of them pulled back from a confrontation that neither had intended and neither wanted. ''You're the military man and I am under your command. I wouldn't dream of interfering. I wouldn't know what to do. That's why I asked to speak to you in the first place. There has to be something useful I can do besides weather control. I can create illusions if that would help.''

''Don't worry, Sir Jarrod, I'm sure there'll be plenty of things for you to do. You're too valuable an asset to waste. I just have to see what we're up against, and then we'll put our heads together and figure out what to do about it.''

Jarrod felt a surge of liking. The man was obviously sincere and he treated him like an equal. It would be a relief to talk to someone sympathetic.

''To tell you the truth,'' he said impulsively, ''I feel ambivalent about this whole thing. I know that Marianna told you about the things she had discovered at the battle of Stronta, and I know that you weren't entirely convinced . . .''

''I believe my daughter,'' Darius said without reproof. ''At least I believe that she believes what she says and that comes to the same thing.''

''She's telling the truth. The colts backed her up. When the Outlanders pulled back, such a long way back, it made sense. They had us unhorsed and down and they walked away. Leave us in peace and we'll leave you in peace. Then they take Fort Bandor and nothing makes sense anymore.''

''Trouble is that we don't know anything about the enemy. You are guessing that they could have finished us off and decided not to. It's just as possible that they were exhausted. The Umbrians inflicted a costly defeat on them and they may not have had any reserves left. They could have withdrawn because they needed a breathing space.''

''That still doesn't explain the attack on Bandor.''

''Perhaps they are not so different from us. Perhaps they have factions and one faction is tired of the war. A coup brings the peace party briefly into power, but now the army is back in control and the war goes on. Then again, the withdrawal could have been a feint to lull us into precisely the kind of thinking you were talking about.'' He smiled at the look on Jarrod's face.

''I could also make a case for their being provoked by the Umbrians, but it's all speculation. What's important is that no matter what the reasons behind it are, it is a particularly shrewd thrust. They've penetrated the Causeway and they've taken an outpost that we thought was impregnable. The fall of that outpost has reduced the Isphardis to panic and confusion, and that, in turn, brings trade to a standstill. I don't know what your opinion of merchants is, but, like it or not, it's trade that counts. I couldn't maintain my estates if I couldn't sell my surplus crops. So it doesn't matter what we think, we can't let this one go by.''

Jarrod sighed. The man was right. There was no getting away from it. He had been making assumptions without proper proof. Greylock would have been merciless. Even if Marianna was right, it wouldn't help to get Bandor back.

''It all comes down to that, doesn't it?'' he said.

''I'm afraid so. We can't permit them to hold Fort Bandor. If I have to wait for the Umbrians to be able to storm it, I'll wait. So you can see that I shall be grateful for any help you can give me, and that I can't afford to squander your Talent.''

''You can count on me, Sir.'' Jarrod was caught by a yawn. ''I'm sorry. Riding on a cloudsteed all day oughtn't to be tiring, but it is.''

''We ought to be turning in anyway,'' Darius said. ''We've another long day's flying in front of us tomorrow.'' He collected his utensils together. ''I'm glad we had this talk. You've given me a lot to think about.'' I must remember that he's still recuperating from the battle, he thought. I'll have to be doubly careful how I use him.

''Good night then,'' Jarrod said, taking his cue and rising. ''I'll see you tomorrow.''

He's not a bad sort, really, he thought as he made his way back to his bedroll. At least he doesn't talk down to me, which is more than can be said of his daughter.

The weather held, and they approached the Gorodontious from the South-Southwest to take advantage of the prevailing winds. The last time Jarrod had approached a range like this, he had been on foot, leading a horse, and the mountains had seemed impossibly high. Now he was high in the air on a cloudsteed and the peaks still seemed unreachable. They rose, ruffed in cloud, to deny them passage.

He had heeded the Wing Commander's advice and donned as much clothing as he could. He felt constricted, as if he were a boy again and growing out of last year's hand-me-downs. Still, he was warm; all but his feet. The cloudsteed ahead angled up more steeply still, and his reliable old mare followed smoothly. The smoke of her breath streamed back.

Jarrod's own breath was beginning to freeze inside his

helmet. The air burned in his lungs and cold seeped in through the folds in his cloak. He dropped the useless reins and flailed his arms across his chest. He clapped his gauntlets together and got the feeling in his fingers back. The effort made him pant. Though he could not know it, he was doing as well as anybody else and a great deal better than Darius. His trips through Interim had accustomed his body to bouts of bitter cold.

Even the cloudsteeds seemed to be having trouble flying at this altitude. He could swear that they were flying more slowly. The mountainside filled his sight and the crags lingered before disappearing down. Then there was a gap. Jarrod craned his neck back and looked up at the thrusting, broken teeth of the mountain top. The cloudmare glided in on the meager air. His hands, feet, ears, and nose were on fire, but he scarcely noticed them.

Ice ledges rose on either side as the Wings funneled through. There was scarcely room for two abreast and, after the open expanse of the skies, the passage was shockingly confining. Dark fissures jagged their way through the packed and wind-polished snow no more than forty feet below the hooves. Jarrod suddenly felt that they were flying very fast indeed. The col condensed into a succession of images; patches of gray rockface where the ice had fallen away, winged shadows flashing over white, and mountain peaks crowding in overhead.

The vista opened abruptly and they were out over the valley of the Izingari with the summits of the Central Range below them in the distance. The cloudsteeds swung out and went into a long, Northward glide up the bright path of the river.

chapter 24

Three shapes, camouflaged in white cloaks, crouched on a reach of granite looking down on Fort Bandor. Wing Commander Dahn's face was a gelid mask. Darius was swearing quietly and fluently. That's where Marianna learned it, Jarrod thought, as he contemplated the brown fog that hid the battlements below. His throat muscles spasmed. It was bad enough to see the stuff out away across the plain, but here, in an otherwise clean and peaceful wilderness, it was obscene.

Darius broke off his monologue. ''Well, gentlemen, I think we can assume that the motherless bastards are in residence. That looks like a permanent base to me. There's no way to take them by surprise in that soup.'' He swore again. ''What wouldn't I give for a brace of Umbrian cannon now. This is worse than anything I had imagined. How in Strand did they get the stuff here?''

At the words something clicked in Jarrod's mind. ''They're making it. They're producing it on the spot.''

''You guessing? Or do you know for sure? And why are we whispering?'' Darius asked.

''I can feel the machines,'' Jarrod answered in a normal tone. ''I've felt the same thing before.''

''Worse and worse. They must have their defenses on the other side or at the foot of the mountain. There are no signs of sentries on this side.''

"I'll send a man up to reconnoiter as soon as we get back to camp," Dahn said. "He'll be able to come in with the sun behind him for another couple of hours yet."

"What happens if it clouds up?" Jarrod asked. "This is uncontrolled country and the weather changes fast in the mountains."

"He'll have to take his chances."

"My offer still stands, General."

"Thank you, Sir Jarrod," Darius replied, misunderstanding deliberately. "It would be most helpful if you could keep the skies clear."

"That wasn't what I meant, Sir," Jarrod began patiently.

"Excuse me, gentlemen," Oster Dahn interrupted. "Reconnaissance is my responsibility."

"The Mage offered to accompany the scout and render him, render both of them, invisible," Darius explained reluctantly. "He thinks that a lone, apparently wild, cloudsteed wouldn't alarm them."

"I see." Dahn sounded dubious. "Begging your pardon, Excellency, but what happens to the scout?"

"Happens to him? Nothing happens to him. Well," he amended, "that's not quite true, but nothing that will affect him; during the spell or after."

"You have to be on the cloudsteed?" The Wing Commander was not reassured.

"Yes, I do."

He studied Jarrod silently. "Reckon it's worth the risk," he said at last. "I'll have to be the one as flies. I wouldn't ask any of the men to do it. And you'd have to agree to do exactly as I tell you once we're aloft."

"Willingly."

"There are other considerations," Darius said.

Jarrod caught the underlying note of tension. "It is, of

course, up to you, Sir, but there is another reason to let me go besides the Magic."

"Let's hear it." There was a challenge in the General's voice.

"Whoever goes will have to be quick about it even if the enemy doesn't decide on a bit of target practice."

"So?"

"I only have to see something once to remember it exactly." Jarrod paused to see what effect he was having. Not promising. "I won't tell the Queen if you don't," he said, with an attempt at humor.

Darius's face relaxed. He held Jarrod's gaze and then he smiled. "All right," he conceded. "We'll try it this once, but if there's the slightest hint of trouble, you're to head straight home. You're our only wild piece and I can't afford to have you taken out of the game this early. Dahn, I hold you responsible, hear?"

"Yes, Sir." The words had the clean precision of a salute.

An hour later Jarrod was holding on to the back of Dahn's saddle. He was sitting on a pad behind the Wing Commander and they were airborne. He could see to the sides on the cloudsteed's downstroke, but didn't feel much like looking. Riding bareback, or as close to bareback as made no difference, was all very well on the ground, but winging over a valley without stirrups was frightening. He had almost balked when he had realized that there was only one saddle. Now he wished he had. Darius probably wouldn't have thought less of him for it. Dahn's undoubtedly just as nervous about being part of a spell, he thought. He hoped he was.

The Wing Commander turned his head as if aware of Jarrod's thoughts. "The fort's coming up. I'm going to glide down crosswind. You keep watching to the right on both passes. That way you'll see both sides."

"Hang on!" Jarrod yelled. "I'm going to make us invisible. You won't feel anything. I'm just going to change the way we reflect the light."

"Better be quick about it."

Jarrod sat back on his pad. He breathed deeply and focused on the image of two riders and a saddle. "See the picture and the frame, Hold them till they are the same." The old jingle ran through his head as the underlying structures came clear. He made his adjustments and clamped the new reality into place. His head throbbed. The machines below sawed at his concentration. They were stronger here than they had been on the other side of the fort.

"How much longer?" Dahn yelled over his shoulder.

"All done."

"I'm still solid."

"Not from down there. Trust me."

The angle of flight sharpened as if in response, and the brown dome rose to meet them. Jarrod's stomach twinged. Concentrate, he urged. Think of the surfaces; linen, wool, leather, metal, flesh. His inner eyes saw them all in molecular detail while his outer eyes scanned for the battlement that ought to be below. The gates were gone, that much was obvious. Brackish clouds puffed out of the ragged opening. Then the fort was behind him.

The world tilted as the cloudsteed swooped round. Jarrod grabbed Dahn's cloak and then locked his arms around the sides of the saddleback, not caring what the man might think of him. The cloudsteed leveled out and started back toward the sun.

Jarrod peered forward over Dahn's shoulder. There was another patch of Outland air growing at the foot of the mountain; a rank puffball against the snow. From it, a line snaked its way uphill. There one second, gone the next.

They make the muck down there and pump it up, he thought as the nag of the machinery pulled at him.

"Want another look?" Dahn asked.

"Not for me, but I can keep us invisible if you want to go back."

"Home, then. How many of those little black boxes did you count?"

"Eight."

"Right. Hold on, I'm going to bank."

Jarrod gripped the cantle and looked back one last time. The dark path of the pipeline was interrupted as it climbed through a ravine and then it was hidden entirely as they tacked across the headwind. The normal world pressed to reassert itself and a tight band formed around his forehead. He allowed the patterns to revert and felt the tightness drain out. The headache was gone, only to be replaced with an awareness of the cold. He wanted to flail his arms around to get the circulation back, but the thought of letting go of the saddle was enough to deter him.

They circled over the empty clearing from which they had taken off. The only sign of the Wings' presence was the trampled snow and a mizzle of smoke. Jarrod squinted down at the packed whiteness. The landing area looked very small from up here. The view tipped as the cloudsteed went in, and he clamped his thighs tight. The back was too broad and he couldn't get a real purchase. He slid forward as they descended and the jolt of the landing bounced him backward off the pad. His arms were flailing in earnest now, but their brief parody of flight did nothing to break his fall. The air was punched out of his lungs when his back slammed into the snow.

Hands were helping him up. They supported him as he bent double in his fight for breath. His back was numb, but that was secondary.

"Easy now. Easy does it. Try to straighten up. That's

it. That's better.'' Darius's voice rumbled in his ear. ''Let's get you where it's a bit warmer and have a look at your back.''

Jarrod waved away the help and, taking long draughts of air, moved his shoulders around. He turned to one side and then the other. Everything seemed in the right place. He walked slowly to the trees. Greylock would want him to maintain his dignity, for the Discipline's sake. He permitted his arm to be taken as they moved into the forest.

''How do you feel?'' Darius asked, as cloaked and hooded men gave up their places by the fire.

''My back feels as if it were made of wood, but I'm all right otherwise. Lucky thing that I waited until we were on the ground before I fell off.'' He forced a smile.

''Let's have a look.''

Jarrod unfastened his cloak and let it drop. He tried to unhook his flying coat, but his fingers were stiff and awkward. A cloudsteedsman stepped forward and took over the task. The coat was eased off his shoulders. Darius turned him so that his back was to the firelight and then lifted up the flannel shirt. There was a stifled exclamation.

''These scars are new. Who did this to you?''

''A keepsake from an Umbrian press-gang,'' Jarrod said as cold fingers prodded him. Feeling was creeping back.

''Press-gang? Where?''

''In the Saradondas.''

''And Marianna . . . ?'' The question was urgent.

''They didn't catch her. Didn't she tell you about it? She and Sandroz rescued me.''

''Not that part. I would have remembered that. What happened?'' Darius let the shirt fall back.

''From what I could gather, the Umbrians send out regular raiding parties to capture men to work in their mines. As you saw, they aren't gentle about it. It's not an episode I'm very proud of.''

"It's an outrage," Darius said, "I'll see something is done about it when we get back." He broke off as Dahn came up.

"Are you all right, Excellency? That was a nasty spill."

"There's nothing soft about snow," Jarrod agreed. "I'm going to be sore in the morning, but I was lucky."

"You certainly gave me a turn," Darius said. "Were there any problems in the air, Wing Commander?"

"No, Sir. Clean flying; not a peep from the enemy. I reckon I owe that to the Mage."

"Spell worked, then?"

"You'd better ask his Excellency. I was solid enough."

Darius looked his query at Jarrod.

"It worked," Jarrod said, and went back to the task of rehooking his jacket.

"Any surprises?"

"Reckon you could say so, Sir. They've another base at the foot of the mountain. There's eight of what I take to be those battle crawlers guarding it. It's covered in muck just like the fort."

"That's where they're making the stuff," Jarrod put in.

"You saw that?"

"No, but that's where most of the machinery is and there's a pipe running from it up to the fort."

"Any sign of sentries? Any suits working outside?"

"I saw none," Jarrod said.

"Nor I."

"Bastards must be feeling pretty confident." He broke off at the sight of two 'steedsman approaching with a stocky figure between them. "Hello, what have we here?"

The 'steedsmen halted and saluted. "We found him in the woods, General, or rather he found us," the one on the right said.

"Am Sandroz. Chief Garrison Scout." The words were flat, devoid of nuance.

Jarrod's head came up at the sound of the voice. There stood the Songean guide. He had known, at the bottom of his mind, that the man had been headed for Fort Bandor when they had parted company, but he hadn't recalled it until that minute.

Sandroz pushed his cowl back and looked at Jarrod dispassionately.

"Still here?" he inquired.

"You know this man, Sir Jarrod?" Darius asked.

"He was our guide when we were searching for the unicorns." Jarrod kept his voice neutral.

"You find?"

"Yes," Jarrod said, and left it at that. Sandroz had forbidden them to climb the Anvil of the Gods and they had disobeyed him.

The Songean showed neither surprise nor pleasure. He merely nodded, and Jarrod felt somehow deflated. Here was someone who had seen him at his worst and knew him for what he really was.

"Chief Garrison Scout, you said," Darius resumed. "Did you escape?"

"Was hunting," Sandroz replied laconically. "When I return, suits everywhere. No good in trees; too clumsy. I kill six. Wait till night and slip inside fort. Soldiers dead; many suits. I leave."

"Do you have any idea how many there are?"

"About sixty in fort. More in valley."

Jarrod listened with mixed feelings. Sandroz was the best possible ally in these circumstances, but he remembered the quarrels the two of them had had and the man's prejudice against Magicians. He's just an ignorant savage, he told himself, but he knew that it wasn't true.

"Did any of the garrison escape?" Dahn asked.

"I find four outside. All dead. Burned."

"Come and warm up," Darius said. "The chai's still hot and you look as if you could do with some."

Sandroz moved forward toward the fire and Jarrod made room for him. Mugs were handed round and the men stood cradling them in their hands for warmth.

"It seems that we're evenly matched up here," Darius said, breaking the silence. "But there's nothing we can do about Bandor for the moment, not while it's filled with that filth. Tell me, Wing Commander, what did you make of the base at the foot of the mountain?"

"Difficult to say, Sir. It was covered in fog. It's not that big; about the size of a middling keep, would be my guess."

"Protected by the crawlers to the North and by the mountain and the fort in the rear. Doesn't sound too promising, does it?"

Jarrod followed the conversation, a picture of the area clear in his mind. He followed the pipe up the mountainside and a little detail snagged his attention. There was a deep shadow high up on the scarp. It was well out of sight of Bandor. He concentrated on it. There was a broad lip of rock, and the shadow was caused by the cliff above it. His inner eye traveled back down the mountainside. There was a good chance that the ledge was hidden from the camp below. If he could get down to it, he would be able to work unobserved. If he used the Spell of Unbinding . . . He turned from the fire and caught Darius's eye.

"I've remembered something and it's given me an idea. Mind you, I don't think you're going to like it."

"Isn't one bad spill enough for the day, Excellency?" Sandroz's eyebrows rose at the title.

"Hear me out, General. There's a smallish cliff, fifty feet high or thereabouts, with a good broad ledge at the bottom. It's completely hidden from the fort and I'm fairly sure that it can't be seen from the other installation. Best of all, the pipeline that connects the two runs close by."

"Does it, indeed? And can we get to this place?"

"An experienced climber could, and if you wanted to get to it unobserved, it would be best to do it on a moonless night, but I can provide that."

"Are you sure?"

"About the moon? Absolutely. I can't be certain about the climb, but I told you before, I have no desire to die." He saw the color change in Darius's face and smiled.

"You have no desire?" Darius stressed the first word. "I might have known it. I thought we agreed that if I let you go on that scouting flight, you'd stay out of trouble." He's as reckless as a young Umbrian, Darius thought.

"I told you you wouldn't like it, but you yourself just said that there was nothing you could do while the foreign muck was all over the fort. The numbers are even up here at the moment, but you don't know how many more of them there are at the bottom.

"I've got a plan that might solve both those problems." The strategem had come to him all of a piece, like a revelation, and he had absolute confidence in it. "The beauty of it is that if I fail, and I don't for a minute think I shall, it will look like a natural disturbance. You'll be no worse off than you are now."

"Go on, then," Darius growled, "but this better be bloody good."

Jarrod looked round the group and then bent down so that their heads were close together. He began to speak rapidly.

chapter 25

It was black beneath the trees. The bulk of Fort Bandor was more a presence than a shape as Jarrod and Sandroz crouched and watched. Nothing moved. The silence was absolute and oppressive. There must be night stalkers other than themselves abroad, but the snow muffled everything. Sandroz tapped his companion on the arm and motioned.

They circled Westward until the ground dropped away. Somewhere below, the valley yawned. They roped up, and Jarrod moved his belt pouch round to the back. He wasn't feeling so certain anymore. He nodded to Sandroz and followed him as he crabbed his way down in the dark. Jarrod's back complained and he set himself to ignore it.

They were about fifty feet below the shelf that had been carved out for the fort, and they began to move sideways across the mountain. Under normal circumstances it would have been an easy traverse. There was no wind to distract them, Jarrod had made a point of that, but there was no light and it was cold. It was difficult to make out crevices, and his fingers soon lost their sensitivity. His feet had no sensation in them, and every time one of them slipped, his heart plummeted.

He could feel the Outlander's machines working, above him and below him. Fear began to creep in. Take your time, he told himself. Take it slow and easy. He swallowed. Sandroz is an expert climber, he's been doing this all his life. He won't let me fall. Just go from one handhold to the next. How much longer before we can stop and rest? The machines intruded again. I'll smash them! he thought. Obliterate them! A flicker of hatred warmed him briefly.

Pebbles rattled and he hugged the icy rock. There was a tug at his waist as the line went taut, but it slackened almost immediately. Jarrod let the air out of his lungs. He felt as if time had been stretched. He had been creeping across this motherless mountain for an eternity. Hand, foot, hand, foot, on and on and on. The sudden touch of Sandroz's glove made his heart leap.

"We climb down," the Songean hissed.

Jarrod looked to his left, over Sandroz's head, and saw the pipe, a darker line against the night. He glanced down. What he could see of the slope looked manageable. He nodded to Sandroz and eased his left boot out of the cranny he had wedged it in. Fifteen minutes later he was standing on a platform of rock. The cliff he had seen from the air rose behind him with a rope dangling down it. He leaned back, took his gloves off, and wiped the sweat off his forehead. His fingers were still cold and he tucked them into his armpits.

"Any idea how long that took?" he asked.

"Hour maybe."

"That's all?" He didn't try to mask his surprise. Jarrod calculated. If Sandroz was right, and he always was on things like this, there ought to be a couple of hours left before dawn. He pushed himself up and slid the pouch around. He took out some of the timothy and fennate mixture he had made, added orris root and galingal, and started to chew. He stooped and scooped up a handful of snow and bit into it. His lips went numb. He chewed on and swallowed, repeating the process until it was all gone.

Not exactly the traditional way to prepare a potion, but he had no other choice.

"It'll take about half an hour to start working," he said quietly. "I'll start as soon as it gets light enough to see by. Get some sleep if you can." He sat down and leaned against the rock. His back was aching. He wouldn't notice it once the simples began to take effect, but that was no consolation now.

The Songean grunted and watched as the younger man's shoulders drooped and the head nodded down. The boy had changed, no doubt about that. He didn't look like a boy anymore, and he'd handled the big Arundelian well, with none of the indecision that had marked him on the earlier trip. The lad had turned out to be unexpectedly hardy, too. There had been long odds against that pair making it all the way back to Belengar with the Season of the Moons coming on. Still, it was difficult to imagine that the same boy was capable of inflicting the kind of damage that he had talked about.

Fate, Sandroz mused as he settled himself for the long wait, was an unpredictable mistress. The job of guiding two young boys through the mountains had been unexpected, and he never had found out what they were looking for. That business about unicorns was such a transparent lie that it made him uneasy. That was nothing new. The tall one had always made him uneasy. The height had something to do with it, of course, but it was the Magic that was the real cause. The boy hadn't said anything about it, but he'd known. And now he was proved right. He hawked and spat into the dark. Didn't do to contemplate what was ahead too closely. Fate would take care of that, too.

Jarrod was pushed back to the surface by the pressure to Make the Day. He blinked, yawned, and stretched. The unorthodox potion had done its work and he felt strong and rested. He looked up at the unreadable sky and then closed his eyes and let his perceptions range Southward. Clouds covered the area as they were supposed to. A lowering of tension told him that he had located the center of the pattern. It is mine, he thought, to do with as I will. He directed some of his new found energy at the core and nudged it around. The winds shifted obligingly and began to funnel up the valley. Satisfied, he gave himself over to the diurnal ritual, and when he emerged there were stars overhead. There was a green tinge in the Eastern sky. It would be light soon.

He got up and went and stood close to the edge. He could make out the pipe, but the pumping station was lost in the gloom. Dim starlight showed him that the immediate slope was extremely steep. So much the better. He turned, crossed to Sandroz, and shook him awake. The little man had a knife in his hand before his eyes were open.

"It's time," Jarrod said calmly. "You know what to do." Sandroz rolled to his feet and went to make his own inspection.

The sky was going pale and the stars were retreating. He was as ready as he was going to be. He felt confident, but there was a fibrillation of nervousness at the bottom of it. This time he was alone. Sandroz didn't count. There were no unicorns, no Greylock, no Staff, even the spirits of the Place of Power had withdrawn. He would find out how good a Magician he really was.

He faced the pipe and followed it down its length until it disappeared. The Outland installation would be below it. He closed his eyes and the mountainside was still there. The Canticles of Correlation began to purl through his mind, blotting out the throb of the engines in his blood. The picture blurred as he sought the underlying structure. The pipe was of a glasslike material that he had never come across before. There was more of it at the foot of the mountain, but that shape eluded him. The irregular layers of rock in between, by contrast, were crystal clear.

More wind, he thought. When that pipe shatters, there are going to be a lot of poisonous fumes spewing out. He turned his blind attention to the sky. New clouds were already scudding North. He projected himself upward and felt the wind streaming through him. He traveled down it to Lake Grad, where the core of the storm drew its strength. He spun around it, making the waters churn, and increased its speed. That done, he rode the winds back to Bandor.

He looked down and observed the dance that held the rock together. There were two dolls perched on the surface below, oblivious of the movement that whirled beneath their feet. One of the dolls had its arms aloft and he knew that it was himself. The mannikin's mouth was open and he felt, rather than heard, the words. They gave him added strength.

The storm was beginning to catch up with him. There were distant gnars of thunder. Time to put the first part of the strategy into action. Freeze the pattern and then unbind it. He concentrated on the slope below the pair. The dance of the universe defied him and would not be stilled. Jarrod gathered his energies anew. The power of the Staff is my power, he thought. Without me it has no force. Nature mocked his presumption. Who was he to think that he could impose himself on what was meant to be? He was a mote, an insignificant dot of empty imaginings.

Not so! Not so! Jarrod fought back. He was Mage of Paladine, discoverer of unicorns and friend to them as he had been to those who had governed the Place of Power. They had named him Keeper Designate and they were more than earth and stone.

Certainty flooded him and he narrowed the thrust of his

will. The whirlagig slowed and then surrendered. The mountain was his. He worked with deliberation to minimize the danger to the little men. He unpicked the web, layer under, layer over, until all he needed to do was to insert a tendril of control. A fissure opened and ran downward. There was a creaking and groaning that welled up through the howl of the wind as the crevasse widened protestingly.

Riven boulders began to tumble and the chasm gaped on down, a snake with jaws unhinged to swallow its prey. The pipe vanished and the brown spume it left was whipped into tatters and dispersed. The world was wail and thunder, and the ground beneath Jarrod's feet trembled. He was aware of his body again and of the dust rising around him. His arms were outstretched and his hands curved down and out. The hooked fingers were pulling at the air as if it were solid. His arms ached with the effort and sharp pains lanced across his shoulders. Too soon for that. He still had work to do.

He put forth another effort and felt the fabric tear and knew that the foot of the mountain had been transformed into a talus. He dropped his arms and stood panting until the swirling dust drove him back from the edge. Sandroz steadied him and guided him to the base of the cliff. Pebbles bounced around them, but Jarrod ignored them. He sat down with his back against the rock, Sandroz did likewise, but Jarrod noted with amused detachment that he left a healthy distance between them.

"There's a big storm coming," he said, but the words came out as a croak, even in his own ears. He cleared his throat and tried it again. Hoarse, but intelligible, he decided. "I'm not sure that I'll be able to control the wind once it really gets going. We ought to be protected from the worst of it here, but you never know."

Sandroz rose and brought the spare rope over. He tied

it round Jarrod's waist and then tied the other end around his own. Jarrod took a plug of his simples mixture and chewed on it. Not too much time left. What snow there was on the ledge was covered with dust. No help there. He swallowed and massaged his throat to help it down. He closed his eyes and went within.

He was aloft again and the storm loomed in his consciousness. It was a big one, driving snow before it in almost horizontal lines, and closing fast, drawn by the heat of the wounded mountain. He looked down. He had been right. There was nothing at the bottom except a skirt of broken rock. He turned his attention to the fort.

The pall that had shrouded the battlements was gone and, as he watched, was replaced by a veil of driven snow. If he could slow the tempest's onrush just a little, the effect on the fort would be greater. The courtyards were probably clear, but there would be corruption inside the buildings still. He spread himself and damped the massive thermal generated by all the energies he had loosed. The magnet was gone, but the speed was not so easily checked.

He pushed against it, but to no avail. The new dose of herbs was sustaining him, but his strength had waned. Tiles were flying from the roofs of the fort and a chimney went crashing down. He abandoned his efforts and rose higher. He chilled the upper layer of the clouds and watched them sink. Hailstones began to bombard the fort, hammering at windowpanes until they shattered.

A pleasant lassitude stole over him and he recognized the signs. He allowed himself to drift back down to his body. He was tired now, infinitely tired. It was time to let go. There was no more that he could do. He was floating on elation. Most of it was the aftermath of Magic, but he had earned the feeling of accomplishment. Greylock would be proud of him. He had made the transition from the Spell of Unbinding to Weather Magic smoothly and had reknit the one while performing the other. That wily old stoat Ragnor had been right. He was the kind of cloth that Mages were cut from.

He curled up in the lee of the cliff, unmindful of the storm. He was happy. He had done it on his own. The power had come from within him. Something had responded to the potion, crude though it was, and when he had summoned it, the energy was there. It was truly his. He smiled at his own presumption. There was no power now. He drifted off with the smile still on his face.

The tempest dwindled. The wind swirled about, but there was no real menace left in it. The sun came out and warmed the rock around the huddled men. Sandroz looked out from his cloak and then pushed his way to his feet. He looked around carefully. The Excellency was still asleep. There was rockdust in his hair. He went over, squatted down, and brushed the hair lightly. The liberal dusting of white stayed put and he snatched his hand away. He bent forward so that he could get a look at the face. It was old and wrinkled.

Sandroz retreated a couple of paces and made the sign to ward off evil spirits. He was comfortable with the idea of the supernatural. His people had always lived close by the gods. The spirits of the great raptors dwelled in certain trees. He'd known shamans before, the Magus of his clan knew the secrets of Nature and spoke with the gods, but this one was different. This one had commanded Nature and she had obeyed. He had needed no ceremony, no headdress, no sacred colors. He had torn the mountain apart with his bare hands and seized the winds from Gyrastor, Father of Storms.

This was not the youth he had known. That one had sulked like a bad-tempered child and had allowed the Umbrians to take him without striking a blow. This one had been afraid on the climb, no mistaking that odor, but then he had become a towering force that tossed boulders about as if they were so much straw. There was much that Sandroz did not understand, but one thing was clear. Twice now the protection of the Paladinian had been entrusted to him. He went back and checked for a pulse. He grunted and sat aback on his heels. The heart was strong.

Protecting him did not appeal, but it was not possible for a mortal to gainsay the gods. They had permitted him to see the weakness that is the other side of strength so that he might better serve this strange master. From the look of him, it shouldn't be too long an assignment. He went over and retrieved the rope that had been shaken down during the morning's happenings.

A shadow swept across the rockface, and Sandroz looked up, shading his eyes against the sun. A cloudsteed flew by almost on a level with him, and he waved at the 'steedsman. He gestured to the sleeping Jarrod and pointed upward, hoping the man would understand that he needed help, then he set himself to watch his charge and guard his rest.

chapter 26

Darius was not good at waiting. His boots squeaked on the patches of fresh snow. The light under the trees was gray. There had been a couple of hours of sun, but now the snow was back. It wouldn't matter if the Mage had managed to obliterate all the Outlanders, but the fort was still occupied. The scouts who went out after the storm reported seeing small parties of suits working to clear the debris from the courtyards. It did not sit well with him to give the enemy time to recover, but he could do little with the cloudsteeds grounded. He turned and paced back towards the fire with his head down, watching his footing.

Still, he reassured himself, there was nowhere for them to go now, no crawlers to escape in, and the surprise factor was still intact. They couldn't possibly attribute an earthquake to human intervention. He wouldn't have believed it himself if Courtak hadn't told them in advance what he intended to do. Even then, it had taken the Songean's terse report to dispel the thought of coincidence.

No doubt about it, Courtak had done his part and done it well from all accounts. The misbegotten pollution was gone and there was nothing but rock rubble where the base camp had been. There was extensive damage to the fort, though that, he warned himself, was probably the result of the initial assault. No telling what kind of weapons the bastards had used. Mustn't go all superstitious and attribute everything to Magic. If only Courtak had managed to keep the skies clear, it might all be over.

"General." Darius's head came up at the quiet hail. He found that he was closer to the fire than he expected. Wing Commander Dahn detached himself from a group of officers.

"Hello, Oster. Any change?"

"Not since the last time you asked, Sir, though the Mage seems to be recovering. At least, the Songean came and got some soup for him."

"Well, that's a relief. He looked all in when they brought him back. I thought we were going to lose him."

"It's the first time I've been close to really big Magic," Dahn said in a careful voice. "They always say as how it exacts a price, but I've never seen the results before."

"The aging? I know what you mean. He looked, well, he looked at least sixty—not a good sixty at that. I suppose we ought to go and see him and present our compliments." Darius didn't sound enthusiastic. "I don't think I should like to have that man angry at me," he added in an attempt to lighten the mood.

"You've got nothing to worry about, I bounced him off the back of my 'steed," Dahn said, as they passed groups of men clustered around the fires. "I've got to admit," he added, "that I completely underestimated him. I mean, apart from his size, he's so—ordinary. Or at least he was."

"You're not the only one to think that. The Queen said much the same thing to me. My daughter doesn't seem to have too high an opinion of him either, not that I understand too much about her these days."

"You, too? I've a boy as wants to move to Arundel and take up farming. I've nothing against farming, mind, but we've been 'steedsmen for five generations." Dahn was talking to cover his uneasiness.

"The whole world's gone topsy-turvy," Darius agreed,

happy to have the subject changed. "There's no predicting anything anymore. I tell you, Oster, I've enjoyed the challenges that have come my way, but nothing's certain anymore and I miss that."

"Young people today certainly don't behave the way they used to when we were lads. If I'd have talked to my father the way my boy talks back to me, I'd have, well, I'd never have dared do it." He broke off. "Ah, here's his Excellency."

"Give you good day, Sir Jarrod," Darius said formally. "I trust that you are recovering." His eyes scanned the seated figure, taking in the pallor, the lines, and the hair.

Jarrod looked up and gave a slow smile. "I am fortunate in that there are no looking glasses here," he said, equally correctly, "but if the General is using the formal mode, I must appear to be at death's door." He held up a hand to still protest. "I know it must be a shock for you, but I am, in fact, feeling better. I shall get younger as my strength returns."

He smiled up at Dahn. "Give you good day, Wing Commander. Will you gentlemen join me?" He waited until they were seated on either side of him. "Sandroz tells me that my efforts were successful. He is not an easy person to pry details out of."

"You've done remarkably well," Darius said, lapsing into the informal. "Far more, in fact, than I'd expected."

Jarrod warmed to the praise. "That makes two of us, General," he said.

"You did a bloody fine job, Excellency. You did everything you said you would and more."

"Thank you, Wing Commander."

"You've made an attack possible," Darius agreed. "We'll roust them in the morning if the snow lets up."

"Yes, I'm sorry about the snow. I should have finished things off when I had the storm to work with, but there was so much going on that I forgot that I had more to do to the castle."

"Forgot what?" Darius asked, puzzled.

"The effects of the Outland air. It's been all over Fort Bandor for sennights, and we all know what happens to animals that stray into the Barrier Lands."

"We'll take our chances, Excellency. It comes with the profession."

"It'll be safe enough for those flying, Wing Commander, but if the General plans to get into the fort itself, it would be wise to give the place a thorough washing down."

"I don't see how we can do that, Excellency."

"I'll do it. I'll use the snow. I'll need my Staff, of course. I don't have enough energy left to do it by myself. Besides, it would be a shame to bring it all the way here and not use it." The voice was thin, but confident.

"There's no need for you to put yourself out," Darius said quickly. "You've already done more than enough."

Jarrod disconcerted him by chuckling. It was a dessicated and scratchy sound. "You do intend to use men on the ground, don't you?"

"Yes. From the scout's description, there's no way a cloudsteed could land inside the fort now, and they won't have cleaned it all up by tomorrow."

"You intend to lead them." It was more a statement than a question.

"Of course."

"That's why I have to do it. And not just for you and the other men. If anything happened because I was careless, I shouldn't like to face the Queen—to say nothing of Marianna."

Darius was caught off guard and smiled appreciatively. Dahn looked from one to the other, feeling left out.

"What are the plans for tomorrow?" Jarrod asked.

"Weather permitting . . ."

"Oh, the weather will permit. I promise you that."

"Very well. As soon as the light's strong enough, we'll mount a two-tine attack." He leaned forward and addressed Dahn across Jarrod. "You'll harass them from the air, and I'll take advantage of the confusion you cause to get through the front gates. A cloudsteed attack ought to be unexpected, but if they think anything like the way we do, understandable. I'm counting on them to think that an attack on foot is impossible." Dahn nodded, and Darius shifted round to warm a different part of his body.

"Is another way." The trio at the fire was so intent on the business at hand that the bass voice startled them. Sandroz came forward and squatted down beside them without waiting for an invitation.

"Can you open the rear gates, Scoutleader?" Darius inquired.

"No. Is another door. Forgotten now. For the dead once. Only open from the inside, but I leave bolts back."

"A triple attack," Darius said, rising hope in his voice. "Distract them from the air, draw them to the front, and then destroy them from the rear. By the Mother, but we've got 'em now." The man was alight again.

"Then it's time for me to go to work," Jarrod said. "I'll get my Staff and some herbs that I need." He pushed himself slowly to his feet and accepted the helping shoulder offered by Sandroz. He looked down at the other two.

"I shall need a large fire. We shall just have to hope that the enemy is too preoccupied, or too tired from their exertions, to notice the smoke. I shall need a pot of boiling water, Wing Commander, and I should be grateful if both of you assisted me in the spellcasting." He enjoyed the startled look the two exchanged as they scrambled up.

"I am sure that you are aware that this is a rare opportunity for you," he added. "We do not normally include members of the laity in such matters, but at this juncture I have no choice.'' He started to smile and then cut it off.

Something nagged at his mind, causing him to tighten his grip on Sandroz's shoulder. He loosened his fingers immediately and looked round for the cause. There was no hint of anything unusual: men were going through their normal rituals. The pressure persisted. It seemed to come from the Southeast. He nodded to the military men and steered Sandroz toward the perimiter. The little man went along with him without question.

It was almost as if . . . No, that was ridiculous. The unicorns were hundreds of leagues away, Jarrod told himself, but his feet forced him round the fire toward the darkness of the forest. And yet. . . ? Could there be some other creature that he could connect with? Perhaps all these months of contact with the unicorns had sensitized him. This could be a wild warcat.

On the other hand, he had found the unicorns in Songuard and there was nothing in Naxania's verse that limited the number of unicorns. Could this be another of them? His heart raced at the thought, and he found he was squeezing Sandroz shoulder again. He forced himself to relax. Mustn't let my imagination run away with me, he thought. I'm just tired. His feet took him on.

Spellcasting always ages me, he acknowledged wryly as the pressure seemed to increase with every forward pace, but this is the first time it's affected my mind.

'What passes for a mind.' The comment popped up unbidden and stopped him dead in his tracks. Sandroz rocked to a halt, but Jarrod wasn't aware of him. That hautbois tone was unmistakable.

'Nastrus?'

'Sorry to disappoint you, but it's about time. I've been calling you for a long while.'

Jarrod peered into the blackness beneath the trees. *'Where are you?* he asked. *'Are you in Stronta?'*

'Hardly. I'm not far away now.'

'If I stay where I am, can you find me?'

'Of course I can.' The tone was scornful. *'And from the sound of you, you better stay where you are. You humans are pathetically weak.'*

Jarrod was too pleased at the thought of seeing Nastrus again to rise to the bait. He waited, and Sandroz waited uncomprehendingly with him. It suddenly seemed to the Magician that he had been sundered from the colts for a very long time, and he wondered at his ability to put it out of his mind these past few days.

'Typical,' Nastrus snorted in his head.

'I even missed you, you little monster.'

'The feeling was mutual,' Nastrus replied as he rounded a tree trunk and came into view.

Jarrod staggered forward, arms outstretched, and clung to the unicorn's neck, tears stinging his eyes. Sandroz dropped to his knees. For Jarrod it was a moment of intense joy, but for Sandroz it was a revelation and an epiphany. This was a clear manifestation of the gods. There could be no doubt that this incandescent creature that made even new snow look drab housed a divinity. And the Magician was its friend, embraced it without fear or harm. There could be no clearer sign that he was a chosen one and he, Sandroz, had been given the honor to serve him. He bowed down until his forehead touched the snow.

'Emotions, emotions, always emotions,' Nastrus remonstrated, but the warmth of his affection shone though the cynical overlay. *'Now if you've finished being sloppy, I'd like to get warm and have something to eat. You know how hungry Interim makes me, and there's precious little that's appetizing around.'*

'You're always thinking of your stomach.' Jarrod's accompanying chuckle startled Sandroz.

'Let's get to the fire then and find you some oats.' Jarrod turned and was instantly aware of the impact their meeting had made. His eyes took in the frozen scene with the kneeling Songean in the foreground. Every man in the clearing was standing and each one was stock-still. The only moving things were snowflakes and firelight.

'Well, you seem to have had your customary effect. Oh, stop feeling so pleased with yourself. I'm afraid I shall need your support to get back to the fire, so please take it slowly. I'd hate to spoil this impression by falling flat on my face.'

They approached the obeisant clansman and Nastrus stopped as soon as the thought formed in Jarrod's mind. "Get up, Sandroz, and come stand on my right. There's no need to be worshipful around this unicorn. He's too full of himself already."

'He won't believe you, you know,' Nastrus said smugly as the trio set off again.

'More's the pity. Now, how did you get here? Were you looking for me? Is anything wrong at home?'

'Easy, boy, easy,' Nastrus replied, using a phrase that Jarrod was wont to use on him. *'Let's take them one at a time. I didn't come looking for you and there's nothing wrong at Stronta. I decided to take this trip because I was bored. A daily gallop with your female and back to the stables; day after day.'*

'She's not my female, and if you weren't looking for me, where were you going?'

'Where d'you think I was going? You know how trips through Interim work. There have to be coordinates in the Memory for us to be able to get to a place.'

'The Anvil of the Gods.'

'Oh, very good. Give the man enough time and he'll come up with an answer—usually the wrong answer.'

'Shut up and steer toward that fire over there. See that man with the white beard? That's Marianna's father.'

'I know that. He's been introduced to us before.'

'He has? When?'

'When we were in that castle in the South. Where you stuck us in the cellar.'

'I didn't know that.'

'You never asked and it didn't seem important.'

'You still haven't explained why you are here,' Jarrod said, as 'steedsmen moved away from them as they approached.

'I'm not quite sure. Something bent the Line of Force I was traveling along. I can only guess that something around here was giving off a tremendous amount of energy.'

'Then I'm probably the thing responsible.' It was Jarrod's turn to sound smug.

'You?' And Nastrus's turn to be astonished.

'Yes, me—and you don't have to sound so surprised. It just so happens that I was performing some very powerful Magic.'

'D'you think you could materialize some fodder?' Nastrus tried to seem dismissive, but Jarrod could sense respect.

They came to a stop before Darius and Wing Commander Dahn. Unlike the rest of the command, they held their ground; both saluted.

"Gentlemen," Jarrod said in the formal mode, "this is my friend Nastrus, who has traversed all the long leagues from Stronta to give us courage."

'I did nothing of the kind.'

Jarrod turned his head towards the unicorn, a polite,

artificial smile on his lips. *'Just make the nice bow you used at the banquet,'* he thought.

'Is this really necessary?'

'It is if you want to eat.'

The right forehoof shot out immediately and the unicorn inclined its head. The horn caught the firelight and gleamed as it descended.

"Sandroz, would you be kind enough to find a blanket and a nosebag for my friend?" Jarrod dropped into the vernacular, and the little man bowed and scurried away. "If you gentlemen will permit, I have to sit down. Snow is tiring stuff to walk through. You needn't worry about Nastrus, he's quite tame. He won't run away."

'I am not tame!'

'Well, the only other word I can think of is 'domesticated' and you certainly aren't that.'

The two men stepped aside to let Jarrod settle himself by the fire and then, with a nervous glance at Nastrus, squatted down beside him.

'What does this portend, Excellency?' Darius asked. "Did you send for him?"

"No, as a matter of fact I didn't. He took it upon himself to visit us. He came to put heart into the men for their assault on Bandor."

'I did no such thing.' Nastrus shook his mane and the two soldiers looked up at the sound.

'Would you rather I told them that you got lost? No. I thought not. All I'm doing is making the best use of a lucky coincidence, so just let me be.' He could tell that the unicorn was still dubious, and he turned his attention quickly back to the officers.

"I think we'd best let him feed, and then we can get on with the spell I promised you."

"By all means, Sir Jarrod," Darius agreed. "I take it,"

he added, "that now that, ah, now that your friend is here, you won't be wanting us to help you?"

"Oh, but I shall." Jarrod had no intention of letting them off the hook. "Unicorns are miraculous creatures, but they lack arms." He retrieved his Staff and levered his way to his feet. "Well, I must get on with my arrangements. Don't forget the boiling water, Wing Commander." He left them, well pleased with himself and knowing that they were staring after him.

He made a little ritual out of the preparation of the tisane. He had an audience to satisfy. Every man in the command who was not on sentrygo was gathered in the clearing. They stood in silent groups at a respectful distance from the central fire. Jarrod was glad that he had changed into the blue robe, even though it wasn't nearly as warm as the flying clothes he had been wearing. The warmth of the brew made up for the difference and began to take the tiredness away.

He flexed his shoulders and moved his neck around. His muscles were still tight from the climbing, but he knew that he would be unaware of them before too long. This was an easy spell and wouldn't take much out of him, but there was no need to let the others know that. He'd dress it up a bit so that they got their money's worth. They would be fighting come morning, and a flashy display of Magic should give them added confidence. This was one time when the Archmage's theory really applied.

'I thought I was the one who was supposed to be putting heart into them,' Nastrus commented from behind.

'You are—just look at them. Some of them are going to get killed tomorrow, but there isn't a one who believes that. You're too potent a talisman to permit doubt. I have to perform this spell to make it safer for them inside the fort. I thought I'd give them a bit of a show to go along with it.'

There were still questions in the back of Nastrus's mind, but he let them be.

Jarrod put his cup down and beckoned the two commanders over. He positioned one on his right side and the other on his left. He could sense their nervousness as they stood there in the sifting snow. The mouths were tight and they shifted their weight from foot to foot. It's good for them to be intimidated for a change, he thought.

"I'm going to make it rain over the fort," he said aloud. "Heat is the key to weather, and I'm going to take the heat from this fire and transfer it to the keep." He smiled confidently from one to the other. "It's important that I remain on my feet during the spell, and I'm counting on you to hold me up if I begin to falter. It will be quite safe to touch me while I'm spellcasting, but I'd avoid the Staff if I were you." He smiled again and saw that they were not reassured. Too bad. "All right gentlemen, here we go."

Jarrod turned to the fire and planted his Staff. He began the chant that deepened his concentration, singing the words out for the benefit of his audience. He applied the lessons of the Voice that Greylock had taught him. It would be a night that none of them would forget. That done, he dismissed them all from his mind and focused on the heart of the fire.

The chant died and was replaced by a more urgent litany. The curve of the Staff vibrated in response, and threads of color grew along it. There were no gasps. This was a hard, disciplined group. The play of lights reached over Jarrod's head to the top of the Staff and curled back down the curved shaft. The fire leapt and crackled, drowning out the first murmurs.

He felt an orderly flow of power enter him. He was surprised. Energy usually whirled into him and had to be tamed before it could be put to use, but this time it was as if the Staff knew his physical limitations and was exercising the control for him. He felt a surge of affection for his instrument and watched as the middle of the blaze turned white.

He needed a picture of a keep. The fort had been hidden under a thick brown head when he had flown over it, but his memory supplied a lithograph. It provided no associations to support the image, but Jarrod knew from experience that it was right. That was a picture of Fort Bandor's keep. It had a simple, circular pattern that was easy to reconstruct. The Staff was warm and vibrant in his hand. He decided to give the watchers something more to remember. He rotated the image of the building until he knew the least of its details and then he projected it outwards. He had told Darius that he could create illusions and he would give them an illusion.

A replica of the keep, complete with miniature steps, appeared in the fire. This time there were gasps. He added the details; doorway, arrowslits, all the way up to the bunglebird cote on the roof. It stood tall in the smoke and flame as the base began to turn red. Jarrod intensified the heat and the color spread upward. The mind-model became a fierce orange and then an eye-watering white. In the distance there was the drumming of rain.

The group at the fire's edge was still. The tall Mage in his plain robe with the still taller Staff was flanked by the two leaders, their arms half up in anticipation. The unicorn stood behind them. The flames and the runelights provided the only motion. The Mage's voice pealed on and the building glowed. Then the voice stopped and the silence was shocking. The snow continued to fall, but the sound of rain was clearer now.

Gradually, the werelight dimmed and the Staff became a black arc against the brightness of the keep. The flames fell back like a spent wave and the diminutive building shone on alone, surrounded by ash and embers. Then it was gone, and the dark rushed in and claimed the space. The Mage sagged, unseen, into the waiting arms. He was lowered to the ground, still clutching his Staff, and covered with two cloaks. They left him by the burned-out fire and Sandroz moved in to watch over him. The unicorn remained, an enigmatic, guarding presence.

chapter 27

The instinct to Make the Day was not strong enough to rouse Jarrod, but all across the Magical Kingdoms the Talented poured their energies towards the Eastern horizon. The dawn came up clear and cold. Darius, however, was abroad before it. He visited the watchposts and listened to the reports of the freak rain that dowsed the fort while snow fell all around. The waxing light showed a moat of smooth ice around the walls. Magic obviously provided mixed blessings. Word of the arrival of the unicorn and of the night's doings had reached the furthest sentinel and the mood was one of confidence bordering on rashness. That was all well and good, but if the footing inside was anything like this, hand-to-hand combat would be exceedingly difficult. Magic and unicorns were all very well, but the gods be thanked for the Songean and his secret door.

Darius had gone back to the dying fire and spent an uneasy hour with the little man under the unicorn's watchful eye. They had gone over the layout of the fort—kitchens, stables, cellars, everything. He had rehearsed the details of his plan again and again as he waited for sleep, and sleep had eluded him. He blamed the unicorn for that, though he knew that he was being unjust.

The night was behind him now. There was fighting ahead and, while morale was commendably high, there were still men who needed to be brought to the combat point. He went among them, remembering a name, clapping a shoulder, making a joke. He conferred with Dahn and went over tactics with the young Flight Captain who was to lead the attack through the front gates. He had done everything he could to ensure victory, and now it was time to toss the knucklebones and see what the gods of the odds would bring.

Jarrod was up, finally, and submitted to the ministrations of Sandroz, including a bowl of the infamous oat pudding. He had tried to decline, but Sandroz had pushed the bowl back into his hands.

"If oats good enough for unicorn, good enough for you," he said with finality, and had stayed to see that it was eaten before going off to join Darius.

When the Songean had gone, Nastrus came trotting out of the forest.

'Fighting again?' he inquired.

'I'm afraid so. It never seems to end, does it?'

'Not with your species anyway.'

'It isn't our fault,' Jarrod said defensively. *'They were the ones who attacked the fort. If we don't get them out of there, it'll ruin trade and that would mean starvation for a lot of our people.'*

'That's as may be, but you humans never stop attacking them.'

'That just isn't true.'

'Yes it is. You do it out of ignorance rather than malice, I grant you, but you do it nevertheless.' Nastrus was sure of himself. He wasn't playing games.

'And how do you come to that conclusion, pray?'

'You people have a fetish about growing things, don't you? The plants produce more of your kind of air, and it gets bound together every morning. It's as simple as that.'

'Stop being cryptic, Nastrus.' Jarrod bent down and

cleaned his bowl out with snow, and then poured himself another mug of chai.

'I'm not being cryptic, you're just being dense,' the unicorn retorted.

'Then humor me and explain in terms that my feeble brain can comprehend.'

'Oh, very well.' There was a momentary pause while Nastrus marshaled his thoughts. Jarrod knew what he was doing, but it was just a mental blur to him.

'You think of your enemies as discrete individuals like yourselves. That's one of your limitations. You tend to think of everything in terms of yourselves. Well, they aren't at all like you. They are their atmosphere, and your air is constantly nibbling away at them.'

'I still don't follow you.'

Nastrus allowed irritation to surface and a ripple ran over his hide. *'Think of them as mist creatures,'* he said shortly.

'But that's ridiculous. You've seen the suits. They have legs and arms. They drive crawlers and make weapons.'

'That's why they need the suits, stupid. They can't do any of those things without the suits, and they deliberately patterned them after you. 'The killing things' is what they call you.'

'If they need the suits to make things, how did they make the suits?' Jarrod asked, sure that he'd clinched the argument.

'They grew them,' Nastrus replied patiently. *'Haven't you noticed that they don't last all that long in your air?'*

'How do you know all this?' Jarrod asked suspiciously. *'You said yourself that you can't communicate with them.'*

'We can't. I don't really comprehend how they are put together. Human bodies are impractical and inadequate, but at least the components are the same as ours. The others don't even seem to have individual thoughts, at least

none that I could detect, but they do have a—how can I put this—a sort of collective sense of identity, and they do have the same kind of emotions that you do; fear and hatred chiefly.'

'*And how do you know that?*' Jarrod persisted.

'*Your female took us out for exercise when we got back from the funeral—*'

'*How many times do I have to tell you, she's not my female.*'

Nastrus snorted. '*D'you want to hear this or not? I'd just as soon go and watch the other humans.*'

'*I'm sorry. I shouldn't have interrupted. And you're right, we ought to follow the others and see what happens.*'

'*You'd better ride me there,*' Nastrus said, mollified by the apology. '*Besides, if you're going to take part, you'll need my help. You look terrible. Your pelt's all splotchy and your skin—*'

'*That'll do, thank you very much,*' Jarrod cut him off. '*I've promised to stay out of it. Of course, if anything terrible happened . . .*' He let the thought die away.

'*Then you'd better get what you need and we'll be going. We can continue this discussion on the way.*'

Jarrod did as he was bidden, and ten minutes later the two set off after the ground forces. The Staff was resting across the unicorn's back, the ends pointing toward the ground.

'*Where was I?*' Nastrus asked as they threaded their way through the trees.

'*Going out for exercise.*'

'*Ah, yes. This time we went North, through the big wall and out onto the plain. Desolate place, but plenty of room to gallop. Marianna took us as close to where your enemies had been as she dared. They had gone back a very long way, but she was still afraid of the ground they had occupied. There was a very strong impression of them lingering. I know she couldn't really feel it, but I suspect that it affected her anyway. The hatred was very strong. They are afraid of your people. They hate being confined in the suits, and they hate you the more for forcing them to use the suits. It hung over the places they had been like a miasma.'*

"It all sounds so hopeless, sad and hopeless." Jarrod's shoulders slumped. *"There must be something we can do to stop it, but I'm too tired to think properly."*

"This isn't the time for it anyway," Nastrus said practically. *"We seem to be there. Where would you like me to go?"*

Jarrod looked around. *"See that old soskia at the top of the slope?'* He gestured unnecessarily. *'That's as good a place as any.'*

The men were already at the bottom of the incline by the time they had settled themselves. Jarrod watched Sandroz lead them in a flat-footed scuttle across the ice. He waved, but not one of them looked back to see the Mage astride the unicorn. He scanned the battlements anxiously, but there was no sign that the Outlanders were aware of the approach.

The raiding party was huddled now against the base of the corner tower. He could see no doorway, but the pool of 'steedsmen was draining into the fort. A moment later there were only a few to be seen, then a small black rectangle that became a slit before vanishing. The only trace of the fifty men was the scuffing on the ice. He pulled his cloak more closely around him.

'There won't be anything more to see for a while—if all goes well.'

"And if it doesn't?" Nastrus asked.

'I don't really know. It'll be up to us to do something, I suppose. Once the sun's over the Saradondas the cloud-

steeds will attack. For the moment there's nothing to do but wait and hope.'

There was nothing to see in the base of the tower, either. Once the door was closed there was no light. It was as cold as an icehouse, and the air smelled old and musty. A cough exploded in the dark. A paling in the absolute black signaled the opening of another door, and a familiar and dreaded odor seeped in with the dim light. It was the same smell that rose into the skies above the Outland brume.

Darius followed Sandroz out into the corridor and looked swiftly left and right. It was as the man had described it. He looked back over the man's head and saw no signs of the enemy or of their atmosphere, but that was no guarantee that the rooms above were free of pollution. As he was thinking that, the Songean took off Northward and Darius signaled to the men behind him.

The guide stopped at a doorway and waited for the others to catch up. He produced a spindly key with a notched head and disappeared up the stairs. Darius peered upward, waiting for a door to open. Nothing. Then there was a hiss from above, and after a pause, he made his way cautiously up, his hand groping ahead. He felt the edge of an open door and then some kind of cloth. The foreign smell was stronger. A hand took his arm and drew him to one side. Light sprang up suddenly, and when his eyes had adjusted he saw that Sandroz was holding back an arras. He stepped around the end of it and found himself halfway down the mess hall. Something white caught the edge of his vision. He swung into a crouch and had the blade of his throwing knife in his hand and ready to launch as he completed the turn. There was a suit on the floor among the overturned benches. It was crumpled, the life gone from it, and Darius relaxed.

The place bore witness to the fighting that had taken

place. There were scorch marks on two of the walls, charred remnants of furniture, and a lot of dried blood. Only the tapestry seemed to have escaped unscathed. There was glass all over the place, but the windows looked intact at first glance. Then Darius realized that they were covered by icicles. He ducked across the room and peered through a chink in the ice. The rest of his force deployed down the room, bows at the ready.

The courtyard was littered with tiles, pieces of chimney, and stacks of armor, all sheathed in ice. The keep cut off a good portion of the view, and Darius moved toward the open doors at the North end. He stopped at another window and moved a 'steedsman out of his way. The steps up to the door of the keep were ahead of him and there was no ice on them. The landing was covered in ash and the door was gone. He craned to see to the right. Two rows of small windows, all of them broken. That would be the officers' quarters. Debris was piled against the wall.

He was about to try for a better vantage point when a bulky suit lumbered into view. It was obviously bothered by the footing and lurched from one handhold to another. The body was round, as was the head. The sausagelike arms and legs were flexible, and from the way they moved, it looked as if the wearer had jointed limbs. The faceplate was a dark circle.

Darius raised an arm to still his men. He glanced around to check and then craned at the window again. The Outlander had stopped. He had his back to Darius and was tugging at something in the pile of wreckage. The figure took a step back and tucked an object that Darius couldn't identify under its arm. It turned and began its cumbersome journey back. A shadow flashed across the court and a wooden shaft appeared in the convex back. It was instantly hidden by a puff of brown as the figure sagged to the ground. The stricken carcass collapsed forward and more gas jetted out. The attack was on.

Jarrod watched the cloudsteeds swoop down from the East. One minute the sky was home to nothing more interesting than high, hazy, streamers of clouds, and the next twenty winged warhorses, one after the other, were skimming the battlements. They lifted toward the last peaks of the Gorodontious, wheeled with parade precision, and came diving back. The enemy was ready for them this time, and the familiar javelins of red light sped up.

The oncoming line broke and veered to either side, but two of the beams found marks. One steed was hit in the wing and spiraled away behind the walls. The other seemed to stop in midair and then plummeted. The wet smack of contact triggered scenes in Jarrod's mind that he had thought safely under control. He bit his lip so hard that it bled. It had been entirely peaceful only moments ago and now the battle at the Place of Power was back in his mind, reinforced by the anger and disgust emanating from Nastrus.

The death of the cloudsteed and its rider paralyzed Jarrod, but Darius saw it as an opportunity.

"Everybody outside!" he yelled. He paused long enough to draw his sword. "First two squads with the Chief Scout; round the right side and head for the gate. The rest of you men, follow me."

The footing was treacherous and fallen debris had turned the courtyard into an obstacle course. He had to keep his eyes on the ground most of the time, but he heard the cursing from behind him and the yells from the other side of the donjon. He hoped the latter meant that the contingent attacking through the gateway had arrived. Shadows of cloudsteeds raced and jolts of crimson were reflected off the ice. The air had a strange, sharp, metallic smell.

He slowed to negotiate a smashed chimneystack, and when he looked up there were white shapes ahead. He dropped to the ground and the edges of the bricks pushed into his chest. Red flared and he felt the heat of the enemy's shot. Bowstrings thrummed from behind him and suits toppled. Thin beams lanced out in reply and there were screams of pain. The Outlanders, taken by surprise and hemmed in though they were, were extracting their price. They used their fallen comrades for protection where they had to and they were holding the Strandsmen at bay.

The shouting from the gate side of the keep had died out. Not a good sign, Darius thought as he looked carefully around. Small fires were burning all over the courtyard and smoke was curling into the air. They couldn't stay pinned down like this. A loft of arrows curved high over his head, designed to come down on the enemy like lethal rain. He saw his chance and made a sliding, crablike dash for the rear. Clothyards arced to cover his retreat.

"The keep!" he yelled. "With me, men! To the keep!"

Darius plunged on, his back tingling in anticipation of an enemy shot. He was past the impromptu barricades his men were huddled behind and making for the keep steps. There were cries and flickers of carmine, but he was too busy watching his footing to look around. Then the steps were ahead and he skidded to a halt, using his drawn sword to keep his balance. He stood, panting, examining the doorway. No door; no sign of life. There was a yelp and a crash nearby, and the smell of burning intensified. The rest of the men were coming. He went up three steps and turned. They were all the worse for wear and there were fewer of them than there had been.

"Good work, men," he said. "We've got 'em where we want 'em and now we're going to finish them off. We'll have to take the keep to do it, but I know you're up to that. Now, any of you lose a bow, or run out of arrows?

Five of you? Good, I need you to defend the doorway. Can't have the bastards coming up behind us.

"I need the four strongest bowmen up on the roof with me. Any volunteers?" He looked at the upraised hands and laughed. "I like your spirit and your modesty, but there isn't room up there for all of us. I'll take you, you, and the two of you in the back there. The rest of you find yourselves an arrow slit, and don't waste any shafts on punctured suits."

He turned his attention to the four who had shouldered their way to the front. "I haven't seen any shots from this place, but that doesn't mean that they're not in there. Throwing knives, I think." He sheathed his sword. "Let's go and find out." He raised his voice. "Good hunting, men. Make those arrows count."

He took the rest of the steps two at a time. No ice here to worry about. He looked around the lintel. There was ash everywhere, but no sign of the Others. He moved quickly to the base of the wall-hugging staircase and looked up. There was charring around the gap through which it disappeared and something on the floor above had been broached or overturned. The top steps and the wall had been stained by whatever it was. The light through the arrow slits was too dim for details.

He was halfway up before it occurred to him that he should have sent an advance party ahead. Too late for that now. As he neared the top and slowed, he saw that what he had thought was moisture was metal. He tested it with the toe of his boot. It was solid. His head was almost up to the stone floor of the next level, and he eased his way forward. Another round, empty, chamber. He moved to the landing and stepped in. Evidence of fire was everywhere. He looked up and saw why there had been no opposition.

The ceiling was gone. Black holes showed where beams

had been anchored. High above was a circle of sky. Darius swore softly. He signaled to the four archers and resumed his climb. This was the Mage's doing. If there had been Outlanders in here, they would have been consumed. Gave them a taste of their own medicine he thought savagely and put the knife back into its sheath.

He was panting when he reached the top landing and his legs tremored after all those stairs. He leaned thankfully on the crenel and looked down. The broken body of the cloudsteed with its pools of drying blood dominated the courtyard. There were human bodies along the walls and at least forty suits, clumped together for the most part, in between. There were enemy repositioning themselves by the stables, and men were hunkered down around the gate.

There was movement at a second-floor window opposite, and Darius pulled back behind the merlon.

"Stay out of sight," he said urgently. "There's movement above the stables, across the way. Might be enemy. I'll see if I can draw him for you."

He waited while the men positioned themselves on the none-too-roomy landing and then he moved his head out from behind the protecting stone. There was a line of burning light, but it was aimed at the gate and not at him.

"Here," he said to the man at his shoulder. "See the opening into the stable yard? Three windows to the right above it. The one without icicles. There he is. See the white?" He moved aside to give the man more room. For answer, the 'steedsman notched an arrow and drew back the string. He let fly.

"Got him!" the man said with satisfaction.

"I don't see anything."

"Hit him in the arm. He pulled it back in, but he'll be done for."

"Good work. Keep an eye on the window anyway."

Darius edged around the man, mindful of the long drop behind him. "I want you four to watch the battlements and the windows. Keep your eyes peeled and your bows ready until I change the orders."

He made his way back down the stairway until he was at the halfway point. He turned and leaned against the wall. Then he cupped his hands around his mouth.

"Right, men," he shouted, and waited until the echo died. "Loose at will!"

He stepped into an unoccupied embrasure and peered out. The suits that he could see looked like molting hedge-pigs, quills drooping and scattered. A red line made him blink and left afterimages in his eyes. He could hear the twang of bowstrings. A cloudsteed's shadow flew beneath him, up the stables, and over the battlements. Smoke ed-died. Nothing else moved.

A ragged cheer went up from somewhere on the right. He strained to see. Men came into view moving warily, ready to dive for cover. They halted a respectful distance from the fallen enemy. Darius waited for some sort of retaliation. His eyes flicked up to the windows. Nothing. It's over then, he thought. The fort's ours, by the Mother. We've beaten the bastards.

The place would have to be thoroughly searched, of course, but Bandor was in Allied hands again. Why then, did he feel so flat? This was going to be hailed as a great victory. The hated enemy was a heap in the courtyard or buried under the mountain. And yet . . . It's just the usual let down after the danger's past, he told himself and stepped back to the stairs. He looked at the men studded around the walls of the gutted keep. Good men these. They deserved to enjoy their victory.

"Well done, lads! She's ours again!" they cheered.

Cheer yourselves, he thought. Cheer the Mage and the Songean, cheer most of all because it's over and you're alive. He waved at them. Getting old and cynical, he thought. He let the echoes peter out.

"Everybody outside and assemble in squads. Squad leaders meet me at the bottom of the outside steps. There's mopping up to be done." Groans bounced off the walls and he grinned. He waved again and started down the curving stairs.

Stop being so hard on yourself, he admonished. They almost gave you up for dead less than a year ago, but here you are. We've done everything that Naxania wanted, including beating the Umbrians to it. Magic had certainly held its own and Courtak's unharmed. Yes, she should be pleased, and when she was pleased . . . He smiled to himself. It might not be the same as riding into Gwyndryth, but it promised to be a most pleasant homecoming.

By the time he reached the floor, his mood had turned. He waited for the last of the 'steedsmen to file out and then gave them time to get organized. When he emerged from the doorway he saw that the men he had led had been joined by the others. Cloudsteeds circled overhead. The men cheered and he stood on the top step beaming. I suppose I'd better get used to this, he thought and promptly laughed at his own conceit. The troops read their own meaning into that and cheered him all the more.

He looked down at them with affection. They had earned this moment of elation. The war might not be over, but, for the first time in memory, the Outlanders had been handed a clear-cut defeat, and, who knew, the combination of Magic and the military might win the war after all. He looked up at the battlements and saw that the sun was on the downslide.

chapter 28

Darius was the last one through the rear gates of the fort. They had spent the afternoon combing the place for survivors, but they had found nothing. They would bury their dead tomorrow. He knew from experience that there was nothing left of the enemy and that their suits would disintegrate in a day or two. There was no point in posting a guard and no one wanted to spend the night in there. He pulled the gate to behind him and looked up the slope. It was icy and seemed much steeper than it had that morning. He sighed and scanned the top. There was no doubt about it, he didn't have the stamina he had had before the Angorn battle. He spotted the Magician, sitting on the unicorn, and shook his head.

How quickly we become enured, he thought. A year ago I didn't believe in them, and now I look up and say, 'Oh, yes, there's the unicorn.' He wondered why they had stayed behind. No use speculating, it was time that he got up there and found out for himself. He started for the scarp and took the bottom of it at a dogged run. He was soon scrabbling upward on all fours.

Jarrod dismounted, lay down at the lip of the slope, and extended his hand. Darius grabbed it, and Jarrod hauled him up over the edge. They both lay there panting.

"We're both in wonderful condition," Darius said as he got to his feet and started knocking snow off himself.

"When you get to be our age," Jarrod said, knowing full well what he looked like, "you are glad to be able to do this much."

The banter made Darius uneasy. He had thought of Courtak as a boy a couple of days ago, but now that remark was fully justified by his outward appearance. Would it be like this with Naxania? Would he wake up one morning and find a crone in his bed?

"Thank you," he said to banish the image. "I'm glad you were there. It was easy enough going down, but I wasn't sure that I was going to make it back up."

"Everyone had trouble," Jarrod said, getting up and dusting himself off. "You are by no means my first. All the men wanted to pat Nastrus: he seems to be the new mascot. Nastrus enjoys the attention and I couldn't deny the men. I thought we'd stay until everyone was out. Are there any more still inside?"

"No one living. I sent everyone back to camp. I wanted to have the place to myself for a while."

"It was a remarkable victory," Jarrod said brightly, responding to the flatness in the other man's voice. "You did everything that you set out to do."

"We couldn't have pulled it off without the Songean and you," Darius said.

"There's enough credit to go around." Jarrod walked back to Nastrus and rubbed him behind the ear. "We'll all be heroes when we get back. Nastrus's arrival will be made to seem miraculous."

"You're right, of course," Darius replied, making a conscious effort to lighten his mood, "and you know what that'll mean, don't you? Parades, banquets, and speeches."

Jarrod grimaced. "Investitures," he said in a hollow voice. Both men smiled. "And speaking of getting back," he continued, "I think we should be moving along. I'm freezing."

"You ride on ahead. Make sure there's some hot chai waiting for me."

"We can both ride. Nastrus won't mind."

'Who said that Nastrus wouldn't mind?' The indignant question thrust its way to the fore. *'I don't recall offering to transport two hulking great humans.'*

'I'm sorry, I didn't realize that you weren't strong enough. We'll take it in turns, but you can see that the General is all in.'

'I didn't say I wasn't strong enough . . .' Nastrus rose to the bait.

"Are you sure, Sir Jarrod?" Darius asked, unaware of the silent colloquy. "These legs still have a league left in them."

"Quite sure. I checked with Nastrus and he says that he's strong enough."

'That's not fair.'

'Stop being such a grump. All that adulation has gone to your head. Look at the man. He won't make it back to camp if we don't help him.'

'He looks younger than you do,' Nastrus thought sourly.

'All the more reason for you to carry both of us. If it gets to be too much, tell me and I'll get off.'

He turned to Darius. "Would you give me a leg up please? As you can see, there's no saddle and he's a big brute."

Darius made a stirrup of his hands and boosted Jarrod up. He chuckled. "One minute a General and the next a groom. Hold your foot rigid and I'll use it as a step, if I can get my leg up there." He positioned himself. "There. That's it. I'm aboard." He linked his arms loosely around Jarrod's waist, and they set off with Nastrus grumbling in Jarrod's head.

"This had been quite a day," Darius said as they picked their way across the trampled snow. "I've captured my first castle and now I'm riding a unicorn. Who'd have believed it? These are certainly strange times that we're living in."

Jarrod turned his head so that he would be heard. "I agree. So much has happened this past year that I can't take it all in."

"The whole world seems to have gone mad, doesn't it? The Maternites believe that there is a pattern to everything, a grand design woven by the Mother, but I'm damned if I can make sense of what's been going on. Take the Outlanders. They used to start attacking around Greeningale and pack it in when the Season of the Moons got underway. Now it's anybody's guess."

"I've learned a lot more about them lately," Jarrod said. "Thanks to Nastrus," he added hastily.

"I've been studying them for twenty-five years, and they're still like waking up after a nightmare. You know you've had one, but you don't remember what it was."

"That may be truer than you know. Nastrus says that they don't have bodies."

"I'm sorry, I'm not following you. It's been a long day."

"The unicorns say that the Outlanders and their atmosphere are one and the same thing. They don't have bodies," he explained earnestly, "they're made out of gas, or cloud, or something. They really aren't individuals as we think of them."

"That's a little farfetched, don't you think?" Darius sounded tired. "They were solid enough to kill twenty-three of my 'steedsmen."

"Only when they're in suits," Jarrod pressed on. He might never get this opportunity again, and he owed it to Marianna to try. "Look, what happens when an Outlander is hit? The suit gets punctured and gas escapes. The suits are always empty, aren't they? What you see escaping isn't just the stuff they breathe, it's them."

"The unicorns told you this? I'm sorry, Sir Jarrod, I'm not up to tackling this at the moment. Perhaps we can go into it when we've both had a chance to rest."

The rode on in silence. The trees around them, bending under the weight of snow, creaked occasionally. A dogfox barked somewhere off to the right and was answered. They were alone in a pink-tinged world and it was difficult to remember that there had been fierce fighting going on scant hours ago.

"We'll be staying here for a couple of days, shan't we?" Jarrod asked after a while.

Darius roused himself. "Yes, at least that. We've wounded to tend to. Some of them won't be able to fly right away. Besides, we'll have to hold the fort until the Umbrians get here. There's always the possibility of reinforcements coming from beyond the Causeway, so we can't let our guard down."

"If you don't need me for anything, I'd like to borrow an extra cloudsteed and pay a visit to a friend of mine."

"Are you fit enough for that?" Darius was surprised. What friend could he have hereabouts?

"I think so. I don't intend to do anything strenuous, and I may never get the chance again. He's even older than we are."

"Then I can't see why you shouldn't. I'd prefer you to go with an escort. I'm still responsible for you, and you're still recovering from spell making. I've lost enough men already."

"Thank you. I promise to come back in one piece, and it shouldn't take more than a few days." Jarrod smiled to himself. He'd know soon enough if Old King Sig was of a mind to come back with him. If he wanted to stay, there'd be no moving him. Pleas and arguments would be wasted.

'Why are you avoiding talking to him about your enemy?' Nastrus cut across his line of thought. *'Is it because he didn't believe you the first time?'*

'The man's tired and he doesn't want to talk about it now.'

'You didn't explain things properly,' Nastrus persisted. *'What I told you was the truth and the truth has to be believed.'*

'You heard what I said, Nastrus.' Jarrod was irritated. *'What more could I have done?'*

'I do not like it when my word is doubted,' Nastrus retorted.

'And I suppose you could have done a better job?'

There was agreement in Jarrod's mind and then he felt Nastrus reach beyond him. He too was tired, and it took him a beat to understand what was going on.

'Nastrus, stop that! What do you think you're doing?'

A tendril separated itself from the effort. *'I'm trying to communicate with him. Isn't that obvious?'*

'You mustn't do that. You could hurt him. You can't talk to other human beings, you know that.'

'Normally speaking no, but he's very relaxed and receptive. He's almost asleep and his defenses are down.'

'Nastrus, I don't think . . .' Jarrod began and then felt Darius's arms tighten. He froze, not knowing what to do. Anything he did might be harmful.

The Holdmaster was dozing, rocking gently to the rhythm of the unicorn. He felt a pressure behind his temple and hoped that he wasn't going to get a headache. There was no reason for one. He hadn't been wearing a battlehelm. The pressure built.

'Don't be frightened. I mean you no harm.' The thought formed, unbidden. Darius stiffened, nerves tingling. I'm dreaming, he thought. Dreaming that I'm riding a unicorn and hearing voices.

'The unicorn is real and I am the unicorn, but you have no reason to be afraid. My dam does this with your daughter.'

"What do you want with me?" Darius said aloud, eyes still shut.

'I want you to know the truth. Since you will not believe the Jarrod human, I must prove to you that I am reporting accurately. Here, see for yourself.' Nastrus opened his Memory.

"Are you all right, my Lord?" Jarrod asked over his shoulder. *'Nastrus, what are you doing?'* Neither of them answered him. The unicorn continued to plod onward.

'Nastrus, stop it! You'll kill him.' "General, say something!"

'Stop shouting. It's all over and he's perfectly all right. He's not answering you because he's trying to absorb the information I gave him,' Nastrus replied.

'You must never do that again. You may not have hurt him, but you frightened me half to death.'

'Calm down. I know what I'm doing. It's only possible when humans are very relaxed, and they almost never are around us. You wanted him to know about the Others, now he does.'

Jarrod turned back to Darius. "Are you all right, my Lord?"

"What? Oh yes, I'm all right. Your friend has an interesting tale to tell and an unusual way of telling it."

"I'm sorry about that, Sir. I tried to stop him."

"Don't apologize. I'm in honored company, though I must confess that I did not really enjoy the experience. It's the involuntary nature of it that's most disturbing, I think."

"I'll try to see that . . ." Jarrod broke off as he became aware of noise. He faced front again.

The sounds were coming from ahead, a goodly buzz,

punctuated by the banging of metal. He could see firelight through the trees. They were coming in to camp.

"Sounds as if the party's started already," Darius remarked. "You ready to make your first speech? I've made one already, and I don't much feel like making another."

"I'll say something if you take care of the saluting."

"Sounds fair to me."

Jarrod straightened his back as they came to the edge of the clearing. Men were dancing, singing, banging mugs and plates together. He caught sight of Sandroz waiting patiently with a blanket and found it comforting.

"Here's our first parade," Darius murmured as they moved forward.

The dancing stopped as men noticed their arrival and a ragged cheer went up. The sound strengthened as more men crowded in, and Jarrod felt buoyed by it. We won, he thought. We really won. He raised an arm and waved to the jubilant flyers. We have bought time, he said to himself; time to rest, to mend, to put an end to this senseless conflict.

He forgot his aches and pains in the euphoria of the moment. They rode through the stamping, yelling, red-faced men and dismounted by the central fire. Hope was in the air like the smell of the woodsmoke. Truth would prevail, he knew that now. It had to. It was a tradition on Strand.

All Futura Books are available at your bookshop or newsagent, or can be ordered from the following address:
Futura Books, Cash Sales Department,
P.O. Box 11, Falmouth, Cornwall TR10 9EN.

Please send cheque or postal order (no currency), and allow 60p for postage and packing for the first book plus 25p for the second book and 15p for each additional book ordered up to a maximum charge of £1.90 in U.K.

B.F.P.O. customers please allow 60p for the first book, 25p for the second book plus 15p per copy for the next 7 books, thereafter 9p per book

Overseas customers, including Eire, please allow £1.25 for postage and packing for the first book, 75p for the second book and 28p for each subsequent title ordered.

interzone

SCIENCE FICTION AND FANTASY

Bimonthly £1.95

- *Interzone* is the leading British magazine which specializes in SF and new fantastic writing. We have published:

BRIAN ALDISS	GARRY KILWORTH
J.G. BALLARD	DAVID LANGFORD
IAIN BANKS	MICHAEL MOORCOCK
BARRINGTON BAYLEY	RACHEL POLLACK
GREGORY BENFORD	KEITH ROBERTS
MICHAEL BISHOP	GEOFF RYMAN
DAVID BRIN	JOSEPHINE SAXTON
RAMSEY CAMPBELL	BOB SHAW
ANGELA CARTER	JOHN SHIRLEY
RICHARD COWPER	JOHN SLADEK
JOHN CROWLEY	BRIAN STABLEFORD
PHILIP K. DICK	BRUCE STERLING
THOMAS M. DISCH	LISA TUTTLE
MARY GENTLE	IAN WATSON
WILLIAM GIBSON	CHERRY WILDER
M. JOHN HARRISON	GENE WOLFE

- *Interzone* has also published many excellent new writers; graphics by **JIM BURNS, ROGER DEAN, IAN MILLER** and others; book reviews, news, etc.
- *Interzone* is available from good bookshops, or by subscription. For six issues, send £11 (outside UK, £12.50) to: **124 Osborne Road, Brighton BN1 6LU, UK** Single copies: £1.95 inc p&p (outside UK, £2.50).
- American subscribers may send $22 ($26 if you want delivery by air mail) to our British address, above. All cheques should be made payable to *Interzone*.

- -

To: **interzone** 124 Osborne Road, Brighton, BN1 6LU, UK.

Please send me six issues of *Interzone*, beginning with the current issue. I enclose a cheque/p.o. for £11 (outside UK, £12.50; US subscribers, $22 or $26 air), made payable to *Interzone*.

Name ____

Address ____

____